CRASH INTO YOU

Roni wrote her first romance novel at age fifteen when she discovered writing about boys was way easier than actually talking to them. Since then, her flirting skills haven't improved, but she likes to think her storytelling ability has. After earning a master's degree in social work, she worked in a mental hospital, counseled birthmothers as an adoption co-ordinator, and did management recruiting in her PJs. But she always returned to writing.

Though she'll forever be a New Orleans girl at heart, she now lives in Dallas with her husband and son.

Also by Roni Loren

Melt into You

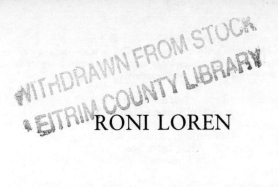

RONI LOREN

CRASH INTO YOU

HARPER

Harper
An imprint of HarperCollins*Publishers*
77–85 Fulham Palace Road,
Hammersmith, London W6 8JB

www.harpercollins.co.uk

First published by The Berkley Publishing Group 2012
A division of The Penguin Group

A catalogue record for this book
is available from the British Library

ISBN: 978-0-00-751113-6

Typeset in Sabon by Palimpsest Book Production Ltd, Falkirk, Stirlingshire

Printed and bound in Great Britain by Clays Ltd, St Ives plc

ACKNOWLEDGEMENTS

First, thank you to my parents, who have always supported me no matter what crazy path I've ventured down. I can't tell you how much your unconditional love and unwavering cheerleading have meant in my life.

And love to my husband and son, who bring the joy to my world and who put up with me even when I'm in obsessive writer mode, which is often. I could never have written this book if you guys hadn't given me the support to follow my dream.

Gratitude also to the wonderful and talented writer friends I've met along the way, both in person and online. For the first time in my life, I feel like I've found the natives of my home planet. Hallelujah.

And finally, hugs to my agent, Sara Megibow, and to my editor, Kate Seaver, for believing in my book, for believing in me, and for helping my dream come true.

To my husband, Donnie.
You are my heart and my very own romance hero.
Thank you for being such a damn good man.

ONE

Don the gas masks and cue the mushroom cloud. Brynn's date was spiraling toward DEFCON 1—imminent disaster. In the brief time it had taken her to down three hors d'oeuvres, her sexy doctor had tumbled from fantasy fodder to potential therapy client.

Dr. Depressed propped his elbows on the table and leaned forward, his brows knitted. "I don't know what I did wrong. One minute we're in love and planning the future, the next I catch her in the copy room with her arms wrapped around the pharmaceutical sales rep."

Brynn frowned as tears gathered behind his glasses. Oh, hell. She couldn't have *another* guy cry on her. That'd be the second one this month. She was becoming the Barbara Walters of dating—taking a perfectly put-together person and reducing him to tears without trying. She reached across the table and gave his hand a quick squeeze. "I'm sorry you had to go through that. It sounds like she took advantage of what a nice guy you are."

He stared at her for a moment, and then released a breath.

"God, what am I doing? I'm breaking that cardinal rule, right? No ex talk on dates. I'm sure you didn't ask me to come to this fund-raiser so you could hear me yammer about my breakup."

"It's fine. Breakups can be tough," she said, giving her therapist half-smile—the one that said *I feel your pain and am* so *not judging you*, even though she was already formulating a hypothetical treatment plan in her head. She drew her hand away and sipped the last of her iced tea.

The lines in his face relaxed, and he leaned back in his seat. "I'm sorry I let it come up. You're just so easy to talk to."

"Occupational hazard, I guess," she said, trying to lighten the mood. But the truth of her statement turned the words to sawdust in her mouth. She enjoyed her work, but did that mean she had signed up to heal every guy she dated? For once, she'd love to worry, like other women did, that a guy had asked her out simply to get her in bed. Instead, she had to worry if someone asked her to dinner because it was cheaper than a therapy session.

A waiter stopped by with a tray of champagne flutes. Brynn accepted one of the drinks, but her companion shook his head. "No thanks, I'm on call. Plus, I don't want to fall asleep on my lovely date before the end of the night."

He gave her a hopeful smile, his brown eyes still red-rimmed from unshed tears. Brynn fought back the defeated sigh that gathered in her throat. If he was staying awake on her account, he shouldn't bother. She didn't care how nice of a guy he was or how hot he probably looked naked. She was not going to be his rebound sex. Nothing like knowing a guy is closing his eyes in bed because he's picturing someone else beneath him. Brynn took a long gulp from her glass.

"Speaking of which," he said, reaching into the pocket of his jacket and pulling out his cell phone, "could you excuse me for a minute? I need to check in with the answering service."

"No problem, take all the time you need." Really, he could take as much time as he wanted because this date was over—sign the death certificate and slap a toe tag on it. Done.

After he strode off, Brynn pushed her chair away from the table and straightened the hem of her black-and-white shift dress as she stood. She needed something stronger than champagne.

She navigated through the crowd and the steady hum of polite conversation, pausing occasionally to smile and shake hands with donors. The Women's Crisis Center of Dallas had a fund-raiser twice a year and, thanks to a very active board, had managed to snag a number of high-dollar supporters for this one. Good thing, considering her job was dependent on the generosity of these strangers. She grabbed a mini quiche off a passing waiter's tray and shoved it in her mouth, hoping her obvious chewing would deter more people from stopping her to chat.

Brynn spotted a familiar face near the bar. Melody, her co-worker, flipped her auburn hair over her shoulder and laughed at something the bartender said. Brynn walked over but hovered behind her for a moment, not wanting to interrupt Mel's flirting. The woman was a master and seemed to have the young bartender sufficiently under her spell until another party guest pounded a fist on the counter and demanded a refill. With an apologetic smile, the bartender excused himself and Melody huffed.

Brynn tapped her on the shoulder. "Hey, girl, I haven't seen you all night. Where've you been hiding?"

Melody turned around and grinned.

"Hey, I could say the same to you. Although, I have an idea of what's keeping you busy." She nodded toward Brynn's table. "How's it going with the yummy doctor? Are you ready to play nurse yet?"

She groaned. "Seriously? That's the best you can come up with?"

"Look, I'm three drinks into this. My comedy skills suffer when I'm tipsy."

Brynn set her champagne on the bar, and then turned back to her friend. "It's kind of a disaster. He almost cried already."

She cringed. "Oh, no."

Brynn held out her palms and shook her head before her friend could go into pity mode. "I don't even want to talk about it. I'm apparently cursed to be a thirty-year-old born-again virgin."

"Oh, screw that. You just need to stop looking for the perfect guy and find *a* guy to have some fun with. You could ask out that lawyer who's starting at the crisis center," she suggested. "I think he's Cooper's friend. And believe me, I mentally undressed him a little while ago and liked what I saw."

"Oh, *really*, you got to meet him?" Brynn asked, scanning the crowded room to see if she could spot Cooper and her new coworker.

Mel sipped her drink. "Mm-hmm. I ran into Coop a few minutes ago and he introduced us. Apparently, the guy's starting Monday, so you have two nights to get around your I-don't-date-people-I-work-with policy. Just enough time for a dirty little fling."

She rolled her eyes. "Right. I think that'd make for an awkward staff meeting on Monday."

"Or an interesting one. I'd bet Mr. Dark and Dashing would know exactly how to break you out of your dry spell. You should see the size of his hands," she said, holding up her palm with a knowing nod.

Brynn snorted. "If he's so great, why aren't you weaving your wicked web around him by now?"

"You know I like mine blond—feeds my Leonardo DiCaprio fantasies. Plus," she said, nudging her shoulder, "you need the action more than me."

"Good Lord, could you make me sound any more pathetic? It's not like I'm going to shrivel up and die if I don't get laid."

Her expression turned deadpan. "You may. The lawyer may

be your only chance before you spontaneously combust from sexual frustration."

"Oh, please." Brynn bent down to fiddle with the strap on her shoe. Damn thing was cutting into her ankle like razor wire. She loosened the strap and rubbed her reddened skin. "I'm not going to combust. Who needs the lawyer when I have a perfectly functioning vibrator at home?"

Brynn expected to hear a witty retort, but there was silence. She froze, her gaze still on her shoe. Mel, a former sex therapist, would never stay quiet after a comment like that, especially when her tongue was loose from alcohol. Unless . . . *Shit.* She closed her eyes briefly.

"Hey, ladies, hope I'm not interrupting," Cooper said, her boss's baritone voice barely concealing amusement.

Brynn straightened, finding Cooper wearing a shit-eating grin and Melody biting her lip like she was three seconds from bursting into laughter. Brynn slapped on a smile and tried to keep her voice light. "Hey, Cooper. Not interrupting a thing."

"Good, 'cause I wanted to introduce you to the new lawyer." Cooper nodded at someone behind Brynn. "This is Reid."

Brynn's response lodged in her throat, the all-too-familiar name ringing in her ears. *No, couldn't be.* But a sinking feeling settled in her gut. She'd only met one Reid in her life, and that Reid was a lawyer. She closed her eyes and took a steadying breath before she turned around to face her new coworker.

Reid's blue-eyed gaze met her head-on, hitting her like an air bag to the chest. She sucked in a breath and fought the old instinct to lower her eyes in deference. *Son of a bitch, where had that urge come from?* She ticked up her chin and gave him her best I-hate-you-but-will-be-polite-because-I'm-the-bigger-person glare. "Hello."

Cooper walked around Brynn and clapped Reid on the shoulder. "Reid, I'd like you to meet our other social worker, Brynn LeBreck."

Reid nodded, his expression annoyingly unreadable. "Brynn, pleasure to see you again. It's been a while."

Not long enough. Three years had passed since she'd last seen him. His inky hair was longer on top and a few lines creased the corners of his eyes, but time hadn't softened her warring responses to him. The urges to pummel his face and strip naked before him held almost equal weight. Luckily, the venue was too public to give in to either. She feigned an air of indifference. "It has."

"Still as beautiful as ever, though."

The warm notes of his voice stirred the dark recesses of her memory, further inciting the old longing. She shifted in her heels as hot tingles crept from deep in her belly and moved downward to settle between her legs. *Un-fucking-believable.* Her body was a whoring traitor.

Melody stepped next to Brynn as if sensing her need for support, and Cooper's eyebrows rose. "You two know each other?"

Boy, did they—in just about every way a man and woman could. She searched Reid's face, and he tipped his head infinitesimally, as if giving her permission to answer the question. Her eyes narrowed. "Used to. Long time ago."

Cooper smiled, either oblivious or unperturbed by the tension zipping through the air between her and Reid. "Great. Guess introductions weren't needed then."

Nope. Not needed. Brynn knew exactly who Reid Jamison was. A first-class bastard.

Reid tucked his hands in his pockets, his relaxed confidence taunting her. "How've you been? Weren't you working with kids the last time I saw you?"

So this is how he was going to play it, like they were old buddies. Fine. She nodded. "I was. But after my mother's murder, I decided I should work with troubled women. Someone needs to be on their side."

Reid's jaw tightened. "Of course."

She swallowed the scoff that threatened to escape. Of course, her ass. He'd been all too happy to take on her mother's killer as a client. Who gave a shit about guilt or innocence if the paycheck was good, right? The ridiculous hormonal surge he'd caused turned frigid with the memory. She shot a pointed glance in the direction of her table. "Sorry I don't have more time to chat, but I can't leave my date waiting."

Reid's mouth curved upward, the effect more predatory than friendly. "No worries. We'll have all kinds of time to catch up now that we'll be working together again."

Together. Every day. With Reid. The words felt like shackles locking around her limbs. She attempted a facsimile of a smile, exchanged good-byes with everyone, and then hurried back to her table. Dealing with a weepy date suddenly seemed like cake compared to spending one more second under the knowing gaze of the guy who, once upon a time, had brought her to her knees with a single, charged glance.

———

Reid watched the swaying ass of Brynn LeBreck as she hightailed it away from the group and returned to her date. Poor bastard. He'd overheard Brynn say something about her vibrator, so he assumed the guy wasn't going to be asked in for "drinks" tonight. For some reason, knowing her date didn't do it for her gave him an odd sort of satisfaction. It'd even been on the tip of his tongue to tell her that if she was in need of a good toe curling, he'd be more than happy to cuff her to *his* bed tonight—no battery-operated intervention needed.

But he figured the whole hating-his-guts thing would probably get in the way of her accepting his invitation. If time was supposed to heal all, Brynn definitely hadn't gotten the memo. The fury that had flared in those green irises of hers could've set his suit on fire. Unfortunately, sharing air with the sexy blonde again had set other things aflame as well. His dick had jumped to attention like a soldier reporting for duty.

And he wasn't even going to acknowledge the little flip his heart had performed in his chest. Stupid.

It'd been a few years since he'd seen her, ten since he'd touched her, but he remembered the feel of her curves and the taste of her skin as if he'd been buried inside her luscious body yesterday. He yanked at his collar, his tie suddenly feeling like a noose. Maybe it hadn't been such a good idea to take Cooper up on his offer of cheap rent in exchange for some pro bono work. He'd hesitated when he'd seen Brynn's name listed on the brochure for the crisis center, but he'd figured he'd be immune to the woman by now. Plus, the deal had been too good to pass up. But now that he'd seen her again, he couldn't deny that the residue of his old attraction still clung to his bones. *Fuck me.*

"Well, boys, I'm off," Melody said, dragging Reid's attention back to the two people standing beside him. "These shoes were made for dancing and the night's almost over."

Cooper turned to him after Melody traipsed off. "Man, you look like you need a beer."

Reid's shoulders relaxed a bit, and he gave his friend a half-smile. "You have no idea."

Coop got the bartender's attention, ordered two Shiner Bocks, and handed one to Reid. They moved away from the busy bar, but remained on the fringes of the milling crowd. His friend took a swig of his beer, then nodded in the direction of Brynn's table. "So what's the deal with you two?"

Reid shook his head. "Long story. Shitty ending."

He chuckled. "I'm guessing there was nakedness involved. I've never seen her look so horrified to see someone. Although, I'm having trouble imagining the two of you dating. Brynn's, uh, not exactly into guys like us."

Reid eyed his friend. "Guys like us?"

Cooper gave him a wry smile. "The bossy type. I know it's been a while, but I doubt you've changed *that* much since college."

Reid absentmindedly rubbed the spot on his finger where a ring used to be. No, some things couldn't be changed, no matter how hard he'd tried. Too bad he hadn't figured that out before he'd married a woman who thought he was some kind of deviant for wanting to take control in the bedroom.

"I guess you're right." However, Cooper's assessment of Brynn confused him. Back when he'd known her, she'd been exactly the kind of girl for his flavor of kink.

Coop pointed his bottle at him. "Well, I don't know what's between you two, but I suggest you clear out that old stuff quick. The last thing we need at the crisis center is drama between the employees. Believe me, our clients provide enough of that."

Reid gave a curt nod. "I'll take care of it."

Now he just had to figure out how. This was supposed to be his fresh start, both from his failed marriage and from the stress of working in his family's high-profile practice. Tiptoeing around Brynn and being on edge at work were *not* part of the agenda. He'd done enough eggshell walking over the past few years to last him a lifetime. That stopped now.

The way he saw it, she'd ripped his heart out ten years ago and then he'd let her down during her mother's trial—they should be even. So whether she liked it or not, the two of them were going to dump their ugly history on the table and deal with it.

Based on previous experience, that kind of discussion would either end up in a screaming fight or a screaming fuck. Regardless, he wasn't waiting until Monday to have it with her. To hell with her date—and her vibrator. There would only be one guy driving Ms. LeBreck home tonight.

TWO

ten years earlier

Brynn fought the urge to roll her eyes as the other girls in the campaign office fawned over the senator-to-be's nephew. Reid had only been in the building for ten minutes and already her fellow coeds had provided him with cupfuls of coffee and an eyeful of cleavage. Not that Reid looked like he minded. He leaned back in his desk chair and graced the two women with his sly smile, holding court.

Brynn shook her head. Must be nice to have things handed to you without having to work for it. College paid for, a cushy summer job, and designer jeans that probably cost more than her entire wardrobe—all because you were lucky enough to win the family lottery.

She dropped her gaze back to the pink notepad in front of her and scribbled down the message from the phone call she'd taken a few minutes earlier. She tore off the sheet and put it on the growing stack of "while you were out" notes for Davis Ackerman, the campaign manager. Her neck ached from cradling the phone to her ear all morning, but she wasn't going to complain.

This new receptionist gig sure beat running the register at the Chicken Fried Chick down the street. She'd take sore muscles over hair that smelled like fryer grease any day.

The sound of a throat clearing made her raise her head. Reid propped his hip on the edge of her desk and peered down at her, his dark blue eyes analyzing her. "Brynn, right?"

She sat straighter in her chair in an attempt to look more professional. "Yes, sir. Brynn LeBreck."

His mouth curled at the corner. "I'm hardly old enough to drink. I don't think you need to call me sir, although it sounds kind of good coming from you. You have a nice voice."

She groaned inwardly. All these girls tripping over themselves and he was going to turn that southern charm on her? Super. Not that he wasn't nice to look at, but she didn't have time for guys right now, especially ones who were related to the man who signed her much-needed paycheck. She forced a polite smile. "Guess that's why they hired me to answer phones."

He shook his head. "No, my uncle said he offered you the job because you were giving an unruly customer the what-for when he went in to get lunch one day. Figured you'd be able to handle all the craziness around here just fine."

She smirked at the memory. The redneck had quickly regretted ogling her and asking if there was an up-charge for large breasts. "Yeah, not my proudest moment, but that customer deserved it."

He raised an eyebrow. "Uncle Patrick said you insulted the dude's manhood . . . and his mother."

She threw up her hands. "Well, the guy was being a dick. What else was I supposed to do?"

He pressed his lips together as if holding back a laugh.

She cringed. "Sorry. Sometimes my mouth opens before my brain gets involved."

He chuckled, the deep sound so genuine the tension in her

shoulders relaxed. "Don't censor yourself on account of me. I didn't hire you. I can't fire you. So no filter necessary. Talk dirty to me anytime you want."

The corner of her mouth lifted. "If that's your pick-up line, I'd work on it."

He frowned, his brows furrowing. "No good?"

She sat her chin on her hand and shook her head.

"Really? Huh." He looked over his shoulder. "I'd bet Molly or Krista over there would eat that shit up."

She leaned back in her chair and crossed her arms over her chest. "I'm sure you could recite the Pledge of Allegiance and the sorority twins would turn cartwheels."

He nodded, his face serious. "That's true. They do recognize my innate awesomeness. Too bad having a conversation with them is about as interesting as alphabetizing my CD collection."

She glanced over at the two girls in question. Both were giving her versions of the stink eye. He followed her gaze, and they hurriedly looked away. "I have a feeling I'm not getting an invite to girls' night now."

He turned back to her, his eyes sparkling with mischief. "So, if I were to need a decent pick-up line to entice, let's say, a smoking-hot blonde who likes to talk dirty to have a burger with me, what would you suggest?"

Her cheeks heated, unable to fend off the effects of his easy charm. No wonder he had girls following him around like ducklings. She glanced down at her desk, wishing she could say yes, but knowing she couldn't. She and Reid Jamison lived on different planets. She didn't have time for flings or dating. She needed to work, get through the summer, save every penny, and hopefully have enough to afford the move to Austin for school in the fall. She looked up at Reid. "I would suggest you find someone who has time to say yes."

"Not even enough time for a simple burger?" he asked.

She tapped her desk calendar. "I'm in high demand these days. Gotta book months ahead."

He snorted. "Good thing I wasn't talking about you then."

She fought a smile. "Good thing."

He rose from his perch and gave her a quick grin. "Just know that I'm a pretty thick-headed guy. Takes me a while to get the point."

She straightened the papers he had mussed on her desk. "I'll keep that in mind."

He gave her a mock salute. "Nice to meet you, Brynn LeBreck. Be seeing you."

━━━

Reid bumped a shoulder against the entrance to the guesthouse and tried to get the humidity-swollen door unstuck. When it didn't budge, he gave it another hard shove and it released, banging against the inside wall. "Piece of shit."

"If it's such a hardship, you could always move back into the main house," said a female voice.

Reid startled and nearly dropped the sack of groceries he'd been carrying. "Jesus, Aunt Roslyn, what are you doing in here?"

His aunt rose from his couch and crossed her arms over her chest, her face as tight as the bun in her dark hair. "You got a package today."

He set the bag of food on the counter of his efficiency kitchen and stared at the large cardboard box in front of her. "Okay. I appreciate the heads-up, but no need to personally deliver it."

She picked up the box and flipped it over, dumping the contents onto the coffee table. A slew of items spilled across the surface and Reid groaned. Handcuffs. Floggers. A blindfold. A few brightly colored vibrators and a number of other things even he couldn't identify. *Son of a bitch.*

She turned her angry-parent death stare on him. "What the hell is going on, Reid? Do I need to call Dr. Leonard? I know he only sees patients until eighteen, but he may make an exception for us."

His jaw clenched, the ridiculous suggestion making his blood curdle. "Back off, Aunt Ros. This isn't even my stuff. Jace must've had it sent here since he's staying with his sister right now. And what are you doing opening my packages anyway?"

Her stern expression didn't soften. "The label said R. Jamison. And I have the right to open anything that's put on my doorstep."

He scrubbed a hand over his face. He was going to kill Jace. Beyond the embarrassment factor of being in the same room with his aunt and box of sex toys, he knew where this was headed. "I'm sorry. He should've never sent this here."

She eyed him with her trial lawyer shrewdness. "Reid, I don't have to remind you how important it is that you do nothing to bring attention to yourself during this campaign. Your uncle is running on a family values platform and I refuse to let your . . . issues put that at risk." She sighed and shook her head. "I thought we were past this."

"My *issues*?" he bit out. "What the hell? I haven't gotten in any trouble since high school. And even then, it was just stupid shit. You act like I'm a goddamned criminal."

She walked around the coffee table and came to stand in front of him, her diminutive stature doing nothing to diminish her powerful presence.

"But your father was. And this"—she cocked her head toward the emptied box—"was his specialty."

Like he needed a reminder. "It's not my stuff. And even if it were, I would never hurt a woman. I'm not him."

"Genes are a powerful thing, Reid. Don't underestimate them." She touched his shoulder, her tone gentling. "I know you can overcome them, but don't put yourself in bad situations. I'm only looking out for you."

And the campaign. She didn't say it, but he knew that's what she meant. "Right."

"Get rid of this stuff. I can't even imagine what poor Vanessa would think if she saw you with this filth. Don't mess things up with her—she's a fine young lady."

Vanessa. He hadn't thought about her all day. Hell, he hadn't thought about any woman since the new receptionist had started at work. He didn't know what it was, but something about Brynn held him captive. He'd barely gotten a lick of work done in three days.

But he definitely couldn't tell his aunt about Brynn. He knew Ros had heard wedding bells the minute he and Vanessa had started to see each other a few months ago. Both she and his uncle tag-teamed him regularly, pushing for him to make the relationship with the mayor's daughter exclusive. He crossed his arms over his chest. "I'll take care of it."

"Thank you." Ros gave his shoulder a quick squeeze, and then headed past him. He didn't unclench his teeth until she'd clicked his door shut behind her.

Stalking to the couch, he pulled his phone from his pocket and hit speed dial.

His best friend answered on the first ring. "Hey, brother."

"Jace, not only am I going to kill you, I'm going to do it slowly and painfully." Reid sank onto the couch.

Jace laughed. "You must've gotten my present."

"What were you thinking, sending this crap over here?" He lifted the handcuffs and examined them, heat rising in his gut as an image of him sliding the cool metal over the narrow wrists of a certain blonde receptionist filled his mind. He dropped them on the table. "My aunt opened it before I got home."

"Oh, shit."

"Yeah, now she's ready to sign me up with the kiddie shrink again, because I'm apparently a rapist-in-training."

Jace groaned. "Dude, I'm sorry. I just wanted to make sure my sister didn't see it. I told them to have it delivered to the guesthouse."

Reid didn't even want to ask what Jace could possibly need with all that stuff. He had enough crap to throw a goddamned orgy. "Just come and pick it up. I don't need her bringing my uncle over here to see it."

"Hey, look, take whatever you want from the box to keep," he suggested. "It's top-quality stuff. Consider it my apology for getting you in trouble."

He eyed the different items that had tumbled out of the box—things meant to restrain a woman, to cause pain, to bring pleasure. He wet his lips. "It's not my thing."

"Uh-huh," Jace said, his tone sly. "So you wouldn't want to try some of that stuff out on that pretty receptionist you were drooling over today?"

He coughed, his throat threatening to close as erotic images crowded his brain. "It's not for me."

Liar. Imagining Brynn bound and naked had his cock straining against his pants. Hell, talking to her that afternoon had done as much. But he couldn't tell Jace that—couldn't tell anyone. He'd kept those urges in check for as long as he could remember, and he definitely wouldn't risk screwing that up, especially with someone like Brynn. He liked her. Liked her enough not to inflict his darkest desires on her. No, with Brynn, he'd have to be extra careful.

THREE

now

Brynn waved as her date drove out of the dark parking lot. He'd received an emergency call and had to head to the hospital, saving Brynn the awkward end of night, this-ain't-gonna-happen conversation. She leaned against the brick wall outside the banquet hall and rubbed her hands over her face. What a disaster of a night.

Thank God tomorrow was Sunday. At least she could sleep in and pretend the outside world didn't exist for a little while. Maybe a day of pajamas, HGTV, and massive amounts of junk food could make her temporarily forget about facing Reid on Monday . . . and every workday after that. She groaned and tapped the back of her head against the wall, hoping maybe this was all some nightmare and she'd wake up.

"Sent him packing, huh?" The deep drawl caused her eyes to snap open. Reid leaned his shoulder against the wall, a hint of a smile playing on his lips.

She crossed her arms over her chest and straightened. "He got called into work. Not that it's any of your business."

He rubbed the back of his neck and looked at the half-empty parking lot. "Let me give you a ride home. It'll give us some time to catch up."

She couldn't help the derisive laugh that bubbled to her lips. "No thanks, I have my car, and please tell me you're not suggesting we need to catch up like old friends. Even you can't be that dense."

He angled toward her and planted a hand against the wall, right next to her head. His face moved to within inches of hers. "You really hate me that much, sugar?"

His calm, commanding tone and the old nickname sent goose bumps along her skin. She pressed her back against the wall, her heartbeat switching to double-time. *Here it comes.* She sucked in a ragged breath, and the smell of his cologne wrapped around her like a familiar blanket. Her muscles stiffened, bracing for the panic attack she knew would hit her at any moment. Being cornered sent all her fear triggers firing.

But the terror never came.

Instead, she couldn't take her eyes off the sensual curve of his mouth. She remembered all too well the things he could do with those lips, that tongue—how he could tease her body without mercy and then when she'd thought she'd go mad with need, send her rocketing into oblivion. A heated shudder rumbled through her and a sharp ache settled between her thighs.

His finger slipped under her chin and tilted it upward, so that she had to meet his eyes. "Well?"

His voice was so close it was as if he'd climbed inside her head. She wet her lips. "I—"

The blaring ring of her cell phone jolted her from her haze. Reid frowned down at her purse and shoved away from the wall.

She dug through her bag with shaking hands and grabbed the phone. "Hello?"

"Brynn, it's me."

She sighed. Late-night calls from her sister usually meant one of two things: she needed money or she was in some kind of trouble. "Hey, Kelsey. What's going on?"

"Are you busy? I know it's late, I'm sorry, I just . . . I need to talk with you and I couldn't wait until morning, and I . . . Can you talk?"

Shit. A rambling Kelsey—never a good sign. Brynn glanced at Reid, who was now sitting on the railing of the handicap ramp, watching her intently. She turned her back to him and faced the wall. "I have a minute, what's up?"

"No, I mean, like, talk in person. Something's going on, and I . . . well, I may need to get out of town for a while. But I want to talk to you first."

"Hold up. Leave town? What are you talking about?" She lowered her voice. "Kels, are you on something?"

"No. It's, I . . . Can you just meet me at my apartment? It's important."

Brynn pinched the bridge of her nose to ward off the sudden pounding in her head. The last thing she felt like doing was traipsing across town at midnight to go deal with what would surely be unfounded drama, but what else could she do? Her sister had been making slow progress toward bettering her life. If she was having a bout of paranoia or had slipped up and gotten high again, Brynn had to help her through that. Plus, Kelsey had no one else to go to—never had. "Sure, I can be there in half an hour."

Kelsey breathed a sigh of relief. "Thanks, B. Hurry, okay?"

"Will do. Just hold tight." Brynn clicked her phone shut and tucked it back in her bag. She didn't want to turn around. She could feel Reid's stare burning into her back. God, why had she let him get so close before? She needed to institute a five-foot rule with him—anything closer than that and her hormones could not be trusted. He'd probably seen the arousal written all over her flushed face.

"Your sister okay?" he asked.

She straightened her shoulders and turned around. "Eavesdrop much?"

He shrugged, unapologetic as usual.

"She's fine. She just wants me to stop by," Brynn said, rummaging through her purse for her keys.

"Right now?" He looked down at his watch.

She threw him a what's-it-to-you look, grabbed her keys, and headed in the direction of her car. His hand caught her upper arm when she passed him. "We need to talk."

She wiggled out of his grip, the skin-to-skin contact too much for her frazzled nervous system to handle. "I don't have time for this tonight. My sister needs me and it's not a short drive to Quincy Heights. So this little come-to-Jesus is going to have to wait."

His frown dipped deeper. "Quincy Heights? You can't go there at this hour. That neighborhood's a war zone."

She snorted. "I grew up in neighborhoods like that. I'll be fine."

She started walking again, but he hopped off the railing and caught up with her. "I'll drive you. I promise not to speak . . . much."

"Yes, because a hotshot lawyer in a Brooks Brothers suit is really going to scare off the bad guys." She halted her step and turned to face him. "Look, Reid. The last time I asked for help, you told me no. I don't plan on asking again. So, go home. Stop acting like there is some discussion we need to have. There isn't. Everything's been said. Just come to work on Monday and pretend like we've never met. 'Cause that's exactly what I'm going to do."

He eyed her, his jaw visibly flexing, but didn't say anything else.

Good. She'd take his broody silence as agreement. She spun on her heel and didn't bother to look back. Reid Jamison might've been able to bend her to his will when she was twenty, but if he thought his sexy smile and whispered commands would get him anywhere with her now, he was more delusional than her clients.

———

Brynn turned her car onto her sister's street. The apartment complex was the last residential holdout on a street littered with pawnshops, bail bondsmen, and strip clubs. Reid hadn't been off base in his assessment of the neighborhood. The Quincy Heights area probably had more hookers, drug addicts, and shootings than any other part of the city. Unfortunately, that type of area was more familiar to Brynn than the middle-class suburb she now called home. The part of Fort Worth she'd grown up in hadn't looked much different than this.

She parked along the curb, then opened her glove compartment to grab her mace. She may have told Reid she could handle it alone, but she wasn't stupid. She wasn't going to go out on these streets this late at night with only a few self-defense training classes under her belt. Weapons were better. She tucked the mace in her purse and climbed out of the car.

Besides a woman in stilettos and spandex standing on the corner a few yards away, the sidewalk was empty. Brynn clicked the alarm on her car and hurried to the stairwell of the three-story apartment complex. She had tried to convince her sister to move closer to her—even offered to help with the costs—but Kelsey had been dancing at the club down the street and said she was perfectly fine here.

Brynn suspected Kelsey's reluctance had more to do with her fear of being under Brynn's watchful eye than commuting convenience, but Brynn hadn't pushed. Her sister was making baby steps in the right direction, and she didn't want to scare her off by being overbearing.

Her feet ached by the time she reached the top floor. Strappy black pumps were not meant for hiking up three flights of stairs. The 3B label on her sister's door was peeling off around the corners. She smoothed her fingers over it, but the ends curled back up again. She took a deep breath, steeling herself for whatever state her sister was in, and knocked on the door.

No answer.

She knocked again, but got the same response. With a huff, she pulled out her cell phone and called her. It went straight to voice mail. Terrific. Kelsey had probably gotten over whatever crisis she had called her about and now had gone out.

Or.

Anxiety crawled up her spine. She'd had nightmares of getting that call in the middle of the night—the one that would say something had happened to her sister. She'd received a call like that about her mother three years ago, and she'd sworn to herself at the time that she would do all she could to make sure she never got that kind of call about Kelsey. Unfortunately, Kels hadn't always been so cooperative in helping Brynn keep that promise.

Brynn sorted through the keys on her key chain and found the one for her sister's apartment. If nothing was wrong, Kelsey would be pissed that she'd gone in without asking, but Brynn wouldn't be able to sleep tonight if she didn't make sure everything was okay. She closed her eyes and said a silent prayer she wasn't walking into a real-life version of one of her nightmares. But when she swung open the door, the only thing that greeted her was an empty apartment.

She hadn't been to her sister's place in over a month, but her mouth dropped open over the change. The last time, everything had been in disarray—empty cans and take-out boxes littering the counters in the tiny kitchen, dirty clothes piled on one side of the couch, and a layer of dust coating the few remaining surfaces. Now the only things that seemed out of place were a few cardboard boxes on the kitchen table. Everything else looked neat and freshly cleaned. Her sister had even draped bright afghan blankets over the shoddy brown couches, giving the room an almost cheery vibe.

"Kels," she called out. "You here?"

Brynn stepped inside and closed the door behind her. When she received no answer, she made her way across the small living room and tapped on the slightly ajar bedroom door. "Kelsey?"

She opened the door a bit and peeked inside. The bed was unmade, and a shirt and pair of jeans were strewn across the flower-print comforter, as if her sister had stripped them off in a hurry. Her mirrored closet door was open, revealing more empty hangers inside than clothes. Hell, had Kelsey been serious about leaving town? She barely had enough money to make rent each month, how was she going to afford a road trip?

Uneasiness settled over her. After another failed phone call to her sister, she headed back to the front door. Maybe Kelsey had gone by the club where she worked. Or, at the very least, maybe someone there would know where she was. Brynn locked up behind her and made her way down the stairs, her brain swirling.

The stench of stale alcohol hit her too late. A sweaty hand clamped over her forearm as she stepped off the last stair. "Hey, sweetheart, where ya going so fast?"

Brynn sucked in a breath, her heart stuttering in her chest. "Let go of me."

She tried to yank away from the man's grip, but he dug his fingers in tighter. A smile edged his thin lips. He couldn't have been older than his mid-twenties, but his face had the hardened look of a longtime drug user. "It's okay, I wouldn't hurt a pretty thing like you."

Yeah right, and she was the queen of England. She jammed the pointy heel of her shoe into the top of his foot, putting every ounce of her strength behind it. "I said, let go, asshole."

A slew of curses flew from his cracked lips, and his green eyes turned feral. Instead of releasing his grip like she'd hoped, he shoved her back into the darkened stairwell and slammed her against the wall, knocking the wind out of her. He leaned in close, his sour breath making her gag. "Well, I was just going to ask if you could spare a little cash, but now you've gone and pissed me off."

She swallowed hard, trying to ward off the oncoming panic attack, but it was too late. She gasped for breath, her lungs' capacity seeming to shrink in her chest. Sweat dampened her skin, and her head spun. She squeezed her eyes shut. *Breathe, Brynn. Think.*

The man's hand grasped the strap of her dress and yanked, tearing the thin piece of material.

Her knees went weak beneath her. She tried to think of the self-defense moves she'd learned, but she couldn't focus on anything except the fact that she was trapped. That this was happening again. She wouldn't survive a second rape. Her mind had barely survived the first. Her words tumbled out at a frantic pace. "You can have my purse, I have cash in my wallet. Please don't do this."

"Should've thought of that before you broke my fucking toe," he growled. His hand pulled harder on the torn strap, exposing her bra. She opened her mouth to scream, but he smacked her hard across the face, her ears ringing from the blow.

"Don't even think about it, or I'll make this much worse."

The image of his face blurred as tears pricked her eyes. Then, it disappeared from view.

"What the—" the man started, but was interrupted by a sharp crunching sound.

Brynn swiped at her eyes to find the guy on the ground, holding his bloodied nose, six feet of suit-clad lawyer standing over him with rage on his face. The man jumped up and started swinging at Reid, landing a fist to his chin. He was much smaller than Reid, but Brynn knew drugs could make a person pretty powerful.

"Shit." She pulled herself out of her shocked state and plunged her hand into her purse. Her fingers curled around the can of mace, and she ran toward the fray. The two men were punching and swinging at each other in a violent dance. She didn't know how to help. The wild-eyed man noticed her standing there and lunged at her. She reacted without thought, emptying the can of mace in his general direction.

"Motherfucker," he cried, grabbing at his eyes.

She almost smiled, but then heard a deep groan from Reid. "Son of a bitch!"

Brynn glanced at Reid and cringed when she saw he was also reaching for his eyes. The would-be rapist stumbled past her, out of the stairwell, and onto the street, apparently admitting defeat. She hurried to Reid's side, her throat itching and eyes watering from the residual spray. "Oh, God, are you okay?"

His face was red and tears streamed out the corners of his closed lids. He opened his mouth to respond, but went into a coughing fit instead.

She wiped at his face and patted his back, not sure what to do. "I'm so sorry. I panicked. I didn't mean to get you."

"Where'd he go?" he asked between coughs.

She looked back to the street. "He ran—he's gone. What can I do to help you?"

He moaned. "Water? Fire hose? Something to flush it out."

"Right, okay." She grasped his elbow. "Come on, I have a key to my sister's apartment. Let me get you up there."

———

Reid leaned his head sideways over the kitchen sink as Brynn poured another cup of cool water over his eyes. They still burned like the fires of hell, but at least his vision had returned and he could speak again. She brushed her hand over his forehead, pushing his hair out of the way. "Any better?"

"I think I'll live," he said, straightening. She handed him a clean dish towel, and he patted his face with it. "Next time aim for the bad guy, okay?"

"Which one was that, again?"

He shot her a withering look.

She gave a sheepish smile. "Kidding. I got him, too."

"Good, I hope he stumbled into the street and got hit by a goddamned truck," he said, his anger firing up again in his belly. Fucking bastard. The guy was lucky Brynn had sprayed her mace. Otherwise, Reid might not have been able to stop himself from beating the man into an early grave. The way Brynn had been shaking. Jesus. From wildcat to kitten with the flip of a switch. "We need to call the police. Report him."

She rubbed her bare arms and nodded. "Yeah, although I'm sure he's long gone by now."

"He may have to go to the hospital for the nose. They could check for him there."

She sank into one of the dining chairs, her cheek still scarlet from where the jerk had struck her. "What were you doing there anyway?"

He smirked and propped a hip against the kitchen counter. "Because a hotshot lawyer *can* take care of the bad guys in a pinch, so I followed you. I wasn't going to let you come out here alone at night . . . looking like that."

She glanced down at her dress. "Like what?"

His gaze traced the delicate line of her neck, the deep V-cut of her dress, and the swell of her breasts. His mouth watered at the memories of how that ivory skin tasted—like sugared strawberries. He cleared his throat and looked down at the now bloodied dishtowel clenched in his fist. "Never mind. It's just not a place you should come to by yourself."

"Hell," she said, getting to her feet again, "I didn't even notice your hand. You're bleeding."

"I'm fine."

She grabbed his biceps and guided him back to the sink. "Rinse it with soap and water. I'll go and see if Kelsey keeps any first aid stuff around."

She disappeared into the bathroom, and he turned on the faucet. The soap stung, but the cuts seemed minor, although his knuckles were already starting to swell. He shook his head. That'd be great for first impressions with clients on Monday. *Yes, let me help you with your domestic violence case. Oh, yeah, don't mind the black-and-blue knuckles. I'm really a good, responsible professional.*

Brynn emerged from the bathroom with a handful of Band-Aids and a bottle of hydrogen peroxide. She pointed to the dining room table. "Sit."

He dried his hands with a paper towel and fought a smile. She always had been a bossy little thing. But he knew the truth. Underneath all that tight control was a woman who, at least when he'd known her, loved handing over the reins. He swallowed hard, tamping down memories he didn't need to rehash at the moment.

He dropped into one of the chairs, and Brynn sat across from him, her knees bumping against his. He widened his legs, and after the briefest of hesitations, she scooted forward, allowing his thighs to frame the outsides of hers as she reached for his injured hand. She circled her fingers around his right wrist, his pulse jumping at her touch, and brought his hand up to her face to examine it. His fingers itched to reach out and trace the bow of her lips.

Dammit. He took a deep breath, trying to keep his desire to touch her in check, but the citrus scent of her shampoo drifted to his nose and sent a bolt of carnal need straight to his groin.

He stared down at her. One quick grasp of her waist and he could lift her to straddle his lap, bunch up that dress, and slide his cock right into her sweet heat—kiss away all the tension furrowing her brow, drive her to that place of wild abandon he knew she could reach.

Without thinking, he lifted his other hand and twined her broken dress strap between his fingers, brushing the backs of his sore knuckles across her collarbone in the process. The small catch of breath in the back of her throat made his balls tighten. Such a feminine sound, so close to the noise she would make as he entered her.

But she didn't raise her eyes to him and beg him to take her like he secretly hoped she would. She simply took the slip of material from him and tucked it under her bra strap to hold it in place, sending her message loud and clear. *Not yours.*

Not anymore.

"This may hurt a little," she said, her voice tighter than it had been. She laid his hand on the table, moved her chair back a notch, and dampened a cotton ball with disinfectant.

He winced when the cotton touched his open skin, the sting helping to drag his mind back from the depths. He shifted in his seat. "So where is your sister anyway? Isn't she the whole reason you rushed out here?"

She glanced up, her green eyes glinting with worry before she dropped her focus back to her task. "She wasn't here when I arrived, and I can't get her on her phone."

He frowned. "Is it standard MO for her?"

She shrugged, but the motion seemed tense instead of casual.

"Is she still . . ." He paused, not knowing how to phrase it politely.

Brynn smirked at him. "Fucked up?"

Looking at this refined blonde in her elegant outfit, he'd forgotten where Brynn had come from. She'd never been one to mince words. He nodded.

She rose and returned to the adjoining kitchen, turning her

back to him as she opened the freezer. "After the murder, she really took a turn for the worse, blamed herself. And she was still convinced the asshole you defended was innocent."

The muscles in his neck bunched. Hank Caldwell was innocent—*is innocent*. Unfortunately, Reid had failed to prove that to the jury, which was the first in the trifecta of lost cases that had led to his demotion from lead attorney. Now Hank sat rotting away in prison with a life sentence, waiting for Reid to pull a miracle out of his ass for an appeal.

However, he knew better than to preach Hank's innocence to Brynn and throw a match on that powder keg. The one time he'd approached her during the trial to see if he could interview Kelsey for the defense, Brynn had jumped his shit like he was the devil asking for her soul. She'd wanted him to drop the case entirely, but of course he couldn't do that. Not when he knew in his gut that Hank wasn't the guy.

The stark betrayal that had flashed in Brynn's eyes that day had sliced right through him. He'd seen the switch flip—the look of total dismissal. *You no longer exist to me.* So if she had any clue he was actively working on Hank's appeal now, she'd probably shove him out of Kelsey's third-floor window.

Luckily, Brynn continued on without waiting for his input. "But the last few months, she's been making some progress. I got her to go to a detox program and a few therapy sessions. And she's been sober—at least she was the last couple of times I saw her. But tonight, she sounded a little freaked out, paranoid."

He flexed his fingers, which were quickly stiffening. "Any idea where she could be?"

"Here, this will help with the swelling." She handed him a plastic baggy full of ice. "I honestly have no clue. It's not like her to ignore her phone. I was headed over to the club where she works to see if anyone knew anything when that asshole attacked me."

"Speaking of which, we need to put in a call to the police." He dug in his pocket, but she waved him off.

"I got it. I saw him up close and personal. I'll be able to give a better description." She walked into the tiny living room and pulled out her phone, putting as much distance between the two of them as possible.

Her voice didn't waver as she relayed the information to the police, but she paced around the room, wearing a track into the already threadbare carpet. Occasionally, she would stop to peek through the blinds of the front window as if to will her sister to appear.

Reid stood and tossed the bag of ice onto the counter, Brynn's nerves setting him on edge. Why would her sister drag her out here then bail without even calling her back? He eyed the boxes on the dining room table, then flicked a quick glance at Brynn to make sure she was sufficiently absorbed in the conversation. He hooked a finger into one of the boxes and slid it closer so he could peek at the contents.

Papers, envelopes, a small notebook—all shoved in there in no apparent order. He rifled through some of the papers, then picked up the notebook and flipped through a few pages. There were a couple of initials and random phone numbers, one of which was for Cowgirls, the strip club down the street. He set the notebook to the side and rifled through another stack of papers.

As he reached the bottom, he froze, a familiar company name catching his eye. *Grant Waters, Inc.* To the rest of Dallas—the wealthy vineyard owner and producer of Water's Edge Wines. But to those in the know—someone completely different. The yellow paper was the carbon copy of a background check form Kelsey had filled out.

A sinking feeling settled in his stomach. Last he'd checked, Kelsey was no farmhand. He set the form aside and grabbed the notebook again, flipping back to the number for Cowgirls. Maybe the strip club would have some information. He pulled his phone out of his pocket and dialed the number.

"Cowgirls, this is Nina," a cigarette-roughened voice said over the blaring background music.

"Hey, is Kelsey performing tonight?" he asked.

"Oh, honey, Kiki isn't here," she said, smacking her gum loudly. "But if you like blondes with d-cups, Alexis is going on in about half an hour. She'll get you going as well as Kiki could've."

He sighed in mock disappointment, making sure the girl continued to believe he was a customer. "Is Kel—I mean, Kiki, on vacation or something?"

She laughed. "What is it with that girl? You're, like, the third call I've gotten asking about her. I'm sorry, but she quit a few days ago. Said she got a better-paying gig."

"Do you know where?"

"Ooh, you got it bad, huh? She didn't say, but I know it's not one of the clubs around here. I would've heard."

"All right, Nina. Thanks for your help."

"No problem, sweet thing."

He clicked the phone shut and turned back toward the living room. Brynn was leaning on the back edge of the couch watching him, her lips pressed into a grim line. "She's not there."

He shook his head. "Quit a few days ago. The girl said Kelsey took another job."

Brynn's threw her hands out to her sides. "Why the hell wouldn't she tell me she'd changed jobs?"

"I may have some idea," Reid said, glancing at the background form again. "Do you know if Kelsey is into anything kinky?"

She glanced at the table, then back to him, a little crease between her brows. "Well, stripping isn't exactly run-of-the-mill."

He shook his head and met her confused gaze. "No, I mean, like the D/s scene."

Her eyes shifted away and he could almost visualize porcupine quills popping out of her skin. "How the hell would I know that? 'Do you let a guy use you like a whore?' is not exactly a question that comes up in sisterly conversation."

He cringed, the words wrenching his gut. "Is that what you think it was? You think I used you?"

She crossed her arms over her chest and glared at him. "What exactly would you call it, Reid? I bet you weren't tying up and ordering around that debutante girlfriend of yours—you know, the one you forgot to tell me about."

She was right. He hadn't been topping Vanessa. She would've sent her father after him with a shotgun if he'd done so much as copped a feel. But he'd had to toe the line—parade around with the girl he was expected to date. He blew out a breath and raked a hand through his hair. "It wasn't like that."

"No, I get it. Do the depraved stuff with the chick whose mother is a hooker, do the respectable things with the girl you want everyone to see on your arm. It's an old story," she said, sounding tired. "I was just too naive to see what role I was playing in the game."

His jaw clenched. "I don't know how I ended up the bad guy in all this. I seem to recall I wasn't the only one you were *playing* with."

She sighed and all the fight seemed to leave her stance. "Look, it doesn't matter, okay. What's done is done. I just want to know what all this has to do with my sister."

He stared at her for a moment, part of him wanting to hash out their past, drag everything out in the open, and deal with it head-on, but the lines of worry in her face stopped him. He crooked a thumb at the boxes. "I looked through some of your sister's stuff. She filled out a background check form for Grant Waters' company."

Her forehead scrunched. "Who the hell is that?"

"He owns two big vineyards outside of town. And he runs The Ranch."

"Is that another strip club?"

He shook his head, tension taking root in his shoulders. "No, and I'm not sure on the details. But what I do know is that it's a BDSM retreat. Elite, exclusive, and if someone wants to disappear for a while—a good place to hide."

She chewed her lip, as if mulling over the information. "But if it's so exclusive, how would Kels get in?"

He shrugged. "Your sister's a beautiful girl who's not afraid to show her body. My guess is that they probably hired her on as a server or attendant of some kind."

She crossed the few steps to the counter and grabbed her purse and keys. "Well, then, what are we hanging around for? Let's go to this stupid place and get her."

"Brynn." He grabbed her wrist before she reached the door.

She glanced back over her shoulder, urgency rolling off her. "What's wrong?"

"I have no idea where this place is. And even if I did, you're not going to be able to get in without an invitation . . . or a master."

All the blood drained from her face. She glanced down at his fingers circling her wrist and jerked her arm free. "What? I can't—"

"Look, calm down," he said, frowning down at her. "We can't do anything tonight, but I know someone who may have a connection there. Let me see if I can get any information—find out if your sister is even there. In the meantime, you can go home and call anyone you can think of—her friends, boyfriends, whoever. Someone has to know where she is."

Brynn chewed her lip, considering him, then nodded. "Okay. I guess that's the best we can do tonight."

He walked her down to her car, keeping an eye on their surroundings to make sure her attacker hadn't decided to hang around.

She pulled open her car door and slid in, looking up at him

with tired eyes. "Thanks for your help. I take back the comment about you not being able to scare off bad guys."

He smiled. "Thanks, and I don't mind helping."

She dug in her purse and pulled out a business card. "Here. My cell is on there. Call me if you find anything out."

He took the card from her and slipped it into his pocket, then feigned a grimace. "Shit."

"What's wrong?"

"I must've left my cell upstairs."

She moved to climb out of the car. "Oh, well, I can go grab it for you."

He held up a hand. "No, it's late, and the sooner you're out of this neighborhood, the better. Why don't you just give me your sister's key and you can leave? I'll get the key back to you on Monday."

She paused, evaluating him for a moment, then glanced down the darkened street. "Yeah, okay, but just make sure everything's locked when you leave."

She slid the key off her key chain and handed it over. Trusting him.

Guilt flooded him, but he charged forward with his plan anyway. "No worries. I'll just run in and then lock back up. And I promise I'll touch base with you tomorrow if I can find anything out."

"Thanks." She pulled her seat belt across her chest. "Good night, Reid."

"Drive safe, sugar." He shut her door and waited on the curb, watching her taillights fade around the corner. As soon as he was sure she was far enough away, he jogged back up the stairs and let himself into Kelsey's apartment, locking the door behind him.

Surveying the room, his eyes honed in on the boxes he hadn't been able to explore while Brynn was there. The ones labeled

Mom's things. Thinking about what could be in those boxes had made his heart pick up speed. Last week when he'd visited Hank in jail, he'd told Reid that Kelsey had called him—said she may have found something that could help him get an appeal. Reid had planned to contact Kelsey to see what she had come across, but now . . .

He tapped down the guilt about being there uninvited and went into the kitchen to grab a pair of rubber gloves from under the sink. If he found anything of use, he didn't want his fingerprints all over it. He hoped what he needed was in one of those boxes. But if it wasn't, he wasn't going to leave the apartment until he'd searched every inch of the place. If Kelsey had some key to getting Hank out of jail, he was going to do every damn thing possible to get his hands on it.

Even if that meant he'd have to hunt down Brynn's sister himself.

FOUR

then

Mr. Jamison stepped out of his office with Reid not far behind. Brynn smiled as the older man stopped in front of her desk.

"Ms. LeBreck, it's almost seven, what are you still doing slaving away?"

She held up a stack of envelopes. "I told Mr. Ackerman I would stay late tonight and stuff these."

He leaned over her desk and looked at the piles of flyers on the floor. He shook his head. "You work late all the time. You're too young to work that hard. Go home, my dear. Take a night off. I'll make sure you get paid overtime for the evening."

Reid broke into a wide grin behind his uncle.

Brynn smiled. "That's really nice of you, but I don't mind staying."

He tapped his palm against the desk. "That's an order, Ms. LeBreck. Get out of here. I'll close up behind you."

Well, she wasn't going to argue with that. Mr. Jamison strolled off toward the copy room, and Reid replaced him at the front of her desk. She raised an eyebrow at him and pulled out her purse. "What's with the shit-eating grin?"

"I have a date tonight."

She choked back the bitter taste that stole across her tongue, knowing that she had no right to be upset. She and Reid had fallen into a comfortable friendship at work over the last few weeks— their playful banter the bright spot in her long days. But she'd never given him any indication she was interested in anything more or told him that when she finally lay in bed at night, that it was his face she pictured, his hands she imagined on her when she touched herself.

She couldn't tell him. Their lives were so far apart from each other, they might as well belong to different species. She gave him a stiff smile. "Good for you."

He laughed and held out his hand. "Come on, LeBreck. Let's go."

She stared at his open palm. "What are you talking about?"

He smirked. "I'm talking about a date—me, you, some food, all congregating in the same general area. You told me the day we met you didn't have time for a burger. Now you've been given two hours you didn't plan on having, so you owe me a date."

She sighed and pushed her hair behind her ears. "Reid—"

He wagged his finger at her. "Nope, can't turn me down. You don't want to be responsible for crushing my fragile ego, do you?"

She snorted, but slipped her hand into his and let him help her to her feet. "Your ego is about as delicate as a freight train."

He pulled her closer to his side and guided her toward the door. "It's just a burger, Brynn."

A few minutes later, Reid turned his truck into the drive-thru at the Burger Haven and ordered their meals. She shifted in her seat, the leather sticking to her bare legs. "I thought we were going to eat here."

He pulled up to the window and paid for the food, then

handed her the greasy paper bags. "The grub here is good, but the ambience leaves a lot to be desired."

She snuck a fry from one of the bags and popped it in her mouth. "So where are you taking me, then?"

He waggled his eyebrows. "My evil lair."

"No, seriously."

He laughed. "And I thought I was a control freak. Relax. We're not going far."

Reid drove a few miles off the highway and parked next to a tree-lined pond, shutting off the engine right as the final edge of sun slipped beneath the horizon. Brynn peered out the window at the small park, its only occupant a lone goose wandering around one of the benches that lined the water's banks.

"Looks like a real popular place," she said, unbuckling her seatbelt.

He chuckled. "It is during the day. People just don't realize how cool it is at night."

She looked out the window again. Obviously, coolness was in the eye of the beholder. "Yeah, I bet serial killers and drug dealers find it very appealing."

That earned her a snort from him before he stepped out of the truck and came around to her side to open her door. "Come on, I'll show you."

She handed him the food and stepped down, the warm breeze lifting her hair off the back of her neck. He grabbed her hand, his fingers interlacing with hers. She couldn't fight the smile that played around her lips. Reid was making an effort for this to feel like a date, which she appreciated. She'd been out with a few guys during high school, but usually the "dates" consisted of hanging out at each other's houses and having awkward make-out sessions before their parents came home. Although, in her case, she always made sure she went to their place instead of bringing them to hers.

Reid placed the bags in the bed of the truck and unhitched the tailgate. "Hop up."

She frowned. "Not the best day to wear a skirt."

"Funny, I was thinking it was an excellent choice."

She rolled her eyes.

"Come on, I'll help you. I promise not to peek." He put his hands on her waist and hoisted her up as if she weighed nothing. The wind caught the light material and sent her skirt fluttering upward, no doubt revealing her underwear in the process. She tamped it down with her hands, but not quickly enough. Reid grinned and put a foot on the tailgate, stepping up in one fluid motion.

She punched his thigh. "You are such a liar. You totally looked."

"Hey," he said, rubbing his leg and laughing. "It happened too fast. And they're pink panties. It was like a tractor beam. How am I supposed to turn away from that?"

She groaned. "Guys are all the same."

He unlocked the truck's steel storage bin and pulled out a flannel blanket, smiling as he spread it out. "When it comes to the chance to see up a pretty girl's skirt, you're probably right. I'm sorry. Guess I shouldn't have made a promise I couldn't keep." He took the burgers and fries out of the bags, uncapped the two bottles of soda, and then patted the spot next to him. "Still willing to eat with me?"

She should've been annoyed—the wicked glint in his eyes said his apology was less than authentic. But instead, his unrepentant playfulness only drew her to him more. Even with the effect he had on her hormones, something about him put her at ease— made the air around her feel lighter, the stress of the day not as daunting.

If she hadn't been working with him, she would've assumed this was how Reid went through life—always cracking a joke, enjoying every moment, not a care in the world. But she hadn't missed his switch in demeanor when his aunt and uncle were around. As soon as one of them walked through the office, it was as if Reid had a steel rod shoved up his back and all that easy confidence seemed to drain away.

Brynn wasn't sure which version of Reid was the real one—the self-assured charmer or the wary political son. Maybe neither.

She scooted over to his side and unwrapped her sandwich. "So what's so cool about this place?"

"Besides the fact that *we're* here?" He sipped his drink and glanced at his watch. "You'll see. Should start anytime now."

They ate their burgers for a few minutes, the song of the cicadas and frogs providing the only chatter. She wanted to lean into him, to know what it would feel like for him to wrap his arms around her, to taste his kiss, but she glued her butt to the spot. This was just a burger. He'd said so himself. She needed to enjoy it for what it was. And even without him cuddled close, an unfamiliar feeling of contentment settled over her.

Every evening she either ate her meals on the run or in her room after she had cooked for her sister. Having someone to sit with was nice. She turned to Reid to tell him how much she appreciated him bringing her here, but a loud whooshing sound cut her off. "What in the world—"

"Here we go," Reid said, and put a hand on her shoulder. "Lie back and look up."

She set her sandwich down and lay next to him, her gaze going to the stars. The roaring grew louder, until it was almost deafening. She winced, but just when she thought her ears couldn't take any more, the inky sky disappeared and the silver underbelly of a plane replaced it. The massive aircraft seemed as if it was going to land on top of the truck, but instead zoomed past them and touched down on a runway hidden behind the trees. The leaves around them shook and warm air gusted over her in the jet's wake.

She turned to Reid. "Wow."

He grinned, his face inches from hers. "Awesome, huh?"

She laughed. "Scared the hell out of me at first, but yeah, definitely. I had no idea you could get this close."

His gaze scanned her face, pausing on her lips, tracking down her neck, then back up. "Yeah, the view's pretty amazing this close up."

Her body warmed under his stare, her heartbeat picking up tempo. She turned back toward the sky, hoping her voice would come out steady. "So can the people in the plane see us down here?"

"No, I don't think so. Not at night. I've landed on this runway during the day and all you can see of the park is the pond and trees."

"Must be pretty neat to see it from that perspective. I've never been on a plane," she said, an unexpected wistfulness tingeing her tone.

He shifted onto his side, propping himself up with his elbow and looking down at her. "More of a road-trip girl?"

She shrugged. "I don't exactly have room in my life for vacations."

His eyes searched hers. "No time for trips, no time for dates, what's got you so busy, Brynn LeBreck? You're not secretly working undercover for the FBI or something, right?"

She laughed. "Why? You have something to hide?"

He leaned in a bit, like he was going to tell her a secret. "Only that I've got a mad crush on a girl who won't even tell me the littlest thing about herself."

The balmy notes of his voice moved over her like a caress, turning her insides liquid. She attempted a lighthearted smile. "There's just not that much to tell. I've been going to community college for two years and am working to save money so that my sister and I can move to Austin in the fall. I have a scholarship to UT. That's about it. My life isn't exciting like yours."

He sniffed. "You think my life's exciting? I go to summer school, and then play the political game for the rest of the afternoon."

She turned onto her side, mirroring his pose, needing to get some space between them. "You don't seem to mind playing the role at work."

"Being good at something and enjoying it are two totally different things. I hate the whole song and dance of politics. Drives me nuts. I just want to tell all those people who are trying to kiss Uncle Patrick's ass via mine to fuck off. But he's done a lot for me, so I smile and shake hands like I'm supposed to."

She cocked her head to the side. "Why do you live with them?"

"They're the only family I have around here." A glimmer of sadness crossed his features. "My mom died of cancer when I was twelve. Aunt Roslyn took me in, and she and Patrick adopted me officially a year later. Hence, the Jamison last name."

"I'm sorry. Losing your mom that young had to be hard."

"Yeah, I didn't handle it so well. Gave my aunt and uncle hell for a few years. I was pretty angry at the universe. But then I realized my mom would've kicked my ass if she saw how I was behaving, so I got my act together." The corner of his mouth tilted into a wistful smile. "I wish she were still around. She was awesome—really got me, you know?"

Brynn nodded, although she had no idea what it must feel like to have someone like that.

"But at least I had somewhere to go when I lost her, even if it meant dealing with all that goes along with filling the role of the Jamison son." He leaned over and tucked a stray lock of her hair behind her ear, sending goose bumps down her neck. "That's one of the things I like about you. You don't seem to give a damn about who my family is, so I can just relax around you."

She laughed. "Yeah, once I found out you couldn't fire me, you lost all shot of me kissing your ass."

He slipped a hand onto her hip and pulled her closer, their

bodies almost touching. "So what's your stance on kissing other things?"

Every muscle in her body strained to move forward, to close the sliver of distance between them, but she held still. "Probably not a good idea since we work together."

He smiled and shook his head. "See, you're always such a half-empty kind of girl. Working together means we'll get paid to hang out with each other."

"And everybody in the office will think I'm hanging out with you for the wrong reasons."

He shrugged. "That's why we don't tell. It's none of their business anyway."

She chewed her lip. "I like you, Reid, but I don't know . . . it's just complicated. I've got a lot—"

He put a finger over her mouth, hushing her. "Stop overthinking things, Brynn. It doesn't have to be so complex. I know you don't bullshit, so I'm not going to either. Since the first day I met you, I haven't stopped thinking about what it would be like to touch you." He cupped her chin and ran his thumb over her lips. "To taste you. I leave the office every day fighting a hard-on because just hearing your voice sets me off."

She swallowed hard, the blunt words and his finger on her lips throwing gasoline on the flickering flame of longing she'd been fighting since they'd left the office.

"So in about three seconds, I'm going to kiss you. If you don't want that, you tell me to stop, and I'll never try again." He curled his hand around the back of her neck, his gaze tattooing her. "One . . . two . . ."

"Three," she whispered.

He leaned over and touched his lips to hers, a deceptively gentle press that, from someone else, would've seemed sweet, innocent even. But the heated grip on the back of her neck and jolt of awareness that sizzled down her nerve endings were something else altogether. With a maddeningly slow pace, he tasted each part of her mouth—the corners, the bow at the top, the line where both lips met—like he was cataloguing every nuance of her skin, each flavor. She gave a little whimper of protest and he pulled back, holding her gaze for a moment. "Changed your mind?"

She should stop him; that'd be the smart thing to do. But her hormones claimed veto power over her brain. She reached for him, gliding her fingertips over the hint of stubble on his cheek, then down his neck to his collar. She gave it a gentle tug and pulled him with her as she rolled from her side to her back. If she was going to be stupid, why do it halfway? "Kiss me like you want to kiss me. I can feel you holding back."

The blue in his eyes darkened as they swept over her face, her neck, lower. "Be careful what you ask for, sugar."

She shivered beneath his hungry perusal. "I trust you."

Something unidentifiable flickered across his features before he dipped his head and claimed her mouth again, blanketing her with his upper body. This time, there was no tentativeness, no teasing. Only white-hot rawness.

Just like in the fantasies she weaved in the privacy of her bedroom, Reid took control—his kiss as unapologetic as the man himself. Commanding fingers twisted in her hair, and his tongue coaxed her lips open, exploring her mouth with an adeptness that made her ache for more of him. Her nipples tightened against the thin material of her bra at the mere thought of what Reid's talented tongue could offer them. She fisted the back of his polo shirt and arched into him.

He dragged his teeth against her lower lip and then nibbled along her jawline, making his way down to her neck. "God, you taste better than I could've imagined . . . so sweet."

She writhed under his attention. The thought that he had

imagined what she would taste like sent a ridiculous giddiness through her. Her voice came out in a whisper: "You've thought about this? About me?"

He groaned. "Every fucking day, Brynn. I can't get you out of my mind. Every time you even look my way at the office, all I can think about is how bad I want you, wondering what it would be like to have you come apart beneath me."

She shuddered against him, and a murmur of pleasure passed her lips before she could stop it. She'd never had a guy talk so blatantly about sex, but instead of offending her, it made the throbbing between her thighs more unbearable.

He chuckled, the sound low and dark. "And you like dirty talk. Sugar, you're going to make me lose my damn mind."

He moved lower, pressing soft kisses to her collarbone, then to the vee of skin exposed by her blouse. His fingers toyed with the first button and paused for a second, as if waiting for her to say something. When she didn't, he unfastened the top two and opened her shirt. Gentle hands caressed her over her bra, providing just enough stimulation to whet her need, but not enough to satisfy. She closed her eyes, her voice a quiet plea. "Please."

"Unhook it for me, show me what you want," he said, his seductive tone like warm cashmere against her skin.

With clumsy fingers, she released the front clasp of her bra, baring her curves to him and the muggy night air. A lazy smile crossed his face as he cupped one of her breasts and ran a thumb across its peak. "I could spend all night just focusing on these. Look how hard and pink they are for me already."

He pinched one of her nipples and rolled it between his fingertips, the sensation rocketing straight down her abdomen to the swollen bundle of nerves between her legs. She bit her lip and whimpered.

Before she could suck in another breath, the hot cavern of

his mouth closed over one nipple. Tongue and teeth alternately laved and nibbled, the twining pleasure/pain combination making her back arch. She threaded her hands into his dark hair, gripping hard, trying to hold on to the shred of self-control she still had.

She wasn't this kind of girl. Despite what the high school rumor mill had said once people found out what her mother did for a living, she'd only slept with one guy. But right now, she couldn't think of anything she wanted more than Reid inside her, claiming every part of her.

His head lifted as his teeth nipped her ear, his hot breath marking her neck. His hand moved to her knee and then slid up her leg at a languid pace, pulling her skirt with it. She parted her thighs, so ready for his touch she thought she would hyperventilate if he didn't get there soon.

Recognizing the invitation, he ran his palm against the outside of her panties, rubbing the soaked satin against her clit. She rocked against his touch, and he slipped his hand below the waistband, sliding his fingers along her hot button before dipping lower.

Her head tipped back, sharp darts of pleasure shooting through her. "Oh, God."

Reid groaned and pulled his hand back.

A flutter of panic seized her. Why was he stopping? "What's wrong?"

He stared down at her, lines of strain etching his face. "Brynn, tell me to stop."

She wet her lips, her throat going dry. "Why?"

"Because this isn't why I brought you here." He raked a hand through his dark hair. "And because if you don't, I'm going to strip you bare and fuck you until you scream so loud the people flying overhead will be able to hear you come."

"The hell you are," said a booming, southern voice.

Brynn jumped at the stranger's words, scrambling to pull her top closed and her skirt down. "Shit, shit, shit."

The beam of a flashlight pierced the darkness, and Reid put a hand up to block his eyes. "Hello?"

A stern, middle-aged face peered over the side of the truck. The state trooper adjusted the brim of his hat. "What the hell do you two think you're doing?"

Reid sat upright, scooting in front of Brynn. "Evening, Officer. We were just, uh, having a little dinner."

"Uh-huh," the man said, shining the flashlight on Brynn as she fastened the last button on her shirt. "I have a feeling I know what's on the menu. Do you kids know I could arrest you for indecency in a public park? Or worse." He turned his light back to Reid. "You didn't give this young lady money for her services, did you?"

Brynn's mouth dropped open. "Jesus, I'm not a prostitute. We were just kissing."

The cop quirked an eyebrow at her. "Well, then I suggest the two of you try to conduct yourselves in a more respectable manner. If I catch either of you out here again, I'll take you both in."

Reid raised his hands and gave the officer a smile that dripped with sincerity. "We are so sorry, Officer. It won't happen again. We'll get right on out of here. Thank you for letting us by with a warning."

The cop grunted and crossed his arms over his chest. Waiting.

They hurriedly gathered their things and climbed into the cab of the truck. Brynn's cheeks burned so hot, she was sure she had turned a shade of purple. God, how had she let that get so out of hand? She'd never lost control like that with anyone. One kiss and she'd been ready to screw Reid until the sun came up. All the reasons of why a relationship with him was a terrible idea had evaporated from her mind the instant his lips had touched hers. Dangerous.

Reid merged onto the highway and after a long stretch of silence, cleared his throat. "You okay?"

No. "I'm fine. Just a little embarrassed."

He gave her a rueful smile. "Sorry about what happened."

She turned to look out the window, afraid that he'd be able to read her thoughts on her face. "Not your fault. I'm just glad he didn't take us in."

"No kidding. I can't even imagine how happy the media would've been over that—candidate's nephew gets arrested for public indecency. My aunt and uncle would've had a shit fit."

She stared out the window as cars whizzed by, feeling like she was in some alternate universe. Reid's biggest worry about an arrest was media coverage; hers was that she'd have no one to post bail to get her out. The contrast would've been laughable if it wasn't so damn depressing.

He reached out and gave her hand a quick squeeze. "I promise less mortification and threat of arrest on our next date."

She closed her eyes and leaned against the headrest, hoping he would take the hint she didn't want to talk. She'd thought that maybe she'd be able to keep it light and have a little fun, but an hour alone with Reid and she'd been ready to lose herself. Something she couldn't afford to do with someone like him. She couldn't tell him right now, but no matter how much she liked him, there would be no second date.

FIVE

now

Reid ordered another coffee and dumped some salsa on his huevos rancheros while Detective Will Green examined the papers Reid had given him. Reid knew not to bother the man once he'd retreated into the zone—that place where cops go when trying to put all the pieces together. But he couldn't help but watch every tick of the cop's expression, hoping Will saw as much potential in the documents as he had.

One refill and a clean plate later, the detective looked up, lines of frustration cutting into his dark skin. "Where did you get this?"

Reid dodged the question, not ready to tell the detective he'd found the ledger—via illegal search—in a hollowed out dictionary in Kelsey's nightstand. "Kelsey, the vic's youngest daughter, contacted Hank about the evidence a few days ago. I think she found it when she went through some of her mother's old things. I just got ahold of it last night, but from what I can tell, the ledger lists all of the victim's client appointments and payments going back two years before her death. Including a big transaction scheduled for the day she was killed."

He nodded. "Yeah, I saw that. Not sure what a hooker could do to warrant a twenty-five-thousand-dollar fee. No lay is *that* good."

Reid gave him a humorless smile. "Celia LeBreck used to work in the high-end strip clubs. Not until after she had her second child did she start turning tricks on the street. Maybe she still had connections to someone she met in her glory days." He pointed at the photocopies he'd made of Celia's appointment book. "This J. Kennedy person listed on the last day. He's in there a number of times before that, but only for a thousand bucks at a time."

Will's eyes narrowed. "Maybe she had something on him and was upping the ante."

"That's what I'm thinking," Reid said, nodding. "And maybe he didn't want to pay up."

"This definitely throws suspicion away from your client. I never did believe that kid was the guy, but I don't know if this is enough to get you an appeal." The detective stared at the copies again, rubbing his chin. "Unless we can figure out her code and actually get some solid suspects. Every name in here is a fake one."

Reid sank back in the booth and sighed. "Yeah. J. Kennedy, C. Eastwood, S. Poitier, A. Lincoln. All celebrities or historical figures. Smart lady—protecting her ass and her clients."

The waitress stopped by and refilled Will's coffee cup. He dumped a few packets of sugar in and stirred, the contemplative look crossing his face again. "My guess would be that she didn't pick the names randomly. If this was her way of keeping people straight, she probably had some reason to assign each name. Like Sidney Poitier probably isn't a young white guy."

Reid nodded. "Right. And she may have let clients pick their own code names as well."

"Was Kelsey any help with who the names belonged to?" he asked, sipping his coffee.

Reid shifted in the booth. "Well, I haven't exactly been able to talk to her about it."

Will nailed him with shrewd eyes. "You have her evidence, but haven't talked to her? How's that work, Counselor?"

Reid cleared his throat. "Um, well, I sort of had the opportunity to get this from Kelsey's apartment . . . without consent."

Will titled his head back as if he were going to shout at the heavens. "Jamison, what the fuck? I know this case has eaten at you, but you're breaking and entering now?"

"No, no, nothing like that. I got ahold of a key from the other daughter. She just didn't know my intentions."

He groaned. "Still makes the evidence inadmissible."

"Unless Kelsey agrees to give it to me, which I think she would do—if I could find her."

"You don't know where she is?"

He rubbed his eyes, the all-nighter starting to catch up with him. "She's kind of disappeared. She called her sister last night and then never showed up to meet her."

His pissed-off expression switched to concern. "Uh-oh. You think something's wrong?"

He shrugged. "I'm not sure. Kelsey doesn't have the best track record. She's got a drug history and from what I gather, a habit of being flighty."

"Well, if she doesn't show up by the forty-eight-hour mark, her sister needs to report her missing—just to be safe. Although with the overload at the department, I don't know how much focus it will get." Will frowned and added even more sugar to his cup, as if the sweetener could make the bitter situation easier to swallow. "That girl was still living at home when all this went down. She's the only one who may have a shot at identifying some of the people behind these names. Without her and her permission to admit this ledger as evidence, you ain't got shit."

Acid burned in his stomach. "Tell me something I don't know."

This case had ruined Reid's reputation and had continued to keep him up at night. There was no way he was going to let such potentially explosive evidence go by the wayside. No, he needed to find Kelsey and find her fast.

Reid's cell phone vibrated against the table, and he picked it up to check the caller ID. Ah, just who he needed to talk to. He plunked a few bills on the table and slid out of the booth. "Will, I gotta take this. Thanks for your help. I'll be in touch."

"No problem." He lifted his coffee cup in salute. "Hope you find your girl, Counselor."

———

A bloodcurdling scream wretched Brynn from the depths of sleep, and she jolted upright, nearly hurling herself off her living room couch. She glanced around frantically, her chest heaving with choppy breaths, but found nothing amiss in her sunlit living room.

She sank back against the arm of the couch and put her hand to her sweat-slicked neck, the rawness in her throat confirming where the scream came from. "Dammit."

She hadn't had a nightmare in over a month and had dared to hope she was past them. But the blanket twisted around her legs and her pounding heart confirmed otherwise. She rubbed her eyes with her hands, the familiar images from the awful dream seeping through now that her mind was fully awake.

Unwanted hands. Being trapped. Darkness. Flashes of the always-faceless rapist now mixing with the image of the man who'd attacked her in Kelsey's stairwell.

She released a groan of frustration and threw the blanket off her. "I am so *sick* of this shit."

She wanted to holler the words, throw something through the sunny window, shake her fists at the fates. But she knew none of it would do any good. And right now, she didn't have time to bellyache about her own problems.

She glanced at the clock on her DVD player. Right past noon.

She'd stayed up all night, calling Kelsey's friends, the clubs she'd worked at in the past, hospitals, and even put in a message with her police contact. But so far, she didn't have squat and was at a loss as to what her next step should be.

Pound the pavement to talk to people in person? Report her missing?

She shook her head. Part of her wished she could just shrug the whole thing off and chalk it up to Kelsey being irresponsible. But she couldn't shake the feeling that something was really wrong. Why wouldn't Kels have called her or left a note, something? She'd sounded really freaked out on the phone. Was she using again? Was that what this was about? She hoped to God that wasn't the case. Last time her sister had gone on a bender she'd nearly killed herself.

The memory clenched Brynn's chest in a vise grip. Kelsey was the only family she had left. If she lost her . . .

She gave herself a mental shake and took a breath. No. She wouldn't go there. Would. Not.

She grabbed her cell phone off the coffee table and checked the screen. No messages. With a sigh, she leaned forward to set it back down, but it rang in her hand. The sudden noise made her jump, but she had the phone to her ear in record time.

"Hello?"

"Brynn, it's me."

Reid. Even after ten years, he apparently didn't feel the need to say who it was. Like he knew she'd be able to identify his voice from any other man's. She could. "Hey."

"Any word from your sister?"

"No one's seen her or heard from her. I'm running out of people to call. What about you? Did you find out anything?"

Papers shuffled, like he was turning the page of a notebook. "I talked to someone who's a member and found out that The Ranch does hire attendants and pays them well. A person gets a bonus of ten grand when he or she completes the intense training pro-gram, which apparently involves a few weeks of total immersion in each side of the D/s relationship."

"Wow, that's a lot of money."

"Yeah, no kidding. It could be pretty tempting for someone like Kelsey."

She tucked her legs beneath her. "So how do I find out if she's taken a job there?"

He sighed. "That's the problem. The place is like Fort Knox. The only way you're going to find out is if you go there yourself and look for her. My friend said he could probably get you in as a guest."

She swallowed hard. "How would that work?"

"They don't allow doms to come in as guests, only as full mem-bers, so your only option is to go in as a sexual submissive. You would have to be willing to submit to a member."

Her fingers curled into the twisted blanket on the couch, the material still damp from her sweat-inducing nightmare. A bone-deep shudder went through her. "Reid, I don't . . . I can't . . . do that."

The line went quiet, and she wondered if the call had dropped, but then he took a breath. "I could go with you. Save you the stranger part."

Her throat seemed to close. Not just submit, but submit to *Reid*? The idea sent her brain and body into a tailspin. Her gaze darted to the picture on her side table—the last one she and her sister had taken with their mom. Before the murder. Before the trial. Anger stirred in her belly.

"Brynn?"

"No," she bit out, her voice finally returning. "No fucking way."

He snorted. "Calm down, LeBreck. It was just an idea. If you'd rather hand yourself over to some stranger, I'm sure there will be many at The Ranch happy to oblige."

She closed her eyes, bile burning the back of her throat. No way would she survive either of his suggestions. "Let me make a few more calls. I'll let you know if I need your friend's help."

"You know where to find me."

———

"Why'd I even bother?" Brynn hung up her office phone and rubbed her forehead, a piercing headache hatching behind her eyes. Two days with hardly any sleep, and her body was no longer responding to caffeine.

A light tap on her open door made her lift her gaze. Mel stepped into her office, lines of concern creasing her forehead. "Still no word from your sister?"

Brynn shook her head. "I just keep calling her like all of a sudden she's going to come to her senses and answer her phone."

Mel plopped into the chair across from Brynn's desk. "So what now?"

Brynn sighed, her shoulders sagging. "I have no idea. I've talked to everyone I can think of, and I can't even officially report her missing to the police until tonight."

"What about Reid's friend? Have you given any more thought to trying to get into that resort? Sounds like a good lead."

Her stomach flipped over. "Mel, I don't know if I could pull that off. I thought I was past all this crap. I did the therapy, took the self-defense classes, but the minute that guy put his hands on me the other night, the panic sucked me in. I was completely useless."

Mel eyed her for a long moment, and Brynn could almost hear the gears grinding in her friend's head.

Brynn pursed her lips. "Why are you looking at me like that?"

"What if . . ." Mel said, then waved her hand. "Never mind."

"Oh, no," Brynn said, shaking her head. "Just say whatever it is you're thinking. It's not like you've ever held back before."

She leaned forward and straightened the papers in Brynn's out-box, adeptly avoiding eye contact. "I don't know, it's just, maybe this is exactly what you need, you know? Exposure therapy."

Brynn stared at Mel as if her friend had sprouted antlers. "Are you being serious? Exposure therapy?"

She shrugged, but still didn't raise her eyes.

"Don't you think turning myself over to some stranger's sexual demands is a bit of an extreme prescription? I was raped, Mel. It's not like I'm trying to kick a fear of spiders or something."

She cringed. "I'm sorry, B. I'm not trying to minimize what you've been through. I just wish I could help you get past it. Exposure therapy is brutal, but you know it can be effective."

Brynn waved a dismissive hand. "I already did the protocol with a therapist where I went through a retelling. The exposure stuff hasn't worked. It didn't even get the nightmares to stop."

"Experiencing the memory in the counselor's office isn't the same as putting yourself in your most feared situation. And it wouldn't be like getting raped again. They have rules at places like that. You could make the person stop at any time."

Brynn pinched the bridge of her nose, the pounding in her head getting worse. "Mel, I love you, but you're talking crazy. Not only does the whole idea make me feel like I'm going to puke, but I'm not going to hand my body over to some stranger who gets off on hitting women. I spend all day working with my clients trying to get them away from men like that."

She sighed. "Dominance and abuse are two totally different things. You and I both know that."

Brynn quirked an eyebrow. "Sounds like you're speaking from experience."

She shrugged, and then focused on picking invisible lint off her black pants. "I may have gone to one of those kink clubs once during grad school."

"And you didn't tell me? What sort of roommate leaves that kind of choice information out? I told you everything that was going on with me."

"Oh, like that was so scandalous," she said, looking up and smirking. "You were dating an accounting major for God's sake. I didn't want to freak you out. And anyway, I just went for research purposes. I didn't actually participate in anything."

Brynn propped her elbows on her desk and placed her chin in her hands. "So what exactly did you do if you didn't join in?"

Melody rolled her eyes. "Duh. Watched."

Brynn leaned back in her chair. "Oh, hell, I hadn't even thought about that part. Even if I had the guts to try to get in the club, I forgot about the fact that others could see me."

"Hey, that's not necessarily a bad thing." Mel's voice took on a saucy tone. "Some people find it exciting to be watched. You never know, you may be an exhibitionist under that good-girl facade."

A long-dormant memory tickled the back of Brynn's mind, making her cheeks heat. Her best friend had no idea how, once upon at time, she'd been far from angelic. She cleared her throat. "Sounds like my personal nightmare, not a fantasy."

Mel gave her a sympathetic smile. "Fair enough. Just know I'm not trying to tell you what to do, hon. You need to figure out what feels right for you." She stood and gave Brynn's hand a quick squeeze. "But either way, Kelsey is lucky to have a sister who still cares enough to worry about her. A lot of people would've given up on her a long time ago."

Mel's words hung in the air long after her friend stepped out, wracking Brynn with guilt. Mel was wrong. Her sister was far from lucky. The only person in the world who cared about her was sitting on her ass in her office too scared of her own demons to try to help. A useless coward.

She pressed the heels of her hands to her forehead, turning

Mel's suggestion over in her mind again. *Exposure therapy.* Full immersion in her fear. The idea sounded padded-cell crazy, but what if her friend was right? What if the only way she was ever going to get past this was to jump off the proverbial cliff and plunge into her nightmare?

She was so tired. Tired of being scared. Tired of waking up in a cold sweat. Tired of letting what some monster did dictate so much of her life.

Maybe this was the answer. God knows nothing else had worked.

Her phone rang, startling her from her thoughts. She fumbled for the receiver. "Hello?"

"Brynn, it's Tony Flores."

Her contact with the police department. Thank God. "Hey, Tony."

"Sorry I'm just getting back to you, but I had to check on a few things before I talked to you. Do you have a minute?"

She sat up straighter at the cop's grim tone. She worked with Tony regularly for her clients' domestic violence cases, and knew he only reserved that tone for bad news. "Of course, what's going on?"

"I didn't get your message until last night, but I ran your sister's name through the system to make sure she hadn't been arrested or hadn't gotten in an accident or something. And I didn't find either of those to be the case, but her name did pop up under something else."

Her grip on the phone tightened. "What do you mean?"

"Saturday night we got called out to work an assault. Guy by the name of Nick Camden got himself beat up pretty bad."

Kelsey's on-again-off-again boyfriend. The knot of anxiety in her stomach grew larger.

"According to the report, the paramedics said your sister showed up a few minutes after the attack, running late to meet Nick. They asked her to wait for us to get there so we could talk to her, but she bailed before our officers arrived. Nick didn't see his attacker, but he's convinced it's Raymond Miller, one of the big dealers in the area. Dangerous guy." He sighed heavily. "Nick told us your sister owes this guy a lot of money. He thinks she was the intended target."

"Oh, my God." She sank back in her chair.

"Have you heard from your sister yet?"

She closed her eyes. "No, she's not answering her phone, and I've called everyone I can think of. No one has a clue where she is."

Another sigh. "Look, we have our guys trailing this Miller guy. He drove by your sister's apartment this morning."

"So he's still looking for her?" The thought sent goose bumps across her skin.

"Looks that way," he said, sounding tired. "The good news is he doesn't seem to know where she's hiding out. The bad news is we don't know where to find her either. We want to offer her some protection if she's willing to cooperate with us. We believe she has vital information that could put this guy behind bars. But we can't do anything until we get a hold of her, and I don't have the manpower to hunt her down. Unfortunately, Miller might."

Brynn pinched the bridge of her nose once more. Kelsey cooperate with the police? Not likely. After their mother's murder and Hank's arrest, she'd developed quite an aversion to the boys and girls in blue. No wonder her sister had run off. She was hiding from the bad guys *and* the good guys.

"Tony, I promise I'll keep doing what I can to find her and will let you know if I hear anything."

"Thanks, Brynn. And I'll call you if I have any news on this end. Just be careful poking around. You don't want to end up on this guy's radar, too. Lie low."

Another thought hit her. "Wait, one more thing. Did Nick happen to say how much Kelsey owed this guy?"

The clicking of a keyboard, then: "Looks like somewhere in the neighborhood of ten or fifteen grand."

Her head tilted back against her chair, the conclusion she'd spent the last day and a half trying to deny taking shape. *Shit.* "Thanks."

She hung up the phone with a trembling hand and sucked in a few long, steadying breaths to quell the adrenaline rushing through her. She knew what she had to do. For her sister, and hell, maybe for herself, too. The only question was if she could actually do it without having a total mental breakdown in the process.

She stared at her desk calendar, the names of the women she counseled staring back at her. Women who she encouraged to take charge of their situations, to tackle their fears, to stand on their own feet and claim their lives.

She was such a goddamned hypocrite.

Her fists clenched and something strong and steely wrapped around the ball of fear in her chest, stifling its hold on her and straightening her spine.

Without giving herself time to reconsider, she stepped around her desk and headed out of her office. One foot in front of the other. The steady clicking of her heels against the linoleum and her pounding heartbeat the only things filling her head. She didn't stop until she had knocked on his office door.

"Come in," Reid called, and she pushed open the door. He glanced up from a box of files on his desk. Despite the temporary truce they'd forged over the weekend, she had avoided him after the obligatory greeting at the communal coffee pot that morning. If he was surprised to see her, he didn't show it. "Hey."

"Hey." Brynn squared her shoulders, trying to hold on to her newfound determination and ignore the swirl of emotions the lawyer incited in her. Seeing Reid on a daily basis was going to take some getting used to. Why couldn't he have lost all his hair and sprouted man boobs by now? Then, she could just focus on hating him and wouldn't have to deal with the attraction that seemed burned into her DNA. "All moved in?"

He tapped the box in front of him. "Last one to sort through."

She nodded and folded her arms across her chest, lingering in the doorway, anxiety leaking into her system again. "That's good."

He pulled a few files from the box and set them on the desk. "Any new leads?"

She chewed her lip. "I'm pretty sure Kelsey's at The Ranch. I talked to my friend at the police department and found out Kels owes a lot of money to a local dealer. They think he's after her to pay up."

He frowned. "Well, The Ranch would be a great place to hide, especially if she's looking to make some cash quickly."

She nodded, her throat threatening to close. Her flight response was kicking in just thinking about asking the question. *Dammit. Get it together, Brynn.* She reached for the doorjamb to hold herself steady.

His blue eyes evaluated her, and his mouth sunk into a deeper frown. Before she could force out a word, he rose from his chair and crossed the room, his focus never leaving her face. She wondered if he was going to embrace her, ward off the panic. The thought seemed both appealing and abhorrent all at the same time.

But he didn't hug her. Instead, he slipped his hand into the inside pocket of his jacket and pulled out a small white card. When she didn't make a move to take it, he grabbed her hand and with a gentle pressure uncurled her fist. He placed the card in her palm. "I told my friend to expect you around eight tonight."

She lifted Reid's business card, flipped it over, and read the handwritten address. "But how did you know to make an appointment? I hadn't even decided to do it."

The corner of his mouth tipped up. "Ten years may have passed, Brynn, but I still know you."

Anger at his knowing glance chased away the burgeoning panic. "What? That I'm a girl who willingly jumps in bed with anyone?"

His expression hardened. "No, I was going to say because I know how protective you are of your sister. But maybe your assessment is more accurate."

She flexed her fingers, wishing that she'd taken the kickboxing class instead of the self-defense one because punching Reid's smug face would have been *so* satisfying. But she really didn't need to get fired for interoffice violence on top of her already shitty day. "Screw you, Reid."

He smirked, tilting his head closer as if he were going to share a secret. "You already did that, sugar. And from what I remember, you loved every minute of it. All you have to do is ask and I'll come along with you."

Heat rushed to her cheeks, but her tone turned icy. "Don't misconstrue my appreciation for your help this weekend with forgiveness. You lost the right to touch me a *very* long time ago."

"Suit yourself." He rocked back on his heels and tucked his hands in his pockets. "Good luck with your stranger, Brynn."

Your stranger. Her lunch threatened to make an encore appearance, and she turned on her heel, striding away before Reid could see how much he'd gotten to her.

SIX

then

Brynn flinched as Davis Ackerman slammed his fist on his desk, a strand of perfectly gelled hair falling across his forehead.

"Dammit, Brynn. How could you leave the governor on hold that long?"

She stared down at her skirt, worrying the hem between her fingers and wishing—not for the first time—that she worked directly for Reid's uncle and not for the power-happy campaign manager. "I'm so sorry. I . . . um . . . I had an emergency call on the other line. I got distracted."

"What call could possibly be more important? He's the goddamn governor!" Davis's face turned the color of the cinnamon gum he incessantly chewed.

Tears brimmed her eyes, but she blinked them back. Explaining to him that her sister had called her in hysterics a minute after she thought she'd transferred the governor's call would not win her any points. She cleared her throat. "I promise it'll never happen again."

"You got that right," he said, rising from his chair, his hand still clasping a copy of the e-mail the governor had sent to him about sitting on hold so long he'd hung up. "I know Patrick has taken a liking to you, but this kind of thing will not be excused. No more mistakes, Ms. LeBreck."

She breathed an inner sigh of relief. Thank God. No pink slip today. She nodded and stood. "Yes, sir, I understand. Thank you."

She yanked open the office door and escaped in such a hurry she didn't notice Reid until she barreled into him. A stack of papers dropped from his hands. "Whoa, there."

"Shit," she said, sinking to her knees to gather the mess. "I'm sorry, I didn't—"

He knelt next to her and laid a hand over hers, stilling her frantic pace. "Hey, chill. It's okay. What's wrong?"

She glanced up to meet his gaze and died a little when a hot tear slid down her cheek. *No, please, not in front of him.* She wiped the moisture from her face and pulled her other hand from beneath his. "I'm fine, just in a rush."

He glanced at the closed door behind her. "Did Davis upset you?"

She shook her head and straightened the documents into a neat stack before handing them to Reid. "It's nothing. I made a mistake, and he was talking to me about it."

Reid stood and set the papers onto a nearby desk, his blue eyes narrowing. "More like yelling. I could hear him from across the office. God, that guy can be such a prick sometimes. He thinks just because he landed a management position at thirty he can piss on everyone else."

She walked past him and grabbed her purse from underneath the reception desk. "It's not a big deal. I deserved it. I shouldn't have messed up."

"Hold up." He caught up to her and grasped her shoulder, spinning her to face him. "It doesn't matter what mistake you made. You never deserve to be yelled at."

His touch burned through the thin material of her blouse, and the worry in his eyes made her want to cry again. She shrugged out of his reach. She *would not* let Reid see her shed tears. And she certainly wasn't going to tell him why Davis yelling was the least of her worries at the moment.

She had managed to maintain her friendship with Reid, even while dodging his repeated invitations for a second date. She refused to ruin it by letting him see who she really was. "I appreciate your concern, really. But I'm fine. And I have to go. I have a bit of a family emergency to deal with."

She hurried past him and headed for the exit door. Home. She needed to get home. Kelsey had blubbered through most of the conversation. But Brynn had gotten the gist. And she wasn't looking forward to what she would face when she arrived.

She climbed into her '88 Chevy and turned the ignition, but the engine didn't fire. She gritted her teeth and twisted the key again. Nothing. Not even a click. The damn car wasn't even trying to start. She banged her fists against the steering wheel, the tears finally escaping. "You're going to die on me *now*?"

A sharp tap on the window made her jump. Reid peered in and mouthed, "You okay?"

God, couldn't a girl get a moment alone to wallow? She grabbed a tissue from her purse and dried her face before shoving open the door. She climbed out and forced a smile. "Ever have one of those days where you wish you had just stayed under the covers?"

He grasped her elbow and pulled her into an all-encompassing hug, the sudden contact stunning her into silence.

Her first instinct was to pull back. For the last few weeks, she had carefully avoided touching Reid again, protecting herself from the internal longing she knew his touch would incite. But the warmth of his embrace was too delicious to reject. She couldn't remember the last time anyone had really hugged her. He smoothed her hair, and for a few luxurious seconds, she let her cheek rest against his solid chest.

He sat his chin on top of her head. "Whatever it is, sugar, let me help."

She closed her eyes and took a deep breath, inhaling his cologne, imprinting the feel of him on her brain so that she could access the memory later. She slipped from his hold and stepped back. "I don't need help."

He eyed the powder blue heap behind her. "I could call you a tow truck."

She shook her head. She couldn't afford to pay for a tow or for anyone to fix it once it got to the garage anyway. "Um, no, that's okay. I'll get a friend to come take a look at it tomorrow."

He shoved his hands in the pockets of his jeans. "Well, then I'll give you a ride home."

She cringed inwardly. No way was she letting him see where she lived, much less witness what would greet her when she got there. He'd either be appalled or, worse, feel sorry for her. The thought turned her stomach. "I'm just going to take the bus, but thanks."

He shook his head and crooked a thumb toward the shiny black pickup behind him. "Get in the truck, Brynn. You said you have a family emergency. If that's the truth, then you don't need to waste time on the bus. Stop being so hardheaded."

She put her hands on her hips, ready to tell him to shove off, but then remembered the frantic edge in her sister's voice. Her shoulders sagged as she said a silent good-bye to the friendship she and Reid shared. Once he saw who she really was, he'd bail like all her other friends always did. She gave him a dejected nod and followed him to his truck.

When she told him her address, she expected a raised eyebrow, but his face remained stoic. "I know where that is."

They rode in silence, the muscles in Reid's forearms flexing as he gripped the steering wheel. Clearly, she had done something to annoy him, but she didn't have the energy for conversation. Instead, she stared out the window, watching the state of the neighborhoods decline as they passed each exit—from upper class to barely getting by in a mere fifteen miles.

By the time Reid pulled into the driveway of her family's shoddy rental, she was burning with embarrassment. She grabbed the cool metal of door handle and didn't dare look at him. "Thanks for the ride."

The automatic locks clicked, preventing her from escaping.

"I'm not leaving until I know everything's all right." His tone brooked no argument.

She bit her lip, not knowing what to think of this version of Reid. The power that radiated off him made her insides twist with an emotion she couldn't pinpoint. She took a steadying breath. "Okay, stay out here. I'll come back out and let you know if I need you or not."

He stretched an arm across the back of the seat, as if settling in for the wait, and nodded.

After disengaging the lock, she scooted out of the truck and said a silent prayer as she pushed open the front door. The small puddle of blood on the vinyl tile of the entryway and the sound of soft sobbing sent panic through her. She dropped her purse and ran for the kitchen. Her fourteen-year-old sister's tear-stained face lit with relief when she saw Brynn. "Ohmigod, what took you so long? She wouldn't let me call 911."

Brynn turned toward the kitchen table. Her mother sat slumped in one of the chairs, her head resting against the back wall, one eye swollen shut.

"Holy crap, Ma, what the hell happened?"

"Hmm?" She lifted her head and peered at Brynn with her good eye. "Is that you, baby?"

Brynn groaned at the slurred words and knelt in front of her mom to check her over. Her low-cut top had been torn slightly at the vee and finger-shaped bruises marked her upper arms. The puffiness around her eye was already turning a sickly shade of purple. "Jesus."

"Is she going to be okay?" her sister asked, wrapping her arms around herself.

Brynn frowned. Kelsey was a tough kid, but no one should have to see their own mother like this. "She'll be okay, Kels. Thanks for calling. I'm sorry I got stuck late at work."

"S'okay," she said, shifting from one flip-flop to the other. "I was supposed to sleep at Becca's tonight 'cause we have a school project to work on, but I didn't want to leave until you got here. I can stay and help if you want."

"Is her mom going to be home?"

"Yeah. And she said she'd drive us both to school in the morning."

Brynn cocked her head toward the back door. "Go ahead. Just ring the phone when you get there so I know you arrived safe."

She nodded, her shoulders noticeably relaxing. "Okay, are you sure?"

"You'll only be three doors down. I'll come get you if I need you, all right? Go get your stuff."

Kelsey turned to head to her room, then yelped.

Reid put his hands up as he filled the doorway. "Sorry, didn't mean to scare you." He looked at Brynn. "I was getting worried out there."

Brynn glanced from Reid to her mother to the stack of empty liquor bottles on top of the counter.

Now he knew. She wanted to fold in on herself and disappear.

———

Reid tried to keep his expression flat as he took in the scene. He didn't know what he had expected to find when he'd barged into Brynn's place, but finding her with a bloodied and bruised woman had not been it.

Brynn turned her back to him but not quick enough for him to miss the horrified expression on her face. She grabbed a cloth off the table and patted beneath the woman's nose. "I'm sorry, I forgot you were waiting. We're fine. You can go now."

Reid moved out of the way as the younger blonde, Brynn's little sister he presumed, hurried past him. He shoved his hands in his pockets and took a breath. "What I can do to help?"

Her shoulders dipped as if she were carrying sandbags on them, but she didn't turn to look at him. "Just leave. Please."

Yeah, like that was going to happen. For the last few weeks, he had let Brynn get away with her casual rebuffs and subtle distancing. He had deserved it after the way he'd lost control on their first date. But he'd be damned if he was going to let her push him away from something like this. "I'm not going anywhere."

She swung her head around, her eyes filling with tears and her face red with shame. "Can't you take a hint? You're making this worse. I don't want you to be here to see this."

He closed the distance between them and put a hand on her shoulder. "Don't be embarrassed. I just want to help you."

She winced. "I don't need your help. I've been handling my mother for years, I'm a pro. So why don't you leave, pretend you never saw this, and I'll see you at work. Okay?"

Ignoring her request, Reid turned and walked to the refrigerator, then pulled open the freezer door. Except for the three cheap bottles of vodka, the contents were slim, but he found what he was looking for. He brought a bag of frozen corn back to Brynn. "Put this on her eye, it will help with the swelling. Does it seem like anything's broken?"

Brynn took the bag and stared at him for a long moment before standing up and placing it on her mother's black eye. "I don't think so."

"Do you think she needs to go to a doctor or the police?"

"She'll refuse to see either."

He nodded. "Okay, then why don't we get her somewhere she can rest and sleep it off?"

Brynn sighed and stood. She gave her mother's shoulder a soft squeeze. "Ma, I'm going to help you get up and walk to your bedroom, okay?"

Her mother reached up and patted Brynn's hand. "Thanks, baby."

Reid went around the opposite side from Brynn and gently grabbed her mother's upper arm to help her to her feet. She stumbled a bit, but managed to stand with their assistance. With slow, steady steps they led her out of the kitchen and down the narrow hallway. Brynn bumped open one of the doors with her elbow.

The room was barely bigger than the closet in Reid's own bedroom and looked way too neat to belong to a woman who was clearly out of control. He wondered if Brynn had led him to her own bedroom to protect herself from more embarrassment.

Brynn pulled back the sheets, and the two of them helped her mother to sit on the edge of the bed. She bent down and slipped off her mom's heels, then placed them on a rack in the closet. Reid frowned. This wasn't Brynn's room, but apparently she played maid to her mother along with everything else.

"Who the hell are you?" said a slurred voice.

Reid turned to see her mother squinting at him with her uninjured eye.

He crossed his arms over his chest. "Your daughter's boyfriend."

She snorted. "Right."

Brynn hurried to her mother's side and shot him a withering look. "Come on, Ma, let's get you into your nightgown."

"He'll only break your heart," she said. "Cheating bastards—all of 'em. Believe you me. They all do it eventually. I'd be broke otherwise."

"You are broke," Brynn muttered, and glanced at Reid. "I'm going to get her changed. I'll be out in a minute."

He nodded and stepped into the hallway, shutting the door behind him. As he made his way back to the living room, his heart broke for the girl who had quickly become the sole focus of his days. No wonder she didn't have time for a burger. She was taking care of everyone around her. He sank into the well-worn couch and ran a hand over his face.

After his last date with Brynn, he'd thought she might be the girl he could share his secret with, but now he knew he had to keep his lips sewn shut. The last thing she needed was to hear about his sordid fantasies. Her opinion of men had already been warped enough.

No, what Brynn needed was a hero—a guy who would treat her with the respect no one showed her mother. The only question was, did he have enough self-control to be that guy?

━━━

Brynn clicked her mother's door shut and took a moment to gather herself before facing Reid. She didn't want to discuss what had happened, but she couldn't just kick the guy out with no explanation after he'd been decent enough to help. She smoothed the creases in her black pants, straightened her shoulders, and walked toward the living room.

Reid was sitting forward on the couch, forearms on knees, and his mouth in a grim line. His black tailored shirt and expensive jeans looked out of place against the faded flower pattern of their secondhand furniture. He looked up when she sank into the love seat. "Got her in bed okay?"

Brynn kicked off her heels and tucked her legs beneath her. "Yeah, she's already out. Thanks for helping me get her to her room. I'm beyond embarrassed that you saw all of this."

He shook his head. "Don't be. It's fine."

She scoffed, the sound holding no humor. "Fine? Yeah, I'm

sure this is exactly how you spend your evenings—cleaning up an alcoholic after one of her *dates* decides she didn't do enough to earn her money."

Deep frown lines etched his face. "That's not what I meant."

"Why did you tell her you were my boyfriend?"

He shrugged. "It just came out. I guess it's because I'd like to be."

Brynn groaned. "You must be a masochist. Look around, Reid. This is my life. I'm not like the other girls at the office. I have a lot going on and hopefully am leaving for college in a few months."

His brows dipped. "Leaving?"

"I told you that on our first date."

"I know, but how are you going to do that with all that's going on here?"

She shrugged. "That's why I'm busting my ass with overtime at work. I'm going to get an apartment and take Kelsey with me—file for guardianship."

He blew out a breath. "Wow."

"Yeah, see what I mean? You need to go find some chick like Molly or Krista who can go and do all the fun things people our age are supposed to be doing. I'm not that girl."

"Oh, right, 'cause those airheads at the office are awesome."

"No, I'm serious. I mean, look, one evening with me and I bet I've completely messed up your plans. Isn't Thursday college night at all the bars?"

"Come 'ere," he said, motioning for her. Reluctantly, she rose and stepped closer to him. He grabbed her hand and pulled her down to his lap before she could protest. "I don't want some chick. I want you. Get over it."

She sighed. The thought of having Reid, of affording herself that little luxury for a few months, was so tempting. But their worlds existed on different orbits. "I like you, Reid. I just don't know how anything between us could work. You have political mixers and frat parties, I have a household to run and now, apparently, crime scene cleanup. There's no way—"

"Shh," he said, smoothing her hair. "Stop overanalyzing everything. Don't you ever shut off that busy brain and let yourself feel what you feel?"

"No."

He laughed. "What about that night in my truck? You seemed like you were able to let go a bit. Weren't you acting on feelings then?"

She smirked. "Well, yeah. I don't get half-naked for guys as a personal hobby. Of course I felt something."

"So what was different?"

She thought back to that night—the confident way he had touched her, the dirty talk, the way his kiss had made her senseless. She shifted in his lap, suddenly very aware of how close they were, and dropped her focus to her hands. "I don't know. You took control, I guess. I didn't have to make any decisions for a change, and it was kind of a relief."

He put a finger under her chin and tilted her face toward him. "So why don't we try that again? You stop worrying, we'll order pizza and hang out tonight. You won't have to decide on anything except meat lovers or vegetarian. Although, if you pick vegetarian, I may rethink this whole wanting to be your boyfriend thing."

"No, I'm sure you had plans tonight. I don't need a pity parade."

He curled a lock of her hair around his finger. "This isn't about pity. I want to be with you and it's you who keeps coming up with excuses to get rid of me. I'm going to develop a complex."

"Uh-huh. You look crushed."

"I am. Shattered, really. So to help me recover, you're going to get on that phone and order us a pizza. Then we're going to relax, forget the previous few hours, and watch some horrible made-for-TV movie."

She laughed, unable to maintain her foul mood around him. "So now I'm the pizza wench?"

He pointed at the phone sitting on the side table. "Yes, woman. I'm wasting away here."

She rolled her eyes, but climbed off his lap and grabbed the phone.

Two hours and an entire pizza later, Brynn curled into the crook of Reid's arm, feeling more content than she had in a long time. Despite the crazy evening, cuddling with six feet of yummy male made it hard to hold on to stress. And the more time she spent with him, the more her resistance to trying something with him crumbled.

Yes, they were far apart in the social stratosphere, but did that mean they couldn't enjoy each other's company for a little while? She'd hopefully leave for Austin at the end of the summer, he'd return to law school. With all that she had to deal with, a summer fling could be the one treat she allowed herself.

She craned her neck to look up at Reid. "So is this, like, your pitch to date me?"

He gave a low chuckle. "Only if it's working."

She sniffed. "You're doing an okay job, I guess. It's a very extensive interview process, I'm afraid."

"Oh, really? What areas do I need to work on?"

She chewed her lip, then decided if she was going to go for it with Reid, she may as well do it with gusto. She scooted from under his arm and shifted around so she could straddle his lap, earning a raised eyebrow from him. "Well, you haven't even tried to kiss me tonight."

The playful expression on his face dissolved. "I know. I'm trying to make up for the mistakes I made on our first date."

She frowned. "What do you mean?"

He sighed and rubbed her upper arms. "I took things too fast, and I should've never talked to you the way I did. I don't know what I was thinking. I got caught up in the moment."

The corner of her mouth tilted up. "I wasn't exactly stopping you. I think we both lost our heads a bit."

He pushed her hair back over her shoulders. "Why don't we start over? Take things slower?"

A small twinge of disappointment gnawed at her belly. Yes, she had let things go too far that night, but part of her had enjoyed the rawness of it, the abandon. She nodded. "Sounds like a plan. As long as kissing is still part of the agenda."

"Oh, definitely. Item number one, in fact."

He curled his palm around the nape of her neck, drawing her closer, then brushed his mouth against hers. The move was sweet, a simple whisper of his lips against hers, but her body shuddered in response. She'd spent so much time the last few weeks keeping a careful distance from him and trying to forget the night in his truck that even the minute contact sent her nerve endings alight.

His fingers threaded in her hair, gently tugging her head back, allowing him access to her neck. The tender force behind the movement caused an odd thrill to rush through her. They had agreed they both wanted to take things slow, but the tension in his grasp made her think he was fighting the urge to charge forward. He kissed the tender skin behind her ear, then her jawline, leaving goose bumps trailing along her skin. Her eyelids fluttered closed as she relished the delicious decadence of his touch. By the time his mouth found its way back to hers, her whole body had flushed with heat.

His hands moved down to her waist, then braced against the tops of her legs, his thumbs making circles on her inner thighs while his tongue explored her mouth. His fingers bit into the soft flesh of her legs through the cotton of her pants. Unraveling restraint, that's what it felt like. Like he was riding the edge of his control and if she made one wrong move, he was going to throw her down on the coffee table and rip off her clothes—an idea that frankly sounded all kinds of enticing at the moment.

Even though she told herself they were simply going to kiss, her body refused to believe it. Slick moisture flooded her sex and desire, sharp and wicked, clouded her thoughts. Unconsciously, she spread her legs wider, and Reid's growing erection brushed against her. A low murmur of pleasure escaped her, but was quickly swallowed by his kiss.

Reid pulled back, his breathing heavy. "God, I can't even kiss you."

She blinked at the sudden break in contact. "What do you mean?"

He tilted his head back and raked his hands through his hair. "I think you know."

She moved her hand to his crotch, his cock as hard as steel against the denim of his jeans. She ran her nails along the scratchy material, loving the fact that she could turn him on so quickly. "It's okay. Apparently, we're not so good at slow and easy."

He groaned. "I'm trying to be a gentleman."

She smiled and moved her fingers under the edge of his dress shirt, walking her fingertips along the ripples of his abdomen. "I just want you to be you—whoever that is."

He lifted his head, his eyes darkening. "No, you don't."

He grasped her wrists and gently removed her hands from beneath his shirt, then placed a soft kiss on each one. "You've had a long, emotional night. I'm going to leave before we take this too far again."

Her jaw fell open. "You're leaving?"

He grabbed her shoulders and eased her off his lap, his expression pained. "I'm not going to risk you hating me in the morning. We'll go out tomorrow night on a real date. If you still want this by then, I'm all yours."

She crossed her arms over her chest, anger bubbling in her

belly. "Don't patronize me, Reid. I'm not some flighty chick who is going to jump in bed with someone because I had a bad night. And I'm not some virgin princess either. You don't have to treat me with kid gloves. Anything I do with you is because I want to."

Reid's eyes turned stormy, the vibe rolling off him almost animalistic. He opened his mouth to respond.

"Brynn? I need you." Her mother's scratchy voice drifted from the hallway and scraped across her ears.

Fucking hell.

Reid's expression smoothed into an unreadable mask, and he leaned over to kiss Brynn on the forehead. "We'll talk about all of this later, sugar, when we're both thinking more clearly. See you tomorrow at work."

She hauled herself off the couch and stomped down the hallway. The self-righteous bastard could find his own way to the door.

———

Reid collapsed onto the couch of his darkened living room, his head still spinning from his disastrous make-out session with Brynn. Fuck. What was wrong with him? Thank God her mother had interrupted them. He'd been about half a second from throwing Brynn down and taking her right there—with no mercy, no restraint. He shifted his position, his dick straining painfully against the zipper of his pants.

He thought he could control himself around her, but she stirred dark urges he'd long been trying to suppress. Something about her made it next to impossible for him to act like a sane person. Brynn had been through hell—she deserved to be cherished, respected, treated like the amazing girl she was. But all he wanted to do anytime he was around her was tie her up and fuck her until she was hoarse from screaming his name and limp with satisfaction.

He tilted his head back against the couch, staring at the ceiling. Maybe his aunt was right. Maybe he needed to stick to a girl like Vanessa—one that he had no trouble controlling himself around.

But at the moment, he couldn't even recall Vanessa's face.

Instead, erotic images of Brynn on her knees, blindfolded and bound, flooded his mind. He groaned and closed his eyes. Automatically, his hand undid his fly and he released his straining erection.

Brynn had such a hot mouth, he knew her lips wrapping around his cock would be nothing short of heaven. He would tangle his fingers in her silky hair and command her to take all of him, to let him fuck her mouth with abandon while she held his gaze. Then he'd have his turn on her—tasting her, teasing her, pushing her limits until he brought her to an edge of bliss that, at least for a few moments, would take her away from all the ugliness in her life.

His balls tightened as the forbidden fantasy played in his mind, and in the darkness of his quiet living room, he fisted his cock and gave it long strokes from root to head. He didn't allow himself any gentleness or finesse. Hard and rough—just like he wanted to take Brynn. He imagined her sucking him hard, scraping her teeth along the tender skin, licking the drops of fluid from the tip, offering him her sweet and utter submission.

Sweat beaded his forehead, and with one last stroke, he let out a guttural moan. Hot fluid splashed onto his shirt and abdomen, and he sank against the sofa, his breath coming in short pants.

God, he was a sick bastard. Even with his best efforts, he couldn't fight the dangerous craving within him.

Maybe pursuing a relationship with Brynn hadn't been such a good idea after all. She had enough demons in her own life; he didn't need to unleash his on her, too. But now that he'd gotten close to the beautiful blonde, he didn't know how to turn off his desire to be with her. He was going to have to find a way to slay this burning need he had before he crossed the line and scared off Brynn.

And he knew the very person who might be able to help him with that.

SEVEN

now

Brynn looked down at the address on the business card one more time, then raised her eyes to the storefront. "You've got to be freaking kidding me."

The elegantly scrawled sign for Wicked blended in with the upscale shops around it, but its name left no question about the store's purpose. Leave it to Reid to fail to mention that the uptown address he'd given her was a sex shop. She sighed. What else would it be? She wasn't exactly applying for membership to the PTA. She slung her purse over her shoulder and fed a few quarters into the parking meter, pleased her hand didn't shake during the process.

The tapping of her high-heeled boots silenced as she stepped from the sidewalk to the posh carpet of the store's entrance. Wine-colored walls and soft music enveloped her, giving her the sense that she'd stepped into some private boudoir. The only indications of the store's wares were the gorgeous black-and-white erotic photos that adorned the walls.

Brynn's eyes traveled over each one, the bondage scenes sending a hum of electricity through her nervous system. How something could be so beautiful and frightening to her all at the same time was a wonder.

She drifted closer to the picture on her right—a photo of a woman on her knees, back to the camera, arms laced in intricate strips of leather behind her. The woman's head was dipped forward in deference to the mysterious man in front of her. The photographer had kept the focus on the girl and left the dom blurred in the distance, a strong and imposing force despite the fuzzy edges. Unconsciously, Brynn lifted her hand as if to touch the picture.

"Beautiful, isn't it?" said a friendly male voice.

Startled, she instantly dropped her hand and stepped back from the art. "What?"

A young, raven-haired man came around the register positioned on the back wall and walked toward her. "That one is one of my favorites. I love how she's showing such trust in the face of the unknown."

A nervous smile jumped to her lips. "Um, yes, it's very . . . powerful."

"Indeed." He nodded, emanating a sage energy that didn't match his boyish looks. "So what can I help you with today? Are you looking for art or something else?"

She shifted her weight to the opposite leg and resisted the urge to wipe her sweaty palms on her pants. "I was supposed to ask for Jason."

One of his perfectly groomed brows twitched a bit, but he quickly smoothed his expression. "Of course. My name's Marius. Let me take you upstairs where the main store is. You can look around while I go get him for you."

"Thank you," she said, and followed his lead to a narrow staircase. "So the whole store is upstairs? Why rent the downstairs space as well?"

He glanced back at her and smiled. "A lot of people prefer the privacy of knowing that those walking by on the street can't peek in and see what they're shopping for. Many of our customers have conservative jobs or public images. So that's important. Plus, I doubt the neighborhood would've agreed to allow this type of store if our merchandise was going to be on display."

"Makes sense," Brynn said, climbing the last step and walking into the main shop. The décor matched the bottom floor, but instead of erotic photography, there were rows of sex toys, bondage equipment, and high-end lingerie.

Marius crooked a thumb behind him. "I'll go get Jason for you. Feel free to browse. You have the store to yourself right now. We usually don't get busy until after ten or so."

"Thanks." She waited until he disappeared before she took him up on the browsing offer.

Brynn wandered down the first aisle, trying to keep her mind off the conversation she was about to have. She eyed the collection of vibrators, the shear variety astounding her. She shook her head. Dolphins, rabbits, butterflies. Why were they all named after animals? What was sexy about that? If she invented a line, she'd name them after movie stars. The Mark Wahlberg. The Brad Pitt. She smiled. Maybe she had missed her calling.

She turned the corner to the next aisle and sucked in a breath. Rows of black leather restraints, paddles, and whips lined the shelves along with loads of things she couldn't identify. The photo from downstairs flashed through her brain. This was what she was signing up for—complete submission to a stranger. A golf-ball-sized lump lodged in her throat.

She picked up one of the items, a flogger according to the tag, and threaded her fingers through the soft strips at the end of the handle. The leather felt cool against her skin, but she imagined the material would heat up quickly when wielded by a strong hand. She resisted the urge to smack it across her palm to test the theory.

She'd never done anything with actual equipment. She and Reid had both been new to the idea back then and hadn't ventured very far into this world. They'd worked with whatever they had around. She drew the leather across her hand again, and images of Reid standing behind her, flogger in hand, invaded her thoughts. A hot tingling fired up in her belly and crept lower.

She shook her head—God, she was so twisted up with this. Her body hadn't forgotten what it had been like with Reid, how unbelievably explosive the sex had been. But the same thoughts that got her body slick and ready made her mind want to splinter into a thousand pieces.

"My God, Brynn LeBreck," said a genial voice, startling her from her errant thoughts.

She looked up, fumbling to put the flogger back on the rack, and her breath caught.

"I didn't think it was possible for you to get more gorgeous," Jace said, green eyes sparkling. "But clearly I was wrong."

"Jace?" she asked, her mind still processing his presence as the broad-shouldered man gathered her into a crushing hug.

He stepped back, smiling. "Didn't you know that's who you were coming to see?"

She shook her head. "No, Reid didn't mention it, and I didn't realize your full name was Jason."

He laughed and scrubbed a hand through his surfer-style blond hair. "That shithead. I'm sorry. I thought you knew."

No, but it would've been nice to be warned. She was going to kick Reid's ass when she got back to the office tomorrow. She took a deep breath and smiled. Her problem was not with Jace. He'd never been anything but kind to her. "No, it's fine. Actually, better than fine. It's great to see you."

He motioned for her to follow him. "Why don't you come on back to my office so we can chat?"

When he reached his door, he swung it open and let Brynn

walk in before him. The space was large, but cozy, resembling a sitting room in a fancy hotel more than an office. Only the massive cherrywood desk gave away the room's true purpose. She settled into the cushioned wingback chair. "Beautiful office."

"Thanks. I'd take credit for the decorating, but this was my sister's project. She was starting an interior design business, and I was her guinea pig." Instead of sitting behind his desk, Jace dropped into the matching chair across from her. "So how the hell have you been? Reid tells me you're a therapist now."

She crossed her legs and tried to give the appearance of being at ease, although her insides were knotted into a pretzel. "I am. I work at the Women's Crisis Center."

He grinned. "That's awesome. I always knew you'd do something great. You were the only one who took your job seriously when we were working for Reid's uncle. The rest of us were just a bunch of slackers. I only lasted a few months before Roslyn told me I should *explore other opportunities*."

She laughed. "Well, I didn't have much choice. It was work hard or head back to 'Would you like fries with that?'" She glanced around the posh office again. "Looks like you're not slacking anymore. Although, I'm a little surprised at the business choice. Weren't you supposed to become a financial planner or something?"

He leaned back in the chair and smirked. "Yeah, the fam wasn't too thrilled with my little venture. They've cut me out of the family fortune. But my finance jobs were soul sucking. I needed to follow my passion."

She raised her eyebrows. "And your passion is selling whips and vibrators?"

A warm chuckle rumbled from deep in his chest. "Among other things. But yeah, I enjoy helping people indulge in their fantasies."

She nodded and fiddled with the clasp of her watch, not sure what to say next. Was she supposed to just come out and ask? *Hey, Jace, can you help me get into that super-duper fancy kink club?*

He sat forward, his mop of blond hair falling across his forehead. "Relax, Brynn. Reid told me about your sister and why you want into The Ranch."

She blew out a breath she didn't know she'd been holding. "Oh, thank God."

"Look, I'll be honest. I'm a little nervous about sneaking you in. Grant, the club owner, is one of my biggest customers and if he found out I brought someone in under false pretenses, not only would I lose my membership, but a big chunk of my business."

"Oh, Jace. I don't want to put you in that position. I just—"

He held up a hand. "No, it's okay—I know if my sister was in trouble, I'd want to do everything I could to help her, too. I was even willing to go look for Kelsey for you, but Reid said she's not going to trust a stranger."

She sighed. "Yeah, she's hiding from some pretty scary people, so there's no way she's going to talk to someone she doesn't recognize."

"So that means it's up to you. We just need to make sure you pull this off flawlessly."

She wet her lips. "Flawlessly?"

"Yes. Grant Waters is crazy good at reading people. It makes him a top-notch master, but it also means he can sniff out bullshit at a hundred paces. You can't go in playing sub—you need to *be* a sub. Really surrender."

She uncrossed her legs and tucked her hands in her lap, trying to keep them from shaking. "Right."

He gave her knee a quick reassuring squeeze. "I'm not telling you this to scare you—just to help you understand what needs to happen. The key is going to be not to overthink it. You know what to do."

"I do?"

"Well, it's not like it was a big secret that you and Reid were experimenting with D/s back when I knew you. You're not a novice."

She clenched her jaw. "Yes, apparently Reid was quite free with that information."

His tilted his head. "Really? I thought I was the only who knew."

No, at least one other person knew. And whoever that someone was had used it to their ultimate advantage to hurt her. Unless . . . She stared at Jace for a moment, a sick feeling rolling through her. What if he had been the one?

No. She dismissed the thought as quickly as it appeared. Jace didn't have a cruel bone in his body. He would've never violated her that way. She shifted in her chair, shaking off the ridiculous idea. "It doesn't matter. Ancient history."

He paused for a moment as if he were going to push further, but the look on her face must have made him think better of it. He crooked a thumb toward the mini-fridge next to his desk. "You want something to drink? Beer, soda? I would offer wine, but despite the décor, I'm not that refined."

The corner of her mouth tilted up. "A beer would be great."

He stood, turning his back to her. "So, are you saying you haven't continued to explore the Scene?"

The Scene. What an innocuous term for something that had the potential to rip her apart from the inside out. "No, I dropped the whole idea after Reid and I broke up."

He grabbed two bottles from the fridge, twisted off the caps, and handed her a beer. "Wow, really? I'm surprised."

She took a sip, the fizzy liquid easing the dryness in her throat. "Why is that?"

He shrugged and sat on the edge of his desk. "We were all new to it back then, but it didn't take an expert to see how well you took to the sub role. I was all kinds of jealous that Reid had you all to himself. Too bad he was such a selfish bastard—things could've gotten much more interesting."

Brynn wet her lips and gripped the bottle with both hands as images more erotic than the art downstairs filled her mind. She knew Jace's kink back then had extended beyond D/s and into ménage. And even though she'd always viewed him as more of a buddy than a lover, she couldn't deny that the handsome blond could get her hormones hopping.

She cleared her throat, trying to shake the images from her brain. "Perhaps. And that's part of the reason I'm here. Beyond wanting to get to my sister, I also think I need to do this for myself. There are some things I need to work through, and I think this type of thing could help."

"What do you mean?"

She shifted her gaze away, trying to come up with something—anything—other than telling him about the rape. "I don't know, it's just lately, I've found myself—"

"Unsatisfied?" he suggested.

She nodded, goose bumps pricking her skin. She had wanted her lie to sound authentic. But hearing it out loud hit a bit too close to home. Shit. She hadn't needed to make up a fib. Unsatisfied was exactly what she was. "I thought maybe this could be the answer."

"And you're willing to go into this blind, with a stranger?"

"Yes."

His eyebrows knitted. "You sure? I could try to get Reid a membership if you want."

"No," she said, shaking her head.

"How come?"

She sighed. "Time doesn't heal everything, Jace."

He swigged his beer, keeping his eyes on her. "You realize that going into a place like The Ranch is the real deal. What you and Reid did back in the day was dabbling. The members at this place vary from one end of the spectrum to the other. You might find a dom who's just looking for a little casual play, but many others are seeking total submission."

Her heartbeat seemed incredibly loud in the quiet intimacy of the room. "Meaning?"

"Meaning guys who want to break down every barrier you have—physical, psychological, sexual—until you're totally and completely theirs to command. Master and slave. It can be an incredible rush to get into something like that, but also can be seriously overwhelming for the inexperienced."

Sweat beaded her back, and she shifted in her chair. "Is it safe?"

"The club is very selective about membership for doms. They do background checks, there are income requirements, and you have to have a clean bill of health. And as for the play itself, there are safe words and surveillance cameras to make sure people only take it as far as they mutually want to."

"Oh, that's good." A little flash of relief went through her, not just for herself but for her sister.

He shot her a stern look. "But that's not across the board, Brynn. They don't broadcast it, but be aware that there are also unmonitored areas you can get into if you sign a waiver. You need to promise me you won't venture into any of those areas until you've established a trusted relationship with someone. Only the assholes will try to get you into an isolated place this early in the game. And *that* is dangerous."

"Right." *Shit.* "So what happens when I go to The Ranch?"

He set his beer down on the desk. "Well, if you go in as a single, guest sub, you'd be presented to the members who were interested in taking you on, and you would get to select which one to be with. Then you'd have to demonstrate your submission to him in front of the group."

"Why would I have to do that?"

He shrugged. "It's a way to make sure you're serious. Some

members of the club are pretty important people. If a reporter or private investigator tried to sneak in, they'd have to *really* want to get a story to go through public submission. Grant will be there looking for that kind of thing, so that's why you have to make sure you're absolutely convincing."

Her knuckles turned white against the bottle. "And what exactly does public submission involve?"

"Whatever the hell your dom wants."

She nodded slowly, then glanced up at him. "I'm kind of freaked out about the whole thing. What if I can't convince that Grant guy?"

He smiled and stepped closer to her, placing a warm hand on her shoulder. "I have faith in you. All you need to do is channel whoever you were back when you were Reid's sub. You have it in you. The key is going to be to not focus on anything but your own personal reasons for being there. Give yourself over to the experience. Once you're past initiation, you can worry about tracking down your sister."

"Right," she said, trying to convince herself.

"You'll be fine. I bet after a few days there, the sub role will become second nature to you again."

"Wait? A few days?" she asked, her voice coming out too high.

He stepped over to his desk and grabbed a few papers. "The Ranch is a retreat, not a drop-in club. You can't sign up for anything less than a three-day stay."

"Shit."

"I had to pull some strings to get you in this quickly." He handed her the documents. "Fill these out and fax them back to me by tomorrow morning, and I can get you in for the retreat starting on Wednesday. There is also a rule sheet in there for you to go over."

She set her beer on the side table and took the pages from him. A hopeful thought hit her. "Are you going to be there?"

He gave her a rueful smile. "Doll, I'd love to take you on as my sub for a while, if you'd have me, but I can't bail on the store without more notice."

Her shoulders sagged.

He sighed and kissed the top of her head. "You're going to be fine. Just trust your instincts and don't be afraid to use your safe word if someone pushes you too far."

She managed a shaky smile and stood. Now she needed to make sure she pulled off this ruse to the nth degree for yet another reason. She definitely didn't want to get Jace in any trouble with the club or screw with whatever business dealings he had with The Ranch.

"Thanks, Jace. I really appreciate you risking your hide to help me."

"You're welcome, doll." He pulled her in for one last bear hug. "Make sure you call me and let me know how it goes. And don't be a stranger. I can get you discounts on all kinds of naughty stuff."

She laughed. "It's good to have friends in high places."

"No doubt."

Jace sank into his desk chair with a groan. He'd been looking forward to seeing Brynn again, but he hadn't anticipated the raging hard-on she would inspire. The hopeful look on her face when she'd thought he might be able to go to The Ranch with her had sent him over the edge. God, he'd love to be the guy who got to experience the sweet submission he knew she was capable of. But he was under strict orders.

He adjusted the crotch of his jeans, then picked up the phone to dial a familiar number.

"How'd it go?"

Jace tilted his chair back and closed his eyes. "It's done. She'll be there on Wednesday."

"Thanks, man."

"Dude, are you sure you want to do it this way? I kind of feel like a dick."

Reid sighed. "Trust me. I know what she needs even if she doesn't."

Jace snorted. If he were a betting man, he'd put his money on Reid's balls getting handed to him on a plate, but he'd learned long ago not to try to change his friend's mind once he had it set on something. "I hope you're right. For both your sakes."

EIGHT

then

Brynn rolled her wrist, her hand aching from all the notes she'd taken during her boss Davis's staff meeting, and sank back into the conference room chair. She glanced around the oval table and noticed everyone's eyes had glazed over. Davis stepped around the whiteboard he'd been scribbling on and stood behind Brynn. "Any questions, people?"

Most shook their heads.

Davis's hands settled on Brynn's shoulders and squeezed, the unexpected touch jolting her from her daze. "Did you get all of that, Brynn?"

She cleared her throat and tried not to squirm beneath the unwanted touch. The man didn't like her, so his seemingly friendly gesture was all for the benefit of the other workers. "Uh, yes, sir, of course."

"Excellent. So Brynn will type up the notes for everyone and e-mail them to you before the end of the day," he said, patting her shoulder one last time before heading to the door and swinging it open. "Thanks for all your attention this afternoon."

Brynn gathered her things and followed everyone out. She'd hoped to pin down Reid earlier in the day to discuss the previous night's disaster of a make-out session, but they'd all been so busy it'd been impossible to say more than a few passing words. So she was happy to see him veer toward her desk instead of his own as they trailed out of the meeting.

As she slipped into her seat, Reid sank into the chair at the front of her desk, his customary grin noticeably absent. "Hey."

"Hey, yourself," she said, dropping her legal pad and pen on her desk. "I was beginning to wonder if you were avoiding me."

He frowned. "Course not, just been busy. But I do have to confess, I'm here to deliver a bit of good and bad news."

"Uh-oh, why don't you start with the good?"

He dug in his pocket, then tossed a key onto her desk. She picked it up and examined it. "What's this?"

"It's for a rental car. I have a friend whose dad owns a repair shop. He owes me a favor, so they're going to try to fix your car for free. If it can be fixed, that is. In the meantime, he was able to hook me up with a loaner for you, so you don't have to take the bus."

"Oh, wow, you didn't have to do that," she said, stunned by his gesture.

"No problem, and hopefully, it will make you less mad at me for the bad news."

She sighed. "Lay it on me."

He sagged in the seat and blew out a haggard breath. "Something's come up, and I'm going to have to move our date to tomorrow night."

"Is everything all right?"

He nodded, but his frown lines didn't match his assurance. "Yeah, it's fine. I'd forgotten I'd promised to go to this thing tonight. I don't want to back out."

Brynn kept her expression smooth, though her chest tightened. She'd seen more people bail when they found out about her mother than stick around, and Reid's change of plans sounded suspiciously like the warning shot before the classic cut-and-run. Maybe fixing her car was her consolation prize. "What kind of thing?"

He shrugged. "Nothing you'd be interested in. Otherwise, I'd bring you along."

Sure he would. Right. She pasted on a smile. "No problem. Have fun."

Roslyn stepped behind Reid and laid a hand on his shoulder. "Reid, dear, stop pestering Brynn. She has a lot of notes to type up before the end of the day."

He glanced over his shoulder at her. "Yes, ma'am. I'll be done in a second. She's just clarifying something from the meeting for me."

The dark-haired woman pursed her lips, but walked off without another word. Reid leaned forward and kept his voice low. "I promise we'll do something tomorrow night."

Brynn propped her legal pad next to her computer screen. "All right, sounds good. And really, thanks again for my car. I really appreciate it."

He paused as if he were going to say something else, but then apparently decided against it because he rose and headed back to his desk. Yep, no doubt, he was going to bail. His whole essence screamed guilt. She clicked her fingers along her keyboard with a little more force than necessary. Well, better now than later. At least her heart hadn't latched onto him yet.

She glanced over to his desk and tried to ignore the way her gut churned at the thought of him returning to the status of co-worker only. Okay, so maybe she was a little attached. Nothing she couldn't handle. She'd learned long ago that everyone lets you down eventually—it was just a matter of when.

———

Reid sat in Jace's living room, nursing his second beer and staring through the TV, not really seeing the baseball game. He shifted forward in the overstuffed chair, bracing his arms on his thighs. He couldn't get comfortable. Not in the room. Not in the chair. Not in his own fucking skin.

Maybe this was a bad idea.

Something nicked him in the head. "What the—?

He raised his hand in defense as Jace launched another peanut at him. "Calm the hell down, dude. You're stressing *me* out."

Reid set his beer down and wiped his damp palms on his jeans. "I think I'm just going to go."

"The hell you are," he said, lowering the volume on the television and angling himself on the couch so he could face him. "Look, she's going to be here in a few minutes. You asked for my help, so don't punk out on me. And what guy is going to bail when a beautiful woman is on her way over to fulfill your sexual fantasies?"

He groaned and sank back against the cushions. What had he been thinking? Jace had agreed to hook him up with a girl he knew—a girl who supposedly liked things a little rough in bed and preferred two guys to one—so that Reid could work through his shit.

Last night the whole idea had seemed like the perfect solution to his problem—a pretty girl who didn't mind some kink, Jace there to keep Reid from crossing any lines, and no strings. But now that he was here, neither his heart nor his dick were onboard.

He needed to go.

The doorbell rang.

Fuck.

Jace grinned. "Right on time."

Jace hustled to the door, leaving Reid with his warring thoughts and pounding heart. Part of him wanted to sneak out the side door and not look back. But the other part was still holding on to the hope that maybe this would fix it. Fix him.

However, when Jace pulled open the door, and Reid heard the voice on the other side, his blood seemed to halt in his veins.

Mother. Fucker.

He hopped up from the chair and crossed the room in three strides, stepping up behind Jace. Brynn's eyes locked with his over Jace's shoulder, her teeth tugging at her full bottom lip.

"What are you doing here?" Reid bit out, then grimaced when he realized how rude his question sounded.

"Oh, hey," she said, shifting her gaze between the two of them, looking as unsure of herself as he'd ever seen her. "I was just telling Jace that Roslyn found your wallet on the floor in the office. She, uh, knew where you were and asked if I would drop it by on my way home. She didn't want you driving home without your license."

He automatically grabbed for his back pocket—of course, nothing was in there. "Damn, how did I lose that?"

She shrugged, and then stuck out her hand, giving him the wallet.

"Thanks." His fingers brushed hers as he took it from her, and his dick—which hadn't twitched all night despite the upcoming threesome—instantly stirred to life.

God, what was it about this girl? Seeing her there, feeling the heat her presence alone fired within him, slapped him with hard reality. He was so screwed. He could fuck his way through sorority row and then hit every whorehouse on the way home afterward, but it wouldn't matter. Nothing was going to slake the dark desire Brynn inspired.

The realization burned an aching hole in his chest. Maybe he'd never be able to trust himself around her.

She pushed her hair behind her ears. "So, yeah, I guess I'll get going. Y'all enjoy your boys' night."

"You can stay and have a beer if you want," Jace offered. "The Rangers game is on."

He whipped his head in Jace's direction. Had the idiot lost his goddamned mind?

Brynn snuck a tentative peek at Reid. His horror must've been obvious on his face because she quickly waved a dismissive hand. "No, I'm not going to interrupt. Far be it from me to interfere on dude time."

Headlights flashed through the darkened street, and she glanced back as another car pulled into the driveway.

Reid's heart leapt into his throat. *Oh, shit.*

"Right," he said, stepping forward, his words tumbling out. "You're probably not a baseball fan anyway. And the game's a blowout so far. Why don't I walk you to your car?"

Her brow furrowed as he took her elbow. "Yeah, okay."

But as they turned to head down the sidewalk, Leah exited her car and sashayed into their path, looking like a teenage boy's wet dream. Shorts hugging her ass, legs up to her ears, and non-God-given tits spilling out her top. Definitely not a baseball-watching outfit. Definitely not a dude. Facts not lost on Brynn.

She stiffened in his grasp and halted her step.

Goddammit. And goddamn his aunt for sending Brynn here. Even without trying, Ros had managed to meddle like she had some sixth sense on how exactly to fuck with his life.

Leah's glossed lips pulled into a seductive smile as she approached. "Jace didn't tell me we were bringing in a fourth, but . . ." She gave Brynn an up-and-down perusal. "I guess I'm open to new things."

Reid closed his eyes, wishing the sidewalk would crack open and swallow him up. *Fan-fucking-tastic.*

Brynn's fingers curled into fists, her nails digging into her palms, but she forced herself to choke down the rest of her reaction. She would not give Reid the satisfaction.

She eased her elbow from his grip and gave the supermodel-like girl a polite smile. "Thanks, but I was just leaving. I think I may be exactly one too many. Have a good night."

Brynn hiked her purse strap further up her shoulder and traipsed past the woman.

"Brynn, wait—"

But she pretended she didn't hear Reid and kept walking, her steps picking up speed. She just needed to get in her car, lock all of this out before she embarrassed herself. She had no claim on Reid. Had no right to feel so possessive. No logical reason to want to yank that bitch down by her ponytail and scratch her eyes out.

Two steps more.

A hand clamped over her forearm and spun her around. "I said wait, goddammit."

"No, Reid," she said, her voice losing its calm edge. "Let me go. I want to go home."

"Look, just let me explain."

She snorted and glanced back toward the house. Jace and Barbie had gone inside and shut the door. "I think I can figure it out. I don't need a diagram. Thanks."

"No, it's not like that." But the guilty shift of his eyes said otherwise.

She sighed. "Reid, it's fine, okay? It's none of my business. But I think it's a good idea if we just end whatever has been going on with us right now."

"Brynn—"

"No, seriously. It's not like I was expecting exclusivity or whatever, but I think I'll have a hard time scraping the image of the three of you from my brain." A flash of the beautiful girl wrapped around Reid's naked body went through her mind, making her want to heave.

He latched his other hand on her opposite arm, squaring her to face him, his blue eyes fierce. "But I don't want her, I want *you*."

She jerked her arms from his grip, no longer able to keep the lid on her boiling anger. "Oh, right. Because cancelling a date with me to go tag-team fuck some other girl is exactly the way to show me you care. You should write goddamned Hallmark cards."

He ran a hand over his face, his expression stricken. "No, it's just . . . complicated."

She smirked. "No, I think it's pretty simple. Now you know why I didn't want you to come inside my house. My life is ugly. I wouldn't want to get involved with me either. Good-bye, Reid."

She turned her back to him and stuck her key in her car door.

"Screw it. You want to talk about secrets?" he asked, his volume rising. "Let's do that, then."

She turned the lock and reached for the door handle.

"You know why that girl is here? Because I'm screwed up, Brynn. When I look at you, I don't just want to play nice and date you. I don't just want to fuck you. I want to *own* you. Tie you to my bed and do whatever the hell I want to you. Use you."

Every muscle in her body stilled and some foreign emotion stirred low and deep in her belly. She couldn't turn around; she just stared back at her own wide-eyed reflection in her car window.

"And it scares the hell out of me because I can't keep that desire in control when I'm with you. I don't trust myself not to hurt you, to take it too far."

The sad current of his words made her chest ache. She swallowed past the dryness in her throat, hoping her voice would still function. "I don't understand. Why that girl?"

He sighed, and she could picture his chest heaving with the weight of what he had revealed. "I asked Jace to help me find a way to get rid of this insane need so that I could be with you. Have a normal relationship. That's what tonight was about. Brynn, I'm so sorry. I just—I didn't know what else to do."

She should get in her car and go. Not look back. Her mother had always told her that when people told you who they were, you should believe them. If Reid thought he was dangerous, maybe he was. But the anguish in his voice tugged at her. This man wasn't violent—every ounce of her God-given instincts told her that.

She took a deep breath, turned around, and met his stormy eyes. "What if I tried to help you?"

"What?" The shame on his face turned to confusion. "What do you mean?"

"You said tonight was about getting this out of your system. Maybe you're right, maybe that will help," she said, trying to keep her voice steady. "But you don't need that girl. You could try with me."

Something unreadable lit his features, but then he grimaced. "No way. You have no idea the things that go through my head, the stuff I want to do—"

"So show me," she said, cutting him off, her courage rising. "I know you think you're scaring me off, but the only thing that's going to do that is you lying to me. So you have some stuff to work through. I have a lot of baggage, too. Maybe we can do this, get you past it, and then move on and date like normal."

He shook his head. "We can date like normal without doing this. If you're still willing to give me a chance, I can leave this behind. I think you knowing about it will help me control the urge better."

She gave him a half-smile. "That's not how it works. My mother makes her money fulfilling the fantasies guys keep from their partners. If we're going to date, I don't want to be wondering if you're secretly sneaking off to feed that part of you."

"I wouldn't do that to you. I swear I won't lie to you again."

He said the words fervently, like he truly believed them. But she knew him wanting the statement to be true wouldn't actually make it so.

She had no idea if there was a certain protocol in his slave-girl role-play, but she put her hands out to him, palms up. "I'm giving myself to you tonight. Let me help you check this off your fantasy list."

Storm clouds gathered over his face. "Stop, Brynn. You don't know what you're signing up for."

She held his gaze, refusing to look away, despite the anxiety hammering through her. "Like I said, show me."

"No."

"Fine." She let her arms fall to her sides and turned back to her car. "Have a nice life, Reid."

His deep groan cut through the night and strong hands landed flat on the roof of her car, his muscular arms imprisoning her on each side. "Don't do this."

Heavy footsteps sounded behind them. "Is everything all right out here?"

Jace.

"It's fine," Reid said through clenched teeth, his fierce tone rippling over her and awakening her senses.

His quickening breath was hot on her neck, and his body heat radiated against her back. She should've been scared; she could sense his dwindling self-control—the man's easy-going facade being stripped away by some dark, primal instinct within him.

But something inside her wanted it. Wanted to push him over the edge. Her voice came out as a whisper. "Don't let me leave, Reid."

The muscles in his arms flexed and bunched as if the war within him was raging in every sector of his body. He remained silent for agonizingly long seconds, then pushed himself away from the car. "Fine, you think this is what you want? Then lose the dress, Brynn."

"Wh-What?" She spun around, looking from him to Jace, who stood a few steps behind him with raised eyebrows, then to the area around them. Jace's driveway was protected by hedges and trees and far off the road, but did Reid actually expect her to take off her clothes out here? In front of his best friend?

Reid's lip curled up. "What's wrong?"

"But—"

"You said you wanted to give yourself to me, to know what this is about. Well, you're getting your wish. If this isn't what you want, then say 'stop,' and we'll go to dinner and have a date like normal people."

She ground her teeth. So that's what this was about? He wanted to prove he was right. That she couldn't handle him. Well, screw that. She reached behind her and unzipped her dress, then slipped the narrow straps off her shoulders. After one fortifying breath, she let go and the material puddled onto the cobblestones at her feet, leaving her in her sheer bra and panties.

A pained expression flitted over Reid's face, and Jace's eyes lit with male appreciation.

"Jace, is the guesthouse unlocked?" Reid asked, his voice disconcertingly calm.

"No, but I can go grab the key and open it for you."

Reid nodded. "Thanks. Do that."

Jace jogged toward the side of the house, and Reid walked toward Brynn with deliberate steps, his eyes not leaving hers. The moonless evening and the soft garden lights cast his face in a combination of light and shadow, but the intensity of his expression was clear. She held her breath, her heart beating so fast she worried it would hop out of her chest and flop onto the ground between them.

When he reached her, his hand cupped her bare shoulder. "Turn around and close your eyes."

She followed his instruction and faced the car. Soft cotton brushed against her face, then tightened over her eyes—her dress, now a blindfold. His fingertips caressed the back of her neck, making her shiver despite the muggy night air. "You're mine tonight. I let Jace look at you, but he gets nothing else now, you understand?"

She nodded, relief flooding through her. She liked Jace, but it was Reid she wanted touching her. Even if this version of Reid was one she hadn't quite met yet.

He kissed her shoulder blade, nipped at it. "You remember what you called me the first time we met?"

She paused, trying to wrangle in her buzzing brain so she could concentrate. What had she called him? Reid? No. She wet her lips. "Sir."

His hand curled around her waist, caressing her bare stomach. "That's right. Tonight, that's what you call me."

The feel of his fingers and the seductive confidence of his voice hypnotized her. She nodded again.

"Tell me you understand," he said, his voice low but firm.

"Yes, sir."

"Good, girl. Let's go."

In one swift movement, Reid lifted her off her feet and into his arms as if she weighed nothing. She grabbed for his neck, disoriented from the blindfold. "Whoa."

"I've got you, sugar. I won't let you fall."

Sounds drifted to her ears as they made their way across the yard—crickets, frogs, the rustle of the leaves as the breeze touched them. She wondered if the landscaping continued around the side of the house or if she'd be exposed to the neighbors. The idea that people might see her half-naked, being carried by this powerful man, should've bothered her, but she was at ease in his arms.

She had given herself to him, so if he wanted her exposed to others, then that was up to him. Tonight, he owned her.

Damp heat pooled between her thighs at the thought.

Uh-oh.

What had she gotten herself into?

———

What the hell had he gotten himself into? Reid sat a blindfolded Brynn down on the edge of the bed and tossed her purse by the footboard. "Don't move."

He stalked back to the doorway of the bedroom and leaned against the frame, watching her. He had fully expected her to bail the minute he'd asked her to strip in front of Jace—that had been his intent. But she'd shocked him, calling his bluff. And the minute he'd seen her bend to his will, he'd gotten an intoxicating rush so strong, it had made his head spin.

Jace laid a hand on his shoulder, keeping his voice low. "The room's yours. Leah and I will hang out in the main house. You need anything else from me? Do you want me to stay?"

Possessiveness ripped through him like lightning, and he had to dial it back before responding. "No. I'll be . . . fine."

Now if only he could believe that.

Jace's gaze flitted to Brynn, then back to him. "Just trust yourself. She does."

Reid nodded, the weight of that knowledge settling over him. "I know."

Jace closed the door behind him, shutting out his last safety net. Reid stared at Brynn. Even in the soft lamplight of the room, he could see the rosy buds of her nipples peeking through the lace of her bra. His cock strained against the denim of his jeans, hardening to the point of agony. Since she'd shown up on Jace's doorstep tonight, he'd been trying to hold back, trying to prove to himself he was over this stupid fantasy. But seeing Brynn offer herself to him so naively had only served to conjure familiar images of her collared before him. God, he was so fucked.

His mother had always taught him you could tell everything about a man based on the way he treated a woman. She'd spent her life as an advocate for women's rights. And now here he was, unable to resist the urge to dominate Brynn like she was some kind of slave. His mom would've been so ashamed.

But he was done questioning it for the night. He had to cleanse this from his system, and Brynn needed to see why she shouldn't jump into things she knew nothing about. By the end of this, they could both move on. They'd either go forward and start a normal relationship, or more likely, she would run away completely freaked out and want nothing to do with him. Either way, tonight he was giving himself over to it.

He walked over to her and caressed her cheek with the back of his hand. She startled at the touch.

"Easy," he whispered. "I'm right here. I'm going to take off your blindfold. I want to be able to see your pretty face."

She nodded. "Yes, sir."

The sweet femininity of her voice went straight to his gut. This girl was so tough, but there was an untouched innocence in her that made him want to take care of her, protect her. He untied the dress and let it fall to the carpet. She blinked up at him, her cheeks tinged pink, her lush bottom lip swollen from her biting it.

"You can still back out."

She shook her head, her green eyes defiant. "No, sir."

No going back now. The steely voice that passed his lips was unrecognizable to his own ears. "Stand up."

———

Brynn swung her legs to the side of the bed and rose on shaky knees. Reid's hands moved up her arms as his eyes traveled over her. She'd never seen this side of him before—so focused and serious. Her nipples tightened beneath his hungry gaze, and the response didn't seem lost on him. He skimmed his finger along the edge of one cup of her bra, sending tiny shivers through her. "Take it off."

The quiet authority of his voice melted over her like chocolate, soothing some of her twitching nerves. She reached behind her back, undid the clasp, and let the bra fall to the floor. Reid gave her a slow smile and reached out to cup one of her breasts, running his thumb across its hard peak. "Gorgeous."

She shuddered and he bent his head to draw the opposite nipple into his mouth, while continuing to strum pleasure from the other with his hand. The combination of sensations sent liquid fire straight to her core. She closed her eyes and let out a soft whimper, his tongue caressing her with painfully gentle strokes.

God, was he going to be this slow and deliberate with everything? She'd burn into a pile of embers by the time he got to the actual sex. He drew back a bit and circled her areola with the tip of his tongue, carefully avoiding what she most wanted. She threaded her hands in his hair and urged him forward, wanting more, needing all of his mouth again.

Cool air replaced his touch as he backed away.

She blinked. "What's wrong?"

He pressed a finger against her lips, quieting her. "I'm in charge of your pleasure, not you. Trust that I'll take you where you need to go."

Her throat went dry, but she nodded.

"Take off your panties."

He stepped back and put his hands in his pockets, watching her, making her feel both wanted and vulnerable all at the same time. Her hands hovered near her hips, suddenly nervous about standing naked before him.

"I'm not going to ask twice, Brynn," he said, his voice calm but firm.

She took a slow breath, then hooked her thumbs in her panties and shimmied out of them. His gaze ate up every inch of flesh, and the impressive bulge in his jeans twitched. Her body tingled beneath his clear approval. She yearned to reach out and touch him, to undress him and feel his skin beneath her fingertips, but she fought the urge to take over control.

His hand cupped her hip and he dragged her against him, the stiff material of his jeans brushing the soft curls covering her mound. He pressed his lips to the pulse point below her ear, his palm sliding from her waist to the curve of her ass. Warm breath lapped over her skin like ocean water. "You know how many times I've imagined you stripped bare for me like this? How many nights I've stroked my cock just at the thought of touching you again?"

The words turned her insides molten, the juices of her arousal coating her sex. She edged her hips toward him, seeking relief.

He trailed his fingers along her backside, the cleft of her ass, the small of her back—each touch unbearably delicate. His voice was barely a whisper. "Have you ever touched yourself and thought about me?"

Her face flooded with heat. She had. More times than she could count since she'd met him. But she had never admitted to masturbating to anyone. She swallowed hard. "Yes."

He groaned and buried his forehead against her shoulder, the first sign that maybe she was affecting him as much as he was her. She bit back a pleased smile.

"When was the last time?"

She wet her lips. In for a penny, in for a pound. "Last night, after you left."

"Fuck." He lifted his head, his eyes meeting hers. "Like this?"

His hand glided along her tender skin and dipped inside her channel, finding her wet and wanting. She tilted her head back at the sweet invasion. "Oh, God. Yes, like that."

"Mmm, so hot and ready for me, aren't you?" The pad of his thumb found her clit and massaged.

She bucked against the contact and let out a soft moan, sharp darts of pleasure shooting up her spine and radiating outward. Her nails sunk into his shoulders as she tried to keep from tipping over to orgasm. How could she be so close to the edge with just one touch?

He chuckled, low and warm. "Don't come yet, sugar. I haven't given you permission."

He pumped his fingers in and out in a languid rhythm, and her knees began to quiver beneath her. "Don't know if I can control that."

Without warning, he pulled back, removing all physical contact and halting her galloping journey toward release. She opened her mouth to protest, but he hushed her, using his fingers to gloss her parted lips with her own cream. He cradled her cheeks and dipped his head to claim her mouth in a scorching kiss. All her muscles seemed to liquefy, and she had to grab onto the bed behind her so she wouldn't end up in a puddle at his feet.

Far too soon, he eased back and gave her a chastising smile. "Hmm. Guess you'll have to learn how to control it. Otherwise, you're not going to get what you want."

She managed a nod, her head still spinning from the kiss. "Yes, sir. I'll do my best."

He lifted her chin with his finger, forcing her to look up at him. "So, what is it that you want, sugar? Tell me."

She willed her voice not to shake. She knew he expected her to ask for her orgasm, but she yearned for something more than that. Something she thought about every day and ached to do anytime he was within ten feet of her. "I want to touch you. To please you."

Feral desire flared in his eyes, mixing in with the tension still rolling off him, an internal battle playing out in front of her. He ran a thumb over her cheek, staring at her for a moment more, then his expression turned resolute. He moved his hand to her shoulder, pushing down. "On your knees."

She lowered herself onto the plush carpet, keeping her focus on his face. He was trusting her with his dark side, showing her what he didn't want anyone to see. Something stirred deep within her chest, warming her. Never had she imagined she would let a guy command her this way, like she was his whore. The idea should have been appalling considering her mother's profession, but something deep within her ached to please Reid, to be his safe place.

He circled around her, stalking, like he had to see her compliance from every angle. The air seemed to charge and spark between them, making every fiber in her body hum in anticipation. Finally, he stopped in front of her, his stance wide, and unbuttoned his jeans. Her tongue darted out and moistened her lips as he freed his impressive erection from his boxers. He stroked his cock and stepped forward, bringing it within centimeters of her face. "Open that pretty mouth of yours. I'll show you how to please me."

Her lips parted and he grabbed a fistful of her hair, pulling so tightly her scalp tingled. He tilted her head to the angle he wanted and without any additional warning, slid his cock into her mouth with a deep, satisfied groan. His utterly male flavor filled her mouth and she closed her eyes, savoring the taste of salt and musk and arousal. Slowly, she ran her tongue along the thick, smooth shaft, taking as much as she could, then eased back to lick the head. He twisted his fingers deeper in her hair and thrust forward, causing her to cry out around him. Not from pain, but from the heady feeling of him *taking* what he wanted from her.

"Don't close your eyes, sugar. Look at me while you suck me."

Her eyelids flew open and she lifted her gaze to him. His face was ravenous, like a man possessed. The laid-back Reid had left the building. Intense power and calm control sizzled off him, drowning her, arousing her. He stroked her cheek with his free hand as he eased deeper into her mouth. "That's good, sugar. You're going to take all of me. Relax your throat."

She followed his instructions, focusing on releasing the muscles and accepting him. Soon, he buried all the way to the hilt, a shudder stealing over him. "Ah, shit. That's right." He moved in long, steady thrusts, tapping the back of her throat with the smooth head. "God, your mouth is even better than I imagined."

Unable to resist touching him any longer, she reached up and palmed his sac as she dragged her tongue along the thick vein on the base of his cock. He moaned, then abruptly pulled out, releasing her hair. "I didn't say you could touch me yet."

She blinked, shocked by the sudden absence of contact. "I'm sorry, I thought it'd be okay."

"Ah, there's your mistake. Your job isn't to think. It's to listen. To obey. You're mine, remember?"

"Right. I mean, yes, sir."

He grasped her chin. "Maybe you should've gone home. A night alone would've been a lot easier on you than dealing with me is going to be."

"I don't need easy. I want you," she said, the steadiness of her voice not betraying her spiking anxiety.

"Be careful what you ask for." He dropped his hand from her face. "Get on the bed. Facedown."

She grabbed the edge of the mattress and climbed onto the bed with wobbly limbs. As she scooted along the sheets, the cool cotton caressed her burning skin, making her hyperaware of her nudity. Reid's eyes followed her progress, and he made no attempt to hide his perusal of her most intimate areas. Her body ached for those heated gazes to turn into touches.

Once she reached the center, she flipped over and settled on her stomach. Nerves skittered down her spine, the intense vulnerability of the position testing her resolve to follow his instructions.

What exactly was he planning to do? She trusted the Reid she'd become friends with, but this version of him was unfamiliar—dangerous. She knew he was trying to prove a point to her, but how far would he take it?

The loud sound of ripping fabric filled the room. She craned her neck around and found Reid tearing a pillowcase into strips. He also had removed the tieback cord from the drapes and had that hanging around his neck. "Eyes down, LeBreck."

She turned to face forward again, and he walked to the side of the bed. Strong fingers lifted her left wrist, and smooth material wrapped around it. She peeked at him from underneath her lashes as he knotted the makeshift bindings. The question bubbled to her lips before she could stop it. "What are you doing?"

He gave her a sidelong glance and tightened the strap. "You just can't give up the control, can you?"

"I—I'm sorry."

Without another word, he took another strip of pillowcase and smiled. A blindfold. *Shit.* With swift movements he slipped it over her eyes, pulling the knot taut in the back. Then a loud crack broke the quiet of the room, and her ass cheek lit on fire. She cried out, the sound muffled by the mattress.

"Learn to keep your questions to yourself."

She balled her fists, ready to end it, to insist he stop. He'd *hit* her. But then warm, pleasant heat replaced the stinging in her skin, and her pussy throbbed in response. Fuck. What was wrong with her? She wasn't supposed to like this. This was to help it get out of his system, not to inspire interest in hers.

Footsteps padded on the carpet, and another strip wound around her right wrist. Reid's hot palms slid up her arms, then moved her hands to rest above her head on the bed so he could bind her wrists together. Something silky brushed against the tops of her hands—the braided cord from the curtain. With a grunt and yank on the cord from Reid, her muscles were stretched, drawing her arms taut above her and securing her to the headboard.

Instinctively, she tugged back, but the restraints only provided a hair of slack. She buried her face in the sheets and tried to steady her breathing. She was at his mercy. Blind and bound for whatever he chose to do to her.

"Get on your knees." He gripped her waist and helped her tuck her knees beneath her. Her face and breasts remained against the sheets, the restraints not allowing her to rise any higher. A gentle hand caressed her ass, smoothing over the area he had hit. "Do you know how fucking sexy you look with my handprint marking you?"

She shook her head, but didn't dare speak.

His finger traced the cleft of her ass, brushing across her most private opening. She automatically tensed. "I have to tell you, Brynn. Spanking such a beautiful ass could get addictive. I'm not sure if I got enough out of the first time."

Before she could process what he was saying, the flat of his palm landed a sharp blow on her opposite cheek. She bit her lip and moaned, the pain/pleasure mix rocketing through her. "Can you take it, sugar? Handle what I'm planning to dish out?"

She braced herself as his hand came down again and again, covering her ass and the backs of her thighs with stinging heat. He never slapped the same spot twice, but instead methodically covered every inch of virgin skin with his attention. Her back arched and she writhed, the heady buzz of pain and endorphins overloading her system and fogging her brain. To her mortification, hot moisture leaked down her thighs as if her body were begging for more.

When the spanking ceased, gentle hands moved over her skin, soothing her. His voice was choppy, his breathing quick. "Have I scared you enough yet, Brynn? Are you ready to run?"

She moaned into the sheets, half out of her mind with need. "For the love of God, please touch me."

His hands stilled as if he was shocked by her words. "What?"

She parted her knees, opening herself to him, not caring at the moment what kind of girl that made her. "Please."

Tentatively, he moved his hand between her legs and dragged his fingers down her folds. Her entire body trembled, and a deep groan rumbled from his chest. "Jesus. You're soaked."

Her hands flexed and fisted in the bindings as he pulled away. If he didn't do something soon, she was going to lose it. Her words came out in a barely coherent jumble. "I need . . . I . . . You're killing me."

"*Son of a bitch.*"

The sound of clothes rustling filled her ears. Lord, she wished she could see him and touch his bare skin, but she knew she wouldn't be granted that privilege tonight. He was trying to punish her, to scare her away. Only it wasn't working. She wanted him more.

The crackling of what she assumed was a condom wrapper replaced the other sounds, and the bed dipped around her. Strong hands grasped her hips and lifted, raising her backside fully and spreading her thighs to bare everything to him.

"Is this what you want, Brynn?" The blunt head of his cock pressed against her opening.

She tried to back into him, to force him into her, but the arm bindings bit into her wrists, holding her in place. "Yes."

"Tell me," he growled. "Tell me what you want me to do to you."

Her breath quickened and the ache inside her hit the point of pain. "Fuck me, Reid. Please, *fuck* me."

With one swift thrust he buried himself inside her, causing her to arch and gasp. Her tissues stretched taut, trying to accommodate his size. She'd only been with one other guy, and he hadn't been nearly this big. Being filled so completely was overwhelming.

Reid hummed with pleasure, but held himself still inside her. "Fuck, baby, you're tight. Am I hurting you?"

The small break in his hardened demeanor made her melt beneath him. She shook her head, all of her senses on fire. "Don't stop."

He grunted and the bed dipped again as he leaned down and draped his hard chest against her back. One hand slid down her stomach to her pelvis and parted her curls. With a roughened finger, he stroked her clit, and began to pump into her from behind. Lightning rushed through her veins as she tiptoed on the edge of release. In and out. The sweet glide of him against her delicate tissues driving her mad. She gritted her teeth, trying to hold herself back from falling into the abyss. She would wait for his permission. Would prove that she could do it.

Sweat slicked their bodies as Reid picked up the pace and relentlessly fucked her, stroking her hot button all the while. "You ready, baby?"

Her body quivered beneath him, no longer in her conscious control. "God, yes."

"Come for me, Brynn." His fingers pinched her clit and rolled it between his fingers, eliciting a scream from deep in her throat. Her nerve endings exploded, electric bliss crashing over her in all-encompassing waves.

She continued to cry out with each ripple of climax, her voice turning hoarse way before she was able to quiet herself. Reid increased his tempo, diving into her with frantic thrusts. Her body rippled around him, milking him with her orgasm, and a low moan sliced through the air as he found his own release.

When they both had gone silent and their breathing had slowed, he pressed his lips to the spot between her shoulder blades and eased out. Her legs collapsed beneath her, and she sank fully into the bed, too exhausted to even lift her head. She had no idea what Reid was doing, but at the moment she didn't care. Her eyelids fluttered closed behind the blindfold.

"Hey, wake up, sugar," Reid said, putting a hand on her shoulder.

Brynn blinked, the lamplight of the room burning her eyes. "Did I fall asleep?"

He brushed the dampened hair off her forehead, his expression guarded. "Just for a few minutes. I tried to let you rest for a little while, but we should probably get out of here. Jace's sister will be home in a few hours."

She lifted herself on her elbows and saw that she was no longer bound and that Reid had thrown a blanket over her. "Can you get my clothes?"

He stood and grabbed her things from the floor. "Here, do you need me to help you?"

She smiled. "I think I can handle it."

She pushed the blanket off her and rose to her feet, shivering from the sudden chill. Reid shoved his hands in his pockets, looking like he'd rather be anywhere else in the world but here. She slipped her panties on and the material brushed against her the tender skin on her bottom. "Ouch."

Reid cringed and dragged a hand through his already disheveled hair. "Hell, Brynn, I'm sorry. I can't believe I did this. I don't know what I was thinking."

She moved closer to him and wrapped her arms around his waist. "It's fine. I asked for it. I wanted you to."

He sat his chin on top of her head and rubbed her bare back. "I promise I won't ever let it happen again. I'm done with this."

She put her hands on his chest and stepped back. "Bullshit."

His eyebrows scrunched. "What?"

She grabbed her bra off the floor and put it on, then hauled her dress over her head, anger tainting the mellow afterglow she'd been enjoying. "You're saying you didn't enjoy yourself?"

He blew out a breath and leaned against the windowsill. "I hit you, Brynn. Used you. Talked to you like I owned you. You don't deserve that."

She zipped up the back of her dress and narrowed her eyes. "You loved it."

His frown lines dipped deeper, and he turned his back to her, looking out the window toward the swimming pool outside. "I don't want to be like this. I want a normal relationship with you."

She crossed her arms over her chest as she toed on her shoes. "And I don't want to be with someone who's lying to me. If you want to date me, you either come into it as you are—quirks and all—or go find someone else to play pretend with."

He raised his head, staring at her in the reflection in the window. "What are you saying?"

"If you want to explore this, I'm game. It's not like we're signing up to get married. We have a summer. I like you, you like me. And tonight was . . . pretty incredible. So, you decide."

His jaw tightened. "And if I just want to go back to a normal relationship?"

She shrugged. "It won't be with me. I don't want to spend my time wondering if you're satisfying this need with some other girl while playing Mr. Perfect around me."

His shoulders slumped. "Be careful on your drive home, Brynn."

Fury boiled low in her belly and her cheeks burned. "You're not even going to walk me out?"

He didn't turn to look at her. "It's for the best."

NINE

now

Soft classical music wrapped around Brynn as she inhaled deeply through her nose, counted to five, then blew the breath out through her mouth.

"Relax your hands, sweetie. You've got them clenched so hard, you're going to make your palms bleed," Melody said in a quiet voice.

Brynn sighed and sat up from her reclined position on the couch. "This isn't working."

Mel frowned and crossed her hands in her lap. "It's relaxation therapy, not surgery. Maybe you should take a Valium."

She rolled her eyes. "Yeah, 'cause that's what I want to do—be drugged up when I hand myself over to a stranger."

Mel pressed her lips together. "Good point."

Brynn gathered her hair in her hands and held it off her neck, trying to cool her sweating skin. "I'm going to frigging faint. Right there in the middle of a sex club. Like one of those goats."

She raised an eyebrow. "Goats?"

"You know, the ones who freeze up and faint when they're startled."

"That sounds hilarious," Mel said, then waved her hand. "I mean, the goats, not you, of course."

Brynn sank back into the couch and let her hair fall around her shoulders. How could she treat countless clients for post-traumatic stress and not even be able to talk herself down from a panic attack? She ran her hands over her face. "I'm going to lose it."

Mel stood and crossed the few steps to Brynn, then kneeled in front of her, taking her hands in hers. "Brynn, you are the most kick-ass chick I know and are stronger than this fear. You're going to be able to do this. If not for yourself, then for your sister."

Brynn gave her hands a squeeze. "Thanks, Mel."

A light tap sounded on the door, and Mel rose to unlock it. Cooper poked his head in. "There's a car here for you."

Brynn nodded. "Thanks, tell them I'll be right there."

He looked from Mel, then back to Brynn. "You gonna be okay, darling?"

Her eyes narrowed. "Mel told you."

He shrugged. "I dragged it out of her. We're all just worried about you. You know how the safe word thing works, right?"

"Hell, Cooper. I don't want to discuss this with you. I'm mortified that you even know where I'm going."

He leaned his shoulder against the doorframe. "Really, don't worry about it. I've been to a club before. I would never judge you."

She raised an eyebrow, but kept her questions to herself. She didn't need to know that much about her boss. "I need to get going. They apparently start initiations promptly at eight."

Both Mel and Cooper gave her tight hugs, and she shuffled off to her office to grab the suitcase she'd brought into work. The Ranch had insisted on a driver picking her up, saying that only members were allowed parking spaces. But she suspected it was really just another way to show her submission to the process.

She walked past Reid's office, but the door was closed. Just as well. She'd been avoiding him since Monday, and the last thing she needed was for him to see her in this state. He'd be able to pick up on her fear from thirty yards away. Even after all these years, the man still seemed to be able to read her as if she were wearing a billboard with emoticons on it.

She rolled her bag out of her office and into the front lobby where a lanky, young man waited in one of the chairs. When he saw her, he rose to his feet and straightened his pinstripe suit. "Ms. LeBreck?"

She nodded.

"I'm Adam, I'll be driving you this evening. Here, let me take your bags."

She passed the handle of her suitcase to him. "Thanks."

She followed him outside and shivered. The air had turned cooler, and she wished she'd chosen to wear something besides a sleeveless blouse and linen pants. She rubbed her arms as she rounded the building and turned toward the parking lot. A sleek limo waited for her at the curb and her stomach tightened. She was really going to do this.

Adam pressed a button on his keypad and popped open the trunk, loading her things inside, then turned to her. "You ready, Ms. LeBreck?"

"Guess so," she said, her voice wavering a bit.

His lips tilted up, the gesture softening his dark looks. "It's normal to be nervous. But just go with it. The anticipation can enhance the experience."

Or kill her. One or the other. She gave him a wan smile, and he yanked open the door for her. With one last steadying breath, she stepped forward and climbed in. To her surprise, Adam slid in right behind her. She cocked her head. "Did you need something?"

"I have to prepare you," he said, grabbing a small bag from the floorboard.

She inadvertently scooted backward. "What do you mean?"

He dug through the bag and pulled out a pair of handcuffs and a blindfold. He held them in front of her. "Your submission starts now, Ms. LeBreck. The safe word at The Ranch is Texas. Now please put out your hands."

"I'm not even going to get to see where the hell you're taking me?"

"Hands, Ms. LeBreck. You asked to participate. These are the rules."

Son of a fucking bitch. She gritted her teeth and held out her arms. With two quick clinks, he locked the cuffs around her wrists.

"Turn around."

She parked her bound hands in her lap and moved to face away from him. The silk sash slid over her eyes, blocking out all remnants of light. She forced herself to take deep breaths as her nervous system threatened to go into red alert mode. Adam grabbed her shoulders, and she almost jumped out of her skin. "Relax. I'm just leaning you back, so I can get your seat belt on."

She squeezed her eyes shut behind the sash and fought the frightened tears that brimmed her lids. This man wasn't going to hurt her; he was doing his job. She had to calm down or she was going to blow it before she even got to the damn place. "I'm sorry."

He finished strapping her in, and the seat dipped as he moved away. "Settle in. We have a bit of a ride in front of us."

———

Jace sat on the edge of the couch in The Ranch's staging room, his foot tapping. Where was she? Had she changed her mind? She should've arrived by now.

He knew the other members were already starting to fill up the common room in anticipation of the new subs coming in. There would be three tonight, but Jace only cared about one. He'd lied when he'd told Brynn he wasn't going to be at The Ranch for this retreat. He couldn't let her know he'd be available to be her dom because he knew she would've taken him up on the offer. Subs weren't allowed to make many decisions, but the one they had complete control over was who to play with.

No, he couldn't offer himself as a choice. He sank back against the sofa and groaned. Let no one ever accuse him of not keeping a fucking promise.

"I thought you said she was scheduled for pickup at six," he said, glancing at the man sitting on the opposite couch.

Grant chuckled and propped his boot-clad feet on the coffee table, looking every bit the laid-back cowboy. "This one's important to you, huh?"

"Just an old friend. I know she's kind of nervous about all this."

He nodded and took a sip of his soda. "She should be here any minute. I'll go easy on her."

Jace didn't buy that for a second. Grant Waters hadn't built this level of privacy by chance. He was a master at reading people and didn't let anyone walk into the place without a thorough observation. Brynn would be no exception. He just hoped to hell Brynn could pull off the whole thing without Grant sensing she was hiding something.

A quick knock on the door made Jace sit up straight again. One of the staff girls poked her head in. "Mr. Austin, your girl just arrived. Are you ready for her?"

Jace rubbed his palms on the legs of his pants and nodded. "Sure, Annalise. Just make sure they don't tell her my name. She's a friend and I'd rather her not know who's preparing her."

The raven-haired girl arched a pierced eyebrow but kept her opinion to herself and nodded. "No problem."

A few minutes later, Adam led a blindfolded Brynn into the small room. Even in the soft light, Jace could see the anxiety cloaking her body. Her hands clenched and unclenched in the cuffs and her bottom lip looked puffy, like she'd been gnawing on it.

Adam made sure Brynn was steady on her feet and released her elbow. "Ms. LeBreck, one of our masters is going to get you ready for the initiation while Mr. Waters, our owner, talks with you for a bit. Do you remember your safe word?"

Her throat muscles visibly flexed as she swallowed. "Texas."

Adam squeezed her shoulder and nodded at Jace. "Enjoy yourself. We'll make sure to take good care of you."

Jace rose and crossed the room, the sound of his shoes echoing off the dark wood floors. He walked around Brynn slowly, knowing she'd be able to sense him there and feel the vulnerability of her position. He needed to make this experience as authentic as possible.

Grant's low drawl came from behind him. "Welcome to The Ranch, Ms. LeBreck. What name do you want to use while you're here?"

She startled at the sound of his voice, but recovered quickly. "Um, Brynn is fine."

"Very well, Brynn. Now I just want you to relax. Master J is going to help get you ready for our members. And I'm only here for the pleasure of seeing a new sub prepared for initiation."

"Wh-What exactly is involved in preparation?" she asked, her words catching in her throat.

Jace frowned. He wanted Brynn to be keyed up. That was a normal sub response. But he hadn't expected her to be this frightened. He touched her elbow and she flinched.

"Shh," he soothed.

Grant interrupted, saving Jace from having to reveal who he was by speaking. "He's just going to get you changed. He won't step over any lines because you aren't his, you understand?"

Her shoulders dipped and she nodded. "I'm sorry. I'm just a little freaked out."

"How come?" Grant asked, putting his feet on the floor and sitting forward, his gaze no doubt taking in every nuance of Brynn's demeanor. "Your file says that you've had a previous D/s relationship. Is it fear of not knowing who your partner is going to be?"

She gave a stiff shrug, and her lip began to tremble.

Oh, hell. Was she going to cry? Jace didn't know if he'd be able to keep his cover if she crumbled in front of him. A crying chick was his kryptonite. He pitched his voice lower and risked speaking. "You okay?"

She sniffed and pulled her shoulders back, apparently fighting to keep her composure. "I'm fine. I just haven't been able to give over control to anyone for a long time. You can start getting me ready. I won't stop you."

He nodded, even though he knew she couldn't see him. His fingers trailed down her arm and then pressed the release on her cuffs. She rolled and stretched her wrists, while he moved his hands up to her neckline. He started unfastening her blouse, while Grant continued his questioning. "Why do you think you've resisted giving over control?"

Jace reached the end of the buttons and slid her shirt off her shoulders, letting it fall to the floor. Goose bumps rose on her ivory skin and she shivered. He rubbed her bare arms with his palms, trying to chase the chill for her.

She wet her lips. "I don't know."

There was a long pause, and Jace could tell Grant was measuring her every word.

"That's not true," Grant said finally, his tone as smooth as silk. "You're holding something back."

Shit. Jace shot a warning glance over his shoulder. What had happened to going easy on her? But it was too late. Grant had that look in his eye—the one that said he'd switched into master mode.

"Tell us the real reason, Brynn."

She began to quiver beneath Jace's hold on her.

"I . . . I was raped."

His hands stilled against her. *"What?"*

She shook her head. "It was a long time ago. I really don't want to talk about it. But that's why I'm here. I want to get past the fear."

Jesus. That was the personal reason she'd alluded to in his office? So many questions rose in his throat—who, when, and did Reid know? He'd bet his left nut Reid had no idea. Otherwise, his friend would be in jail for killing the fucker who'd hurt her. Shit. No wonder she was shaking like a frightened puppy.

Grant rose from the couch and came to stand in front of Brynn, his normally unreadable face full of concern. "Do you want me to tell my members what you're dealing with so they can take that into account?"

She wagged her head. "No, please don't tell anyone. I can't even believe I told you. I just want to blend in. No special treatment. And please," she said, her voice edging on desperate, "Master J, keep going."

Jace bent to slip off her heels, his mind still reeling, and Grant reached out and laid a gentle hand on her shoulder. He leaned forward a bit as if he was making eye contact with her despite her blindfold. "Brynn, you're extremely brave to come here and do this. But you need to be careful. I'm as concerned about the mental wellbeing of my customers as their physical safety. I don't want you to push yourself too far. You understand?"

"Yes," she said, her voice sounding tiny in comparison to Grant's firm tone.

Grant continued, "If at any time you need out, a break, whatever, you use that safe word. There is no shame in exercising that right."

She nodded, straightening under his touch. "Thank you. But I've given this a lot of thought. I want to do this. I *need* this."

"Well, then I hope we can provide you with what you're seeking. I'm going to let Master J finish getting you ready, but if you need anything while you're here, don't hesitate to ask me."

"Thank you."

Grant stepped away and slipped out of the room, nodding at Jace as he left.

Jace eased her pants down her legs, then ran a palm along her calf to indicate she should step out of them. Once he gathered all her things from the floor, he rose and took in the view.

God, she was a gorgeous girl. Even though years had passed, she looked as sexy as she had that first night he'd seen her strip for Reid in his driveway—all curves and soft femininity, her creamy skin standing out in contrast to her black satin bra and panties. But who knew under all that softness was a woman tough enough to suffer a rape, then come to a place like this to try to heal herself. He shook his head in awe.

Whomever she ultimately decided to give her submission to was one lucky bastard.

He just hoped to God she'd choose correctly and not hand herself over to someone who could exploit her fear.

Brynn could feel Master J's eyes on her and wondered what was going through his mind. She couldn't believe that she'd told him and Grant about the rape. But now she was glad she had. Despite her raging anxiety, telling them the truth about why she was here—or at least part of it—had somehow managed to ease her down from a panic attack.

"I'm going to bind you now, Brynn. Just relax," said Master J, who'd been silent most of the time she'd been in here.

She tilted her head, something about the way he'd said her name giving her pause, but then the thought flew from her mind when his fingers touched her throat.

Master J wound something around her neck. The smell of new leather filled her nose, and fingers of fear wrapped around her windpipe again. After a quick clink of metal, he tugged at the collar. "Is that too snug?"

She swallowed past the tightness in her throat. "It's fine."

His footfalls echoed off the floor as he moved behind her. A warm hand gathered her wrists and bent her arms behind her back into L-positions. Leather cuffs locked around them and when she tested the hold, the collar around her neck pressed against the hollow of her throat, causing her to cough.

"Easy. It's all connected to a strip down your back. Move one thing, it moves all of it."

Officially trapped. She bit her lip and nodded. She would . . . not . . . cry. This was just sex. Sex. It was supposed to be fun. Used to be great. None of these guys were here to rape her. There were rules and surveillance cameras. She had her safe word.

"It's time, Brynn."

Her stomach threatened to heave.

Master J clasped her upper arm and eased her forward on her bare feet. "I'm going to walk you into our common room. All the members interested in taking on a new sub will be there. You are to remain on your knees with your head down until someone addresses you. If someone wants to take you on, they will stand in front of your post. Only after everyone has made their selections will your blindfold come off. At that point, you'll be able to choose who you want to be with. Understand?"

"What if I don't want any of them?"

He sniffed. "Then you go home."

The squeak of a door swinging open made her suck in a breath. The soft buzz of conversation washed over her as the air temperature around her warmed. They had arrived. A crowded room, and she was half-naked and bound for all to see. Her legs wobbled beneath her, and Master J's grip tightened on her arm to keep her from falling. "Almost there."

A few more steps and he halted her. "On your knees."

He helped her bend, and her knees landed on a soft pallet. His hand ran along the back of her hair. "Choose wisely, doll."

She reared up like someone had pinched her. Only one person had ever called her doll. She turned her head and opened her mouth to ask the question, but he cut her off.

"No more talking." And with that she heard his footsteps fade.

Well, hell.

A sharp tinkling sound cut through the hum of voices—metal on a wine glass she guessed. "Members, it's time for the initiation. For those of you participating tonight, please step forward. For those here to watch, please have a seat."

Brynn sat back on her calves and flexed her fingers, her arms starting to tingle from the restricted position. This was it. No turning back now. She said a silent prayer that she'd get someone who would go easy on her. Heavy footfalls circulated around her, and the air shifted as people stepped into her space, bringing a mix of male scents to her nose—cologne, soap, sweat. She set her mouth in a firm line and kept her expression smooth, determined to keep her fear hidden.

A finger pressed under her chin, lifting her face to some unknown suitor. "What's your name, beautiful?"

Her heart crashed against her ribs, her panic rising like mercury in a thermometer. She cleared her throat and tried to keep her voice even. "Brynn."

"Have you been in a D/s relationship before?" asked another male voice.

"Once, a long time ago."

There were a few murmurs of approval, and the first man released her chin. Then a third voice, deep and melodic, chimed in. "Did you love the guy or was it a casual relationship?"

She wrinkled her forehead, confused by the question. "Does it matter?"

"Answer the question, sub."

She clenched her jaw. "I loved him."

"But you think you can keep it casual now?" asked the first man.

She nodded. "I know I can."

The men asked a few more questions, then the sound of the clinking glass hushed everyone again. "Time to choose."

Brynn's head swam and sweat beaded her skin. She dug her nails into her palms and started counting backward from one hundred in her head, a habit she had picked up as a child when she'd wake up from nightmares in an empty house.

Ninety-nine.

Feet shuffled around her.

Ninety-eight.

The strong smell of cigar smoke filled her head as someone else neared.

Ninety-seven.

What if she couldn't handle it? What if she was repulsed by all her choices? Tears gathered beneath her lids.

Ninety-six.

She tightened her fists and focused on the image of her sister when she was little—blond pigtails and wide, trusting eyes—before she and Kelsey had been tainted by the world around them. Brynn tilted her chin up.

Ninety-five.

It didn't matter who was standing in front of her. She would do what she needed to do. She was tired of living with this crippling fear. And on top of that, her sister needed her. If she fainted like one of the damn goats, then so be it. A hand touched the back of her head and yanked at the knot on her blindfold.

Ninety-four.

The wisp of silk fluttered to the floor, and Brynn blinked as her eyes adjusted to the low lighting of the room. Three sets of shoes came into vision.

"Lift your head, Brynn, and choose your master."

Brynn raised her eyes and stared into the familiar blues of Reid Jamison.

TEN

then

Brynn yawned as she lifted the stack of files and set them on her desk. She hadn't gotten a lick of sleep the rest of the weekend. Every time she'd laid her head down, images of her night with Reid had flooded her senses. How could the guy walk away from something like that? Why couldn't he just accept that he'd enjoyed it? Yes, it was a little . . . alternative. But so what? Didn't people always say that the college years were the experimental ones?

She glanced over at Reid's work area. He had his head turned toward his computer screen and was typing away. He'd barely looked in her direction all day. She plopped into her chair with a huff. What an asshole. Even if he didn't want to pursue anything with her, it was shitty to ignore her after he'd slept with her.

She picked up the date stamp and started stamping each file with a little more vigor than necessary. The silent treatment was going to drive her mad. He should at least have the balls to face her and not cower behind his computer all day. *Men.* She finished the files and moved them to the side of her desk, then spun in her chair to grab the other stack off the floor.

"You stamp those things any harder, you're going to rip through the paper. I can hear you pounding away at them from across the room."

Brynn jumped at the interruption and swung around to face Reid. She slammed the new pile of folders on her desk with a heavy *thunk*. "So sorry, did I break your concentration?"

He leaned down, palms splayed on the top of her desk. "Am I sensing some hostility here, sugar?"

"Boy, you're bright."

He gave her a half-smile. "I'm sorry I sent you away. I needed to get my head straight."

"I don't think it worked. It's apparently still stuck up your ass."

He sighed. "I guess I deserved that."

She glared at him and went back to stamping. Flip page. Stamp. Flip page. Stamp.

He grabbed her wrist, stilling her hand. "Don't shut me out, Brynn."

"Interesting request, considering you're the one who can't seem to bear a glance my way today."

He dropped her arm and scrubbed a hand over his face. "It hurts to look at you."

She smirked. "Gee, you really know how to flatter a girl."

"Come on, Brynn. You know that's not what I mean. It's just every time I see you, I'm reminded of how I treated you this weekend, how I lost control."

She shut the file folder and met his gaze. "Seems like you were pretty in control to me."

His closed his eyes, and she noticed the deep bags beneath them for the first time. "I'm so sorry. I know I probably made you feel like shit."

She blew out a breath, his remorse taking the wind out of her tirade, and touched his arm. "Hey, stop making assumptions. Yes, you pissed me off sending me home without even walking me out. But you know what I felt before that?"

He looked up, his expression wary. "What?"

"Alive."

He opened his mouth to respond, but she cut him off.

"No, I'm serious. You don't get how it is for me. I spend my days worrying about if I'm going to have enough money. Am I doing right by Kelsey? Is my mom going to be okay if I leave and take my sister with me? And on and on it goes. The noise inside my head can be deafening."

"Brynn—"

She raised her hand, letting him know she wasn't finished. "But, for some reason, when you took control in the driveway, all those worries and stresses that race around my brain all day quieted. From that moment on, all I had on my mind was you and how you made me feel. It was . . . freeing."

"But the way I talked to you, the things I did . . ."

"Were all things I could've stopped at any moment. But I didn't want to. I knew you wouldn't hurt me." She wanted to reach out and grab his hand, but was afraid people in the office would start raising eyebrows. She placed her palms on her lap. "I'm not scared of you. Or of what happened this weekend."

"But I am. I don't want to be that guy," he said, his tone making her chest ache. "I don't want to turn into some monster."

"You're not a monster," she said, believing it with every ounce of her being.

"You don't understand."

"Then help me understand, Reid, because I can't be the only one who felt the . . . rightness of what happened between us."

He tilted his head back and groaned. "Look, go tell Davis you're leaving for your lunch break, then meet me in the parking lot. There's something I need to show you."

Fifteen minutes and one painfully silent drive later they turned onto the winding driveway of the Jamison estate. Brynn had no idea what Reid was bringing her here to see, but getting a chance to check out where he lived was motivation enough for her. She'd heard more than one story in the office about how amazing the Jamisons' house was. And the reality did not disappoint.

The sheer size of the plantation-style home astounded her— the garden alone taking up more space than her rental house. She half expected Scarlett O'Hara to pop her head out one of the windows and ask them inside for coffee and biscuits.

Reid had told her he lived in the guest space over the garage, so presumably the massive white mansion housed two people. Two! She shook her head. What must it be like to grow up with such luxury, such security? Never wondering if the lights were going to get cut off at the end of the month of if there would be enough money left over to buy groceries for the week. She couldn't even imagine.

"That's some house."

He smirked and shot the house a derisive glance. "No one would ever accuse my aunt and uncle of doing anything halfway." He parked his car in front of the closed garage. "Come on."

He led her up a flight of stairs on the side of the garage and unlocked his door. She stepped inside the apartment, and he bumped the door shut behind them. The living room was small, but cozy, and was open to the small efficiency kitchen. Camel-colored couches and dark wood furniture, a big-screen TV in the middle of the biggest wall. Practical, unpretentious. Probably the complete opposite of what resided in the main house.

"This is a nice place," she said, running her fingers along the back edge of the suede couch.

"Thanks, it works for me. Gives me a little privacy from everything." He tossed his keys on the kitchen counter. "Sit wherever you'd like."

She maneuvered around the front of the couch, but before she could sit, the purr of an engine outside made them both turn their heads. Reid stepped toward the window next to the door and peeked through the blinds. "Shit. Aunt Roslyn's here."

"I thought she was supposed to be at a luncheon today."

"Yeah, me, too," he said, still peering through the window. "Dammit, she noticed my car and is headed this way."

Her heart picked up speed. "Crap. She can't see me here."

"Hurry. Go in the bedroom and lock the door. I'll get rid of her."

Brynn hustled through the small living area and into the bedroom, clicking the door shut behind her. She held her breath when she heard Roslyn's voice. The last thing Brynn needed was for the senator's wife to know she was . . . Well, she didn't know exactly what she was doing with Reid, but she doubted the woman would approve regardless.

Unable to resist, she pressed her ear against the door.

"What are you doing home? You didn't cut out early did you? I told you no special privileges at the office," Roslyn said, her words clipped.

"I'm on my lunch break, Aunt Ros. Calm down."

"I called the office to talk to you and Molly said you left with the receptionist."

Brynn cringed on the other side of the door. Fucking Molly.

"Brynn needed a ride to pick up her car. It's been in the shop. It was on my way here, so I offered."

"Is she here now?"

"No, I dropped her off already."

There was a pause, and Brynn imagined Roslyn was deciding whether she believed her nephew or not. "Is that all there is to it—a friendly favor? Don't lie to me, Reid. I've noticed how chummy you've gotten with her."

"With all due respect, how is that your business? I'm not sixteen anymore."

"I don't care how old you are. I know you probably don't know a lot about that girl. Brynn's a decent worker, but we've done background checks. Her family is . . . less than desirable." Roslyn had lowered her voice to where Brynn could barely decipher the words. "And the press would have a field day if they found out you were . . . cavorting with her."

He snorted. "Cavorting? Come on. Nothing is going on, all right? We're friends. She needed a ride. End of story."

Another pause. "You better not be lying to me. I know she's probably a lot looser with her morals than the girls you're used to, but don't fall into the trap. Women like her have one thing on their mind when it comes to boys like you—a paycheck. Touch her and she'll either be filing sexual harassment or getting pregnant and petitioning for support faster than you can say 'goodbye future.'"

"We're *not* together. And anyway, she's not like that."

Roslyn's tone turned icy. "They're all like that. You need to get your head out of your pants and get things back on track with Vanessa. You're going to end up ruining your chance with her."

Reid made a frustrated sound, and Brynn stopped listening. She stepped away from the door and sank onto the edge of Reid's unmade bed, deflated. Was she ever going to escape her family background? Even a woman who treated her with the upmost politeness to her face secretly believed Brynn was a whore-in-training. Tears lined her lids, and she swiped at her eyes. She knew she should be used to the judgment by now, but hearing it from the lips of someone she respected wrenched her gut.

The door cracked open and Reid peeked in, quickly noticing her tears. "Sugar, what's wrong?"

Brynn shook her head and tried to smile. "Nothing, I'm fine."

He strode over to her and put an arm around her. "You heard what she said."

She shrugged. "I'm okay."

"Look, Vanessa is just a girl I was seeing at the beginning of summer. I'm not with her anymore."

She shook her head. "No, it's not that. It's just hard to hear what people really think of me."

"That's not what everyone thinks of you," he soothed, rubbing her arm.

"Isn't it though? The girls at work know I don't have money, so they think I'm trash. Your aunt thinks I'm trying to tempt you with my wanton ways. And you think something's wrong with me because I enjoyed the other night. Hell, maybe I do have warped morals."

"Enough," he said, his voice soft but firm. "I don't think there's anything wrong with you."

"Right, I'm not screwed up, yet you believe there's something the matter with *you* because of what happened between us. Your logic sucks, Reid."

He groaned. "Listen, that's why I brought you here. Maybe I can help you understand. You're not the only one who wishes they could change their family background."

He rose from the bed and crossed over to a small desk stacked with textbooks and papers in the corner of the room. He yanked open a drawer, rifled through it, and pulled out a manila envelope. "Here."

He tossed it onto the bed and shoved his hands in his pockets, his posture turning rigid. She eyed him warily and picked it up. "What is this?"

"My father's claim to fame."

She slid her fingers beneath the flap to pull out the contents. A yellowed newspaper clipping. The picture on the article was of an older man with Reid's features, but none of his warmth. Cold, gray eyes stared from the page, sending a ripple of uneasiness through her. The headline read *Serial Rapist Caught*. Her stomach flipped over. "Oh, my God."

"Brutalized thirteen women before he was arrested. Tied them up, beat them, raped them." His voice caught on the last part. "My mother was his sixth victim."

The breath left her lungs. Reid was born out of rape? Growing up, she'd thought nothing could be worse than her situation—not knowing who her father was. But man, she'd been wrong. She glanced up and found Reid staring at his shoes, his shame and embarrassment palpable.

She set the article down on the bed and went to him, sliding her arms around his waist, though he kept his hands in his pockets. "I'm so sorry. I don't even know what to say."

He sighed and put his arms around her. "Now do you see why we need to be careful?"

"What do you mean?" She pulled back so she could look at his face.

He threw his hands out to his sides. "I came from a monster, Brynn. Half of me is from him. What if all these urges I have to dominate you are an early version of what he became? What if he started by just wanting to tie a girl up and spank her a little?"

"Oh, Reid, no," she said, shaking her head, her heart breaking for him. "You have as much in common with that man as Molly has with a brain surgeon. You can see it in the photo, that man has no heart, no soul." She cupped his face and met his eyes. "And you—you're all heart and soul."

He stared down at her, his eyes swirling with an amalgam of emotions. "Why do you keep putting your trust in me? I don't know if I trust myself."

She wound her arms around his neck and held his gaze. "My

mom has dated abusive men. When guys like that walk into the room, it's like the air stops moving. My skin crawls and all I want to do is leave. But when you walk into the room, the opposite happens—I'm not scared. All I want to do is get closer to you. And get naked."

A laugh broke through his pained expression. "Is that right?"

She shrugged and stepped back. "But if you're not into me . . ."

He hooked her waistband with one of his fingers and yanked her against him. "Now hold up right there, sugar. I never said I wasn't into you."

"So what are you going to do about it, then?" she asked, her tone challenging.

His gaze met hers. "I'm in."

"What do you mean?"

He sank into his desk chair and pulled her down onto his lap. "I mean, I'm *in*. I'm tired of struggling against my instincts when I'm with you. So, let's try it your way. You want me to be myself, well, here I am."

Her heart did a little twirl in her chest. "Really?"

He cupped her chin and ran his thumb along her cheek. His eyes pleaded with her. "You just have to swear that if I ever do anything you don't want me to, you'll make me stop. We'll come up with a code word that means quit, but even with that, you have to promise you'll do whatever you need to get your point across. Don't let me push you too far."

She leaned forward and brushed her lips across his. "I promise. I will totally kick your ass if you step out of line."

He grinned, the tension lines in his face softening and the heaviness in the air seeming to lift. His hand curled around her hip, and he put his forehead to hers. "Thank you. I've never told anyone about my dad besides Jace. I thought for sure you would run for the hills."

She lifted her head and shrugged. "I refuse to believe that we're doomed to our parents' fate. If I bought into that logic, I may as well slit my wrists now."

"Your outlook on life is such a ball of sunshine," he teased.

She tapped her temple. "Yep, like I told you, it's all rainbows and unicorns in here."

He gave her a wry smile and closed the space between them to claim her mouth in a heated kiss. Her lips parted, and she could feel the tension draining from both of their bodies as they gave themselves over to the simple pleasure of tasting each other—an acceptance of each other's ugly histories and a promise to move forward despite it all.

He pulled away from the kiss, his cheeks flushed. "You know we still have a half hour before we're due back to the office? Maybe we should practice our new arrangement."

She shifted on his lap so that she could straddle him, and adjusted her skirt. Her panties brushed directly against the hardening erection in his pants, sending a dart of warmth through her. "That isn't very much time."

He shoved her skirt farther up her hips and with a yank, ripped off her panties.

"Hey! I'm supposed to go back to work in those," she protested.

He pulled the swath of material from under her and tossed the panties onto the floor. "I'll buy you some new ones. But for the rest of the day, I want to look across that office and know that there's only this thin skirt between me and what's mine."

His fingers found her heat and glossed her clit with her juices. She tilted her head back, and his other hand unbuttoned her blouse and freed her breasts. His hot tongue sucked a needy nipple through the lacy material of her bra, then he bit hard enough for her to gasp. She moaned and rocked against his hand.

"That's right, sugar. I love how responsive you are for me. I can't wait to take you somewhere tonight, tie you up, and taste every delicious part of you. Make you beg for release."

She shuddered. God, just his words could set her off.

"But right now"—he leaned back, undid his fly, and released his cock—"just hold on."

"My pleasure, sir."

ELEVEN

now

Brynn swayed on her knees, the shock of seeing Reid in front of her hitting her like a bullet to the chest. She stared at him, a hundred questions coloring her thoughts. Why was he here? How had he even gotten in? And what the hell was he expecting—that she was just going to jump at the chance to be with him after she'd explicitly told him she never wanted him to touch her again?

His stern expression didn't answer any one of her silent demands.

"You need to choose your master, Brynn," said a well-dressed man standing to the left of Reid. She glanced at the man's tapered fingers; he held a chain, no, a leash. *Oh.* He was one of her choices, as was another shorter man on Reid's right. Shit. Both guys were attractive enough, but could she turn herself over to them—put her trust in one of these strangers?

Her gaze darted to the second man's waistband where a whip was attached, coiled like a sleeping snake. His fingers toyed with the handle as if his hand itched to wield it. *Oh, hell no. Scratch him off the list.* Anyone that eager to whip her wasn't going to go easy.

She tilted her face and ventured another glance at Reid. His expression remained smooth, but something in his eyes yanked her back in time—back when she wanted nothing more than to give herself over to him, body and soul. Yes, he'd burned her like no man had ever before or since, but he'd also had moments of tenderness that had stilled her heart. He wouldn't physically hurt her. She knew that. Which was more than she knew about either of the other guys.

But could she temporarily seal off the wound that sent slicing pain through her anytime she was around Reid and see him as simply a means to an end for the few days they were here? At least behind closed doors she wouldn't have to pretend with him like she would the others. She inhaled deeply, causing the bindings on her arms to bite deeper into her skin, and held Reid's gaze.

"Looks like she's made her pick," said the man with the leash.

Reid shook his head. "No, I want to hear you say the words, Brynn."

Her fists clenched behind her. Why did he always have to push? Always make things more difficult than necessary? She put as much contempt as possible into her tone. "I choose you, *sir*."

The set line of Reid's jaw relaxed, and he gave a slight nod. The other men looked mildly disappointed, but stepped away and melded back into the shadowed groups sitting around small tables near the bar on the other side of the room. Reid hooked a finger in the loop on her collar and his other hand on her elbow. "On your feet."

"Help me." She eased to her bare feet, relying heavily on Reid for support. She'd never realized how much she counted on her arms for balance. A few feet away, a gangly man who was hauling his own sub to her feet turned his head in their direction.

"You're not to talk without permission unless it's to say 'yes, sir' or your safe word," Reid said, his words loud enough for the other initiation pair to hear.

Oops. She dropped her gaze to the floor. "Yes, sir."

"Better," Reid said, and gave her ass a swat. "Now move."

She gritted her teeth. Was that a smile she heard in his voice? She bet the bastard was marinating in smugness. He'd gotten his way, and now she couldn't even protest—at least not when anyone could hear. She was only one slipup away from losing her chance to stay in the club. And now she was obligated to submit to whatever act Reid selected to demonstrate her submission in front of the group. Damn it all. She must've really pissed off karma in some former life.

Reid guided her to a curved love seat at the edge of the staging area and moved his hand to her shoulder. "On your knees, sugar."

She shot him a steely glare. After being on her knees for far too long already, he wasn't going to let her sit on the plush couch?

He shook his head, a *tsk* passing his lips. "So defiant. You have three seconds to comply, or I'll make sure your upcoming show for everyone is much more unpleasant than what I have planned."

His words splashed over her like ice water. The show. Public submission. Her anger at Reid had momentarily drawn her thoughts away from what she was about to face—humiliation, panic, possible fainting-goat behavior. The contents of her stomach threatened to make an appearance. She dropped to her knees, facing the open area she'd just left.

"That's right." Reid sank onto the couch behind her, placing a thigh on each side of her. He gave her hair a light stroke. "You can sit back on your calves. We're going to watch one of the others go before it's our turn."

She nodded and rested her butt on the backs of her legs, which offered a bit of relief. She wiggled her arms to try to get some of the tingling to stop, but the minute movement the bindings allowed was not enough to accomplish anything. Reid ran his fingers along the leather straps, grazing her skin along with it. His head dipped next to her ear. "I forgot how fucking sexy you look when you're tied up for me—just me."

She stared at the Persian rug beneath her, her jaw tightening. She hadn't missed his dig. He still thought she'd cheated on him. That she'd been playing games with him the whole time they'd dated. She could set him right, but what did it matter? Better for him to think that than know the truth—that she'd loved him with everything she had, only to find out later that he'd been the one who'd had a girlfriend the entire time. Asshole.

She shifted forward infinitesimally, moving away from his touch, and he gave a low chuckle. Maybe she should have gone with the guy who had the whip—that might have been less painful after all. Reid cupped her chin from behind and lifted her face toward the front. "I want you to watch. The show's about to start."

Her gaze lifted and locked on the scene before her. The gangly man was strapping a pixie-sized woman to a large wooden X in the front of the room. He'd stripped off her clothes, and her freckled back seemed to quiver with anticipation each time the man locked another leather restraint in place. Sweat prickled Brynn's brow, and her heart seemed to take up residence in her throat. If Reid decided to strap her to something like that, she'd surely lose it.

Before she spiraled into a full-scale panic, she dragged her stare away from the action and scanned the room, quickly noting with disappointment that her sister was nowhere in the audience. At least twenty other people dotted the tables and couches around them, some talking quietly and sipping drinks, others riveted by the tableau at the front of the room. If not for the provocative clothing and the occasional man or woman sitting at someone's feet, it could have been any high-end club. Glossy mahogany furniture, votive candles or fresh flowers on each table, a few cocktail waitresses milling around, even muted jazz in the background. The fact that all those lovely, refined people were there to watch and participate in public sex acts almost made Brynn laugh. It was all so absurd.

The sharp smack of leather on skin yanked her attention back to the front. The man held a riding crop in one hand and a telltale red mark darkened the woman's left thigh. "No squirming. You take what I give you without complaint."

"Yes, sir."

He dragged the crop along her back, slowly tracing each notch of her spine, the small of her back, the crack of her ass. The woman's back rose and fell with her quickening breaths, and Brynn felt her own breathing pick up tempo. The whole room had gone quiet, the man's practiced patience drawing them all in. He moved the crop between the woman's spread legs, caressing her with the flat of the leather. Gentle. Sensual. Brynn could almost feel the smooth material gliding along her own clit, imagining Reid as the one wielding the crop.

But before she could get carried away with her own images, the man gave a quick flick of the wrist and snapped the leather against the woman's sex, startling Brynn. The woman gave a sharp cry and her fists flexed in her bindings, but her body stayed stock-still.

"Very good, pet," the man said, running his hand along the sensitized skin and earning another, softer whimper from her. He moved to a table lined with what looked like half of Jace's stock from Wicked and selected an impressively sized dildo. "I think you've earned a reward."

He stalked back toward his sub and, not bothering to give her any additional warning, he placed the blunt head of the dildo against her and pushed. Brynn winced, but the ease with which it slid in told her the woman was more than turned on by his treatment. With a slow smile, the gangly dom pulled a small remote out of his pocket and hit a button that sent a buzzing sound through the rapt room.

The woman reared up and let out a desperate moan. Vibrator.

"I said no moving. And don't you dare come." The man lifted his riding crop again and rained blows across her ass, thighs, and back—the smack of the leather filling the room and making Brynn's head spin. The woman's muscles tensed beneath the rapid assault, her pale skin quickly turning pink then red, and her cries becoming mewls of pleasure.

Brynn squeezed her eyes shut, her mind rocketing back to her and Reid's night at Jace's house—how Reid's hands had reddened her bottom, the mind-numbing pleasure he'd coaxed out of her. What would it be like to have him handle her like that again? Despite the fear that still shrouded her, a kernel of heat spread between her tightly closed legs.

She bit the inside of her cheek. No. She was not that girl anymore. She wanted to get past the fear, but this was not a lifestyle she wanted for herself. This was only the tool to get her where she needed to be—to get her to the place where she could have a *normal* life again.

"Who is your master, pet?" the gangly man demanded.

Brynn forced her eyes open, determined to tamp down the dangerous memories.

The girl's back glistened with sweat and blotches of red. Her voice, as tiny as her frame, quivered when she spoke. "You are, Master K."

The man twirled the crop between his fingers. "Are you sure? You don't sound too confident about that answer, pet. Do I need to remind you a little more?"

Her words came out in breathy pants, clearly fighting the orgasm the vibrator was coaxing out of her. "No, sir. Please. I'm yours."

The man smoothed a hand over her ass, his erection straining against his leather pants, and then slid his fingers to her clit. A visible shudder ratcheted through the woman's body and her groan turned guttural. But just as quickly as he'd touched her, the man withdrew his hand and grabbed his remote. The humming stopped. "Not yet, pet. You haven't quite earned that. But I will accept your offer of submission."

"Thank you, Master K. Thank you," the woman said, her whole body sagging against her restraints.

Reid's hand touched Brynn's shoulder and she jumped. "You're all flushed, sugar. Saw something you liked?"

She shook her head vehemently. "No, sir."

His tone dipped. "So if I slipped my hand between those gorgeous legs of yours, you wouldn't be all creamy for me?"

She pressed her lips into a line. He wouldn't call her bluff like that, would he?

"Ah, silence is very telling, Brynn. Guess the girl I used to know is still in there somewhere, huh?" The smile had returned to his voice.

If she were a cartoon character, smoke would have shot out of her ears, but she held her tongue. She refused to give him any additional fodder to make her punishment in front of the crowd worse. Reid had always enjoyed the power position a little too much and apparently he hadn't lost that proclivity.

The gangly dom released his woman from her bindings and slipped a silky robe around her shoulders. She leaned into him, and a trembling smile crossed her makeup-streaked face as he led her past the crowd and out a door at the back of the room. The second they disappeared from view, the crush of anxiety squeezed Brynn's chest. She was next.

A man in a crisp white shirt, dark jeans, and cowboy boots rose from one of the tables and headed to the front of the room. All eyes followed him, and Reid shifted restlessly behind her. The man's casual dress and mussed dark hair did nothing to diminish the air of importance and power that rolled off him. Brynn had the urge to sit up straighter. He graced the audience with a smile that probably melted the panties off most of the women in room.

Reid leaned forward and whispered against her ear, "That's Grant. The owner."

Oh.

Grant glanced in her direction and gave her an encouraging smile. "Ladies and gentleman, our next initiation will be given by a new member. Please welcome Master Reid to our ranks."

Reid rose and clasped Brynn's elbow. "Up."

A quiet smattering of applause followed them as she and Reid made their way to the front. Brynn's arms ached and her legs had trouble remembering how to work. She stumbled slightly before reaching their destination, and Reid drew her closer to his side. Grant shook Reid's free hand.

"Welcome to The Ranch, we're glad to have ya," he said, the now familiar deep West Texas drawl coloring his words.

Reid nodded. "Pleased to join."

"You have a lovely sub there. What do you think she needs for an initiation?"

Brynn kept her eyes on the polished wood floors and began counting. If she looked up or thought about what was about to happen, she'd tip over the edge. Already, her heart was pounding hard enough to splinter a rib. *Please let Reid pick something simple.* A blow job. A quick, unrestrained spanking. She could maybe handle something basic. But blindfolds and handcuffs or helplessness would guarantee flashbacks and panic. She inhaled deeply through her nose and blew the breath out her mouth. In. Out. In. Out.

She didn't want to have to use the safe word, knew from Grant's concerned words earlier that if she broke down, he'd probably send her home—for her own mental health.

Reid ran a knuckle along her cheek. "Well, I think my sub is feeling feisty. She's talked back to me multiple times since I chose her, so a punishment is in order."

Brynn dared a glance up. Talked back? When?

Grant eyed her, evaluating her reaction. "I see."

Reid continued, "I've had the pleasure of spending time with this sub in the past, and I know she's big on the exhibitionism. So I refuse to grant her the pleasure of displaying herself in front of the group. She hasn't earned such a privilege yet."

Brynn bit her lip. What was he doing? Was he actually going to save her from having to deal with this? Oh, please, maybe she had misjudged his earlier behavior.

"But I still want her to demonstrate her submission. So, I'm going to get the one thing that will make sure she knows she's giving herself to me personally and not just any random master." Reid pinched her chin between his thumb and forefinger and forced her to meet his gaze. "A kiss."

Her eyes widened. *What?*

Reid's mouth curved upward. "Release her bindings."

One of the attendants standing near the back of the room stepped up and started unfastening the leather straps as the reality of Reid's request sliced through her. She should've been happy. A kiss was as simple an act as you could get . . . but also the most intimate. If he'd have forced her to her knees and made her get him off, she would've had the outside chance of blocking out what was happening—thought of numbers or England or her grocery list. But how could she zone out with his lips against hers?

Her tingling arms fell to her sides and she balled her fists. Reid was doing this to punish her. What had he said? *To make sure she knows she's submitting to me personally.* God, hadn't ten years been long enough for him to get over her supposed infidelity? She narrowed her eyes at him. Nope, not with an ego the size of his.

Once all the leather had been removed, the attendant and Grant moved away, leaving her alone with Reid. He hooked an arm around her waist and dragged her against him, wickedness glinting in his eyes. "Let's see if this is better than a stranger."

She shot him her best I-hate-you look before he brought his lips down on hers.

Despite his firm grip, his kiss was teasing. His lips moved against hers—nibbling, tasting, drawing her in like a moth to light. The tension in her muscles softened in his grasp, and something white hot and long dormant unfurled inside her. As if on their own volition, her lips parted and granted his tongue access. The taste of mint and Reid danced in her mouth, and her arms looped around his neck. When she pressed her breasts against his solid chest, she couldn't tell if the groan that reached her ears was his or her own.

———

Reid groaned as Brynn's half-naked body molded against his. Shit. He'd thought a kiss would be the safest route to go since he wasn't sure he'd be able to control himself if he'd chosen something more sexual. He sure as hell didn't want to fuck her when she had no option to say no. But he'd forgotten that a kiss with Brynn had never been just a kiss. The moment his lips had touched hers, he'd wanted to strip her down and take her in front of all these goddamned people.

Her superior acting skills weren't helping matters either. She was kissing him back with the fervor of a sub set on pleasing her master. His cock swelled against his dress pants. Fuck, how was he going to make it through the weekend? Regretfully, he slipped a hand into her hair and tugged gently to separate her from their kiss. He sucked in a haggard breath, trying to reclaim his cool control. She stared at him with question marks in her eyes.

He had to clear his throat twice before he was able to speak. "Who's your master?"

As if snapping out of a daze, she straightened her shoulders. "You are, sir."

He tightened his grip on her hair. "Use my name, sub. I don't want you confused on who you're supposed to please."

She narrowed her eyes, defiance flaring in them. "You are, *Master Reid*."

Reid didn't miss the cocked eyebrow Grant gave him at Brynn's snarky tone. He palmed the back of Brynn's skull, drawing her face closer. "You need to drop the smart mouth or you'll force me to gag you."

She didn't drop her gaze.

Dammit. Why couldn't she play by the rules for a change? He couldn't show weakness in front of this group or Grant. "I think you need to learn some manners, sub. You get off on being defiant, don't you? Dip your fingers in that tight pussy of yours and show everyone how wet you are."

Shock crossed her features, and he could hear her silent plea, but he couldn't back off. "Don't make me wait. It displeases me."

Her eyes darted toward the crowd, then to the floor. With a shaking hand, she slipped her palm beneath the band of her panties and dipped her fingers inside. The visual alone sent all his blood rushing to his groin, his cock turning to steel. She removed her hand and raised it to him, shame coloring her cheeks.

The evidence of her arousal glistened along her fingers, the sweet scent of her juices tickling his nose. His zipper pressed into his sensitive skin as his erection flexed against it, begging for relief. Without thinking, he circled her wrist and lifted it to his mouth, sucking the honey from her fingers. He closed his eyes, savoring her flavor and the fact that he could still turn her on even through all that ire.

His eyelids lifted slowly, and he found Brynn's attention riveted on his mouth. He lowered her hand. "Who made you so wet, sugar?"

Her gaze dropped to his feet. "You did, Master Reid."

"That's right. Don't forget who you belong to." Reid pulled a strip of leather from his back pocket and slipped the collar around Brynn's neck. Once it was secured, he grabbed a chain off a nearby supply table and hooked the leash to the loop on the collar. "There, maybe this will remind you of your role. Now let's go."

He led her from the open area to the table Grant was sitting at. Grant gave Brynn a long look, then gave Reid a knowing smile. "I think you've found a good pairing."

Some of the tension in Reid's shoulders eased. They'd fooled the most important person—at least for now. "We'll see. I think she may need some time in my room before I allow her to participate in any club fun, though."

Grant nodded. "I think you're right. Have her sign the waiver then feel free to use your private room however you like. Activities will be going on in the common areas all evening."

"Thanks, I'm sure we'll be around later," Reid said, and tugged at Brynn's chain. "Come on, sugar."

Reid could see the tight set in her jaw, but he knew Brynn wouldn't break character now. She ducked her head in deference and played sub, following him through the crowd of onlookers. Even though he knew it was all an act, seeing the beautiful blonde under his command flipped all his erotic switches.

During his four-year marriage to Vanessa, he'd tried to shut the dominant part of himself off so he could be the man she and his family had wanted him to be. His wife had found the whole idea of D/s abhorrent and hadn't been open to doing anything but once-a-week vanilla sex. The minute he'd even suggested trying anything kinky she'd thrown his father's history in his face, knowing exactly how to make him feel like shit. The whole thing had been miserable for them both.

The only moments of indulgence he had allowed himself was the occasional jerk-off session when he'd let his mind travel back to those few glorious months with Brynn before the bottom had fallen out. Transport himself back to the only time in his life he ever remembered being truly happy.

And now, here she was, right next to him—wet and wanting—a ripe fruit waiting to be plucked. Too bad she despised him. And if she found out he was here to get information from her sister for the appeal and not simply out of chivalry, she'd really be ready to castrate him.

They exited the main room and entered a wide hallway with chocolate brown walls and soft sconce lighting. All noise except the gentle padding of their feet on the plush carpet ceased. He eyed the red lights of the strategically placed security cameras and drew Brynn next to him.

"Why the hell did you make me do that?" she demanded in a hoarse whisper.

"You can't challenge me as a dom in front of everyone. If I hadn't punished you, they would've gotten suspicious. And I tried to pick something that was as . . . non-intrusive as possible. I could've done anything I wanted to you."

Her shoulder sagged against him, the reality of his words settling in. They walked in silence for a few moments before she spoke again, her tone decidedly less hostile this time. "It's like a tomb in here."

"The rooms are soundproof so no one interrupts anyone else's scene. Although, those things that look like mirrors can actually be lifted if the people inside want to allow people to watch."

She shook her head. "Jesus, they're not messing around here."

"Keep your eyes down, sugar. The cameras can't hear us, but they can see us. Make sure you look like a sub."

She followed his instructions, but didn't stop talking. "Why are you here, Reid?"

He sighed and guided her around a corner, guilt about his real reason gnawing at him. "Because I knew you were full of shit when you said you were okay submitting to some stranger. And I figured it'd be easier to find your sister if you didn't have to pretend with someone twenty-four seven. You could've gotten a guy who wanted to lock you in his room for the whole weekend, and you wouldn't have even had a chance to look."

She shuddered at the thought. "But why do you care?"

The muscles in his neck tightened. "Because despite what you may think, I'm not heartless, Brynn. You've been through a lot. I don't want to see you or your sister go through any more tragedy."

At least that much was true.

She glanced up at him, and for a moment, the mask dropped, revealing the stark fear beneath it. The worry in her big green eyes stirred up a fierce protectiveness deep within him. He had the urge to reach out and pull her in for an embrace.

He peeked over his shoulder and dipped his head next to her ear just in case anyone was listening. "It's going to be okay, sugar. I was going to wait to tell you until we got to our room, but I've already confirmed that Kelsey is here."

Her eyes widened, hope filling them. "You've seen her?"

"No, but I flirted with the girl at the front desk earlier. I got her to leave her post for a second and was able to peek at the employee schedules. There's a Kiki listed in the sub training slot."

"Oh, thank God." The relief was visible in every inch of her stance.

"Yeah, the only problem is anyone in training is on lockdown with their master—no outside contact unless the master allows it. So it's not like we can go make a social call at whatever cabin or room she's staying in. We're going to have to wait for her master to bring her out."

She frowned. "What if he doesn't let her out for the whole time she's here?"

"I'd be surprised if that were the case. If he's training her to work here, he's going to want to expose her to as much as possible—public displays, special equipment, et cetera. I think we're just going to have to keep our eyes peeled, try to blend in, and participate in as many of the group functions here as possible."

She nodded, some unreadable expression crossing her face. "Right. Participate."

He shook his head. "Wow, is being here with me really that horrible? You didn't have to pick me, you know."

She turned and started walking again. "Not everything is about you, Reid. Let's just leave it at—I appreciate your help, alright?"

Biting back a sigh, he caught up to her and swung open the exit door, and the damp night air washed over them.

She shivered and crossed her arms over her barely concealed breasts. "Which way are we going?"

"I rented one of the private cabins. It's just a few yards down that path." He glanced down at her and watched goose bumps rise on her exposed skin. He let the door click shut behind them and hooked the leash to his belt. "Hold on."

With quick fingers, he unbuttoned his blue dress shirt and shrugged out of it, leaving him in just his gray slacks. Brynn's eyes darted to his bare chest. "What are you doing?"

He smirked. "I thought we'd have a quick fuck right here against the wall. Break the ice."

She gave him a you-must-be-on-crack look.

He shook his head, glad to be back in comfortable territory. Exchanging barbs with her kept them both safe. Kept him from examining the little whispers of old feelings she'd stirred with that kiss. He handed her the shirt. "Here. I wouldn't be a very good master if I let my woman freeze to death before reaching the room."

She grabbed the shirt and wrapped it around herself, the bottom reaching her mid-thigh. "Thanks. I'm not sure what they did with my clothes."

"Don't worry, they have a closet full in our cabin." He turned his attention to her bare feet, then to the slate stone path leading to the cabins. "Are you going to be okay barefoot? You can hop on my back . . . or my front, if you'd like."

"I think I'll manage," she said, her voice as cool as the air around them.

He laughed, grabbing her elbow and leading her forward. "You're no fun at all anymore. What's the deal with you, LeBreck?"

She stiffened next to him, but didn't say another word until they reached the porch of their little wooden cabin. A white envelope labeled "Jamison companion" was clipped to the front door. She grabbed the letter and held it up. "What's this?"

"Probably your waiver. You have to sign it saying you're okay with being in unmonitored zones."

She raised an eyebrow. "Unmonitored?"

He pulled a key out of his pocket and stepped past her to open the door. "I paid extra to get a room without security cameras. Most clubs would never allow it because it's too risky for the sub, but they're all about catering to privacy here. So there are private cabins and unmonitored zones. No senator or CEO is going to come here and allow some lackey to have video evidence of his carnal indiscretions."

"Jace told me to avoid those areas—that it wasn't safe."

"It wouldn't be if you were with someone you didn't know." He smirked. "What? You scared of me now?"

"No." But the wariness on her face made him think she wasn't being entirely truthful.

"Good, because I went through the trouble of reserving one of these so that you wouldn't have to play the role the whole time."

"So we don't have to pretend in here?" she asked, her whole demeanor visibly relaxing.

He ushered her into the small living room, unhooked her leash from his belt, and flipped on the lights. "Nope, you can insult me as the need strikes."

Instead of heading to the other side of the little living room like he expected, she stepped so close he could feel her quick, little breaths on his naked chest. The awareness in his body sparked like she'd touched him with a cattle prod.

What the hell was she doing?

She slipped her hands onto his waist, pressing herself against his lingering erection, and peered up at him with steely resolve in her eyes. "That's not what I need."

He didn't trust himself to touch her. She had to be setting up some kind of joke or she was going to kick him in the balls. "Okay, then what do you need?"

"For you not to ask questions." She let his borrowed shirt fall to the floor, revealing miles of delicious ivory skin. "And for you not to stop unless I say Texas."

TWELVE

then

Five days. Five goddamned days of Reid gone on vacation, and it was like Brynn's world had tilted off its rotation. Man, she was in trouble. She *missed* him. Really missed him.

She propped her elbows on her desk and pressed the heels of her hands to her brow bone. This wasn't supposed to happen. This was supposed to be a fun fling. Nothing else.

For the past few weeks, she and Reid had kept up their ends of the fun bargain, stealing moments whenever they could to be together. To talk. To laugh. To have hot, sweaty sex in a sundry of places and positions. She'd been having such a good time she'd never let herself pause long enough to think about what could be developing between them. But now that he'd been in Florida with his family for the week, she'd had nothing but time to think. And pine.

Pining. She was pining. Oh, good God.

She peeked over at Reid's desk—empty—just like it had been since Monday. He hadn't called much because he was afraid his aunt or uncle would hear him. But she found herself worrying that maybe he really didn't *want* to call and was using that as an excuse. Maybe he was having too good of a time without her. They were only a fling anyway, right? There were probably loads of girls hanging around the Jamisons' sure-to-be-fancy beach house just waiting to take a shot at her guy.

Her guy. Yep, she was screwed.

With a sigh, she scooted from behind her desk and headed through the darkened office to the employee lounge, hoping a change in scenery would get her spiraling thoughts to go away. She needed to focus and get some work done. Everyone else had left for the day, but she'd agreed to stay late to stuff goody bags for the next campaign fund-raiser. Bad idea. Between her racing mind and her lack of sleep, she hadn't even made a dent in the project. She was going to be here every freaking night for a week at this rate.

Not bothering to flip on the lights, she walked toward the fridge and rummaged around for something with sugar, and preferably caffeine. The people around the office drank coffee like fiends, but she'd never had a taste for the stuff, so she had to rely on soda to get her fix. She saw a glint of red behind all the diet lemon-lime drinks and stretched her arm farther in to reach the cola.

A light squeeze on her ass made her jolt upward, nearly banging her head on the top of the fridge. "What the—"

"Easy, sugar. It's just me," Reid said from behind her as he slid his arm around her waist and nuzzled her neck. "I couldn't resist with you bending over like that."

She spun around in his grasp, the blasting cold from the refrigerator chilling her backside as his body warmed her front. "Reid! You scared the crap out of me."

He brushed a hand over her hair. "Sorry about that."

She tried to catch her breath, not sure if her pounding heart was from being startled or from being so close to him. "What are you doing here? You're not supposed to be back until tomorrow."

"I hopped an earlier flight." He dipped his suntanned face

closer and brushed his lips against hers. "I couldn't stay away from you for another minute. I've never hated the beach so much in my life."

"What? Too many beautiful, bikini-clad girls for you?" She poked his ribs.

"Ooh, jealousy. I like it on you." His thumb stroked the small of her back, her skin coming alive beneath his touch. "And I didn't need to check out the other girls. I already have the one I want."

She stared into the bottomless blue of his eyes, unable to tell if he was being serious or simply being his charming self. How could she be who he wanted? He couldn't even take her out in public for fear someone in his circle would see them. She pushed the ugly thought away and tilted her chin up. "Guess I shouldn't have spent my week working my way through the guys in the office, then. I didn't realize you were going to have such a strict moral code on your trip."

"Oh, is that what you've been up to?" The corner of his mouth tipped up. "I'm not enough to satisfy you? Maybe I should've taken Jace up on his offer to join us for a threesome."

Her eyes widened and retort got hung up in her throat. Reid *and* Jace. Whoa.

He laughed and kissed the tip of her nose. "Don't worry. I told him no. Even though I'm guessing by the way your body just quivered, you're not totally opposed to the idea. Naughty girl. Too bad I'm too selfish to share you."

She shook her head, dismissing the erotic images the crazy suggestion had sparked. "You're more than enough for me to handle."

"Uh-huh. Then why are your cheeks getting all red?" he asked, trailing his fingers along the curve of her ass. "What other fantasies are rolling around in that pretty head of yours?"

Fantasies. She looked down so he couldn't read her expression. Was that all this was about for him? Exploration. Games. Sex.

Or did he get the same fist-to-the-solar-plexus feeling she got anytime she thought about the end of summer?

She hid her thoughts with a saucy smile. "Wouldn't *you* like to know."

"Vicious tease." He dragged her away from the open fridge and lifted her with ease, guiding her legs around his waist. Her skirt bunched around her thighs, and he nipped at her lower lip. "Man, I've missed you like crazy this week."

She couldn't stave off the smile that hopped to her lips, a little zip of giddiness going through her at the obvious sincerity of his words. Maybe he did feel something more. "Really? You missed me?"

"Ah, sugar, you have no idea."

Her heart did a little flip, confirming how far into crazytown she'd strayed. Okay, so this was stupid. Insane. She was getting in too deep. She should run hard and fast. There were a thousand reasons why this couldn't work long-term.

But she couldn't bring herself to turn away from him. No one had ever made her feel this good, this free to be herself. Alive. So she shoved the worries in a mental closet and kicked the door closed. Stressing about the inevitable wouldn't get her anywhere. She would figure out how to say good-bye. Soon.

But not while he was giving her that look that made her insides turn liquid. She kissed along the curve of his neck. "So are you going to show me how much you missed me? Or do I need to call one of the other guys?"

A low growl rumbled from his chest as he swung her to the left and planted her back against the wall. "Well, I was going to take you to get some dinner first. But if you insist, I'll gladly fuck you right here."

"Oh." She'd only been asking for a kiss, but the new suggestion sent a shot of lust-laced adrenaline through her vitals. She glanced at the empty hallway over his shoulder. "There aren't hidden security cameras around, are there?"

"Nope." He dragged his greedy gaze over her chest, and her nipples tightened under the perusal, her whole body going achy with want. "Grab the edges of the shelf above your head and don't let go. I'll show you exactly how much I missed you."

She stretched her arms above her and wrapped her fingers around the cool metal, her heart hammering against her ribs. "Are you sure no one's going to come back here tonight?"

"Nope." He set her on her feet, giving her a dark smile, and shoved her skirt to her waist. "Want me to stop?"

His fingers trailed up her inner thigh, sending hot and tingly desire steamrolling over any lingering worries. She shook her head. "God, no."

"Good." The backs of his knuckles brushed against the cotton of her panties. "Because I don't know if I could make it through a whole meal knowing how hot and wet you are under these already."

She wriggled against his touch, seeking more, needing all of him. Now. "Well, whose fault is that?"

"You're sassy tonight." His hand slid beneath the band of her underwear, dragging heated fingers over her slick tissues and the throbbing bundle of nerves. "Guess I need to remind you who's in charge."

He pinched her clit hard enough for her to cry out, and she jolted against him, squeezing the shelf so tightly her nails bit into her palms. "Yes, like that. Please."

"Did you obey my orders while I was gone?" he asked, continuing to stroke her with firm fingers. "Or did you touch this pretty cunt and come without my permission?"

"I obeyed, sir," she panted, grasping at her unraveling rope of control. She wouldn't last long. He'd told her not to touch herself the whole time he was gone, and for some reason, she'd listened. Now she was like a grenade with a loose pin.

"Good girl." Without finesse, he yanked her panties down, and she kicked off her heels. "Let's see if it was worth the wait."

Her head lolled back against the wall.

She had no doubt he'd be worth the wait, but would he be worth the heartbreak?

———

Reid fumbled with his belt and unbuttoned his pants, the need to claim Brynn burning through him like wildfire. A week without her had been like walking around with a hole in his chest. He'd planned to surprise her tonight, take her to a nice dinner. Talk. But now she was here in front of him, smelling like strawberry shampoo and feminine arousal. Looking like sin. And he was about to lose his goddamned mind. Food and the discussion he wanted to have with her could wait.

Not even bothering to step out of his pants, he rolled a condom on and grasped the backs of her thighs, lifting and spreading her. "I don't know if I can go slow and easy right now, sugar."

Her green eyes met his, the low light of the room not dimming the fire behind them. "Then take me hard, sir."

He groaned and dug his fingers into the soft undersides of her thighs as he thrust forward. Her wet heat closed around him like a velvet fist, causing a bone-deep shudder to wrack his body. "Goddamn, you feel good."

Part of him wanted to stay like this, buried inside her balls deep, feeling her stretching around him, watching how her teeth bit into her full bottom lip as she fought to keep her composure. The tender skin at her neck jumped with the frantic beat of her heart, and he dipped forward to run his tongue along the pulse point.

She moaned and her muscles flexed around his shaft, nearly sending him over the edge before they even started. "Reid, please, I need you."

He slid out until just the head of his cock rested inside her, relishing the view of their carnal connection, then plunged forward, deep and hard. Her feminine grunt of satisfaction, that little catch in her throat, was all it took to strip the last remnants of patience from his system. He hitched her legs higher and rocked into her with the speed and gentleness of a freight train, the sound of skin hitting skin drowning out the mundane noises around them.

She writhed against the wall and sweat slicked both their bodies as he balanced on the precipice before release. He refused to let it end too soon. He wanted to savor the feel of having her in his arms, enjoy the wild look in her green eyes as she hurtled toward her own bliss. "Touch yourself, sugar. I've got you."

Her fingers uncurled from the shelf, and she lowered her hand to her swollen clit, stroking over it with the confidence of a woman who wasn't ashamed to take her pleasure. The move shot lightning through his blood, tightening his balls and dragging him even closer to the edge.

She leaned her head back, her breath turning choppy. "Oh, God."

"That's right, baby. You come for me. Let me hear how much you like me fucking you hard."

"*Reid,*" she ground out, the word rattling out her throat and her inner muscles rippling around him as she flew apart.

Unable to resist the combination of her orgasm and the erotic sound of her calling his name, his entire body tensed, the sweet ecstasy of oncoming release rushing along his nerve endings. His cock swelled inside her, and he crushed her against him as the heated pulse of his own climax jetted through him.

When they both quieted, his legs felt as if they would collapse beneath him. Keeping a snug hold on her, he turned until his back was against the wall and then slid them both to the floor.

She touched her forehead to his and laced her fingers at the nape of his neck. "Okay, so that was worth the wait."

He laughed and kissed the corner of her mouth. "Definitely."

Although he didn't plan on ever making her wait that long

again. The trip had been a mistake. He'd agreed to go with his aunt and uncle for the vacation, thinking it would be a good way to get his head clear and get some perspective on his situation with Brynn. Maybe shake off the feelings she stirred up in him—feelings that had no place in a summer hookup.

But it hadn't worked. Instead, hanging around with his family's hoity-toity crowd had only made him want Brynn more.

For a while, he'd convinced himself their scorching sexual chemistry was the only reason the sun seemed to get brighter anytime she was near. But the week away had burned that theory into a pile of ash. As he sat on the beach night after night, staring at the ocean, he'd realized that the agonizing ache he felt didn't reside below his belt but square in the middle of his chest.

He missed her.

For the first time in his life, he felt comfortable in his own skin, and she was the reason. The people in his world always came with conditions, fine print. But not Brynn. Even after he'd told her about his father, she hadn't judged, only accepted. She'd embraced the dark parts of him as well as the bright spots. He'd never experienced that kind of total acceptance—not even from his mom. And he didn't want to give that up.

Not now. Not at the end of the summer. Maybe not ever.

And he had no idea what in the hell to do with *that* realization.

Asking Brynn to be in a relationship with him was akin to inviting her into a snake pit. The people who ran in his family's social circle could be vicious. They'd slice her apart with their genteel passive-aggressiveness and backhanded comments before she even realized what was happening. Plus, if he and Brynn started dating publicly and the press dug into her background . . . Hell, he didn't even want to think about that. Beyond the fallout from his aunt and uncle over the campaign, he'd never forgive himself for bringing that kind of scrutiny and exposure down on Brynn.

But he was getting ahead of himself.

Even if he could figure out a way to shield her from the land mines in his life, she'd given him no signs that she had any interest in him beyond the summer. Sure, the whole thing was fun and different for her right now. She was trying it out. Just like she'd try out a threesome if he offered one. But would she want this kind of relationship with him for real?

He intended to find out soon. If she felt even an inkling of what he felt for her, maybe they could figure out a way to be together.

He shook himself from his thoughts and smiled. "How about some dinner, sugar?"

Her lips parted to answer, but a noise coming from down the hall made them both freeze.

"Shit," he whispered. He strained to listen. What in the hell was that? "Is that the . . . the copy machine?"

Her eyes widened and she climbed off his lap, hurriedly standing and tugging her skirt down. "Did you lock the front door?"

Had he? He thought he had, but maybe in his rush to see Brynn he'd forgotten.

He buttoned his pants and stood, putting his finger to his lips to hush her. If someone was in the office, he and Brynn could be in trouble for a number of reasons. He didn't want anyone knowing about their relationship, but that was the least of his worries at the moment. If someone had broken in, they could be in much more serious danger.

He leaned next to her ear. "Stay here. Don't come out until I call for you. If I'm not back in ten minutes, call 911."

"*Reid,*" she whispered, latching on to his shirtsleeve. "Don't go out there, what if it's a burglar?"

"I'm sure it's fine. What burglar would use the copy machine?" he whispered, trying to reassure her, but not convincing himself.

He crossed over to the sink and pulled open a drawer but found only plastic utensils. Damn. He bent and opened the cabinet below. He grabbed the small fire extinguisher. It wasn't much, but it would have to do.

He headed toward the doorway and poked his head out into the hallway. Empty. The copy machine was still going at a steady pace in the distance. Click and glide. Click and glide.

He slipped into the hall, keeping his back close to the interior wall, and inched forward on quiet feet. If he could get to the end of the corridor, he'd be able to peer around and see the spread of the main office area. Step by agonizing step he made it closer to his destination, all the while telling himself that the stealth was for nothing. That it was probably just one of the office workers stopping in for something. But the hairs on the back of his neck said otherwise.

As he reached the end of hall, he carefully peeked around the corner. The whole office was dark except for the parking lot lights illuminating the glass doors at the front and the green and white dance of lights under the lid of the unattended copy machine across the room.

"Hello?" he called out. "Anyone there?"

Only the monotonous rhythm of the damn copier answered.

Unwilling to traipse around the place in the dark to search, he reached for the light switch and flipped on the bank of overhead fluorescents. He scanned the room quickly to make sure no one was in sight, then started looking behind desks, keeping the fire extinguisher poised for his lame spray-and-distract plan.

Once he'd secured that area and checked that the front door was indeed locked, he did a cursory search of the private offices. Not a soul anywhere.

He blew out the breath he'd been holding.

Huh. Maybe some weird glitch in the copier.

He stuck his head in the hallway and called out, "Brynn, all clear."

He headed across the room to shut off the annoying contraption that had caused the drama. The machine had been queued up for five hundred copies and was steadily pumping them out. He hit the stop button and grabbed the top page of the stack in the output slot.

His blood ran cold.

A photo filled the center of the page—the two faces in profile easily identified. He and Brynn naked by the lake during a midnight tryst from a few weeks ago, her arms bound behind her, his hand poised above her backside, ready to strike. Underneath the photo, a handwritten message in small block letters:

YOUR DADDY WOULD BE SO PROUD. KEEP FUCKING THE WHORE, AND I'LL MAKE SURE EVERYONE KNOWS ALL ABOUT THE TWO OF YOU AND YOUR DIRTY LITTLE SKELETONS. THINK YOUR FAMILY LOVES YOU ENOUGH TO STAND BY YOU IF THE WHOLE WORLD FINDS OUT HOW SICK YOU REALLY ARE?

"Reid?" Brynn called from the other side of the office, her voice tentative. "Everything okay?"

He ripped the original from underneath the copier's lid and grabbed the stack of printed pages. The papers quivered in his shaking hands. "Everything's fine, sugar."

THIRTEEN

now

"*What?*" Reid asked, his stubbled jaw hanging open at Brynn's proposition.

Brynn stared up at him, willing herself not to turn tail and run after coming on to him. She needed to do this or she was going to spend the whole weekend flinching like a wounded bird.

During the kiss with him in front of the group, she had glimpsed a feeling—a whisper of freedom that she hadn't felt since the day someone had decided to violate her. If she could just rip off the bandage—guerilla-style exposure therapy like Melody had suggested—then maybe she could break the shackles that seemed to weigh her down any time she was near a dominant man.

She wet her lips. "I said not to ask questions."

His eyes darkened. "Last I checked, I'm the dom here, so I'll ask what I want."

"Are you attracted to me?"

He crossed his arms, the muscles in his shoulders shifting and bunching. "Well, I'm not fucking dead."

"Then, please, just go with it. I don't want to talk about the past or why we hate each other. Let's leave all of that outside these grounds for the next three days. You know we're not going to be able to make it through our stay here only kissing in front of people."

He looked left, then right. "There are no people here now. Who is this show going to be for?"

My sanity. At least if she panicked, she wouldn't have to do it in front of the whole club. "Myself. I don't want to flinch every time you touch me. Maybe your breaking-the-ice idea wasn't such a bad one—we could get this first time out of the way in private."

"Get it out of the way. Like I'm a dentist appointment or something?" He smirked, but she didn't miss the weariness in his voice. "Come on, be honest. Why don't you just admit that underneath that big grudge you're holding, you still want me?"

She threw her head back and groaned. "You're such a jerk sometimes, you know that? Yes, I'm attracted to you, okay. I wouldn't offer to have sex with you if I wasn't."

He gave her a triumphant smile, picked up the shirt from the floor, and handed it to her. "Don't worry, sugar. I'll make sure we get it out of the way, but it's not going to happen because I'm some item to scratch off your to-do list. I'll decide when and what happens."

Ugh. Couldn't the man cooperate with anything? She yanked the shirt from his hands. "Screw you."

He walked past her and stretched out on the couch. "Later. I promise."

She balled her fists and fought the inclination to stomp her feet like a child. She'd never met a more frustrating man in her life. How had she ever fallen for such a jackass? Without wasting another breath on him, she stomped past him, down the narrow hallway, and slammed the bedroom door behind her.

Like the rest of the cabin, the upscale rustic theme continued in the bedroom—dark woods, cream-colored fabrics, and soft lighting. It could have been a luxury cabin at any fine resort if not for the metal loops drilled into the walls and a leather and wooden bench contraption at the foot of the bed. She grimaced. This was going to be the longest freaking weekend of her life.

She rubbed her arms to fight off a shiver, and Reid's heady scent wafted up from the shirt, reminding her of balmy nights and twisted sheets. The urge to bury her face in the soft cotton ratcheted through her. Damn it to hell. Why did the jerk have to smell good, too?

All right, enough of this ensemble. Letting the shirt fall to the floor, she headed to the closet and slid the louver doors open. But the contents only inspired a groan. *Frederick's of Hollywood called—they want their inventory back.* She flipped through the satin-covered hangers with a huff. Lingerie, slinky dresses, vinyl getups, and enough leather to outfit a Judas Priest fan club. Terrific. She'd thought the items she'd packed had been sexy enough, but apparently the dress code here required hooker chic.

She grabbed a black bustier and a brief leather skirt and held them up in front of her. At least these would cover the essentials— not a guarantee most of the other options afforded. She tossed the items on the bed and grabbed a pair of knee-high black boots from the floor of the closet. Well, at least those weren't so bad.

A sharp rap on the door sent her bolting upright. "Brynn, you've got five more minutes to pout, then I need you out here. Company's coming."

"What the hell are you talking about?" she called through the closed door.

"Just put your game face on and get out here."

She sighed. "Fine, I'll be right there."

A few minutes later she heard Reid let someone in and the murmuring of male conversation. She gave herself one last glance in the mirror, pulled up the bustier a little more to make sure her boobs wouldn't tumble out, and headed into the living room. The click of her boots earned raised heads from both the men.

Reid's eyes widened as his gaze swept over her new clothes. "Guess you found the closet."

Brynn ignored him and focused on their guest. "Hi, Jace."

"Hot damn, girl, you look smoking," he said, a wide smile splitting his face.

"Thanks." He didn't look so bad himself. Linen pants, untucked button-down shirt, and wavy blond hair pulled back in a short ponytail. If she weren't so annoyed with him, she would've returned his compliment. She settled into the overstuffed chair opposite the one Jace sat in. "So what happened to 'I'm not going to be here this weekend.'"

His gaze darted to Reid, then back to her. "Plans changed at the last minute."

She smirked. "Right."

"Be nice, Brynn," Reid warned. "Jace doesn't do one-on-one stuff—he's known around here for ménage. It would've looked suspicious if he'd taken you on. Plus, he's already doing us a huge favor by getting us in. I don't want to risk him or his business with Grant by dragging him in deeper."

She sighed, conceding. Reid was right. Who was she to be mad at Jace when he was putting himself on the line for her? "Sorry for snapping at you, Jace. I really do appreciate the help."

"No problem, doll. I'm going to do all I can to help you—with everything." His gaze met hers.

She bit her lip and nodded, getting the message and silently thanking him for not bringing up the revelation she'd made in the staging room. "So what's the plan for tonight?"

"That's what we were discussing before you walked in," Reid said, buttoning the cuffs of the black shirt he'd put on to replace the one he'd lent her. "Jace chatted up one of the staff members and found out that new sub trainees are on total lockdown to-night and won't be allowed on the main grounds until tomorrow at the earliest."

"Shit," she said, her hope for finding her sister tonight plummeting. "What the hell are we supposed to do now?"

Reid shrugged. "We need to go out and be seen. Jace offered to have dinner with us and to give us a tour of the main clubhouse so we can get our bearings. After that, who knows?"

She eyed the two of them, getting the feeling that the only one who *didn't know* was her.

———

An hour and two courses later, Brynn still hadn't managed to eat anything more than a few bites of salad. Between the ball of anxiety burning in her stomach and the breath-stealing bustier, she doubted even chocolate would tempt her. They'd toured the building, and she'd seen things that would be seared into her brain forever. Some of the scenes had gotten her heated in all the right places, but others had nearly sent her into a panic attack just watching.

She needed to get this exposure therapy over with now. The anticipation alone was going to be the death of her. She pushed a baby carrot back and forth across her plate as Jace and Reid talked.

Reid speared a piece of steak. "So how serious does it get here? Is it mostly light stuff or do they cater to those who go for the extreme?"

Jace shrugged as he finished chewing his bite. "It kind of runs the gamut. But there are limits. No blood play and definitely no breath play. Grant allows a lot of things, but doesn't want anyone messing with the deadly stuff."

Brynn's fork stilled, but she kept her mouth shut and let Reid continue.

"So besides that, pretty much anything goes, then," Reid said. "Guess I shouldn't expect any less with all the high rollers around here. No one would pay this much money to go somewhere with a lot of restrictions."

Jace nodded. "Yeah, they cater to people who aren't used to hearing the word 'no.' You'll get to see all the bigwigs tomorrow night. There's a Bacchanal planned after sunset to celebrate the grape harvest."

"Oh, really?" Reid said.

"Yeah, Grant only holds it once a year, so I guarantee all the rooms and cabins will be empty tomorrow night. *No one* misses this event."

Reid and Jace both looked at her, confirming the message. Kelsey would probably be there.

She dabbed her mouth with her napkin, and glanced at the nearby tables. They had to be careful about what they said. "Wow. A festival honoring Bacchus at a place that doesn't let you drink alcohol."

Jace laughed. "Yeah, I know. The no alcohol rule is important with all the stuff that goes on here. But believe me, that's the only excess the party won't have." He eyed her, his face turning more serious—no doubt thinking of what she'd revealed to him in the dressing room. "But it can be overwhelming. The rules for D/s don't really hold up in there. It's kind of a free-for-all. Although, the safe word always applies."

She took a long gulp of her tea, digesting the information, nerves skittering through her.

How was she supposed to survive a goddamned orgy? She was jumping out of her skin at even the simplest touch. The thought of an anything-goes night with a crowd of hedonistic strangers made her want to curl into a fetal position and hide. The panic and flashbacks would surely engulf her.

But she didn't have time for a nervous breakdown. That was

going to be her best chance to convince her sister to come home and go to the police.

Brynn straightened in her seat, her decision made. She was going to have to do something about her fear *tonight*, prove to herself that she was stronger than what that monster did to her.

She cleared her throat. "I definitely want to check that out. Sounds like something I shouldn't miss."

"For sure," Reid said, giving her a purposeful nod. "We'll be there."

Jace smiled. "Great."

Reid glanced down at her plate. "Sugar, you've barely touched your food. Do you want me to order you something different? We've got a big night ahead of us. I can't have you fading on me."

She set down her glass, his subtle warning setting her on edge, but she pushed forward with her plan. "I don't need anything else. I'm ready for whatever you guys have planned."

Reid lifted an eyebrow. "*Whatever* is a broad word, Brynn."

She took a breath. *I can do this.* Once upon a time, she'd loved this man, trusted him, and had enjoyed some seriously hot sex with him. She needed to keep that last thing in the front of her mind. Maybe if she could hone her focus onto the physical, indulge the part of her that was still hopelessly attracted to him, she could block out the fear that threatened to undo her and enjoy herself.

"I know, Master."

Reid grinned, wickedness glinting in his eyes. He rose from his chair and dropped his napkin on his plate. "Jace, why don't you head to the nightclub area with Brynn and I'll meet you? I'm going to have them box up dessert to take with us."

Jace stood and Brynn downed the rest of her drink before getting up to join him, wishing it was some of the wine the vineyard produced instead of iced tea. She'd kill for some liquid courage tonight.

Jace slid a hand onto the small of her back as Reid strode off. "Come on, doll. Let's go join the reindeer games."

She bit her lip, but let him nudge her forward. As they passed another table, a man reached out and stopped Jace. "Hey, Jason, I didn't realize you were going to be here this weekend."

Jace shook the man's hand and offered a polite smile to both him and the scantily clad brunette who kneeled on the floor next to his chair. "Hi, Davis. How's it going?"

Brynn's insides chilled as the name and familiar voice dinged bells inside her. She ventured another look at the man's face and then quickly dropped her gaze. Shit. Davis Ackerman, her old boss, and now current city councilman. Just what she needed—yet another person seeing her half naked and collared. She dipped her head down even farther and hoped the man had a bad memory.

"I'm here, so I'd say it's going excellent," Davis said. "And I wanted to thank you for getting that order to me so quickly. I'm really happy with everything."

Jace absently rubbed Brynn's back, and she sensed he was itching to move on from the conversation. "Glad to hear it."

"Pretty sub you have there tonight." Davis's tone made it sound like he was admiring the night's dinner specials. "Are you two looking to join up with anyone?"

Ugh. Not in this lifetime. The thought of that man laying a finger on her made her soul shudder. Jace's palm moved to her hip as he gathered her closer. "Sorry, Davis. I appreciate the offer, but we actually have plans with someone else tonight. I'm sure you'll be able to find an available couple in the group room, though."

"Ah, oh, well. Maybe we'll see you at the festival tomorrow night."

The men exchanged good-byes, and Jace hustled her away. "Sorry about that, doll. Davis hasn't gotten any less annoying with age, but I'd be stupid to get on a councilman's bad side. Plus, he's a steady customer at the store."

"You think he recognized me?"

"Nah, he's so drunk on lust for that chick he's with. He wouldn't be able to pick his own wife out of a lineup right now."

She grimaced. "He's married?"

Jace sighed. "Unfortunately, being single isn't one of the requirements for membership at The Ranch."

A sound of disgust escaped her. Thank God that's not who her sister was paired up with.

Jace gave her a rueful smile as they exited the restaurant and headed down one of the unnaturally quiet hallways. "I know it's not right, but it is what it is. At least you don't have to worry. Both of your men tonight are footloose and fancy-free."

Her steps stuttered. *Both?* "What?"

He paused outside a set of double doors and turned to her. "Brynn, before we go in there, I want to make sure you're okay with this. Reid asked me to join you guys tonight."

Her eyes widened.

"I know, shocked the shit out of me, too, because you know how he is. And don't get me wrong, I'm definitely a willing participant, but if you don't want that or think it's going to freak you out, tell me now. I know you haven't told Reid what you're going through, but I know he wouldn't want to do anything that's going to scare you."

Both of them. *Both of them.* Her heart hammered in her chest, but the rush of adrenaline didn't feel like fear. No, this rush was something *totally* different. After a few moments, she nodded. "I'm okay. I trust you guys."

"You know what to say if anything goes wrong."

"Yep."

"Okay," he said, giving her a smile that suddenly seemed more than friendly. He pushed through the double doors, and pounding dance music drowned out her question. He bent close to her ear and shouted, "Come on, doll. Into the den of inequity we go."

She grabbed his hand and followed him through the throng of people on the dance floor. Couples and groups of every possible makeup—some clothed, some not so much—bounced and writhed to the pulsing beat. Hands and bare skin brushed against her as she and Jace were absorbed into the crowd. The scents of sweat and sex enveloped her, and despite her racing worries, her body jumped to attention.

She mentally grabbed on to that physical sensation—that's what she needed to focus on. She closed her eyes, centering herself, drawing herself down into her senses and into an almost meditative state. *Nothing exists outside this moment. This room. All you need is what your body feels.*

A hot hand cupped her ass and jolted her from her internal chanting. She turned her head to tell whoever it was to back off, but Reid's confident smirk greeted her. "Keep moving."

Once they made it off the dance floor and to the fringes of the room, the music faded to a manageable volume. Jace found the last open couch. "This'll work."

Brynn frowned at the small love seat. No way would the three of them fit on that. Hell, was she going to have to kneel on the goddamned floor again? Jace sank onto the dark brown leather, and after setting a paper bag on a nearby cocktail table, Reid moved past her to take the other spot. She huffed. Guess "ladies first" had no application in this world.

She sighed and started to kneel, but Reid's hand circled her wrist. "Plenty of room for you on my lap, sugar."

Her heart skipped a tick as he patted his leg in invitation. She used to love being on Reid's lap. Back when she'd felt like her whole world was balancing on the edge of a dime, his embrace had made her feel cherished, safe. But right now, she doubted his intent had anything to do with safety.

Before she could respond, he dragged her closer and pulled her onto the tops of his muscular thighs. With ease, he shifted her whole body until her ass was in his lap and her legs were draped across Jace's. "There, that's better."

She looked back and forth between the two men and wet her lips. "But, I'm taking up Jace's space, too."

Reid ran the backs of his knuckles along the outside of her exposed leg, sending shivers along her skin. "I don't think he minds."

Jace's eyes followed Reid's movements. "Not at all. The view is mighty fine."

Reid's palm slid toward the inside of her thigh, and he parted her tightly closed knees, spreading her until Jace could most definitely see up her skirt. "Don't be shy, sugar. You were ready to take Jace on as your dom last week, so I know you're not opposed to letting him have a little fun with us."

She couldn't help the swift heat that nestled between her legs. Maybe staying focused on the physical wouldn't be a problem. She turned to Reid, her brows knitted. "What happened to your no-sharing policy?"

He gave a soft chuckle, even though something akin to pain flashed in his eyes, and kissed the spot below her ear. "Back then I was young and stupid and thought I was in love. Now that it's just sex, I don't mind sharing."

She scoffed. Sure, he'd been in love with her—so in love that he'd been cheating on her the whole time they were together. What a stand-up guy.

Reid frowned and pushed a stray hair away from her face. "But, we're leaving the past behind while we're here, right? Let's not let that taint the experience of 'getting this whole sex thing over with.'"

She opened her mouth to respond, but his finger pressed against her lips.

"Shh, relax and keep an open mind, Brynn. I promise if you do that, this will be way better than a dentist appointment."

Her retort shriveled in her throat. He was right, as much as it killed her to admit it. This was what she had walked in here to do. Beyond the fact that this would make them look like authentic guests, she needed to do this for herself. If she was going to get past this fear and learn to enjoy sex again, what better way to do it than to hand herself over to the most dominant man she'd ever met?

Despite their issues, she knew Reid wouldn't physically harm her. And although she and Jace only had friendship between them, she'd never deny that the man was sex on a stick. The idea of both of them . . . Well, her damp panties certainly indicated that her hormones were a fan.

Her chest rose and fell with deep breaths. This was it. *Take the leap, Brynn. Just be in the moment. You're safe.*

She gave a final nod, mentally slamming the door shut on everything but the feel of the two beautiful men against her skin.

Reid removed his finger, his blue eyes glittering in the club's flashing lights. "Good, girl. Now, I think you're ready for dessert."

Jace's hand curled under her knee and she startled. "Easy, doll. We're going to take good care of you."

She swallowed hard. "I know."

While Reid leaned to the side to grab the bag he had brought with him, a vinyl-clad waitress stopped in front of them. Her heavily lined eyes danced across Brynn's two companions, her interest obvious. "Do you need anything from the bar . . . or from an attendant?"

Reid lifted his head, and Jace continued to caress Brynn's leg. Reid traced a finger along the edge of Brynn's bustier. "I think we have all we need right now."

The girl's bottom lip jutted out a bit, but she nodded and moved on. Brynn sniffed. "I think you guys have a new president for your fan club."

Reid laughed and pulled a pint-sized container from the paper bag. "We'll see. You might want to apply for the job once we're done with you tonight."

She lifted an eyebrow. "Confident, aren't you?"

"Jace, I think our sub has a bit of a smart mouth."

Jace shook his head. "Seems so. I think it's this outfit. It's making her feisty."

Reid yanked at the laces holding the front of the bustier together, sending her breasts spilling out the top. She gasped and her hands instinctively flew to cover herself.

Reid frowned. "Drop your hands, Brynn, or we'll be forced to tie you up."

Her gaze darted around the crowded room. She had known that public display would be involved in this, but knowing it and experiencing it were two different things. A couple sitting a few yards away openly ogled the scene, and Brynn had the urge to grab the paper bag and put it over her head.

Reid's fingers grasped her chin, and he turned her face toward him. "Look only at us. You're here to please me and Jace—no one else gets the privilege of your attention. Now I'm giving you one more chance to drop your hands or I'm pulling out the cuffs."

Cuffs. The word tried to slip through the hold she had on her fear. Restraints equaled panic. She stared into Reid's eyes, feeling his grip on her face, letting his unwavering focus draw her back to center. She let her arms fall to her sides, and her nipples instantly tightened from the exposure.

Reid's gaze traveled over her breasts as if he was seeing the female form for the first time, and she couldn't help but warm beneath the full glow of his appreciation. He kissed her bare shoulder. "Thank you. A body this gorgeous deserves to be worshipped not hidden."

"Amen to that," Jace said, his normally genial face turning serious.

She knew there were far more beautiful women in the room, knew that her belly was a bit too round and her breasts a bit too heavy to call perky. But in that moment, the two men's hungry perusal made her feel like a goddess upon an altar. The traces of panic started to drain out of her completely.

These men wanted her, would take care of her. And suddenly she found herself wanting them back. Really *wanting* them.

Reid pulled off the lid of the container he'd brought and dunked a finger inside. "Ready for dessert, sugar?"

He lifted his hand to her lips, rubbing something thick and warm over them, then lowered his head and claimed her mouth in a slow, possessive kiss. *Mmm.* Reid and the sweet, buttery flavor of caramel glazed her taste buds—a heady combination that sent her inner thermostat inching upward. He sucked her lower lip and removed the last of the sticky confection just as another streak of warmth painted the sensitive skin of her leg. *What the . . .*

He smiled as awareness dawned within her. "Four hands can be so much more efficient than two."

Reid's mouth returned to hers right as Jace's hot tongue glided along her inner thigh, lapping up the caramel sauce and setting a match to her nerve endings. Holy shit. Was she actually going to do this? Two men—no, not just two men, Reid and Jace. Heaven help her.

As Reid's tongue stroked over hers, his growing erection pressed against her bottom. She wiggled against him, and he hummed his approval into the kiss. Jace's hair brushed against her legs as he continued to taste the skin higher and higher on her thigh, maddeningly close to the slow throbbing between her legs. Her knees instinctively parted farther, seeking relief as the combination of the two men's attention coalesced in her core, sending moisture hotter than the caramel straight to her sex.

When Jace nudged the bottom edge of her skirt, Reid pulled back from the kiss and grabbed the container again. Creamy caramel drizzled over each of her nipples, and she arched from the contrast in temperature. Reid's fingers spread the sugared sauce over one of the tightened buds, then tilted her farther back against the arm of the couch, putting her on full display like a buffet to be sampled. Jace slid out from beneath her and moved to the floor, settling at her side. Both heads lowered, and each man latched on to a breast, sucking and laving in tandem—Reid's mouth hot and firm, Jace's more teasing.

She threaded her hands in their hair, pulling Jace's short ponytail free in the process, and let her head fall back. The last threads of resistance burned into wisps of smoke as the call of her body overruled the voice in her head. Heated palms slid up her legs and hiked her skirt to her waist. Reid's teeth scraped against her left nipple sending a shot of pleasure/pain through her before he released it. "I think it's time for something sweeter than caramel."

Jace didn't stop his ministrations but cupped the breast that Reid had abandoned and rubbed a thumb across the tip. Reid scooted from under her and set her ass on the couch. Before she could process what he was doing, he spread her legs wide and ran a finger over the soaked crotch of her panties. "Mmm, I think our little sub likes us, Jace."

Jace lifted his head and smiled down at Brynn, the green of his eyes dark and dangerous. "Is that right?"

Reid grabbed her wrist and moved her hand beneath the waistband of her underwear, the pads of her fingers resting on her mound. "Jace is being so nice to you, don't you think you should give him a little taste?"

Her heart stuttered in her chest, and she moistened her lips. "Y-Yes, sir."

Reid caressed her arm. "Go ahead then, sugar."

After a steadying breath, she lowered her hand and ran two fingers along her slick folds. One brush against her clit and she thought she may tip over the edge right there. Just a few strokes and she'd be there. But she wasn't ready for it to be over yet; she wanted to let the guys decide when it was time.

Jace's hooded gaze never left hers as she raised her hand to him. He grabbed her forearm and brought her glistening fingers to his mouth. With unhurried reverence, he sucked them clean. "Your girl is so fucking sweet, Reid."

Her pussy clenched as if he'd licked her clit instead of her fingers, and a whimper slipped past her lips.

Reid's hands kneaded her legs. "Can't wait to refresh my memory."

Coarse fingers moved to her hips, and Reid tugged her panties off. A low groan rumbled from him. "Jesus, Brynn, you're going to fucking kill me."

She lifted her head to see his hungry gaze trace over her Brazilian wax job—something she'd started doing a few years earlier. "You approve?"

He traced his fingers over the baby smooth skin, making her writhe. "I don't think I've ever seen a sexier cunt in my life. So pretty and pink."

She shuddered and his lips curved upward. "Still love the dirty talk, huh, sugar? I bet that lame-ass date you had the other night would've whispered gentle, polite words to you while he fucked you. Is that what you'd rather have?"

Two fingers slipped inside her channel, and Jace resumed sucking a breast. Her hips bucked against the delicious invasion, and she could only reply with a moan.

Reid's fingers pumped harder, filling her just enough to make her yearn for more, but not enough to satisfy the needy ache. "Answer me, sub. Tell me what you prefer?"

She shook her head, not wanting to give in, even though she knew he knew the answer.

He bent lower and the very tip of his tongue flicked her clit once. Her muscles jolted and tilted her hips upward, seeking more. He kissed her mound, his lips landing right above her slit. "No, darling. You don't get what you want until you answer me."

As if punctuating Reid's point, Jace pinched the nipple he wasn't sucking, hard enough to make her gasp. Reid's fingers slipped out of her, and she squeezed her eyes shut, a second shy of begging. "I like it when you talk dirty."

Reid's fingers moved back inside, and she let her head relax against the arm of the couch again. With his free hand, he positioned her legs over his shoulders "Now you get to come for us, sugar."

His lips pressed against her sex and his tongue swirled around her clit, sending electricity pulsing through her veins. She knew she wouldn't be able to hold on for long. She couldn't remember the last time she'd been this keyed up, this turned on. It'd been so long since she'd been truly sexually satisfied that she'd almost forgotten what the climb felt like.

Her breaths turned to pants as the need for release gnawed at her dwindling control. Jace captured her mouth with his, and the lingering tastes of her own juices and caramel swirled along her tongue. She slid her hand along his muscled chest and twisted her other hand in Reid's hair.

Sensations and scents and tastes whirled into a maddening tornado, twisting inside her, pushing her to the edge of the abyss. Reid sucked her clit into his mouth and dragged his teeth lightly over it. *Oh, God.* A piercing scream ripped from her throat and poured into Jace's kiss, her orgasm shattering her into a million different shards of glittering pleasure.

The men continued pushing her, ratcheting up her volume, until she wondered if the people outside the building could hear her. Then, as if sensing she couldn't take another second, both eased back, giving her a chance to drift back to earth.

After her breathing calmed, her body sagged into the couch, sweat glazing every inch of her. Reid slipped her legs off his shoulders and replaced Jace at his side. He brushed the damp hair off her forehead and her lids fluttered closed. "Beautiful, sugar. Take a minute to relax. We're not done with you yet."

Her eyes blinked open, and he smiled as he took her hand and put it on the impressive erection straining against his pants. "You still have two very hard cocks to take care of."

She ran her hand along the length of him, all brain activity numbed by the afterglow of her rocking orgasm. "Looking forward to it, sir."

He bent down and kissed her tenderly, catching her off guard. "That's my girl."

His girl. The words sent a jagged slice through her chest, ripping through the stitches of the old wound. She turned her head before he could see the stupid tears that jumped to her eyes.

FOURTEEN

then

Brynn slipped off her shoes before she pushed through the front door so she wouldn't wake her sister or her mother with the *click clacking* of her heels. But when she stepped inside, she was surprised to see the light of the television flickering on the walls of the living room, and her mother lying on the couch awake.

Brynn glanced at the time on the VCR—2:21 a.m. Usually her mother went to bed early on her nights off. "Hey, what are you still doing up?"

Her mom sat up, pulling the afghan she had draped over her legs around her. With her blond hair pulled back in a ponytail and no makeup on, she looked younger than her thirty-eight years— pretty, even with the world-weary lines around her mouth and eyes. She nodded in Brynn's direction. "I could ask you the same thing."

"I had a date."

Her mother eyed her outfit, her gaze shrewd enough that Brynn knew she hadn't been drinking tonight. "Where'd you get that dress?"

She and Reid had gone to a restaurant outside of town, and he had surprised her with a new dress for the occasion. Brynn set her shoes by the door, wishing she had come through the back instead of the front. "It was a gift."

Her mother's shoulders rose and fell with a heavy sigh. "Baby, you're treading in dangerous territory."

"What are you talking about?"

"I saw that boy you've been going out with. Saw his clothes, that brand-new truck he's driving. And I can tell you that dress cost at least a few hundred dollars."

She crossed her arms over her chest and dropped onto the love seat. "So."

"So, I've been down that path. Handsome guy. Lots of money. Makes you feel like a princess. It's hard to resist. But relationships with boys like that are bad news."

Anger began to percolate in her belly. "You don't know anything about him."

"I know his type. And his type only dates girls like you for one reason. They use you and then when they get bored, they leave and go marry a girl who's a member of their country club."

"Mom, with all due respect, you're the one who lets guys use you for sex. Not me."

Instead of the angry retort she expected, sadness crossed her mother's tired face. "You're right. I've made more mistakes than I can count. I never meant for my life, your lives, to be this way. But sometimes once you start rolling down a hill, you find there's no way back up it."

Brynn looked down at her hands, unable to bear the tears gathering in her mother's eyes. "I'm sorry. I shouldn't have said that."

"It's okay," she said, her voice soft. "I've earned it. But I've also learned a lot along the way, and I love you too much to watch you follow the same path. You're too smart and good-hearted to let some guy take advantage of you. Go to school. Get a job that allows you to support yourself without any help from anyone. Then, worry about falling in love."

"I'm not in love," she said, maybe a bit too quickly.

Her mother nodded, though the knowing look in her eye said she didn't buy it. "Just be careful, baby."

"I will. I promise," she said, even though her mother had it all wrong. Reid wasn't one of those guys. He'd proven over and over how much her cared about her and wanted to be with her. She climbed off the love seat and headed toward her bedroom, but paused before she left the room. "Mom?"

"Hmm?" she asked, her gaze lifting from the TV.

"I love you, too, you know."

She smiled. "I know, baby."

———

Reid's shoulders tensed as soon as he parked his truck in the driveway and saw the kitchen lights were still shining brightly through the windows of the main house. He checked the clock on the dash. Almost three a.m. Not a good sign that someone was still up. The back door swung open before he'd even cut the engine. Aw, hell. An even worse sign. His aunt was waiting up for him.

With a heavy sigh, he climbed out of the truck and shut the door. "Everything alright, Aunt Ros?"

"We need to talk to you. Inside. Now."

Shit. We.

He scrubbed a hand over his face and slinked inside the house, feeling like he was fourteen again. He squinted in the bright lights of the pristine kitchen. His uncle was perched on a stool next to the marble island, sipping a glass of amber-colored alcohol and his aunt was standing next to him, arms crossed over her chest and lips pressed in a hard line.

"Nice night, Reid?" she asked, her tone cutting.

He leaned against the counter, his gaze hopping back and forth between the two of them. "It was . . . fine. What's going on?"

She grabbed a sheet of paper off the island and flipped it over. She jabbed a finger at it. "How could you do this to us?"

He took the few steps forward to grab the page. *Fuck.* The photo from the lake again—only this time with no message.

"Aunt Ros, I—"

"No!" she said, smacking her hand hard against the counter-top. "I don't want to hear it. I *told* you to stay away from her, that you'd only get yourself in trouble. Get *us* in trouble." She shook her head, her body visibly quivering with her anger. "Do you know what people will say if they find out that our son—that he does *this* to women? We're running on a family values platform, Reid!"

He bit his lip, letting her get her tirade out, his cheeks burning with shame.

His uncle put a hand on Ros's shoulder. "Reid, it's not just the campaign. We're worried about you. These are very dangerous waters considering your history. Did Ms. LeBreck consent to this, uh, activity?"

Reid jaw fell open. "Hold up. You think I *raped* her?"

Patrick's gaze dropped to his glass. "We just want to know what we're dealing with here."

"Of course not! Oh, my God, you guys really think I'm that screwed up, don't you?"

Neither his aunt or uncle met his eyes.

"Unbelievable." He raked his hands through his hair. "She's my girlfriend, all right?"

His aunt cringed, as if him dating someone outside their social circle was just as egregious as committing a rape would've been.

"Well, this has to end immediately," she said, her words clipped. "Whoever left this picture is probably building a blackmail case and doesn't need any more ammunition. For heaven's sake, the girl herself may have told someone to follow you two and grab a picture so she could make a little money off your relationship herself."

"Don't you dare throw accusations at her," he said, his voice rising. "She's not interested in my money."

She scoffed. "Don't be so naive. Everyone's interested in money."

His fists balled. "Just because you judge people's worth by their bank account doesn't mean everyone else does."

"Hey!" his uncle barked. "That's enough. You've had your aunt in tears all night over this, and I will not have you sit here and insult her. This family has done a lot for you. You need to have respect for the people who care about you."

Reid deflated, his uncle's words dousing him like a bucket of ice water. "Look, I'm sorry, okay? To both of you. I didn't mean for this to happen. But Brynn is leaving for Austin in a few weeks, so we'll be out of sight soon. We'll lay low until then."

"We?" his aunt asked.

Reid sighed and shoved his hands in his pockets. "Brynn doesn't know it yet, but I'm going to transfer down to UT with her if she'll have me. I know you guys don't approve of our relationship. But . . . I love the girl."

His uncle downed the rest of his alcohol.

"Oh, the hell you will," Ros said, angry tears brimming her lids. "You are staying right here. I will not have you chasing some tramp to some *state* school. You are our son now, and I will not stand by and watch while you throw your life away."

Steam was ready to burst from his ears, but he kept his tone calm. "It's not your decision. I'm an adult. My trust fund can pay my tuition wherever I want to go. And please don't call Brynn names."

"So that's it?" she said, tears spilling over for real now. "You're just going to leave the only family you have? The family who loves you. Your mother wanted you to be with us."

He couldn't recall ever seeing his aunt cry, and the show of emotion and mention of his mother tugged at his heart. Yes, they were the only family he had. But he sometimes forgot that he was the only child his aunt and uncle had ever had as well. Even though he'd come into their lives late in the game, they'd never treated him like anything but a son.

Fuck. He ran his hands over his face. "Look, I just need some time to think, all right? I love you guys, too, but Brynn is important to me. Why can't I have a life with all of you?"

His uncle gave a world-weary sigh. "Because that's not how the world works. Life is about the tough choices. And you need to make the right one for you, for this family, and for everyone's future."

His shoulders sank with the weight of his words. For the first time since he'd met Brynn, he wished she had the pedigree of someone like Vanessa. A girl who would be accepted into the fold with open arms. Life would be a hell of a lot easier.

But he couldn't help who he loved.

Now he just had to figure out if love was enough.

FIFTEEN

now

Stupid. So fucking stupid. Reid had seen the wince cross Brynn's face when he'd called her his girl. Here he was, preaching about leaving the past behind them, and he had to go and say something to remind her of it. The words had just rolled off his tongue before he could stop them. God, he was an idiot.

Sex. That's what this was. A kinky, no-strings fuck. That's why he'd invited Jace for a ménage. He had to make sure his own head didn't get screwed up being one-on-one with Brynn again. But even knowing that it was for the best, Reid had still wanted to break Jace's fingers the minute he'd touched Brynn. The girl had a way of crawling beneath Reid's skin and flipping his "mine" switch, making him entertain bonehead ideas.

No more relationship shit. The entire four years with Vanessa had been a miserable, expensive mistake. He realized now that fighting his nature had been pointless. His dominant desires weren't going to go away, so he had to accept he'd never be Mr. Ideal Husband for anyone. Long-term love wasn't in the cards. Women wanted him—just not forever. Both girls he'd ever tried to do the commitment thing with—Brynn being one of them—had confirmed it.

Still confirmed it. Based on how Brynn had reacted to having both him and Jace touching her at the same time—the woman's needs still erred on the "more the merrier" side. Which was fine. Once he'd shoved down the wave of possessiveness that had clouded the first few minutes of their encounter, he'd been able to enjoy watching Brynn writhe beneath both his and Jace's attention, had been turned on by it. And he sure as hell was going to enjoy what they had planned next. But all it could be was a fuck. He couldn't let old feelings and sentimentality blur that.

He didn't make the same mistakes twice. Period. He tucked his hands in his pockets. "Jace, help her back into her clothes. We're moving to my cabin."

A few onlookers who had gathered at the nearby tables grumbled. Reid didn't blame them. Brynn had put on quite a show. The woman had no idea how sexy her feisty submission was. His cock flexed in his pants at the memory of her keening orgasm. Hell, if he didn't get her to his room soon, he was going to end up fucking her against the nearest wall. He inhaled a deep breath. *Patience.*

He had Brynn right where he needed her—humming from orgasm, but slightly unsatisfied. He knew as soon as she was sated, that relentless worry segment of her brain would kick back into gear and she'd revert to ice-queen status around him. Tonight he wanted to show her what could've been—what she lost when she went behind his back. Because he sure as hell knew what he'd lost.

As Jace was finishing up with Brynn, Grant strolled over to Reid. The owner had the easy gait of a cowboy, but the shrewd face of a businessman who missed nothing. Grant smiled at the scene, then turned his evaluating gaze on him. "You're a natural dom. Why haven't you applied for membership here before?"

Reid shrugged. "Married a girl who thought this kind of thing was sick and perverted."

"Ah, but you're no longer married?" He said it like a question, but Reid knew the man already had the answer. The background check to get in the place was more intrusive than a goddamned proctology exam.

"She cheated on me with the pastor at her church," Reid said, his voice flat. "Said she'd found Jesus. Who knew he was hiding in that dickhead's bedroom?"

Grant smirked. "Glad to see you have a sense of humor about it."

Reid glanced back toward the couch and noticed Brynn was watching the two of them intently—probably hoping that she'd put on a sufficient display to put any possible suspicions the club owner might've had to rest. "It was only a matter of time. Neither of us could be what the other needed. It was as much my fault as it was hers."

Grant clapped Reid on the back. "I'm sorry that's what brought you here, but at least now you can indulge in what comes naturally to you. And what obviously comes naturally to her as well." He nodded at Brynn. "Now, don't let me hold you up any longer. Enjoy your evening. And make sure to let the staff know if you need any additional equipment in your room. Most requests can be accommodated here."

He shook Grant's hand. "Thanks. I'll keep that in mind."

Too bad he couldn't request that Grant deliver his star witness to his doorstep. Now that would be first-class service.

Although if that happened tonight, Reid's chance to touch Brynn again would be lost. The second she found out he was there to use her sister for Hank's appeal, any truce they'd forged over the last few days would go up in flames. Brynn would officially hate him forever.

Dread settled in his stomach. For the first time since he'd discovered the evidence, he found himself not so jazzed about locating the youngest LeBreck.

———

Brynn shivered as Reid sidled up next to her and slipped a hand around her waist. "Y'all okay with moving this to private quarters?"

She nodded, relieved to know they'd at least be alone if she freaked out. "Yes, sir."

Jace smiled. "Lead the way, brother."

Reid guided her through the crowd and toward a back door. A noticeable tension rolled off his stance, his jaw steadily clenching and unclenching. She glanced back at Grant and quickly shifted her eyes downward when she saw the owner's gaze hadn't left them. She tilted her head toward Reid's ear. "Is everything okay? Did Grant say something?"

He pulled her tighter against him. "Everything's fine, sugar. He said you were a born sub. Doesn't suspect anything."

Her shoulders drooped in relief. Guess she'd been convincing. Not that she'd had to act. Reid and Jace had brought her past the edge of conscious control. Never had she felt so purely carnal, so worshipped and desired. And there was more to come.

Her knees wobbled at the thought. She'd managed to avoid a panic attack so far, but she feared the boys weren't going to leave the toys in the cabin unused. If she could stay focused on the pleasure, on the fact that these two men wouldn't harm her, maybe she could get past the whole thing altogether. Conquer the panic, the flashbacks, the nightmares.

The three of them walked in silence through the quiet night. Without the pounding music and flashing lights, their triad suddenly seemed all the more intimate—Reid with his arm around her, Jace on the other side, clasping her hand. A little current of warmth, having nothing to do with sex, moved through her. She bit her lip. *Stop it.* This wasn't real. This was an act—a means to an end. When the sun rose three days from now, life would go back to normal. She couldn't let herself forget that.

They reached the cabin, and Reid released her to insert his key into the door. Jace let her step in front of him and before the door had even clicked shut, Reid yanked her against his solid chest, and Jace closed in behind her, pressing his heat against her back. She had no time to question, think, or second-guess. A fact for which she was grateful.

Reid's lips sought hers, and Jace's mouth feasted on her neck and shoulders. Being sandwiched between the two virile men sent all sentimental feelings draining out of her and desire fired up anew. Dual erections brushed her front and back, and she ground against them.

Reid broke from the kiss, his breaths ragged, his cool control fraying. "You've got too much fucking clothes on. Fix that, LeBreck."

"But leave the boots on," Jace added, a smile in his voice.

Reid stepped back and Jace joined him in front of her. Both crossed their arms over their chests, waiting, watching. The low lamplight in the room played off the angles in their faces, casting them in shadows, making the two of them look even more foreboding. She hugged herself, rubbing a chill off her arms. "Aren't y'all going to undress, too?"

The corner of Reid's mouth lifted. "All in good time, sugar. In fact, maybe we'll let you do that for us."

Her gaze traced over them—the two friends a study in contrast—dark and light, intense and carefree. But all nice to look at. She looked forward to unwrapping each one of them to see what lay beneath their clothes.

With shaking hands, she made quick work of unlacing her top and shimmying out of her leather skirt. Her panties hadn't made it back on—they were probably tucked in some cushion of the couch in the club. She stepped out of the puddle of clothes and stood their stark naked before them, save for the boots. She didn't know what to do with her hands, lifting them first to cross over her, then dropping them at her sides.

Jace's hungry look slid shamelessly over her, and Reid's fingers flexed as if he were having a hard time not reaching out to touch her. Reid took her hand and pulled her closer to them. "God, you're beautiful. Even better than I remember."

She knew he had to say something like that so she would feel confident enough to stand there and not dash to cover up. But for some reason, she believed he wasn't feeding her a line. Her cheeks warmed and she lowered her eyes. "Thanks, Reid. I, uh, I mean, sir."

He put his finger beneath her chin and tilted her face toward him. "No, it's okay. I like the sound of my name on your lips. Feel free to scream it later."

A small smile fought to show itself—some things hadn't changed. The more turned-on he got, the cockier he became. Somehow she found that little glimpse of the boy she used to know comforting. He ticked his head in Jace's direction. "Why don't you get us out of these clothes, sugar. It's getting a little warm in here."

She turned to Jace, who gave her a quick wink. "Go for it, doll."

She lifted her hands and worked down his white shirt, unbuttoning it until the material gaped open. He helped her work the shirt off, revealing smooth, golden skin stretched over lean muscles. An intricate tribal tattoo covered his left shoulder, snaking down his upper arm. She traced her fingers along the design and let her eyes indulge in him for a moment.

Reid chuckled from behind her. "Don't stare too long, Brynn. He'll start preening."

Jace showed Reid the backside of his middle finger, but amusement lit his green eyes. "She can look . . . and touch whatever she likes."

Brynn bit her lip and spun to face Reid. He'd already unbuttoned his own shirt, so she slid her palms along his broad shoulders and pushed it the rest of the way off. If Jace had the body of a swimmer, Reid was the football player. Strong and solid, arms that could envelop her and block out all thoughts of the outside world.

She walked her fingers down his chest and the planes of his flat stomach until she reached the smattering of dark hair trailing down to his belt. Remembering what lay beneath sent a little shudder of anticipation through her. She'd never admit it to Reid—she'd rather have bamboo shoved beneath her fingernails—but the sex she'd had with him all those years ago had never been topped. Even when they were that young, the guy knew how to wring out every ounce of pleasure from her.

His hands rubbed the goose bumps from her arms, and she moved to his belt buckle. Metal scraped metal as she unfastened it and crouched to ease his pants to the floor, leaving her eye level with the bulge in his boxer briefs. Forgetting that she was supposed to ask for permission, she reached out and stroked him through the soft cotton. He groaned and ran a hand over her hair.

The rustling of Jace getting out his pants sounded behind her, but she kept her eyes on Reid's face while she slipped his cock free of the material. Her fist wrapped around him. Mmm, suede over steel. As if on instinct, she moved to her knees, the need to taste him coursing through her. She swirled her tongue over the smooth tip, tasting the salt on his skin and the bit of fluid that glistened there.

He leaned back against the wall and closed his eyes. "You're breaking the rules, sugar, but fuck if I can bring myself to stop you."

Jace tugged at her collar from behind, pulling her lips away from Reid. "Let me help with that, bro. This will be much more comfortable in the bedroom. And I promise we'll keep that lovely mouth of hers full."

Jace stepped in front of her—his own impressive erection jutting out proudly—and in one smooth motion, lifted her up and settled her face down over his shoulder. A sharp smack to her ass made her jump. "That's for not having patience, doll. Now you've gone and made Reid so hot, he may not be nice enough to wait for you to get off again before we fuck you."

To her horror, a whimper of need slipped out of her. Where the hell had her pride gone? She should tell them to go screw themselves, that she'd be just fine without their help. But the throbbing between her legs didn't believe it. No, her whole body ached for a release that she knew only they could give her. "I'm sorry."

Jace carried her to the bedroom, and Reid's footsteps followed behind. Jace dumped her onto the bed without ceremony, and her eyes widened at the erotic overload of seeing both men standing before her—naked and undeniably turned on. Reid nodded at the wall behind her. "Help me bind her. Facedown. I want that pretty ass in the air."

A ripple of anxiety quivered through her, but she turned to lie on her stomach. She could do this; she *would* do this. Her rapist, whoever that bastard was, would not continue to hold her hostage. Panic wouldn't kill her. She squeezed her eyes shut and focused on keeping her breathing even. *This is not against my will. I want this—want them. I can stop at any time.*

Chains clinked and supple leather wrapped around each of her wrists. Her heart hammered against her ribs. *Breathe.* Each man yanked a bit at the bindings to make sure the cuffs were secure.

"Lift your head," Reid instructed.

When she did, he moved toward her with a satin mask. She reared back, rattling the metal chains connecting her to the wall and shaking her head. "No. No blindfold. Please."

Reid frowned, his eyebrows drawing together as he stared at her. The fear must've been apparent on her face because instead of pushing the issue or telling her she wasn't in charge, he nodded and set the mask on the side table. "On your knees, LeBreck. Eyes closed."

With a sigh of relief, she drew her knees beneath her and laid her cheek against the cool comforter. The sound of drawers being opened and rummaged through filled her ears. She hadn't had time to explore the contents of the dresser when she was in the room before, but she suspected it wasn't filled with socks and T-shirts.

"I saw her eyeing this one in my store," Jace said. "It may make her think twice about disobeying us again."

A loud *thwack* echoed through the quiet room as the leather strips of the flogger striped across her ass. She bucked against the impact, but didn't have time to catch her breath before another blow rained down on her. Her teeth bit into her lip as she waited for the stinging pain to morph into the burn of pleasure.

The bed dipped and Reid's familiar scent moved over her while Jace continued punishing her rear and the backs of her thighs. She moaned as a hot palm slid along her belly.

"Jace is a fucking master with a flogger, but I know you like a little pain, don't you, Brynn?" His fingers parted her folds and buried inside her needy channel. Her body clenched around him, aching for more. She spread her knees wider and the tails of Jace's flogger flirted with the crack of her ass. "Oh, yeah, you're loving it, aren't you?"

Reid pulled his hand back, and she writhed in protest. The strips of leather smacked her pussy and she cried out—the crazy pain/pleasure combination nearly sending her into instant orgasm.

"Fuck," Jace said, his voice strained. "I'm usually good at this whole patience thing, but she's killing me. I've been waiting a goddamned decade to share her with you."

Reid rose from the bed and smoothed a hand over her burning ass. The crackle of a condom wrapper was the best sound she'd heard all day.

A finger tapped her cheek. "Open your eyes and let me under you, doll."

She cracked her eyes open to find Jace fisting his cock and staring at her with a hooded gaze. She rose on her elbows and let him settle against the headboard. Her mouth watered at the sight of his thick erection—the tip glossy. Reid's deep voice rumbled from behind her. "Suck his cock, Brynn. You don't get to come until we do."

She leaned forward and took Jace into her mouth, pressing her tongue along the vein on the base of his shaft and earning a shudder of pleasure from him. "Holy shit. She may not have to wait long."

As she worked her tongue and mouth on Jace, Reid grabbed her hips and pressed his cock against her slick entrance. She canted her body toward him, silently begging. If he didn't get inside her in the next three seconds, she might drop the sub protocol and start yelling at him. Reid plunged forward, filling and stretching her, and she moaned against Jace.

Reid begin to pump forward at a steady pace, but Jace, way past slow and easy, grabbed her hair and fucked her mouth—all the while showering her with deliciously dirty endearments. Reid soon sped up to match Jace's rhythm, and Brynn could do nothing but ride the freight train with them—pushing them all toward mutual oblivion. Knowing she was driving both men to abandon, making the always-in-control alphas lose their shit, only served to ratchet up the intensity of her oncoming release more.

Her insides melted around Reid, the familiar feel of him almost too much bear. As he continued to rock into her, he reached around to tease her clit, sending contagious need to every molecule in her body. She sucked in deep breaths through her nose, trying to hold off on her orgasm until he gave her the go ahead.

Jace's grip tightened against her scalp and he pushed deeper, forcing her to relax her throat. His cock seemed to swell thicker, and with one last strangled growl, hot fluid splashed onto her tongue as he found his release.

"Goddamn," Reid said, increasing his tempo and strumming his fingers along her clit with new urgency. "You look so fucking hot sucking him dry."

Jace scooted back, caressing her hair as she rested her cheek against his thigh, and Reid continued to thrust into her with abandon. Lava flowed through her veins, ready to burst free and send her into the ether.

Reid's hand moved from her hip to her sweat-glazed tailbone, then down to the dimple above her buttocks. "Hmm, should I let you come or should I take you here first?"

His finger slid down the crack of her ass and teased her forbidden opening. Horror twined with the physical pleasure of the stimulation. No, not that. She couldn't handle that. She shook her head, but her voice had left her. The moistened tip of his finger pushed against her muscles and slipped in. Tears pricked her eyes and her breathing turned short and choppy. Her body wanted it, loved the sensation, but her mind had gone on red alert.

His voice soothed as his finger slowly moved back and forth. "Mmm, so tight. Can't imagine how good this would feel around my cock."

Her orgasm came hard and fast, but the panic was right on its tail. Her voice scraped against her throat as she called Reid's name over and over again. Reid, oblivious to the inner battle warring within her, thrust harder and faster, chasing his own release. Her lungs strained for air, but she couldn't seem to catch a breath. Blackness edged her vision.

A sharp ringing began in her ears, and the hands on her suddenly weren't Reid's or Jace's; they were coarse and unrelenting. Unwanted. The scent of sweat and her own fear filled her nostrils, and she was dragged back to a darkened storage room. A stranger invading her.

No. No. No. Oh, God. Dizziness overwhelmed her, and she

struggled for just one tiny breath, but there was no air to be found.

———

Jace's worried voice cut through the end of Reid's orgasm. "Shit, man. Stop. Something's wrong."

Reid lids snapped open as he pulled out of Brynn. Her body collapsed in a limp heap on the bed. What the hell?

"Brynn, sugar, you okay?" She didn't respond, and fear squeezed his chest. "Jesus, check her breathing."

Jace put a hand near her lips. "She's breathing. I think—I think she passed out."

Reid closed his eyes and blew out a breath. *Thank God, she's okay.* He climbed to his feet and laid a hand against her clammy cheek. "Watch her. I'll go grab a cool rag and some water."

Reid returned from the bathroom with the supplies and a robe wrapped around him. He tossed another robe at Jace. "Here, let me get next to her. And get these bindings off her arms."

Jace moved out of the way and went to work while Reid gently turned Brynn over and pressed the moist towel against her forehead. "Come on, sugar. Wake up for me."

He'd sensed a shift in her when he'd touched her ass, but when she didn't use her safe word, he'd thought she was just reacting to a new sensation. Maybe he'd hurt her . . . or scared her. Fuck. Why hadn't he stopped and checked on her?

He cradled her head in his lap, and she mumbled something incoherent. An urge to curl her into his arms and kick Jace out rolled through him. He tamped down the ridiculous thought and put the cool cloth to her cheek. "That's right. Come on."

Her eyes flew open on a sharp intake of breath, and terror crossed her features. She jolted upward but he put a hand on her shoulder and eased her back down. "Shh, it's okay, it's just me. You're okay."

She blinked, her pupils readjusting to the light. "Reid?"

He brushed her damp hair from her face. Her skin had taken on the pallor of the white bedsheets. "Yeah, babe. I've got you. I think you passed out on us."

She winced and pressed the heel of her hand to her brow bone.

Jace sank onto the other side of the bed and tossed a quilt over her. "What happened, doll? You all right?"

Reid helped her sit up a bit and offered her a glass of water. She took a small sip and then shook her head. "I think I may have hyperventilated or something."

Jace squeezed Brynn's hand, an odd expression passing over his face. "Did something trigger that?"

"No." She shot Jace a look of . . . warning. "I guess you guys are just a lot to handle."

Reid's jaw tightened and the wan smile she offered the both of them did nothing to alleviate the bitter taste crossing his tongue. "What the fuck are you two not telling me?"

Jace's eyes shifted away, and Brynn stiffened. "What do you mean?"

Reid rose from the bed and glared down at the two of them. "You've always been a terrible liar, Brynn. Tell me what's going on. Obviously, your best bud Jace knows."

Jace slid off the bed, his frown deep. "I think I'm going to head out and let you two chat." He leaned over and kissed Brynn's forehead. "Thanks for tonight, gorgeous."

Reid stepped out of the way to let Jace exit, but his gaze never left Brynn, who'd gone even paler. She tucked her knees to her chest and wrapped the blanket around herself, vulnerability rolling off her. He walked over to the bed and perched on the corner, then took a deep breath to make sure his bubbling frustration didn't come out in his voice. "What's going on?"

Her shoulders rose and fell with a deep sigh of resignation. "I had a panic attack and hyperventilated."

His brows knitted. He didn't know what he'd expected her to say, but that wasn't it. "A panic attack over what?"

She dropped her gaze, taking an interest in an unraveling thread of the quilt. "Certain things, sexual things, trigger them."

A creeping discomfort tracked up his spine. "Like what?"

"Like blindfolds and like . . ." She continued to worry the string between her fingers.

"Anal sex," he filled in.

She glanced up, her eyes haunted, and nodded. "Yeah."

Back when they'd been together, he'd touched her there before, and they certainly had used blindfolds. So something had changed. A sick feeling settled in the pit of his stomach. "Why, Brynn?"

She shook her head, avoiding his eyes.

"Tell me why," he commanded.

"Because I lied to you back then. I wasn't seeing someone behind your back," she said, her voice dead of emotion. "Someone raped me."

At first, he couldn't make sense of the words she'd uttered—the sheer shock sending his brain into a spin. No cheating? Rape. Brynn. *Raped.* His reply came out in a roar. *"What?"*

She flinched and shrank in on herself even more. "The night I broke up with you, I'd just been attacked."

He shot up from the bed, his body burning with rage. He needed to punch something—no, someone—the bastard who did this to her. His fists balled, and he forced himself to breathe. "Why didn't you tell someone? Call the police? Or for God's sake, tell *me*? I went to you that night."

She shook her head. "I couldn't. He threatened me—my family. And I was so confused. He told me you had a real girlfriend, that I was only your whore. And then when I saw your picture in the paper a few days later with Vanessa, I knew he'd told me the truth."

He raked a hand through his hair and leaned against the dresser. His guts had been torn out the night he and Brynn had broken up. But God, had he been so hurt, so angry that he'd missed the fact that she'd needed help? "Jesus, Brynn. You didn't even let me explain about Vanessa. I would've helped you. And I would've fucking killed the guy who did it to you."

She frowned and rubbed her arms through the blanket. "You wouldn't have had the chance. I still have no idea who he was."

He closed his eyes, a piercing pain slicing through his skull. "I'm so sorry I wasn't there for you back then, but I'm listening now. Tell me what happened to you."

SIXTEEN

then

Brynn thought the blindfold was part of the surprise. Reid had promised something special tonight, but he hadn't clued her in as to what exactly he had in mind. She smiled as the dark fabric blocked out the low lights of the storage room. "You're early."

Lips pressed against the back of her neck. Hot hands caressed her shoulders, her arms. "Shh . . ."

She shivered beneath the touch. So he was going to be Mr. Serious Dom tonight. Alrighty. She wet her lips. "Yes, sir."

He grabbed her forearms with firm fingers and pulled them behind her back. Instead of the usual cloth or rope, something less forgiving circled her wrists—plastic? A quick zipping sound filled the silent room as he yanked on the bindings, tightening them to the point of discomfort. "Ouch, hey. Could you loosen those up a bit?"

With a grunt, he gave another pull, and the zip tie bit into her flesh deeper. She squirmed and tried to turn around, but he gripped her shoulder and held her in place.

"No, come on, I'm serious. That hurts. *Ruby*," she said, using the word Reid had told her would signal to him something was wrong.

His chuckle was low and sent a chill through her insides. "Is that the special word you use with him?"

The unfamiliar whisper made her jolt forward, panic seizing her, but the stranger wrapped an arm around her neck and dragged her against him. A scream ripped from her throat.

His hand slapped her across the mouth and his whisper turned fierce. "Now, now, no yelling. You can fight all you want, that'll make it better. But keep that big mouth shut or I'll find something to shove in it. Got it?"

She nodded, tears flooding her eyes. When he released her mouth, words tumbled out of her. "Please, let me go. My boyfriend's on the way. He'll be here any minute. If you go now, I promise I won't say anything."

"Ah, Brynn. So naive. Your *boyfriend* won't be making it. He's at an event with his real girlfriend, Vanessa."

The wind left her lungs. This asshole knew her name? My God, this was someone she knew? The rest of his statement registered, and she shook her head. "No, that's not true. We have plans. *I'm* his girlfriend."

"Oh, sweetheart. Haven't you realized it yet? You're just his whore." The smile in his disguised whisper rang in her ears. "You think he's going to parade around trash like you on his arm?"

The words stung as much as the bindings around her wrists. She couldn't muster a response.

"Of course not. But even though you're only temporary, whores like you have a way of fucking up the lives of perfectly good men, and I'm not going to let that happen." He pet her head like she was a dog, and her whole body began to shake with terror. "So after tonight, you're going to end things with him. Otherwise, this won't be the last time we meet. Only next time, maybe I'll take that sweet little sister of yours for a ride instead. I wonder if she likes being treated like a slut as much as you do."

An inhuman scream of rage ripped from her lungs, and his hand clamped around her neck with crushing force.

"Shut the fuck up, you stupid bitch, and let's see how rough you like it."

Blackness edged her vision as she fought for breath.

His other hand moved to the neckline of her blouse and ripped downward, shredding the delicate fabric and her world all in one swift motion.

———

Reid tucked the last surprise next to the silver promise ring nestled in the box and smiled. Brynn would probably think he was being high-handed and had lost his mind, but he hoped once she got past that, she'd be excited. He'd agonized over the decision his aunt and uncle had laid at his feet, and he still had a burning ball of guilt in his stomach. But the last few months had been the most amazing of his life, and he couldn't bear to let the woman responsible flit off to Austin without showing her how serious he was about her. He just hoped against hope that if it worked out between them, that one day his family would accept her.

He hadn't said the words "I love you" to Brynn yet; he'd been too afraid to scare her off, but he'd known them to be true since his trip to Galveston. Tonight, he'd tell her—lay his feelings and his plan out there and see what she thought.

He checked his watch—fifteen minutes before he was supposed to pick her up at the office. She'd insisted on working late again to squeeze in any last overtime hours she could get. Too bad he couldn't tell her he already had the apartment she'd been saving up for taken care of. He'd put the deposit down on hers and the one across the hall from it a week ago.

He tucked the box with the key to that apartment and the ring into his jacket pocket and headed out of the house to his car, feeling lighter than he had in days. But as soon as he rounded the corner, the little zip in his step died. Vanessa Thomas was sitting on his hood, a big smile lighting her face. "Ooh, you look nice. But that may be kind of dressy for an outdoor party."

His brows drew together, still processing her sudden appearance. "What are you doing here, Ness?"

She hopped off the car and brushed invisible dirt from her white tennis skirt. "Your aunt said you'd go with me to the Stevens' barbecue tonight. Didn't she mention it to you? Both she and your uncle are going."

"Um, not so much," he said, scratching the back of his head. "And I'm really sorry, but I have plans tonight."

She stuck her bottom lip out as if it held some magic power to change his mind. "But I can't go by myself—how would *that* look? Lauren Gates is going to be there and you know she'll never let me here the end of it if I show up without a date."

Reid closed his eyes and counted to three. *Be nice.* He'd been accompanying Vanessa to events over the summer to make his aunt and uncle happy, and she really was a great girl. But she wasn't Brynn. "Ness, I really can't."

Her pout lifted into a coy smile. "Come on. After the party, we can hang out at my place. My parents went to the lake house for a few days, so we'll have it all to ourselves."

He had to stifle a laugh. So, Miss I-Wear-a-True-Love-Waits-Ring was ready to have him over for dessert. *Guess true love only waits until the parents are out of town.* He shook his head. A few months ago, he would've jumped on the opportunity to entertain the pretty debutante for the weekend. But the thought held no appeal anymore.

The only person he wanted curled up next to him in his bed was Brynn. *His* Brynn. Who was going to be pissed if he showed up late for their big date. "Wow, I appreciate the offer, but I can't break this commitment. I'm sorry you came all the way out here."

As he stepped past her and hit the unlock button on his keypad, she reached out and grabbed his arm. "Hey, wait. My dad dropped me off. I didn't bring a car."

Motherfucker. He glanced at his watch and sighed. The Stevens' house was at least ten minutes out of the way. "Fine, get in, I'll drop you off on my way."

She smiled and lifted on tiptoes to plant a kiss on his cheek. "Great, and maybe you can just stop in for a minute and say hi."

———

Reid took the turn into Brynn's driveway on two wheels. Vanessa had insisted he walk her into the party, and she'd roped him into a photo-op for the society section of the newspaper and half a dozen introductions. Then, his aunt and uncle had dragged him into a conversation with the mayor. Now he was a solid hour late for his date with Brynn. He'd stopped by the office to pick her up, but she'd already left. And she wasn't answering her phone.

Damn it. He'd wanted tonight to go perfectly and he'd screwed that up. Hopefully, once she saw what he had planned she'd forgive him.

He hustled up the sidewalk and knocked on her door, praying that she wasn't too upset with him, but no one answered. *Oh, come on.* Her car was in the driveway, so he knew she had to be home. Was she mad enough not to answer the door? She usually wasn't that easily angered.

He knocked again, and the door finally cracked open. He opened his mouth to launch into his apology speech, but when he took in Brynn's state, the words died on his lips.

Brynn was dressed in gray sweats, her hair damp from a shower, and her eyes bloodshot and puffy.

"Sugar, what's wrong? Are you okay?" he asked, reaching out for her.

She shrunk back before he touched her. "I . . . uh . . . I'm not feeling very well. I think I may have the flu."

He frowned. "Oh, no, that sucks. Is there anything I can do? Obviously, you can't go out, but do you want me to go pick up some soup and we can watch movies or something?"

She shook her head, and he had the impression that she may burst into tears. "No, but can you come in for a minute? We need to talk."

He tucked his keys in his pocket. "Yeah, of course."

She walked back into her living room and he followed, shutting the door behind him. She curled into the chair and tucked her knees to her chest. He had to stop himself from going over to her, picking her up and holding her. He'd never seen her look so miserable.

He sat on the couch. "Look, before you start, I just want to tell you, I am so sorry for being late. I got hung up and couldn't get away. And I tried to call, but then I couldn't reach you. And I feel like a dick."

She looked up at him, her face emotionless. "We've got to end this."

The words hit him like an anvil to the gut and halted his rambling. "Wait, what?"

Her eyes went watery, and she quickly swiped at her face with her sweatshirt-covered hands. "I'm sorry, Reid. But this—us—has to end."

"Us?" His heart began to pound in his ears and panic edged in. Where the hell had this come from? "No. I don't understand."

She looked down, staring at the now damp sleeves of her shirt. "You knew this had an expiration date. We agreed to have a summer thing. Summer's over. I'm leaving."

He sat forward on the sofa, hope entering his voice. "But it doesn't have to end. That's what I was going to tell you tonight. There are ways we can work this out. I can go to Austin with you."

Her head snapped up, her reddened eyes wide. "You want to move?"

He smiled. "Yeah, sugar. I want to be with you. Wherever that is."

She shook her head, her tears returning. "No, you can't."

Screw the flu. He got off the couch and went to crouch in front of her chair, laying a tentative hand on her knee. "Baby, sure I can. I don't know what the future holds. But all I know is I don't want to let you go. Nothing is holding me here, and in Austin, we won't even have to worry about anyone seeing us. We can just be together—wherever and whenever we want."

She squeezed her eyes shut and stayed that way for a moment before taking a deep, shaky breath. Her voice came out flat. "There's someone else, Reid. I have a boyfriend waiting for me in Austin. This was just supposed to be a fling. I love *him*."

All sounds in the room suddenly seemed painfully loud. The ticking clock above the couch, the used car salesman on TV, the hum of the box fan on the other side of the room. His hand slipped off her knee, and he sank back onto his heels.

A lump the size of a grapefruit lodged in his throat. "There's *someone else*? Why didn't you tell me? Why—?"

"The same reason why you didn't tell me about Vanessa."

He sucked in a sharp breath. "It's not like that, she's not—"

"So that's not who you were with tonight?" she asked, her voice more sad than angry.

His stunned silence gave her the answer.

"How long would it take for you to get tired of me? To want someone who fits into your life. We come from different worlds. This just wasn't meant to be." She rose from the chair and gave him one last lingering look before turning her back to him. "Please just go. I won't be returning to work. I wish you the best, Reid."

And with that, the only girl he'd ever loved walked out of his life.

—————

Brynn locked herself in her bedroom and waited until she heard the front door close before crumpling into a ball on the floor, wishing she could shut her eyes and not wake up again. But every time her eyelids closed, the feel of the monster's hands crawled over her skin, and images of Reid's brokenhearted face tore through her.

There was no escape. No safe corner in her mind. Maybe never would be again.

So she cried and stared blankly at the peeling paint on the base-boards, letting the sobs wrack her abused body well into the night, until she was only a husk of the person she had been a few hours before. Until she felt dead inside.

SEVENTEEN

now

Brynn nestled deeper into the crook of Reid's arm, the bed squeaking beneath her, and he ran his palm over her hair. She'd told him everything, dragged out the nasty innards of what had happened to her, and laid it out there unedited.

He'd listened to every word—shock, sympathy, and anger crossing his face at different intervals. But to his credit, even though she could tell he'd had questions, he'd held his tongue and had let her finish without interruption, as if sensing that if she'd paused, she wouldn't have been able to get it all out.

His chest rose and fell under her cheek as he drew in a deep breath and released it. "My God, Brynn. I don't even know what to say."

"It's okay. You don't have to say anything," she said, feeling tired, gutted.

He pressed his lips to the crown of her head, and his voice turned strained. "This was all my fault. If I hadn't been late, I could've stopped him."

"No," she said, sitting up so she could face him. "Don't do

that. The rape was *not* your fault. It was that psycho's fault, who-ever he is."

He shook his head, his jaw set. "No, I could've helped. Could've been there for you."

The guilt in his words tore at her. "I didn't let you. I almost broke down and called you about a week later. But then I saw the photo in the paper of you and Vanessa at that party, and I figured you were probably better off. It's not like I would've been able to continue the kind of relationship we had. You saw what happened earlier. Blindfolds, being restrained, aggressive guys—it all can set off panic attacks or flashbacks for me now."

He grimaced. "Why didn't you tell me when we got here? I would've never made you do all this. We could've done the bare minimum to get by."

"Talking about the details of that night just drags me back there, so I didn't want to open myself up to that again. Plus, I thought coming here could be a cure. Sometimes throwing yourself totally into the fear can fix it." She looked down at her hands. "I'm so tired of feeling this way, letting it interfere with my life. I wanted to see if I could force myself past it, have a shot at a normal life, a chance at finding a normal relationship."

He scrubbed a hand over his face. "I feel like such an asshole. I pushed you harder than I ever have. You must've been miserable the whole time we've been here."

She gave a half-smile. "Well, not the *whole* time. You and Jace made it a bit difficult to focus on anything but the two of you. I thought the rip-off-the-Band-Aid method was working, but then—"

He frowned. "I took it too far. I was so wrapped up in my own crap that I wasn't paying attention to your signals. I'm so sorry."

She shrugged. "It's okay. You didn't know. It was stupid for me to think I could get over it that easily. Clearly, I'm too screwed up for a quick fix. I just hope I can make it through tomorrow night without completely losing it again."

He reached out and rubbed her knee. "Don't be so hard on yourself. You're not screwed up—you've been through hell. The fact that you had the balls to come here in the first place is amazing. If you want to skip tomorrow night, I can go alone—try to track Kelsey down for you."

"No, it's okay. She's not going to be willing to talk to anyone but me. I'll figure out a way to get through it. And if the panic takes over, I'll have you and Jace there to help me."

"I'll be there for whatever you need."

The sincerity emanating from his blue eyes sent hazy warmth through her. She leaned forward and kissed him lightly on the lips. "Thank you."

With this thumb, he swiped away the lone tear that had slipped past her lids. "Thanks for finally trusting me with the truth."

Without considering the consequences, she dipped back down, seeking a deeper kiss. She knew it was dangerous, stupid. But after rehashing the rape, she needed to erase the ugliness of the last hour. She didn't want to think about that night or the daunting task of finding her sister tomorrow or all the reasons why she needed to avoid Reid now. All she wanted to do was bury herself in the feeling she used to get when it was just the two of them—like no problem in the world was too big to tackle.

Reid's eyebrows rose in surprise when her mouth touched his again, but after a second's pause, he slipped his fingers along the nape of her neck and drew her in closer. His tongue parted her lips, and his other hand drifted to the small of her back. Instead of the frantic need that had colored their earlier encounter, he took a languid pace with his kiss and explored her mouth with heated tenderness, savoring her.

He eased back against the pillows, lowering her until her

breasts pressed into the solid planes of his chest. Her muscles melted against him, and she sank into the moment—relishing his flavor, the feel of his stubble against her face, the scent of fading cologne and man. If she could bottle minutes, she would capture these.

Too soon, Reid withdrew and stared up at her with conflicted eyes. He cradled the side of her face. "It's been a long night, sugar. How about I go run you a hot bath?"

She pressed her forehead against his, recognizing a retreat when she saw it. A swift reminder that despite their heartfelt conversation, this situation was only a means to an end and sex. Intimate make-out sessions could lead nowhere good. She rolled off him and stretched, noticing for the first time how her muscles ached. "Sounds heavenly."

He climbed off the bed and belted his robe, his smile warm, but his stance stiff. "Be back in a few minutes, sugar."

True to his word, he returned to the bedroom a little while later and lifted her off the bed. She laughed. "You were a lot to handle, but I *can* still walk, ya know?"

"You wound me," he said with mock hurt. "But I'm carrying you anyway. I've put you through a lot tonight, let me take care of you."

He nudged open the bathroom door with his foot and carried her into the lavish bathroom. Instant warmth kissed her skin. He'd lit the candles around the edge of the enormous Jacuzzi tub and the scent of lavender wafted off the curls of steam rising from the water. "Wow, now that is what I call drawing a bath."

He set her on her feet and pulled off the T-shirt she'd borrowed from him. He smiled down at her, his eyes dark in the flickering candlelight. "Glad you approve."

She tugged at the knot in his robe. "You joining me?"

He palmed her bare hip and drew her closer. "You're in charge right now, babe. You tell me."

She yanked the tie harder and his robe fell open, revealing miles of muscle and rugged male beauty. Her hands moved to his chest, her fingertips exploring the lines of his collarbone, his sternum, the cut of his wide shoulders. She pushed off the robe the rest of the way. "I think I don't want to be alone with my thoughts right now."

He caught one of her hands and brought it to his lips, placing a kiss in the center of her palm. "Then I'd be honored to join you."

With the ease of a child picking up a doll, he swept her back into his arms and carried her to the tub to lower her in. The heat enveloped her and her aching muscles, inspiring a long, satisfied sigh. Once he had her safely immersed, he climbed in and settled behind her, letting her recline against his chest.

She caught their intertwined reflection in the mirrored wall at the foot of the tub. "The mirror isn't steaming over."

"They probably treat it with something so nothing interferes with the view. They think of everything here." He kissed her shoulder. "Comfortable?"

She let her hands drift along the strong thighs that framed her. "You may need to carry me out afterward. I think my muscles have liquefied."

"It would be my pleasure," he said, his voice right next to her ear. "I'll carry you anywhere you want to go."

He reached for a sponge on the side of the bathtub and squirted it with vanilla-scented soap. With slow, methodical strokes, he began to wash her neck and shoulders, working the knots of tension from them. Her mind was a twisted mess, but the combination of shear emotional and physical exhaustion and Reid's skilled hands were swiftly lulling her into a hazy, almost numb state.

He grazed a finger over the scar that marred the back of her left shoulder, and she momentarily tensed. But when he didn't ask about it, she relaxed again, closed her eyes, and leaned forward so he could reach her back. "Aren't I supposed to be doing this for you, *Master*?"

He chuckled, but continued washing. "You can remove that tongue of yours from your cheek, smart-ass. First of all, you're not my slave. Even if this weekend were real, that's not what I'm into. And secondly, you're assuming I don't get pleasure from taking care of you like this. Believe me, washing your naked body is no hardship."

His hands slid over her rib cage, and she sank back against him while he scrubbed circles over her belly. She mulled over what he'd said for a moment. "What do you mean, that's not what you're into? I thought the whole slave thing was what this was all about."

"I love taking sexual control of a woman—especially one who's used to being in charge in the rest of her life. Love bringing her to a level of release she didn't even know she could reach. But I'm not looking to take it outside of that realm or have a partner submit to me twenty-four seven like a lot of the people here. That holds no appeal for me."

She chewed her lip, considering his answer. "So you're just looking to have a good time with someone, then go home to your normal life."

He sighed. "Pretty much. I've learned the hard way that relationships and this scene don't mix well for me. But I can't shut off the desire—it's part of who I am. So yeah, now that I'm divorced, I'll probably join a club and keep the play separate from the rest of my life."

A bitter taste filled her mouth. "And keep it a secret from whoever you're with?"

His hands paused, and she could feel him bristle beneath her. "No, despite what you thought happened when we were dating, I don't cheat. All I'm saying is that I've done the marriage and commitment thing, I don't need to do it again."

She swirled her fingers in the bubbles. "And you think you can be happy just having random hookups at some club?"

His shrug sent a ripple through the water. "Works for Jace."

She pursed her lips, not sure why Reid's plan annoyed her so much. What did she care about how he chose to live his life? Her mind drifted to all the subs she'd passed in the club last night, all the women who had sent envious glances her way. Would one of those women be kneeling at his feet next weekend? The thought made her intestines knot.

"What's running through that busy mind of yours?"

Her eyes traveled to the mirror and met his probing blue stare. She quickly shifted her focus to one of the candles on the side of the bathtub, scrabbling to come up with another thought to share besides the one she'd been having. "It amazes me that people can go into this kind of dynamic with strangers. I mean, for the dom it's not as much of a risk, you hold the control. But for the sub . . . there's so much trust that needs to be there. Even if I wasn't dealing with my panic attacks, I can't imagine willingly turning myself over to someone I didn't know."

He nuzzled the curve of her shoulder. "It's definitely not something to enter lightly with strangers. If you ever get the urge to sub again, you can come to whatever club I join. I'll make sure you're well taken care of."

"Thanks, but I'm not that girl anymore." Even if she could get past her anxiety, she had no desire to live some clandestine double life. Growing up, she'd expended enough energy hiding her mother's secrets and feeling ashamed. Never again would she be the subject of hushed neighborhood whispers.

No, after this weekend, her dalliance with sexual submission was done for good. She would move on and continue searching for the guy who would fit into the vision she had for her future. Nice suburban home, a few kids, maybe a dog—the kind of normal, respectable existence she'd only been able to glimpse from afar growing up.

"Who are you, then?" he asked, his voice quiet.

The question hung in the air, taunting her. How could she reconcile the woman she thought herself to be with the one who'd melted under the commands and hands of the man sitting behind her? One who'd let two men tie her up and enjoyed it? She shook her head, a lump lodging in her throat.

"Shh, never mind," he said, apparently sensing her darkening mood. "No stress allowed in the bathtub."

The sponge moved higher, over her navel, the ripples of her ribs, tickling the underside of her breasts. His movements were gentle, but not tentative—as if he sensed the only way to pull her from her spiraling thoughts was to draw her back into her senses. It was his gift and one of the reasons he'd been so addictive back when they'd dated. He'd always been able to quiet the storm for her, bring her into a place where all she had to do was listen to his commands and feel his touch. A welcome respite from the constant beehive of worries and responsibilities in her mind.

The mild abrasiveness of the sponge crested the curve of her breast and moved over the distended nipples. Darts of pleasure trekked from the point of contact outward, chasing the tension that had tiptoed into her tendons back into the shadows. She let out a little murmur of appreciation and stretched her leg onto the edge of the tub.

A rumble of Jacuzzi jets cut through the quiet room, startling her, and fat bubbles broke through the still water. "Uh-oh, I must've hit a button."

He kept his attention on her breasts, dropping the sponge and soaping the swells with his agile hands. "It's okay. Might as well enjoy all the tub has to offer."

She tilted her head back and arched into his touch. He gave her needy buds a firm pinch and the sensation shot straight to another swelling bud between her thighs.

"Just lay back and relax, sugar." His hands moved down until they slid to the outside of her thighs. She offered no resistance as he tucked his palms under her knees and spread her legs wide, positioning her in the direct line of one of the jets.

"Oh!" She jerked back as the warm current of water pulsed against her already sensitive clit, but he kept her in place, holding her as well as any restraints ever could.

"Let me make up for ruining your pleasure earlier. I promise I won't let you drown." He dragged his tongue along her shoulder, lapping up the droplets of water beading there. "Mmm, and maybe I won't let you dry off after the bath. I might just lick you clean instead."

She moaned at the image he'd painted and at the relentless throb of water against her. Already, the coils of need inside her were tightening to the breaking point. Her body arched, sending water sloshing out of the tub and onto the tiled floor. She dug her nails into his thighs, trying to keep herself from slipping fully under the water. "Reid. I can't—"

"Shh, give in to it. I have you. Just let go, let it all go, and trust that I'm here."

The jets were like legions of hot tongues flicking, caressing, and nibbling her most sensitive nerves all at the same time. Tremors coursed through her, sending bigger and bigger waves of pleasure splashing over her, building toward the tsunami she knew was lingering in the distance.

Reid eased her thighs wider, opening her completely, giving them both a view of her water-slicked nudity in the mirror. He nipped at the back of her neck but kept his eyes focused on the reflection. "You're so beautiful when you let go. Let me watch you come for me."

As if his command willed it, the jets shifted to just the right spot and her nerve endings exploded into bright bursts of sparkling pleasure. A hoarse cry ripped from her throat, echoing off the walls in the room, and her body thrashed against him. He held her in place until she was almost at the edge of sanity, then swiftly kicked off the Jacuzzi and released her legs to sink back against him.

He gathered her closer to him, turning her, and tucked her head under his chin. Her body continued to quiver with aftershocks as he rubbed a gentle hand up and down her back. When she finally stilled, he slipped an arm under her knees. "Let's get you out of here and into bed. It's been a long night."

He set her on the closed lid of the toilet and toweled her off with patient attention. Her muscles felt like wet rubber bands, but the buzzing afterglow of her orgasm and the view of the sexy man before her had entertaining other ideas than sleep. Her eyes traveled over Reid's luscious backside as he bent to grab a T-shirt from his bag. He had slipped on a pair of boxer briefs, but before he had turned, she hadn't missed the ramrod erection he was sporting.

When he spun to face her again, he smirked. "LeBreck, are you checking me out?"

"Can't a girl look?

He laughed as he slipped the shirt over her head. "Sure, I give you permission to objectify me at any time."

She poked his side. "You're an arrogant bastard, you know that?"

He bent and laid a quick kiss on her lips. "You love it. Now come on, off to bed with you."

Reid carried Brynn into the bedroom and settled her beneath the covers. She closed her eyes and for the brief moment, he let himself drink in the view. The polished, put-together professional was nowhere to be found. Her makeup had long since worn off and her blond hair was starting to curl where it'd gotten wet. He loved seeing her like this—her only adornment the flushed hue of a woman well satisfied. If she were his, he'd make sure that she went to bed every night with that look.

He groaned inwardly. There he went again—thinking stupid shit about staking some claim on her. He'd already stuck a toe in dangerous waters, offering to take her on as a sub if she ever wanted to join him at a club. As if she'd ever be open to that after she found out why he was really here.

Didn't matter. She'd recoiled at the idea anyway. And how could he blame her? Brynn didn't want a guy who could offer her a weekend collar; she wanted one that would offer her a lifetime ring. Deserved it.

She shifted onto her elbow and peered up at him from under her lashes. "I think it's time you get a little TLC, too."

Her voice was as innocent as a spring morning, but the suggestion in those moss-colored eyes shot straight to his groin. "Sugar, it's almost three in the morning."

She nodded toward the now aching bulge in his shorts. "Doesn't look like your friend knows that."

He gave her a rueful smile. There'd be nothing he'd like more than to slide in bed next to her and keep her awake until the sun came up, but he knew better. Besides the fact that they needed to be rested for tomorrow, one-on-one sex with Brynn was not an option. "Don't worry about that. He can't help standing at attention anytime you're around. You've already given me more than enough tonight."

Her eyebrows lifted. "Since when have you gotten enough?"

He laughed and kissed the crown of her head. "Since I discovered years ago that you are absolutely insufferable without sleep. I refuse to subject myself or the rest of the resort to that tomorrow."

She pushed her lip out in a mock pout and shifted into a sitting position, bringing her thin T-shirt and the hard points of her nipples into clear view. "I'm not *that* bad."

"Uh-huh." He turned away from her and headed toward the closet, trying to think of anything besides how much he wanted to tear the shirt off her, seize those tight little buds with clamps, and test out that spanking bench taunting him at the end of the bed.

He'd lock her down on all fours, spread her wide so he could enjoy every detail of that smooth pussy, her sweet ass. He'd tease and pinch and nibble until her honey dripped down her thighs—until he knew she was aching just for him. Then he'd take her—utterly and completely—until she was so exhausted that all she'd be able to do when he was done with her would be to curl in his arms and let him hold her while she slept.

His erection hardened to the point of pain, and he had to stifle a groan. *Fuck*. He needed space. Air. Something. Before he broke every rule he'd set for himself coming into this thing. He yanked a pillow and extra blanket off the top shelf of the closet and spun to face her.

"Get some rest, LeBreck," he said, forcing a casual tone. "We have another full day ahead of us tomorrow."

Her attention zeroed in on the items in his hand. "You're not sleeping in here?"

"I'm a rough sleeper. It'll be best for both of us if I use the sofa bed out front." He knew the excuse was lame, knew she would see through it. But at the moment, he didn't care. He needed out of the room. Now.

A cool mask stole over her features, and he could almost see the mental retreat from the openness they'd shared a few minutes earlier. She leaned over and clicked off the bedside lamp, plunging them into shadows. "Don't forget to shut the door on your way out."

He cringed at the icy tone. He'd hurt her. He'd known it would, but if he stayed, he'd hurt her much worse. So without another word, he stepped out of the bedroom and put a solid wooden door between them—hoping it was strong enough to protect them both.

EIGHTEEN

now

Brynn sat on the side of the bed with her knees to her chest, staring out the window as the last glimmers of the setting sun peeked through the trees bordering the back of their cabin. She and Reid had wandered to every possible place on the grounds today—smiling, touching, acting like a couple. Convincing everyone within shouting distance that they were for real.

Almost convincing her.

She rubbed her burning eyes. Absolute exhaustion had overtaken the two of them late this afternoon, and Reid had suggested they come back to the cabin to shower and rest before the festival. He'd managed to fall asleep on the sofa bed. But, she'd only closed her eyes for a few seconds before uninvited thoughts had crawled into her brain and taken over like ants at a picnic.

When Reid had shut the door to the bedroom the night before, she'd been left with a feeling she hadn't experienced in a decade— a hollow, yawning ache deep inside her chest. A feeling of incompleteness. Of wanting. Needing. Forcing her to accept something she'd thought long dead.

She loved Reid. Probably had always loved him. And no matter how many miles, years, chapters of life she'd put between them, she couldn't run from the fact that some door within her only accepted Reid's key. Being with him again had flung that door wide open, yearning for him to step inside and stay awhile.

Only Reid had no interest in stepping over the threshold. Couldn't. He needed something she couldn't give him, and she wanted the kind of life he had no interest in.

She rested her chin on her knees and rocked, letting the realization that she was going to have to let him go all over again roll over her. She knew, technically, she didn't even have him this time. But when he'd held her last night, caressed away her fears, it had felt like he was hers and she his—if just for a few moments. A few perfect minutes.

Now there would be no more. At least not with him.

She prided herself on being able to tough things out in life, but she couldn't grit her teeth through this one. After the Bacchanal, there would be no more playacting with Reid. Every time he touched her, whispered her name, commanded her, she fell a little deeper into the hole. If she let herself tumble any further, she'd never be able to climb out. So before the party tonight, she needed to draw the line between them again so they could move forward and coexist. The only time he needed to touch her was at the Bacchanal. Period.

A light knock on the front door roused her from her thoughts. She stood and wrapped her robe around her. Quietly, she padded down the hallway and peeked into the living room. Reid was still splayed across the sofa bed, the sheets a tangled mess around his legs, and his bare chest rising and falling with heavy breaths. Every muscle in her body strained to move forward, to crawl into bed next to him, and bury her face in his neck—absorb his scent, his heat, his being.

The hole in her chest widened a bit more, and she forced her eyes away from the scene. She hurried to the front door and swung it open. No one was there, but two toga-style costumes were hanging from the hook on the front of the door and two familiar black bags sat on the doorstep. *Hallelujah.*

Careful not to make any noise, she grabbed her suitcase and purse and set them inside the door. A small white envelope with her name fell off the top of the larger bag. She slid open the sealed flap and pulled out the card.

> *Ms. LeBreck, your master informed us that you have earned the privilege of your things. If you need anything additional, please request it through him.*

> —*The Ranch Staff*

She rolled her eyes. So Reid could've have given her access to her clothes last night. Opportunistic bastard. But even as she thought the words, a smile touched her lips.

She lifted the costumes off the door hook and laid them over the back of a nearby chair, then closed the door. Reid flipped over to his stomach, providing her with a buffet of delicious skin and sinewy muscles, but seemed to still be in a deep sleep. Not surprising—the man had always slept like the dead.

She checked the clock over the dining room table. Still an hour before the festivities started. She didn't want to wake Reid yet since it wasn't time to go, but she was starting to feel a bit stir-crazy. Maybe she could take a walk toward the vineyards. All the private cabins were along that path and people would inevitably be heading out for the evening. Couldn't hurt to watch who was coming and going. Maybe she could intercept Kelsey before they even got to the party.

She headed to the bathroom with her costume, changed into the short, wine-colored toga, and twisted her hair into a knot.

Next, she fastened the leather collar that marked her as attached around her neck. The one-shouldered outfit definitely covered more than her ensemble from the night before, but she couldn't help wondering how long the costume would stay on at an event like this. She'd seen paintings of the bacchanals of Ancient Rome in her college art history class. It wasn't the fashion that had inspired lewd comments from the guys in the back row.

She smoothed the fabric with trembling hands and took a deep breath. *I will make it through tonight. I'll talk Kels into coming home with me. Everything's going to be fine.*

She gave a derisive snort, making a mental note to nix her practice of prescribing positive affirmation to her clients. Clearly, it was bullshit.

On quiet feet she made her way back through the living room and to the small dining room table. Reid had set a laptop bag next to one of the chairs and had placed his computer and a legal pad on the table. Apparently, she hadn't been the only one who'd had trouble sleeping the night before. She sat down in the chair and grabbed the pad so she could leave him a note, but frowned when she saw there was no pen in sight. Leaning down, she peered into his unzipped bag to see if one was in there.

She spotted one in an inner pocket and moved aside a few files to unzip the mesh pouch. But when she shoved aside the last one, the name on the manila folder caught her eye. After casting a quick look at Reid to make sure he was still asleep, she snatched the folder from the bag and laid it on the table next to the laptop.

Hank Caldwell. The name alone made acid rise in the back of her throat. Her mother's murderer.

And Reid's client.

Why would he have Hank's file in his bag? The case had been closed for two years, and the guy had gotten a life sentence—so no parole hearings to worry about. She drummed her fingers along the outside of the folder. She knew she shouldn't look. Didn't even know if she *wanted* to look. What if it contained copies of crime scene photos?

She'd seen the horrible scene in person and had done her best to block the images from her mind—though they still showed up in her nightmares from time to time. Her mother's lifeless body, the gunshot wound to the chest, all the blood. So much blood. And the feeling of complete despair that had overtaken her when she'd realized her mother was gone. Taken—right when she'd finally started to work toward a better life.

Her mom had hit six months of sobriety, was looking for a new place and a respectable job. Had even saved some money to get a fresh start. And then, *wham!* Gone forever. All because Hank Caldwell, Kelsey's druggie boyfriend, had heard about her mother's savings and needed cash to get that night's fix. Fucking psychopath.

And then to add vinegar to Brynn's open wounds, she'd shown up that first day in court to see Reid and his aunt Roslyn sitting next to the cold-blooded bastard. Defending him.

Apparently, Hank's wealthy family, who had previously disowned him because of his drug use, had jumped in at the last second to lawyer-up their son and pay the Jamisons' exorbitant legal fees.

She still didn't understand how Reid had stood by that man, touted his innocence, even when she'd begged him to drop the case. Was he really willing to defend anyone if the paycheck was right? She glanced over at him again, having trouble reconciling the guy in the courtroom back then with the man who'd come to the women's center to do pro bono work. Maybe the experience with Hank had changed him.

Regardless, she thanked God that he and his aunt had botched the case and lost. She'd never be able to sleep at night if she knew her mother's murderer was still roaming the streets.

She shook the memory from her mind and stared down at the folder again. She couldn't bear to see the crime photos, but the temptation to find out why Reid was carrying the file around was too compelling to resist. After a few centering breaths, she lifted the edge of the file and opened it.

As she feared, a picture sat on top of the pile of papers, but it wasn't the crime scene, wasn't even the killer. Instead, her little sister's senior yearbook photo stared back at her. Brynn frowned and lifted the black-and-white photocopy, flipping it over to read the writing on the back. Reid's neat, block lettering filled the page in bulleted notes, but the first line glared like neon in Brynn's vision: KELSEY LEBRECK. VICTIM'S YOUNGEST DAUGHTER. SCHEDULE INTERVIEW.

Her fingers gripped the page so hard, it crinkled the paper. She forced herself to read on. Copious notes about Kelsey's whereabouts in the days leading up to the murder. Her drug dealer contacts at the time and her relationship with Hank. Theories on who could've committed the murder and what motive someone may have had. A note that Kelsey had found a list of her mother's clients that may help with the case. Then, the name J. Kennedy circled with the word *killer* and a question mark behind it. Finally, at the bottom of the page, the date of his notes.

Last Sunday.

Rage ripped through Brynn as she shoved the page aside and looked at the next one. Title: Hank Caldwell Appeal.

That son of a bitch.

Reid was working on a way to get that bastard out of prison and hadn't told her? And he was planning to get Kelsey to help him?

Jesus. She put her head in her hands as another disturbing realization hit her. *That's* why Reid was here. Not because he'd wanted to help her. He needed to know where her sister was for his case.

She rose to her feet, almost toppling the dining room chair in the process, and stalked across the room to her bags. Goddamn him for lying to her and making her believe he really cared. Self-serving motherfucker. She slipped on a pair of sandals, barely resisting the urge to ram one right up his conniving ass. But that would wake him up, and she planned to be as far away from possible from him when he woke up.

The sheets rustled behind her and she froze, holding her breath. When no other sound came, she turned her head and saw that he had shifted his face toward her, but hadn't awakened. His breath had become shallower, however. She frowned.

With renewed urgency, she zipped up her suitcase and dug through her purse to find her watch. When she slid the silver Timex over her arm, she cringed. The leather from the night before had abraded her wrist, leaving a ring of sensitive pink skin. She dropped the watch back into her bag, then paused, an idea tiptoeing into her brain. *Hmm.*

Quickly, she moved past Reid and returned to the bedroom. She hadn't had time to explore more than the closet the night before, but she knew the place had to be well stocked. When she opened the armoire that faced the bed, her lips pressed into a determined line. She grabbed what she needed and hurried back to the main room.

Reid had remained in a stomach down, spread-eagle position. Perfect. With the stealth of a thief, she quietly locked a set of fur-lined cuffs on each of Reid's wrists, then fastened the matching cuff of each pair to the frame of the bed. She placed the keys that would release them on the kitchen counter, far out of his reach. Then, unable to resist the vindictive impulses running through her and encouraged by the return of his sleep-heavy breathing, she hooked her fingers into the waistband of his boxer shorts and gently slid them off and tossed them across the room. That would assure he'd try to get out on his own before calling for help.

She glared down at his sleeping form, knowing she should just walk out now, get as much of a head start as possible. But the urge to confront him burned bright within her. He'd tricked her into trusting him, loving him—again. God, how could she have been so freaking stupid? Before she could think better of it, she gave the bed frame a sharp kick, jolting the mattress and Reid. "Wake up, asshole."

Reid's body jumped in response and the muscles in his back flexed as he automatically tried to turn over, but the metal cuffs clinked against the frame. He jerked his hands back, fighting against the restraints. "What the hell?"

Brynn stepped around the side of the sofa bed until she was in his range of vision and tossed the Caldwell file onto the bed next to him. Papers slid out of it and scattered along the sheets. "So is every word that comes out of your mouth a lie or do you just save that for me so you can enjoy fucking me over again and again?"

He blinked in her direction, his eyes widening when he saw the documents in front of him. "Brynn, I—"

"Don't," she said, her voice deadly calm. "Don't even try. I don't need to hear more piles of bullshit."

"Brynn, I know, I'm sorry. I couldn't tell you. You wouldn't—"

"What? Wouldn't have helped you use my sister to free a god-damned *murderer*?" Her voice was rising, but she couldn't stop it. She wanted to scream at him, to pummel him for the betrayal, to make him hurt as much as she was right now. "He *killed my mother*, Reid. Left her to die alone. What part of that don't you get?"

"Hank's not a murderer," he said, his own voice almost meeting her volume. "I know you want to believe he is. Want to know that the killer is locked up tight and that everyone is safe. But *they've got the wrong guy*. All the new evidence points to someone else. And if I don't get this conviction overturned, no one is ever going to look for the real murderer. He could be out there hurting other people as we speak."

"Stop it!" She wanted to put her hands over her ears so she could block out the image he was painting. None of that could be true. Hank was the one. Had to be. He was the only one who had motive and access. The thought that someone else had done it and was still walking around free . . . No. No. No. She couldn't go there. This was simply more of Reid's bullshit. "You just can't let it go because you lost the case. You want him to be innocent, so it must be true. Because God knows the almighty Reid couldn't be wrong about anything. Couldn't actually lose a case."

His face flooded red. "Goddamn it, this isn't about my fucking ego!" The restraints scraped against the metal frame as he attempted—unsuccessfully—to get out of his prone position. "Now come on and uncuff me. We need to talk about this rationally."

She snorted. "Sorry, I'm all out of rational for tonight. Enjoy your evening."

She spun on her heel and headed toward the door.

"Brynn, wait! You can't leave me like this."

"Watch me."

To hell with it all. She'd find her sister on her own tonight. She didn't need Reid or anyone else for that matter. She'd taken care of things on her own her whole life, why stop now. She glanced back at Reid, who was pulling at his cuffs again. The room's phone was within reaching distance if he worked for it, but it would take a while. Perversely, she hoped he had to call someone to find him in this position. She'd love to see how Mr. Big Bad Dominant liked that.

He met her gaze. "Don't do this."

Without another word, she turned and walked out of the cabin.

NINETEEN

now

Brynn stepped onto the porch and slammed the door behind her, ignoring Reid's last plea. Her hand was shaking when she released the knob. *Dammit.* She needed to get ahold of herself. She sucked in a deep breath, trying to quell the angry tremors coursing through her. *Focus on why you're here.*

She closed her eyes and repeated the mantra in her head until her heartbeat slowed to a semi-normal pace. She didn't have time to worry about Reid or her broken heart right now. She'd deal with both of them another day. Tonight was about finding Kelsey.

She straightened her shoulders with renewed resolve and stared out into the night. The air had turned a bit cooler and fog hung low over the dark grounds, giving everything an ethereal feel. If she had been there for different reasons, it would have been the perfect evening to hang out in the rocking chair and sip wine while listening to the sounds of the night come to life. But a normal evening never seemed to be in the cards for her anymore.

With a sigh, she crossed the wooden slats of the porch and headed down the steps onto the slate path. She looked toward the main complex they had come from the night before. All the windows in the house were lit up and paper lamps lined the winding paths that snaked out from the back of the building. The house was modern rustic—an enormous home constructed with dark logs and Texas stone. Anyone driving by would assume it was the vineyard tycoon's mansion. Nothing about it even hinted at its real purpose.

She wrapped her arms around herself and started down the path in the opposite direction, knowing the other private cabins lay closer to the vineyards. The area got darker the farther away she ventured from the main house. Laughter and music floated on the air from somewhere in the distance, but no one seemed to be in her immediate area. Maybe this hadn't been such a great spot to watch for her sister.

She reached the end of the path and the short wooden railing that marked the beginning of the rolling expanse of grapevines. With a sigh, she climbed onto it to sit on the top rung. At least Reid wouldn't look for her here if he managed to escape.

Cabins dotted the land around her, but only two had lights on. The other guests must've already headed toward dinner and the party, ready for a fun night. Fun—what everyone else was here for.

She rested her heels on the middle rung of the fence, set her elbows on her thighs, and put her face in her hands, feeling drained and more alone than she had in as long as she could remember. How had everything gone so off course?

Her mom. Her sister. Reid. Her own life.

Was the universe bound and determined to take everyone from her? Each time she thought she had something to hold on to, it seemed to slip through her fingers like mist.

She hadn't given over to self-pity in years, had sworn to herself that no matter what, she would create a safe and happy life for herself, her sister—help other women do the same. But as she sat on the fence inhaling deep gulps of the earthy air and feeling the darkness of the night closing around her, fat tears tracked down her cheeks.

God, she was losing it.

The breeze shifted and the steady thudding of footsteps joined in with the rustling of the grape leaves. Her heart stuttered—he couldn't have escaped that quickly, right? She lifted her head to find an imposing figure heading her way. She could tell from the sauntering gait that it wasn't Reid, but other than that, she couldn't make out much else. Great, just what she needed, uninvited company.

"Hello?" she called, hurriedly cleaning the moisture from her face.

The man closed the distance between them in a few long strides. "Well, hi there, darlin'. What are you doing out here all by yourself?"

Brynn gave Grant a once-over. Plaid shirt rolled up his muscular forearms, well-worn jeans and boots, stubble that was a few hours past a five-o'clock shadow—all matching up perfectly with that lazy drawl of his. If she hadn't learned last night that he owned the place, she would've taken him for a cowboy who had wandered off a nearby pasture.

She cleared her throat, which had clogged with her tears. "Um, I just needed to get away for a minute."

He stepped closer and into a patch of moonlight. His dark eyebrows dipped low as he took in her appearance. "Is something wrong?"

She sniffed and shook her head. "Um, I'm fine. Just needed a break. I don't think the whole submissive thing is going to work for me after all."

"Brynn, I had the pleasure of watching you with your master and Jace last night. Had you not told me about the fear you're dealing with, I would've never guessed. You take to the role like it's second nature." The side of his mouth lifted a tick. "Are you sure it's the sub part of the equation you're struggling with?"

She shifted uncomfortably, his penetrating stare scattering her nerves. No question which side of the power exchange fence he played on. "Things didn't go well with Reid."

His tone turned deadly calm. "Did he break a rule with you? Push you too far? If he did, it's important for you to tell me. I have no tolerance for that kind of thing here."

She bit her lip. "No, nothing like that. He knows what I've been through and would never physically hurt me. We just . . . clash."

"Ah," he said, some of the tension in his stance easing. "He must be quite a master if he's gotten under your skin this quick. Most doms don't even crack the surface of a sub's defenses until well into a relationship."

She gritted her teeth at his knowing nod. "I'm not going back to his cabin."

His eyes crinkled around the corners. "Fair enough. We can always get you another room. But I hope you aren't going to skip the Bacchanal tonight. We only do it once a year—it'd be a shame for you to miss it."

"I still plan on checking it out. Aren't you going?" She glanced down at his outfit.

He chuckled. "I have to monitor the party to make sure everything goes all right. If I participate, it usually isn't until late into the night, and by then, costumes aren't exactly needed."

Her cheeks heated. "I imagine not."

He reached for her hand. "Come on. You'll walk over to the party site with me. They already have the food laid out. Your master's loss is my gain."

"I really don't think—"

"Indulge me, Brynn. My mama taught me to make sure guests are satisfied. The club has clearly failed in meeting the expectations you had for your stay here, so at least give me the pleasure of putting a good meal in your belly. Our chef Collette makes food so good, I've seen even the scariest doms get on their knees to beg her for seconds."

She knew he'd just given her a command, not a request, but suddenly she didn't want to be alone in the dark anymore. Wallowing would solve nothing. Plus, his easy charm made him hard to resist. He was like one of those drinks with the umbrellas—all that sugar disguising the true power swirling in the depths. Not until halfway through the beverage would you realize it was too late, that you'd already been knocked off balance.

She smirked as he led her back up the path. "I figured the owner of this kind of place would have a harem of beautiful slaves to hand-feed him dinner."

"Only on Sundays. Can't let myself get too spoiled, ya know?"

A snort escaped. "Right. Wouldn't want that."

They took a turn off the main walkway toward the east side of the property, the full moon lighting their surroundings with a silvery glow. Beyond the cabins and expansive vineyards, there was nothing but open land and the low swell of hills along the horizon. Breathtaking and so different from the flat Dallas landscape.

"How far from the city are we?" she asked.

"About an hour west of Fort Worth."

"Huh. Didn't feel like that long on the way out."

"That's 'cause Robbie drives a limo like Satan's on his tail," he said, gently taking her elbow and guiding her to another turn.

The music that'd been drifting on the breeze grew louder and a few hundred yards in front of them the sky filled with an orange glow. "Looks like the party started without us."

"Ah, don't worry. The night is young."

Her heartbeat increased tempo every step they got closer to the revelry—both in anticipation of seeing her sister and in nervousness about her hair-trigger panic attacks. And God help her when Reid got free and made it down here. She was going to have a seriously irate lawyer on her hands. Hopefully, she could talk to Kels before she had to deal with that.

The Bacchanal was set up in a large corner of an open pasture. The few trees that dotted the area had been strung with white twinkle lights, and large tiki torches had been placed strategically around the perimeter of the party to provide additional illumination. Some people were already dancing to the rhythmic beat of the music and some were sitting at the small tables that had been placed at the far end of the space, but most were around the long buffet tables that ran along the fence flanking the right side of the field.

A girl with fiery red hair long enough to cover her bared breasts greeted them with a smile. "Welcome, Master and Lady."

"Thank you, Holly," Grant said, giving the woman a soft, but chaste kiss on the mouth. "Don't you look tempting, tonight."

Holly dipped her head in thanks, then turned to Brynn to place a head wreath made of grapevines on her head. "Enjoy your evening."

"Come on," Grant said, putting his palm against the small of her back and leading her to the food area. "If you plan to enjoy the festivities, you need to make sure you're properly fueled and hydrated."

"Sounds like a sporting event."

He glanced down at her, his eyes glinting. "Oh, darling, this is way more vigorous than any sport."

She forced a smile, but her heart had taken up residence in her throat.

When they reached the food line, Grant handed her a plate and let her go in front of him. Lavish displays of fruit, cheese, and roasted meats filled the tables along with bowls of a creamy orange punch and huge decanters of some aubergine-colored liquid. Half-dressed male and female attendants stood on the other side of the table filling glasses for guests. She pointed at the drinks and looked back at Grant. "What are these?"

"Ambrosia and fresh grape juice."

An Adonis-like man clad in only a swath of material low-slung around his hips ladled some of the ambrosia into a cup for her. She thanked him, then smiled at Grant. "Bacchus may strike y'all down for having his festival with no wine."

He chuckled. "Rules are rules, but we are honoring the harvest. I even have vats of grapes wheeled out later so people can experience crushing them. Wine will be made on these grounds—we just won't be the ones drinking it."

As attendants randomly piled food on her plate, she kept her eyes on everyone around her, scanning faces like she was looking through a line-up book at a police station. Every young blond woman caught her attention. She was seeing Kelsey everywhere and nowhere.

When they reached the end of the buffet, Grant guided her to one of the tables at the edge of the party and excused himself to go make his rounds. She was relieved to be rid of him and put all her focus on watching every partygoer who arrived. She saw a few familiar faces—two politicians, one of the more popular Dallas Cowboy football players, the weather girl from one of the local TV networks. But no Kelsey. And thankfully, no Reid or Jace.

As the minutes passed, the number of attendees grew incrementally and soon workers were folding up the tables to make space for all the dancing. She gave up her perch and was quickly sucked into the crowd. Bodies pressed around her and the air grew thicker—the shift in mood palpable. Fun-loving to down and dirty before she had the chance to catch her breath.

The music increased in volume, and the beat slowed to a more sensual rhythm—one that required writhing instead of bouncing. Men and women brushed along all sides of her body, the crowd dancing as one. She squared her shoulders, determined to keep at the edges of the group so she had an escape route, but the effort was useless. Like a buoy in a churning ocean, her position was controlled by the tide around her instead of her own volition. Soon, she was so deep in the swarm that she'd lost a sense of where she was in the field.

Then, clothes began to come off.

All around her, people were shedding their colored togas and moving from dancing to kissing, touching. The man in front of her poured a cup of the dark grape juice over his lover's breasts and lapped it up as it dripped down her nude body. Brynn's blood began to rush in her ears—the collective body heat and the press of the crowd testing her hold on her panic switch.

She moved through the crowd, desperate to find the edge of the mass again, needing air. A sea of faces and voices swirled around her, disorienting her as to which direction was the quickest way out. Her breath started coming in short gasps. *Shit. Not now. Please.*

"Ooh, look, we have a shy one," a man said next to her. "Have you lost your master, pretty girl?"

She whipped her head around to meet his amused brown eyes.

"Don't be bashful, sweetie," the woman with him offered. She slid her fingers along Brynn's arm and teasingly tugged the one strap holding her toga up. "Join the fun."

"Hey!" Brynn said, batting her hand away.

Before she realized what was happening, the man hooked a finger in the loop on Brynn's collar and brought his mouth down on hers in an ambrosia-laced kiss. She fought to pull away but her strength was no match for his. Smooth hands glided over the thin material covering her breasts and she realized the woman had joined in.

Fear ripped through her, and her knee jerked upward, landing squarely in the man's crotch. He doubled over, wincing and cursing. "What the hell?"

"Texas!" Brynn stepped back but only ran into more people,

more exploring hands. Flashes of her rapist's hands on her pressed against her mind, threatening to unhinge her. She turned frantically in the other direction and shoved her way through the horde using her safe word like a machete in the jungle. "Move! Please. Texas, Texas, Texas!"

Thankfully, the crowd begin to ease back to let her through. She just needed air. Space. By the time she reached a break in the mass of people, her mind was buzzing with terror. Trying not to draw attention to herself, she forced herself to walk at a calm pace until she was outside the ring of firelight. Then, when cloaked in darkness again, she bolted toward a nearby tree and collapsed onto the bench beneath it.

She leaned forward, her eyes squeezed shut, and tried to breathe past the invisible band that seemed to be tightening around her chest. *God, when will this go away? Not everyone is out to hurt you. You're acting like a fucking lunatic. Stop!*

"Not your kind of a party, huh?"

She jolted upright, and a hand clamped over her mouth from behind.

"Shh. Don't want to disturb anyone's good time."

She screamed beneath the grip and attempted to jerk out of his grasp, but the muffled struggle was just a whisper compared to the thumping music coming from the party.

"Better calm down and listen. I have what you want. And she's safe, for now. But if you don't cooperate, I guarantee she won't stay that way."

She stilled, her blood running cold.

"That's right. Good girl." He ran his other hand over her bared shoulder, the scar. "So, have you missed me?"

Jace bent at the waist, hands on knees, and wheezed with yet another fit of laughter.

Reid gritted his teeth. "Are you done yet, asshole? Because I could use a little help here."

Reid had tried unsuccessfully to free himself from the cuffs Brynn had secured him with. But all he had to show for it was a whole lot of sweat and a bent sofa bed frame. Jace had been his last resort before calling staff. Now, he wondered if staff may have been a better option.

Jace coughed, trying to get a hold on his laughter. "Dude, I'm sorry. But this is funny as shit. At least she only cuffed you and didn't stick a plug in your ass or something. What the hell did you do to inspire this?"

Reid laid his head on the pillow and stared at the scattered papers in front of him. "She went through my bag. Saw that I'm working on an appeal for the guy who's in jail for her mother's murder."

Jace's tone turned serious. "And you didn't tell her?"

Reid craned his neck and shot him a lethal glare.

Jace raised his palms. "Okay, okay. Not my business. Let me look for the keys."

After a few minutes of searching, Jace found what he was looking for and released Reid from the bed. Reid wrapped the sheet around his waist and rubbed his reddened wrists. "I seriously fucked up this time, man."

"Well, that's obvious." Jace straddled one of the dining room chairs and frowned. "What haven't you told me?"

Reid sighed, then spilled the whole story. He hadn't told Jace from the start about the appeal because he knew his friend would've never agreed to get him into the club under those pretenses, but he needed to come clean now.

Jace stayed silent a full minute after Reid stopped speaking, his expression neutral as he processed the information. "So you didn't come here to help Brynn and win her back like you told me? You came because you needed to know where your star witness was?"

"Yes. No." Reid scrubbed a hand through his hair. "I don't fucking know anymore. Most of it was because I needed to know where Kelsey was and, I won't lie, part of me wanted revenge on Brynn for hurting me all those years ago—I couldn't wait to remind her what she'd walked away from."

"But . . ."

Reid sighed. "But the other part of me couldn't stand the thought of her submitting to someone else. Couldn't pass up the chance to touch her again."

"And now you're so gone on her, you can't even see straight."

Reid recoiled. "No, it's not like that."

Jace smirked, the simple gesture cutting through all the bullshit Reid had been telling himself.

Reid closed his eyes and shook his head. "Fuck."

His friend's smile turned sympathetic. "Come on, get dressed and we'll go find your girl."

Reid had never seen so many naked bodies in one place. The Bacchanal had only started an hour ago, but the guests hadn't wasted any time getting down to business. Some were dancing, others were sloshing around naked in a large vat, crushing grapes, and the rest were in the grass, fucking in full view. The scent of earth and sex permeated the air, mixing with the sounds of carnal indulgence.

The decadent scene was the stuff of fantasies, but for Reid it was more nightmare than dream at the moment. Finding Brynn in the mass of people was going to be a challenge—especially when she didn't want to be found.

"Looks like we're missing quite the party," Jace said as Reid scanned the crowd for Brynn.

"Do you see her anywhere?"

His friend frowned. "I don't know how we're going to be able to pick her out with all this going on. But Grant's over there by the food. I'll go ask him if he's seen her. That guy doesn't miss much."

"Yeah, good idea," Reid said. "I'll go with you. I'm not going to get anywhere with this method."

Grant smiled at the two of them as they walked up. Unlike everyone else, he was clothed in his usual jeans and plaid shirt. Reid didn't know him very well, but based on his interaction so far, he sensed the man didn't let his guard down very much even at his own resort.

"Evening, fellas. Decided to join the fun?" he asked, sipping on some orange-colored drink.

"Actually, I'm looking for Brynn," Reid said, keeping his eyes on the crowd. "Have you seen her?"

"I figured she'd be back with you by now," Grant said, drawing Reid's attention back to the man in front of him. "I found her sitting by herself on the far side of the property earlier—pretty pissed at you I might add. I got her to walk over here with me, but then she left not long after. I thought she was on her way to find you to work things out."

"No, I haven't seen her." Reid blew out a frustrated breath. "Shit."

"How long ago did she leave?" Jace asked. "Was she by herself?"

Grant shrugged. "'Bout half an hour or so, I'd guess. And yeah, she was alone." He looked back and forth between the two of them, his brow furrowing. "Is everything all right?"

Jace clapped a hand on Reid's shoulder. "Yeah, it's fine. Reid's just gone and ticked off his woman. Nothing new. I'm sure she'll make her way back to the cabin at some point. Let us know if you run across her before we do, though, will ya?"

"Sure, no problem."

Reid was ready to head out on his search again, but the way Grant was looking at him gave him pause. "What's wrong?"

He sipped his drink and frowned. "I know it's none of my business, but you need to be careful."

"What do you mean?"

He shrugged. "You push a girl like Brynn too hard and she'll run like a frightened rabbit. She needs a dom who can draw out her submission without crushing whatever's so fragile inside her."

Reid bristled—who the hell did this guy think he was? The Dr. Phil of BDSM? "Look, I appreciate your concern, but you don't even know her."

The corner of Grant's mouth lifted. "You run a place like this long enough, and you learn how to read people. I'm only trying to help."

Reid nodded, his throat tightening, and turned on his heel to head away from the party. He didn't have time to be psycho-analyzed.

Jace followed behind. "Any thoughts on where she might've gone?"

"Not a fucking clue. I guess we can check each of our cabins first. She doesn't have a car, so she couldn't have gone too far."

As soon as Reid's cabin came into view, his phone vibrated against his leg. He halted his step and yanked the cell from his pocket. Unknown number.

"Hold up, Jace." Reid put the phone to his ear. "Hello."

Silence for a few seconds then: "Reid?"

His shoulders sank with relief. "Brynn, look, we need to talk. I'm sorry about everything. I know I should've told you. I was wrong. Just please, give me a chance to—"

"Reid, stop," she said, her voice shaking a bit. "I don't want to talk about it right now, okay?"

He frowned. Was that . . . road noise in the background? "Where the hell are you?"

A long pause. "I'm on my way home. I—I, uh, called a cab. I couldn't find Kelsey. I don't think she's at the resort after all, so I'm going home."

"You called a *cab*?" He started pacing, and Jace stepped out of his path. "What the hell, Brynn? You know I would've driven you home."

"Don't you get it? I don't want to be around you right now. And I don't exactly have *ruby* slippers to click my way home. So yeah, a cab."

"Brynn—"

"Good-bye, Reid."

The line went silent.

"Son of a bitch!" he yelled to no one in general.

Jace winced. "She bailed?"

Reid kicked a nearby shrub, sending leaves flying. "She's on her way home. Called a goddamned cab."

"I'm sorry, man. That sucks," Jace said, wisely keeping his distance. "Maybe she just needs a little space to cool off."

"Screw space. The minute Brynn gets back into her little world, she's going to talk herself out of everything that happened this weekend. She'll put me back in that little I-hate-you box she keeps me in."

"You'll never catch up with her."

Reid cocked an eyebrow at him.

"Uh-oh, why are you giving me that look?"

Reid flashed his teeth. "No, not in *my* car."

Jace's crossed his arms over his chest. "No way, you're out of your fucking mind. Only my hands touch the steering wheel of my baby. I've seen the dings on your car."

"You either give me the keys or come with me," Reid said, staring his friend down.

Jace sighed and pulled his keys out of his pocket. "Come on, but I'm driving and if my car ends up with so much as a scratch, I'm posting the cell phone pictures I took of you tonight on the Internet."

He narrowed his eyes. "You didn't take pictures."

His lip curled. "Never underestimate my penchant for blackmail."

———

The purr of the engine filled the car as Jace's Dodge Viper devoured the open highway in front of them. Reid punched Brynn's number into his phone again, hoping his persistence or at least her annoyance would make her pick up the phone. But all he got was the same voice mail greeting he'd heard the last three times. He hung up without leaving a message and barely resisted the urge to bang the phone into pieces against the dashboard. "We should've caught up to her by now."

Jace had been driving like a Nascar champion since they'd left

The Ranch, but so far, they'd only passed a handful of cars on the pitch-black road—and no cab. His friend frowned, but didn't take his eyes off the highway. "Maybe they stopped at a gas station or something and we passed them."

"The two stations we've passed so far looked empty. Maybe you just need to go faster."

Jace shot him a you-gotta-be-fucking-kidding-me look. "Any faster and we're going to break the sound barrier. I'm trying to get you to Brynn with all our limbs still intact."

Reid gave a derisive snort and stared at the taillights of the black SUV they were gaining on. Jace cut into the left lane and glanced over as they passed the vehicle. "Huh. Looks like we aren't the only ones skipping the Bacchanal tonight."

"What do you mean?" Reid turned to look over his shoulder, but the Escalade was quickly becoming a black dot in the distance, the large vehicle no match for the high-powered sports car.

Jace shrugged. "That was Davis Ackerman. He's a member at the club."

Reid grimaced. "Seriously? Women actually sleep with that dirtbag?"

"Some," Jace said, his tone wary. "But Grant has had to work hard to find him matches. Davis's proclivities are pretty fucked up from what I've heard."

Reid smirked. "Let me guess, he's into extreme humiliation? He always excelled at doing that at work."

"More than that," Jace said as he passed another vehicle. "He wants the pain sluts—girls who claim they don't have limits. A few weeks ago, Grant had to call in a medic because Davis had bitten a girl's neck so hard, it had gushed blood. He's been warned twice about biting."

"Jesus."

"Yeah, the guy's in his own zip code. I figure it's only a matter of time before he gets kicked out. He ordered a whole shitload of stuff from me a few weeks ago under a fake name, so I assume he's setting up his own private playground."

"Huh. Glad to know he's running part of our city government."

Jace became quiet again, apparently lost in his own thoughts, and Reid tapped his fingers on the armrest as he stared out the window into the night. Jace would slow when they passed gas stations and rest stops, but after another thirty minutes, they still hadn't spotted a cab.

Reid shifted restlessly in his seat, something tugging at his brain. He'd gotten a weird vibe on the phone with Brynn. More than just her anger, something else. But he hadn't been able to pinpoint what had bothered him. He played the conversation over again in his head. What had she said? *I don't have ruby slippers.* Strange statement.

He closed his eyes and leaned his head against the headrest, going over the words again and again, turning and rearranging them. Then, like numbers in a combination lock, they finally clicked into place—one word standing out among the others. All the breath left his lungs. *"Fuck!"*

Jace shot him a wary look. "What's wrong?"

He pressed the heels of his hands to his brows, his head instantly starting to pound. "She used her old safe word and I didn't catch it."

"What?"

"On the phone. She used the word, trying to tell me something." His frustration over not being able to find her now turned to cold fear. He looked at Jace. "What if she's in trouble?"

He gave Reid a sidelong glance. "I think you're getting paranoid and reading too much into things. She's just pissed at you, man."

He shook his head. "No, I don't think so. She used the word specifically. She emphasized it. I was just too shocked over her leaving to catch it. And why would she leave so suddenly—give up on finding her sister so easily?"

Jace's face reflected Reid's worry. "But she was at The Ranch—it's not like the dude who's after her sister could just pop in. How could she get into any trouble?"

"God, I don't know. Maybe someone called her, lured her out. Maybe this drug dealer guy has some contact inside The Ranch." He blew out a frustrated breath. "She could be fucking anywhere. All I know is that she was in a car."

"What do you want me to do? Turn around or keep going?"

Reid stared straight ahead, wracking his brain. Had she said anything else in the phone call that contained a clue? Had anyone at The Ranch seemed like they were paying particular attention to Brynn? A whisper of something danced at the edge of his awareness.

He thought back over the previous night, about each moment he'd spent with Brynn—making love to her, touching her, kissing every inch of bare skin. The conversation they'd had in the tub. Thought about how he'd bathed her, soaped her back, ran his fingers along her spine and over the faint circular birthmark that graced the line of her shoulder blade.

An icy stillness moved over him as he pictured that last moment, the mark on her skin. It hadn't quite been a circle, more like two crescents not fully joined together. And had that been there when they'd dated before? No, not that he remembered.

When he'd touched it during the bath, Brynn had tensed ever so slightly—like she'd momentarily held her breath. He'd thought maybe she was reacting because she was self-conscious about the birthmark, but . . .

A nauseating realization gripped his gut.

No.

Not a birthmark.

A *bite* mark.

Reid gripped the door handle as murderous rage ripped through him, his whole body shaking with the need to maim and dismember. "Turn the car around."

Jace gave him a quick glance. "You sure?"

"Turn the goddamned car around, Jace," Reid said through clenched teeth. "I know who has her. Jesus Christ. That sick fuck is the one who raped her."

The car slowed a bit as Jace turned to him with knitted brows. "What? Who? The drug dealer?"

"No. *Ackerman.* Brynn has a bite scar on her back. She was working for him when she was attacked."

"Holy fuck." Jace's expression hardened, and he eased off the gas pedal so that their U-turn didn't send the vehicle into a roll.

Anger flared up so fierce inside him, Reid was sure he'd breathe fire if given the chance. That monster had his girl. She was alone in her worst nightmare. *God, please let me get to her in time.* And Davis had better start praying, 'cause Reid was ready to send him straight to his fucking maker once he got Brynn away from him.

That psychopath had traumatized and ripped Brynn apart. Had destroyed the relationship he and Brynn had been building. How different would both of their lives be if Reid had gotten the chance to give her the ring that day? That fucker had stolen everything. Reid cracked his knuckles. "If he hurt a hair on her head . . ."

Jace shot him a look of warning. "Take a breath. You can't kill him, dude. You don't even know if it was him for sure or if he even has Brynn right now. You of all people should know circumstantial evidence can be dead wrong."

Reid knew that, but something deep in his bones told him he was on the mark with this one. "I won't kill him. But if he is the one who has Brynn, I'm going to see if the asshole likes receiving pain as much as he likes dishing it out."

TWENTY-ONE

now

Sweat soaked through Brynn's toga as Davis Ackerman continued down whatever road they were on. He'd wrapped bungee cords beneath her breasts and around her legs, securing her to the seat, then had cuffed her wrists and blindfolded her.

Brynn breathed through the panic. She was with her rapist. She'd known the minute he'd whispered to her in the voice from her nightmares. But why did he have her sister? Was he associated with the drug dealer who wanted Kelsey? It didn't make sense. Davis was a respected councilman for God's sake. She cleared her throat and tried to force calm into her voice. "Where are you taking me?"

He snorted. "Oh, so now you're going to make conversation? Last night you didn't even bother to say hi."

She wet her lips. "I wasn't allowed to speak. I was with a dom."

"Yeah, I saw your little performance with your two old friends last night," he said, disgust dripping from his tone. "I guess some things never change. You're still going after the smarmy pretty boys and still willing to spread your legs at the drop of a hat."

She recoiled as if she'd been slapped, and her response tumbled out before she could stop herself. "You don't know shit about me."

He laughed, the sound chilling her blood. "I know how easy it was to tie you up and fuck you before you even realized I wasn't one of your lovers. Maybe I'll make you say my name this time so you don't forget who's inside you."

The world tilted beneath her feet. Nausea shuddered through her and fingers of panic squeezed around her windpipe as she sucked in sharp, quick breaths. She wouldn't survive his touch again.

He chuckled. "Maybe we can do a three-way. I've always fantasized about sisters."

Kelsey. Her sister's name broke through the haze of spiraling fear in her brain. Kels needed her. Brynn couldn't let herself slip into the anxiety attack or pass out from hyperventilation. Her sister would be left alone with the monster in the front seat.

She sucked in a deep breath through her nose and held it for a moment before breathing out through her mouth. *In . . . one, two, three . . . Out . . . one, two, three.* She focused on centering herself, clearing her head. The only chance she had of protecting her sister and herself was if she could wrangle in her emotions.

The SUV made a hard left turn, throwing her weight to the right, and then the sound of crunching gravel filled her ears. She'd lost track of how long they'd been riding, but she knew it hadn't been long enough to reach the city yet. Shit. Where the hell was he taking her?

A few bumpy minutes later, the vehicle pulled to a halt, and Davis shut off the engine. "Things will go much easier for you if you cooperate, so I don't suggest you try anything heroic. And don't bother screaming when we get out. There's no one around to hear you."

"What do you want from us?" Brynn bit out.

"From Kelsey? A little information. From you?" He paused

and she could almost hear the smile in his voice. "We'll just have to see what mood strikes me."

Doors opened and the car dipped twice. Then, the air shifted. Hot breath hit her cheek. "Mmm, you still smell the same. Like fear. You know all that adrenaline rushing through you right now can actually enhance a sexual experience. Add in a little pain and it will send you right over the edge."

She reeled backward in her seat, bile rising to the back of her throat. "Get away from me, you fucking psycho."

He laughed. "Now, no need to be crude. Although, I expect no less from you. I know from experience you're no lady."

His steel grip wrapped around her upper arm, and he jerked her to her feet. "And I expect from this point on, you call me master."

Over my dead body. But she swallowed back the words before they slipped out. At this rate, that might be exactly what he had in mind.

He hauled her out of the car, and she fell forward, her knees and elbows landing hard on the pebbles. She clenched her teeth through the sting, refusing to give him the satisfaction of hearing her cry out in pain.

He grabbed the chain between her cuffs and yanked. "Get up and walk."

He led her from the humid night air into an air-conditioned space. Thick carpet silenced their footfalls as he shut a door behind him.

He guided her another few steps, then untied her blindfold. Brynn blinked as her eyes adjusted and was surprised to find herself in a brightly lit kitchen. A darkened flight of stairs stretched down through a door in front of her. Davis grasped the back of her neck. "Down the steps. Try to stay on your feet this time."

She shot him a hateful glare and moved forward when he nudged her. Slowly, she descended the stairs, her heart sinking as the fluorescent light disappeared behind her and the contents of the basement came into view. No workout room or rec area for Davis Ackerman. Nope. Instead, a full-scale BDSM playground—his very own personal dungeon—spread out before her. A St. Andrew's cross, benches, a wall full of hooks with various tools she couldn't identify.

But the shock of that paled in comparison to the surprise that greeted her as she hit the bottom step.

They weren't alone.

Roslyn Jamison gave her a disdainful look as she casually held a gun at her side. "Oh, hurray, the gang's all here."

Brynn stared at her, trying to connect the dots between the man behind her and the woman in front of her. But none of it lined up. "What the fuck are you doing here?"

She pursed her lips. "You couldn't leave things alone, could you? I should've known. You've been a complication since the day you were born."

"What?"

"Never mind." She waved the gun dismissively.

But Brynn couldn't draw her eyes away from her—her presence too unbelievable to process. The petite woman looked like she was dressed for a political convention instead of a kidnapping. A navy blue, perfectly tailored pantsuit with matching low heels. 1950s-style white gloves. Even a bun with nary a hair out of place. The contrast with the BDSM equipment in the background was almost laughable.

But Brynn's attention was diverted when a light sniffling sound came from her right. She whirled around to find Kelsey, tied to a chair, face swollen from crying and ball gag in her mouth. Brynn lurched in that direction. "Kels!"

Davis grasped her arm. "Not so fast, sweetheart. We need to take care of business before we get to have happy reunion time."

Kelsey's gaze met hers, her terror palpable. Roslyn stalked over to the chair and unsnapped the gag, but when her sister tried to talk only wretched sobs escaped.

"Kels, shh, I'm here. It's going to be okay. We'll figure this out. Shh . . ." Brynn knew the words were empty, but they tumbled out anyway.

Her sister shook her head frantically, her eyes wild. "No, it's not okay. She's the one."

Brynn frowned. "Kels, I don't understand."

Roslyn's tone turned sharp. "Stop the blabbering."

Her sister inhaled a ragged breath and met Brynn's gaze. "She killed Mom."

Brynn's knees went weak beneath her, and Davis began a slow, measured clap.

"You know it only took her three days to figure out the connection. And who said strippers were dumb?" He gave his winning, politician smile.

"Shut up, Davis." Roslyn tucked the gun in her waistband.

"Wait, *what*?" Brynn asked, her thoughts whirling like her brain had been thrown into a blender. She shook her head vehemently, unable to believe what her sister had just said. "No, Hank killed Mom. All the evidence was there. The fingerprints, the stolen money."

Tears freely dripped from Kelsey's eyes. "No, B. I told you. He was messed up, but he wasn't a killer. All the evidence was circumstantial. You knew that."

Brynn squeezed her eyes shut, the news too shocking for her mind to assimilate.

Reid had been right?

"Yes," Roslyn agreed, her tone smug. "Circumstantial evidence the idiot prosecutor had no idea how to present. I never thought it would be so difficult to throw a case. But luckily Hank didn't have the best record. No jury has sympathy for a pathetic junkie."

"Why?" Brynn asked, the question sounding more like a plea. "Why would you kill her?"

Roslyn pressed her lips together, impatience coloring her seemingly ageless features. "Because she didn't know when to quit. My husband paid her fairly for years to keep quiet about you, but when he threw his hat in the governor's race, she saw a bigger meal ticket. Patrick was going to give her whatever she wanted—he's always been soft when it came to you and that bitch—but I wasn't going to put up with her blackmail anymore. Getting knocked up by one of your customers doesn't mean you get a salary for life."

Brynn blinked, dumbfounded. She thought of the man who'd given her a job out of the blue all those years ago—when she'd needed it most. The way he'd always offered her overtime. "Patrick's my dad?"

"Yes, how do you think you landed that receptionist job? His stupid decision to hire you almost sent Reid down the exact same path he had gone. Men are so weak." She shook her head, her tone full of disgust. "But I couldn't stand by and watch my sister's only son make the same mistakes. If I hadn't had Davis fix that *situation*, I'm sure you'd have ruined Reid's future before it even got started."

Brynn swayed on her feet.

The rape had been planned?

Holy God. She and her sister weren't getting out of here. These people had long fallen off the sanity train. She cut a look at Davis. "Why would you help her?"

Davis shrugged as if the question were unimportant.

Roslyn smiled, the effect chilling. "You weren't the first of Davis's problematic dalliances. Let's just say if the world knew of all the girls he'd unleashed his little weakness on, he would've never made it to where he has. Lucky for him, I'm good at keeping secrets if the favor is returned."

Brynn inhaled deep breaths through her nose, trying to fight off the urge to vomit on the shiny tiled floor.

Roslyn stalked around Kelsey's chair, then laid her hands on the back of it. "Now, we were hoping not to involve you, but Kelsey here has been rather uncooperative. We know she has evidence incriminating a J. Kennedy as the murderer, and I can't have anyone figuring out that your mother used to call Davis and I John and Jackie when we met with her, now can I?"

Her sister bit her lip. "I told you where I put the evidence."

Roslyn grabbed a handful of Kelsey's hair and yanked backward. Kelsey's hands automatically flew up, but her bindings prevented her from being able to defend herself.

"And *I* told *you* that I went there and it's not where you said," Roslyn said, her voice smooth. "Which is why Davis brought Brynn over to inspire some honesty out of you."

The loud crack of a whip echoed through the basement as Davis brought it down on Brynn's back, the thin material of her toga doing little to soften the bite. She crumpled to the floor and groaned.

"Brynn!" her sister screamed and tried to launch forward, but Roslyn held fast to her hair.

Brynn clenched her jaw, trying to think through the haze of pain. "It's okay, Kels. I appreciate you trying to protect me all this time, but we just need to tell them. The evidence is at my house. She sent it to me to keep safe."

Kelsey's lips parted, but Brynn sent her a warning glare.

"Is that true?" Roslyn asked, twisting Kelsey's locks around her fist.

"Yes, yes," Kelsey said, frantically. "I couldn't figure out what the names in the logbook meant, and I thought Brynn might be able to help. But I didn't tell you 'cause I didn't want you to hurt her, too."

"If you take us there, I'll give it to you," Brynn said, hoping she sounded convincing. She knew that Davis and Roslyn had no intention of letting them go, since they'd already revealed too much. But maybe if she could get on her own turf, she and her sister would have a shot. If nothing else, she could punch in the emergency code into her security system to activate the silent alarm feature. Maybe the cops could get there before Roslyn discovered there was no evidence to be had.

Roslyn smiled, the expression holding no warmth. "Yes, I'm sure you'd love to get to your own house where you know every nook and cranny. No, you'll tell us where it is, and I'll take Kelsey there with me. You can stay here with Davis until I have the evidence secured."

Brynn's stomach twisted into a pretzel for her own fate, but a little flame of hope flickered for her sister. She nodded. "It's in the back of my closet in a box. But you're going to need my alarm code to get in the house."

Kelsey's face was filled with question marks, but Brynn mustered up her therapist mask to hide her emotions. Roslyn evaluated her with shrewd eyes, no doubt searching for any chink in Brynn's facade. After a few agonizing moments, the woman gave a curt nod and released her grip on her sister.

"I hope for both your sakes, you're not lying to me. If I discover this is a wild-goose chase, your sister will pay the price. I have a hefty overdose of heroin with her name on it. They say relapse is a bitch—can kill you by accident so easily."

No. Please, God. Let the alarm code work in time. If the plan failed, they were both dead.

Roslyn pointed a finger at Brynn, but looked at Davis. "Keep her restrained until I call you."

Davis's thin lips spread into a smile as he idly toyed with the whip, winding it around his fingers. "Gladly."

TWENTY-TWO

now

Reid leaned his head against the headrest and groaned. "Where the hell did he go?"

Jace sighed and pulled over onto the dirt shoulder, a cloud of dust engulfing the car. "We should've met up with him by now. This is where we saw him the first time, and I know he never passed us."

"He must've turned off somewhere."

Jace crooked his thumb. "There's a small lake area a couple of miles up the road. I think there are a few vacation homes and rentals out there. That's the only way he could've gone. There's really nothing else on this stretch of road except cow pastures."

The crush of pressure around Reid's chest tightened. Brynn. Isolated with that whack job. "Do you remember where he wanted the stuff he ordered from you delivered?"

"No, my assistant handled that part. But I'd bet my left nut that he didn't get any of it sent to that fancy house in Highland Park where he lives with his wife. He wouldn't have had to use a fake name if he'd done that."

"Let's check it out, then."

Jace swung the car back onto the highway and a few minutes later, turned onto a narrow, tree-lined road. They followed the winding gravel path, squinting through the darkness at the well-kept houses tucked behind the foliage. As they passed the homes, the car's headlights illuminated each labeled mailbox. The fifth box they passed had Kennedy spelled out in gold letters.

"Ding, ding, ding. We have a winner," Jace said, his tone grim. "That's the name he uses to make his orders."

The world seemed to stop spinning as Reid stared at the mailbox. "Like the president."

"Yeah, arrogant fucker, isn't he?" Jace pulled around the next bend in the road and parked out of view.

Reid barely heard him over the pounding of his heart. He wet his lips. "Jace, do you still keep a gun in the car?"

Jace shook his head. "Oh, hell no. You're not going in there with a weapon. You'll end up spending the rest of your life in an orange jumpsuit."

Reid pinned him with a stare. "The new evidence I found on Brynn's mother's case points to someone with the last name Kennedy as the murderer."

His eyes widened. "Fuck."

"We might have more than a rapist out for a repeat performance. Brynn's sister was the one who originally had the new evidence."

Jace looked toward the house, creases of concern framing his mouth. "You think he's got both of the girls?"

"I'm about to find out," Reid said, his voice resolute, but his insides twisting with worry. Davis had a jump of time on them. What if he'd done something to Brynn or Kelsey already? No. He pushed the thought out of his mind. He would *not* be too late for Brynn this time. If this bastard had her, Reid would do whatever it took to get to her and protect her. "Give me your gun. I won't use it unless I need to."

With a deep frown, Jace leaned over, popped open the glove compartment, and handed him the Smith & Wesson.

Reid checked the safety, then tucked it in the back of his waistband, hiding it beneath his loose T-shirt. "Call the police. I'm going in."

"Let me come in with you. Keep the numbers on our side. Or, why don't we wait for the cops?"

"No, I don't want to waste any more time—every minute could count. And I need you to stay out here to make sure at least one of us can help if something goes wrong."

Jace sank back against his seat and ran his hands over his face. "Fifteen minutes. If whatever Podunk police force isn't here by then, I'm coming in after your ass."

Reid gave a quick nod and pushed open the car door to climb out. After double-checking the gun was secured, he quickly made his way toward the house. He had never shot anything besides a paper target at a shooting range—he'd always been too much of an animal lover to even join Patrick on his biannual hunting trips. But Reid knew if Davis had hurt either one of the women, he wouldn't hesitate to shoot the fucker right in the heart. Or maybe tear him limb from limb with his bare hands. A gunshot might be too humane.

He stared at the door for a moment, not sure if he should try to sneak in. This was Texas—people tended to shoot first, ask questions later. If he had the wrong house, he'd get shot regardless of if Davis was on the other side or not. Better to make sure he was on the right track first. Knowing Davis he'd probably be arrogant enough to answer the door, pretend everything was fine.

He rapped on the heavy oak door as icy calm overtook him.

A minute passed and he thought he heard shuffling on the other side, but the door didn't open. The chickenshit was going to ignore him? Oh, hell no. He pounded on the door with the side of his fist, the wood rattling beneath it. "Open up, Ackerman. We need to talk."

So much for subtlety.

When no answer came, he reached for the handle in frustration and jiggled it. The lever handle gave easily and the lock clicked. He gave the door a tentative push and it creaked open, revealing a darkened living room of whitewashed furniture. Moonlight streamed in from the wall of windows at the back of the room—the lake glinting a few yards beyond the small backyard. Reid slipped his hand behind him, wrapping his fingers around the handle of the gun. He took a cautious step forward, the carpet absorbing the noise.

He paused in the entryway, tuning his ears to each nuance of sound around him—the breeze rustling the bushes outside, the hum of a refrigerator in the nearby kitchen, the click of the air-conditioning shutting off. The ordinary soundtrack of an empty house. But the hair on his arms was standing on end. Despite all the normalcy, something was off.

He closed the door behind him with a gentle snick, shutting out the outdoor noises, and listened more closely. There it was. Underneath all those mundane hums and clicks, a muffled sound that started then stopped in an irregular pattern. He eased the gun from his waistband and moved toward the kitchen with silent steps.

The unfamiliar sound grew a shade louder. He scanned the kitchen, quickly determining it was empty, then approached the only closed door in the room. He pressed his ear against the door and strained to hear what lay beyond. The sound he'd been following increased in volume and hit him straight in the chest. A soft groan. Human and undeniably female.

All caution flew from his brain, and he grabbed at the handle with his free hand. The door eased open and exposed a shadowed flight of stairs. Basements weren't normal in Texas, and Reid could think of only one reason why Davis would have a house built with one—to conceal his dirty secrets.

The pitiful sound of whimpering increased, and Reid had to force himself not to rumble down the stairs like a charging bull. Keeping the gun poised in front of him and clinging to the shadows, he eased down the steps. When he reached the point where the shaft of light from the basement angled too wide for him to stay hidden, he crouched down to peek around the wall blocking his view.

His heart jumped into his throat. Brynn—naked and hanging upside down on a St. Andrew's cross. She'd been blindfolded and ball-gagged, but her choked sobs and moans made it past the blockage. Angry welts striped her torso, breasts, and thighs, and blood seeped from the lashes as her body heaved with her panicked breaths.

Rage whipped through him like a gale force wind. After a quick scan to make sure no one else was in the room, he hustled toward Brynn. She tensed and turned silent, apparently sensing she was no longer alone.

He tucked the gun in his waistband. "Brynn, sugar, it's Reid. I'm here."

A strangled cry escaped from her.

"I'm going to get you off this thing," he said, reaching for the blindfold first, knowing that scared her as much as anything.

When he pulled the material from her, her bloodshot eyes were wide and swollen from crying. Unintelligible noises emanated from behind her gag, but he wanted to get her freed before anything else. He searched for the mechanism to turn the bondage wheel that the cross was attached to right-side up. "Shh, it's okay, baby."

He hoped Davis had taken off when he'd realized he'd been caught, but Reid knew he could still be in the house. They needed to get the hell out of here. Fast.

He found the device and cranked the wheel. The thing groaned and squeaked as he slowly spun Brynn right-side up. Damn, could the thing be any louder? Might as well have a bullhorn announcing his location. He threw a glance over his shoulder, verifying they were still alone.

Once he'd gotten her fully upright, he went to work on the straps securing her wrists. She shook her head frantically and tried to speak. He frowned. "Sugar, it's all right. I'm going to get you out of here. Just try to breathe. I'll get the gag off you in one sec."

His big fingers fought with the intricate fastenings, and he cursed under his breath. He should've brought Jace in; he could've worked the equipment with his eyes closed. Finally, one of the straps came free. Brynn grabbed at her mouth, yanking the ball out of it, as he went to work on the next binding.

"Reid," she whispered, her voice raw.

He kept his eyes focused on the task at hand. "What, baby?"

"Behind you."

Reid whirled around, and Davis stepped off the bottom stair, a pistol trained on Reid's chest. "Oh, look. Company. How lovely."

Reid shifted to the side to stand between Brynn and Davis's steady hand.

"Sorry, I'm late. I had to take care of your friend out there. Can't have him interrupting the party," Davis said, his tone sickeningly calm.

The words hit Reid like one of the bullets in Davis's gun. *Jace.*

The councilman walked toward the two of them with deliberate steps and a satisfied smile. "Step away from my slave, Reid. I don't plan on sharing her like you do."

Reid's teeth ground together, the urge to murder this man a living, breathing thing inside him. "I'm not going to let you touch her."

He smirked. "Roslyn always worried this girl would be your downfall. After all the trouble she's gone through to keep you two apart, she'll be so disappointed to see she's failed."

Reid's focus stuttered at the mention of his aunt's name. "What the hell are you talking about?"

Davis gave a put-upon sigh. "Blackmail, dirty pictures, letting me have my fun with Brynn. I told her you were a lost cause, but she had these ridiculous notions that you could actually make something of yourself."

Reid stared at gun. All the puzzle pieces were crashing through his brain like jagged pieces of shrapnel, ripping through the fabric of his reality, but he couldn't lose sight of the situation at hand. He raised his eyes to meet Davis's. "You're a fucking lunatic."

His voice turned colder. "I'm going to ask you one last time to step aside."

"Go to hell."

He shrugged and cocked the pistol. "Suit yourself. It's not going to be much of a matchup. In man versus gun, gun usually wins."

"Wait," Brynn said, her hand touching the small of Reid's back. "Listen to him, Reid. Let him have me."

———

Reid's back stiffened beneath her fingertips as she made the suggestion, but she prayed he would listen. Davis wouldn't hesitate to kill him. She'd seen the crazy in the councilman's eyes as he was tying her up. The man had no soul.

"I can't," Reid said, his voice strained. "Won't."

"You have to. Please, Reid. Listen to what he says and maybe he'll let us go."

"He's not going to let us—"

She slipped the gun from his waistband and pressed the butt of it into his back, hoping he could feel what she was doing. "Please. Move aside like he said."

"See, my pretty slave wants me to touch her. Now get the fuck out of the way, and maybe I'll let you watch."

Reid glanced over his shoulder, giving her a pointed glace, and mouthed the word "one." She nodded, counting the next numbers in her head.

Two.

Three.

In one swift motion, he took a wide step to the left. Automatically, Davis's gaze and pistol followed the movement, giving Brynn the beat of time she needed to aim. When Davis's attention returned to her, the pompous smile wilted. Without hesitation, she pulled the trigger of Reid's gun, shooting the man of her nightmares squarely in the chest.

But the deafening sound of the shot seemed to stutter as the gun recoiled in her hands—two bangs, not one. She looked down at her weapon, confused. Only when she heard the dueling groans of agony did she realize her shot hadn't been the only one fired. Horror ratcheted through her as she lifted her gaze to find two crumpled and bloodied men on the floor.

"No!" Brynn yelled, and jolted forward, but the waist and ankle straps held her fast to the cross. "Reid!"

Tears pricked her eyes as she set the gun aside and frantically unfastened the bindings. Low moans came from Reid, giving her hope she still had time to help him. She couldn't lose him—wouldn't. Davis had taken so much from her; she refused to allow him to take any more.

She freed herself and raced to Reid. Blood covered the entire left side of his shirt and the hand he had clamped over the wound. She couldn't tell if he'd been shot in the chest or shoulder. She brushed a hand over his ashen cheek. "Reid, can you hear me, baby? I'm going to go find a phone. Can you try to stay awake for me?"

"My pocket," he said through a grimace of pain.

She patted his pockets, then dove in when she felt the cell phone.

She hoped her rushed words to the police conveyed the situation clearly enough. They assured her help was on the way and that they'd send someone to her house to find her sister and Roslyn. They wanted her to stay on the line, but she couldn't focus on the 911 operator. She needed to keep Reid conscious.

She stepped around Davis and the pool of blood spreading beneath him. Her stomach threatened to heave. She'd killed someone. Granted, he'd deserved it, but she knew she'd be seeing this scene replayed in her mind for a long time.

Dragging her focus away from the macabre sight, she hurried to the far wall and grabbed a stack of clean towels off a shelf. She wrapped one around herself, then brought the rest to Reid's side. Gingerly, she lifted his hand away from his shirt and placed a towel against his wound, applying pressure. His bloodied hand settled on top of hers.

"I'm sorry I . . . lied to you," he said, sounding like each word was a monumental effort. "But need you to know, everything between us . . . was real. I—"

"Shh," she soothed. "We'll talk about it later. I'll save your ass-kicking for then."

A choked sound that could've been an attempt at a laugh escaped him, causing him to wince. "Look forward to it."

He went quiet and anxiety clawed at her as his breath turned shallower, but she couldn't let Reid sense her fear. She channeled every ounce of her remaining strength into her voice. "You stay with me, Reid. I don't care how bad it hurts. You're not allowed to go to sleep. You understand?"

His lips quivered into a hint of a smile. "I'll try."

"Trying isn't good enough," she said, keeping her tone firm. His commands had always cleared her mind, sharpened her focus, and she hoped to God it would work the same way for him right now. "I'm done losing the people I care about. You don't have permission to leave."

His mouth curved into a full grin, even as his skin took on a sickly shade of gray. "Yes, ma'am."

But right as the paramedics thundered down the stairs, the grip of his hand on top of hers went slack and the smile faded from his face.

TWENTY-THREE

now

Brynn shifted in the hospital's vinyl-covered chair, pulling her knees to her chest and setting her chin on them. The change in position relieved some of the pressure on the healing welts striping her back, but irritated the ones on her front side. No matter. She'd survive.

The monitors at the nurses' station continued their steady beat, lulling her into a near catatonic state. She hadn't slept in days. Couldn't. Reid's surgery had gone well even though he'd lost a lot of blood, and the doctor had said he should make a full recovery. But watching Reid lie in bed for two days—only waking up for brief, drug-induced moments—had her on edge. She needed to hear from the man himself that he was okay.

She closed her eyes, the insides of her lids feeling like steel wool scraping against them. The scene in the basement kept playing over and over in her mind. All the things she could've done differently. How if she had just stayed and talked to Reid instead of running away to the party, everything could've been avoided.

Running. Always running. It's what she did best.

"Ma'am." The nurse's hand on her shoulder made Brynn jump. The older woman smiled down at her. "I'm sorry, did I wake you?"

Brynn dropped her feet to the floor and shook her head. "No, I'm fine. Just waiting for visiting hours to start."

She nodded at the door. "You're all set. Doctor just finished with him. You can go in now."

Wiping the bleariness from her eyes, she stood and thanked the woman, then moved past her and through Reid's door. She had expected to see the same scene from the previous two days—darkened room, beeping machines, and a pale, sleeping Reid.

But instead, she was greeted with a lopsided grin and a gravelly voice. "Hey, sugar."

Her heavy heart buoyed in her chest. "You're awake!"

"So it seems." He shifted higher on the angled bed, wincing a bit. "How come every time you get near a weapon I end up in pain?"

Awake *and* sarcastic. She wanted to drop to her knees and thank the heavens. "'Cause you're always standing too close to the bad guy."

He nodded, some of the humor leaving his face. "So are you."

She headed toward the visitor's chair, but he patted the side of the bed instead. She sat on the edge near his feet, trying her best not to jostle him any. "How do you feel?"

He shrugged with his good shoulder. "Like I've been shot."

"Right. Stupid question."

The corner of his mouth tipped up. "I'm okay, I think. Doc said the bullet missed all the important stuff."

"That's good." She wondered if the doctor had told him how close to hitting his heart it had been. Her breath left her thinking about the scant inches, the sliver of a miracle that had saved him.

Concerned eyes scanned her head to waist. "And you? Are you . . . okay?"

She nodded. "The welts are healing."

He stared at her, as if trying to find the answer to his next question on her face. "Did he—?"

"No," she said, cutting him off before he could say the words. "He was going to, after he finished the beating, but you got there before he had the chance."

He closed his eyes briefly. "Thank God."

She grabbed his right hand and squeezed. "Thank you. You didn't just save me from that, you saved my life."

His Adam's apple bobbed. "The nurse said Jace is all right?"

"Jace's fine. Davis knocked him out, but he only had a concussion."

"And Kelsey?"

She looked down at her hands and sighed. "The police intercepted Roslyn and got Kelsey to safety, but she's been through a lot. Davis posed as the dom who was supposed to be training her and brought her to his cabin."

"Oh, no."

"Yeah, The Ranch assumed Kels was a no-show, but Davis had her on-site for three days—fooled her into his bed. She figured out he was lying when he started asking questions about the evidence. When she tried to escape, he hauled her off to stay with Roslyn at the lake house and came back to pursue me for the information instead."

"Jesus, is she going to be okay?"

She twisted the ring on her right hand over and over. "Kelsey's tough. Right now she says she's fine. She's even willing to cooperate with the police on both this case and the one with the dealer. But I think when she slows down, all this is going to hit her pretty hard."

"And what about you?" he asked quietly.

"I'm just glad to be alive at this point."

Reid released a long breath. "I thought I'd be too late again—that I'd lost you for good."

She fought against the lump forming in her throat. She'd thought she'd lost him forever, too. The moment the second gun had gone off had been one of the worst of her life. "Nope. You still have to put up with me every day at work."

His fingers laced with hers. "What if I want to put up with you for more than that?"

She stared at their locked hands, the simple connection both warming her and bringing sadness all at once. Her mouth twitched. "You're pumped full of pain meds and not thinking straight."

"No, I'm serious," he said, the firmness in his voice making her meet his eyes. "I've been up since four this morning doing nothing but thinking. I'm sorry I deceived you about why I was at The Ranch. I needed your sister for the appeal, but I won't lie, I also wanted to knock you down a few notches. Get back at you. It was an asshole thing to do. But Brynn, as soon as you kissed me back at the initiation, it's like I was right where I needed to be. Everything that happened after that was a hundred percent real, at least for me."

She chewed her lip, considering him. "For me, too."

His hand tightened around hers. "Then give me another shot to get it right."

Her heart picked up speed, urging her to grab on to what he was suggesting. But she knew better. Nothing had changed since their conversation in the bathtub. "We want different things, Reid."

"I want you."

She frowned and extracted her hand from his. "You know I can't be what you need."

He glanced down at her body as if remembering the scars beneath, and she had the urge to cover herself with her arms.

"You are what I need, Brynn. I know you've been through hell and it's going to take time to work through that. But let me be there with you while you do it."

"What if I never work through it, Reid?" she said, her voice hardening. "What if every time you touch me, I can't help but think of all the horrid things he did to me?"

He frowned. "We'll figure it out, sugar."

"What? You'll just give up being who you are if I can't handle it? Isn't that why you got divorced?"

His jaw flexed. "I got divorced because I didn't love her like I love you."

Her lips parted, the unexpected words halting all her thought processes.

He captured her wrist and forced her to scoot up the bed, then reached to cup her cheek. "My world cracked open when I thought I might never see you again. Give us another shot, sugar."

She blinked back the tears that welled in her eyes. "Reid . . ."

"Yes, I am who I am. You're the one who tried to teach me that all those years ago. And if you're looking for a guy who's always going to be polite and gentle and politically correct, I'm not him. But you have to ask yourself—is that what *you* want? I know you're scared. But I would *never* hurt you. Don't let what that bastard did change who you are."

She dropped her gaze, staring hard at the seam on the sheets. "I'm not the girl you used to know, Reid. Things do change whether we want them to or not."

"Then who was the girl with me at The Ranch?"

"Who was the guy who said he was done with relationships?"

He released a frustrated breath. "A guy who was too afraid to admit he had fallen in love."

She bit her lip to keep it from trembling. "We've been through a lot. Trauma like this can mess with your head—make you think you want things you may not actually want. We're both too emotional right now to make big decisions."

He put a finger under her chin, forcing her to look at him. "Don't give me the therapist speak, Brynn. Sure, shit like this can screw with your mind, but it also can bring things into laser-sharp focus, make you realize what's really important. Can you look me in the eye and tell me you don't love me back? That you don't feel more alive when we're together? Because that's what you do for me."

She swallowed hard, the duct tape holding together her fractured emotions threatening to bust apart. "I can't . . . do this right now."

She moved to get off the bed, but he grabbed her arm, his grip firm and his eyes blazing with determination. "You will *not* run from me, Brynn. Not again. You look at me and tell me the truth."

She stilled, staring at his hand on her, then looked him dead in the eye and said the only thing she knew would free them both. "Texas."

The hurt that crossed his face ripped her guts out, but she pasted on her stoic therapist mask—the only thing that saved her from falling to her knees in a broken heap of emotion. The sights and sounds of the rooms seemed to grind to slow motion, and the fight left Reid's body. His hand slipped from her arm and he nodded.

Without another word, she rose off the bed and walked out the room, the tears falling as soon as she shut the door behind her.

TWENTY-FOUR

now

Reid glanced up as Jace pulled open the sliding glass doors and sauntered onto Reid's backyard deck like he owned the place. "You know, knocking before you come into somebody's house is usually customary."

Jace grinned and handed Reid a beer. "I forgot. That head injury has made my memory shit."

He snorted. "Right. Is that what you're telling the girls you date when you forget their names?"

Jace laughed and sank into the lawn chair next to him. "The benefits of being hit in the head are vast. Although, it won't impress women nearly as much as surviving a gunshot wound to save a damsel in distress."

Reid closed the file he'd been working on and took a sip of beer. "Yeah, I'd have to leave out the part about her saving my ass right back."

"Have you talked to her?"

He stared off in the direction of the setting sun, frowning. "No. Not since the hospital."

And it was killing him. Brynn had been through her worst nightmare, and knowing she was facing all those demons alone kept him awake at night.

But she'd walked away. Didn't love him enough to try. Some things he couldn't command. No matter how much he wanted to.

Jace considered him, his normal humor gone from his face. "What happened in there?"

He sighed. "I told her I loved her."

"And?"

"And she used her safe word."

Jace winced. "Fucking brutal."

Reid ran a hand over the back of his neck, wiping the sweat that had gathered there. "She's terrified, man. That sadistic asshole fucked with her head, and now she's convinced being with someone like me will rehash that terror every time I touch her. She was so close to pushing past her fear when we were at The Ranch, and now she's scrambling backward."

Jace's tone hardened. "Makes me wish we could bring that fucker Davis back from the dead, just so we could have the pleasure of killing him ourselves. Slowly."

"No shit." He swigged his beer. "And this giving her space thing is driving me nuts. I wake up every damn day ready to pound on her door, throw her over my shoulder, and cuff her to me until she gives me another chance."

Jace shrugged. "So why don't you?"

He shot his friend a don't-be-a-stupid-asshole glare.

Jace leaned forward, his forearms braced against his thighs. "Look, I'm not saying you actually kidnap her. But, whether Brynn wants it or not, she responds to submission—to you. She was so scared when I was getting her ready at The Ranch. I thought for sure she'd bail before the word 'go,' but as soon as she was with you, she relaxed and, unless she's the best actress ever, enjoyed it. You need to remind her how it can be with someone who's there for her pleasure not pain. Chase away the ugly associations she has about it by giving her a taste of your dominance again."

Reid shook his head. "She'll just run farther away."

"Maybe, maybe not. And she can't run too far—you'll be back in the office with her on Monday."

Reid gave a noncommittal grunt. He hadn't told Jace, but he'd be looking for a new place to move his office to on Monday. No way would he be able to see Brynn every day knowing he couldn't have her. Masochism was not his kink.

Jace set his bottle down, his expression brightening. "All right, enough of this, I've got an idea."

Reid shot him a wary look. "Dangerous words coming from you."

"No, I'm serious. We're not doing anyone any good sitting here having a fuck-my-life conversation. And it's time for you to stop doing the hermit thing."

Reid tilted his bottle back. "I think the hermit lifestyle suits me. I'd look good with a beard."

He shook his head. "No. Three weeks of house arrest is long enough. It's Friday night, your shoulder sling is off—we should go do something." He checked his watch. "I have a friend whose band is playing tonight. Why don't we grab a burger, then go to their show?"

"Don't you have a roommate you can drag to these things?"

"The department switched Andre to the night shift. Plus, he hates hard rock."

"I don't think—"

Jace hopped from his chair. "I'm changing that from a request to an order. You owe me."

"Seriously?" Reid cocked an eyebrow. "You're ordering me around? That head injury really did do some damage."

He crooked a thumb toward the house. "Come on, don't be a

douche. Go get showered and changed. I've seen homeless people who look better than you."

Reid flipped him off, but rose from his chair. Maybe Jace was right. He'd done nothing but work on Hank's case and worry about Brynn since he'd come home from the hospital. Maybe getting out of the house would help his sour mood. He headed into the house, Jace hot on his heels. He glanced over his shoulder. "Where are you going?"

"To help myself to the rest of your beer supply."

Reid walked into the nightclub already itching to leave. After three weeks of holing up in his quiet house, the blinking lights and heavy rock beat overloaded his senses. He pulled at the sleeve of his black T-shirt, the snug fit irritating the healing bullet wound. Jace clapped him on his good shoulder. "Come on, there's a table over there, next to the dance floor."

Super. Just what he wanted to watch all night—happy couples having vertical sex.

He followed Jace, sank into one of the modern leather chairs, and prepared to brood. As soon as he could wrangle a waitress, he ordered a stiff drink and started his mental clock. One hour, and then he was leaving. His indebtedness to Jace only went so far.

Once the drinks arrived and he had sufficiently drained his and ordered another, he leaned toward Jace. "Who do you know in the band?"

Jace put his hand up to his ear to hear him over the thumping music. "What?"

He cocked his head toward the stage at the female-led rock band. "How do you know the band?"

The corner of Jace's mouth tipped into a wry smile, and he pointed over Reid's shoulder with his straw. "I don't. But *she* does."

Reid craned his neck in that direction and froze. *Son of a bitch.*

"She calls me every day to check on your recovery, you know," Jace said. "I may have asked her what her plans were for the night."

Reid gripped his drink so hard he was surprised the glass didn't splinter. "I'm going to fucking kill you, man. You have no right to interfere."

Jace shrugged. "So don't do anything. Enjoy a few drinks and watch that dude take your girl onto the dance floor."

Reid whirled around again to see Brynn take some yahoo's hand and rise from her seat. He couldn't see her face, but the short hem of her snug black dress taunted him, the sweet skin of her thighs and calves beckoning him to touch, taste, and devour.

But before the fantasies started weaving in his head, the guy's hand slid onto the base of Brynn's spine. Possessive. Presumptuous. Something dark and primal snapped inside Reid. He surged upward, no longer able to hear the music over the blood rushing in his ears.

Mine.

Brynn tried to muster a smile for the guy, Mark or Mitch something, who'd asked her to dance, but she knew she was failing miserably. She could think of fifty other places she'd rather be than here at this stupid club, but she'd promised Melody she'd go out with her this weekend to see her new boyfriend's band. She knew Mel was worried about her and was trying to get her mind off everything, but beyond a lobotomy, she doubted anything was going to accomplish that.

Luckily, the crowded dance floor and loud music saved her from having to make small talk. She moved along with the throng, sweaty bodies bouncing around her on all sides. Mitch/Mark kept a palm on her hip and a pelvis grinding in her direction, the playful spark of interest firing behind his rimless glasses.

She closed her eyes, not having the energy to feign interest back, and turned herself over to the hypnotic pulsing of the bass and the small buzz she'd gotten from her two glasses of wine. *Thump. Thump. Thump.* Her muscles moved in time, but her mind drifted, her thoughts going to the same place they always went these days.

Warmth oozed over her skin as the hands on her hips suddenly became broader, stronger. The amorphous body heat against her back more defined, solid. Tossing her head back, she leaned into the steely wall, inhaling the scent burned into her olfactory glands. *Mmm.*

She didn't want to open her eyes, wasn't ready for the fantasy to slip away.

"Think this jerk-off can make you come apart like I do?" asked the deep, familiar voice.

She startled at the words, her lids flying open. Her dance partner had been absorbed into the crowd and now large, familiar hands gripped her waist from behind. Her movements stuttered off the beat, and her knees almost went out from under her.

His lips brushed against the back of her neck. "You know what it fucking does to me to see some other guy touch what's mine without my consent?"

What was Reid doing here? She had used her safe word, had walked away. He wasn't supposed to be doing this. But she couldn't make herself form a protest. Instead, she tilted her neck to the side, providing him better access, her body acting on its own volition.

The brush of lips became a scrape of teeth. "That's right. Give in to it."

The hand on her waist drew her closer, bringing her ass against the hard ridge in his pants. She let out a little gasp, molten heat flooding her sex. "Reid."

"You feel how much I miss you, sugar," he said, his voice like warm milk on a cold night. "Have you missed me?

His palm slid down, cupping her vee and making her arch against him. "God, yes."

The words came out before she had time to evaluate their consequences. She bit her lip hard as her clit swelled beneath the pressure of his hand. The music continued to thump and people pressed around them, concealing his blatant touch. He worked his hand against her with a slow, methodical rhythm, the lacy material of her underwear sliding against her sensitive skin.

His other hand moved to her ribs, his thumb idly caressing the underside of her breast. Her nipples pebbled against her bra, the buds aching for Reid to yank down the neckline of her dress and take one into his mouth. She sagged against him, and his fingers drifted higher, grazing over her left breast. She bucked with the combination of sensations. Fuck. She was going to come right here on the dance floor and he hadn't even touched her bare skin.

He chuckled against her hair. "Not yet, sugar. Not here."

She squeezed her eyes shut, willing herself not to beg for release.

"The song is about to end. When it does, you tell Melody you'll be back in a little while. Walk out to the parking lot. My car is in the back corner of the lot. You meet me there."

"Reid," she said, her breath catching, the word more a plea than anything else.

"No safe words tonight. You're either by the car when I get there or you're not. I call the shots after that."

She shivered, his hard tone making her belly tighten and her clit ache. Shit. What was he planning to do to her?

The song came to a cymbal-crashing conclusion, and Reid released her. When she spun around, his blue eyes blazed over her. He caught her wrist and brought it to his mouth for a light nip. "Your call, sugar."

He turned on his heel and strode away, his confident swagger and drool-worthy body drawing the attention of every woman he passed on the way back to his table. He didn't grace any of them with a glance and didn't look back to see if Brynn was following his instructions.

On jelly legs, she made her way back to her table. Melody looked up at her, her eyes widening. "Good lord, girl, are you okay? You're all flushed. Maybe you should sit."

Brynn shook her head. "I need some air. I'll be back in a few minutes."

Mel moved to stand up. "I'll come with you."

"No," Brynn said, maybe a bit too abruptly because Mel raised an eyebrow. "You'll miss Terrence's next song. I'll be fine."

Her friend sank back into her seat. "You sure?"

She nodded and before she could think too hard about what she was about to do, headed toward the exit door.

The air outside had cooled and grown heavy since she'd arrived, and the low rumble of thunder promised a rare summer storm. Besides the tap of her strappy heels along the pavement, the lot was quiet, the headlining band enough to draw even the smokers inside. She kept a brisk pace, and her senses tuned to her surroundings. The club was in a good neighborhood, but the parking lot was dark and she was seeing monsters in every shadow these days.

Reid's sleek SUV loomed in the farthest corner of the lot next to an ancient looking oak tree, but there was no sign of the man himself. She paused a few steps from the vehicle, her heart hammering against her ribs. Maybe she shouldn't do this. What if she panicked again and didn't even have a safe word to escape? What if the nightmares she'd had every night since the day in Davis's basement claimed her and Reid didn't stop?

Reid stepped out from behind the SUV and leaned a hip

against the grille. Her crossed his arms over his chest and pinned her with his stare. "You've got four steps of free will left, Brynn."

She eyed the small expanse of space between them and swallowed hard. His very presence soothed something jagged inside her. "I'm not ready to talk about us."

He smirked. "What I have in mind doesn't require conversation, sugar."

Her eyes darted to the large erection pushing against his jeans, and her muscles tightened in anticipation of how it would feel to have him inside her again. *Shit*. This was a bad idea. So bad.

But God, she wanted him.

She locked her gaze with his and took a breath.

One. Two. Three. Four. She crossed the last few steps, not stopping until she stood within inches of his broad chest.

"Good girl," he said, pushing off the car and straightening to his full, intimidating height.

She moistened her lips. "Where are we going?"

He gave her a slow smile. "Who said we were going anywhere?"

Before she could respond, he hooked an arm around her waist, and his lips claimed hers. Hungry and hot, his tongue possessed her mouth—pure, animal need flowing from every pore in his body and into hers. Gone was the sweet, loving guy from the hospital. In his place was Reid's dark side personified. The side he had tried to ignore when they were in their twenties. Dominant. Powerful. Carnal.

She should've been scared, and she expected the panic and flashbacks to slam into her. But instead, her entire being jumped to life and every nerve swirled into a pool of trembling want low in her belly. This man wouldn't hurt her. He would *own* her.

And hell if she didn't want anything more in that moment.

She curled her fingers into his T-shirt as he pressed her against the front of the car, the residual heat from the engine warming her back. His hands traced up her waist, over her rib cage, and then cupped her breasts. She tilted her head back, her moan chasing a clap of thunder.

His forefingers glided up and hooked her spaghetti straps, then yanked them down along with the top of dress and the cups of her strapless bra. Her breasts tumbled out, the nipples already tight and needy when they hit the night air. She gasped as his hot breath slid along her bared skin. "Someone could see us."

"Yep." He circled an areola with his fingertip, the touch sending electric sparks straight to her center. "And I bet you're dripping just thinking about it."

He pinched the nipple between his thumb and forefinger hard enough for her to writhe. "Shit."

He stared down at her. "You've convinced yourself you're a good girl. The social worker in the conservative suits who teaches women about empowerment. But underneath all that, good doesn't get you off, does it?"

She closed her eyes, unable to hold his probing stare.

"Lie down." He grabbed her waist and lifted her to sit on the hood, then pushed her shoulders until she was lying down, her back heating against the warm metal. He smoothed his hands up the outside of her thighs and slowly pushed the hem of her clingy dress up to her hips, revealing her panties.

The sky roared again, and rain began to hit her exposed skin in fat droplets, cool kisses against her breasts and face. Reid grabbed the edge of her underwear and yanked, the thin material ripping immediately. "Let's see how right I am, shall we?"

She squirmed in anticipation of his touch, and he planted a palm against her pelvis, securing her to the hood. His free hand traveled up her inner thigh until his fingers found her wet heat. Losing her last grip on control, she mewled at the contact.

He let out a low, satisfied groan. "It's beautiful how wet you get for me, sugar. How badly you want me to fuck you."

She widened her legs, inviting him, begging him. She'd deal

with what this all meant later. Right now she needed him inside her. Two fingers surrounded her clit and massaged. She pressed the back of her head into the hood, her breath rapid.

"Are you scared, sugar?" he asked, a hint of gentleness entering his tone.

The answer was automatic. "No."

"Good," he soothed. "Because I would *never* hurt you, Brynn. You're safe with me. I'll never push you further than I know you can go."

Tears mixed with the rain that splashed onto her cheeks, the truth of his words resonating over her. "I know."

"Thank you," he said, the relief in his voice evident. "Now come for me, sugar."

He slid two fingers inside her throbbing channel and kept a thumb against her hot button, working her with swift confidence. Thunder rumbled in the sky, matching the lightning flashing through her veins. She squirmed against the car, but he gave her no reprieve. One hand remained splayed over her navel, the other against her pussy. No time to think or worry, just feel. Within seconds, every nerve in her body coiled into a tense, yearning mass, bringing her focus to that single, unbearably beautiful ache in her core—that exquisite moment right before release.

"Let go, love. Let it all go."

On his command, her body tipped over the edge of control, ripping a primal groan from her chest. Her body clamped down on his fingers, and her pelvis arched against his hand. "Oh, God. Reid!"

"That's right, baby. I'm right here."

His words both soothed and heightened her senses as she crested the wave of orgasm, his skillful touch wringing out every ounce of pleasure as the rain continued to pound against her.

When the contractions finally quieted, he eased his fingers from her and draped his chest over her form, shielding her from the now full-fledged thunderstorm. He laid a soft kiss against her brow. "Good night, sugar."

Her languid muscles stiffened beneath him. "Where are you going? I thought we—"

"This is as far as I'm taking you tonight. I won't go any further until you tell me what you want. Who you want."

His clear blue eyes stared into hers, and she knew he wasn't asking what and who she wanted in this moment. But for every moment. Her voice came out in a choked whisper. "Reid."

"Shh," he said, standing up and easing her to her feet. "You don't have to decide anything tonight."

Rivulets of water dripped off his jawline, and his black T-shirt clung to every line of muscle as he helped her set her dress to rights. Unable to resist touching him, she pushed the wet hair off his forehead. "You're soaked."

A hint of a smile played around the corner of his mouth, and he nodded at her saturated dress. "Said the pot to the kettle."

She grabbed the remaining strap of her dress and slid it over her shoulder. "You're not so good at giving up, are you?"

"I told you a long time ago it takes me a while to get a point." He shoved his hands in his pockets and cocked his head toward the club. "Come on, beautiful. Let's get you to dry land."

She stepped to his side and offered him her hand. Without a word, he threaded his fingers with hers and they walked back to the club, only the sound of the pattering rain between them.

TWENTY-FIVE

now

All weekend. No phone call. No visit. And then today, she'd called in sick for work.

He'd blown it.

Reid slammed his shower door shut with his foot, then kicked it for final measure. "Fuck."

He'd thought he'd broken through, thought he'd reminded Brynn how good they were together. But apparently his take-no-prisoners seduction had backfired. He'd given her the full face of his dominance, taken away her safe word option, tried to show her that what they had was stronger than the darkness Davis left behind. But apparently it wasn't enough.

He scrubbed the towel through his damp hair, and then wrapped it around his waist. Maybe he had pushed too hard. Maybe he should've taken the slow and gentle approach, shown her that he was capable of being just as tender with her as he was tough.

He reached for a fresh bandage for his shoulder and all of his supplies toppled off the edge of the sink and onto the floor. He let another string of choice words fly as the bottle of rubbing alcohol landed on its side and sent the strong-smelling liquid flooding over his tile.

Was everything going to fight him? With a sigh, he got to his knees and cleaned up the mess. Great, now his bathroom was going to smell like the hospital ward he wanted to forget. After tossing the soiled towel in the hamper, he finished bandaging his shoulder, and finally headed into the bedroom.

But he only had one foot on the carpet before he ground to a halt.

Sitting in the middle of his bed with her legs tucked under her, was Brynn. Naked, save for the red necktie fastened over her eyes and the small, flat box she held in her hands.

She gave a hesitant smile, apparently sensing his presence. "You all right? Sounded like a Quentin Tarantino movie in there."

The longing that assaulted him sucked all the air from the room and almost brought him to his knees. But he didn't dare move. "Brynn, what are you doing?"

"Giving you my answer."

The golden lamplight of the room gilded every curve of her nudity, making her appear both goddess-like and vulnerably human all at the same time. He gripped the edge of the doorframe. The urge to touch her, hold her . . . *claim* her overwhelming him. But the soft glow couldn't conceal the faint pink of the healing whip marks—a glaring reminder of the deeper, more pervasive scars that lay beneath the surface.

"Oh, sugar." He walked to the bed, sat next to her, and untied the blindfold, barely resisting the instinct to pull her into his lap and cradle her. "You don't have to do it this way. I love you. I only want another chance. I don't need you to push yourself into this part before you're ready."

She blinked a few times, adjusting to the light, then held out the box. "I *am* ready."

He took the gift from her, her words not lining up in his head. "I don't understand."

She gave him a rueful smile. "You were right about what you said in the hospital. I'm always giving you lectures about being true to who you are. That very first night when we made love all those years ago, I told you I wouldn't be with you if you were going to deny your nature. And then I spent the next ten years denying mine."

His heart seemed to pause mid-beat, and his fingers tightened around the box.

"Ever since the rape, I've tried to block the submissive part of myself. Not only because of the fear, but because of what I thought it said about me. Davis told me that night that I'd better get used to what he was doing because I was a born whore. That no decent woman would enjoy a man tying her up and hitting her." She looked down at her hands. "And part of me knew he was trying to be cruel, to humiliate me, but another part of me believed him."

His jaw clenched. "That fucking bastard."

The corner of her mouth twitched. "My career is teaching women to value themselves, to take pride in who they are, and to live the life they want. I thought what that meant for me was striving for some idealistic image I created in my head when I was a kid. But it's not. I'm proud of the person I've become. I'm good at what I do, have great friends, and have made a nice life for myself."

He smiled and pushed a wisp of hair from her face.

She lifted her eyes to him. "But I'm also a girl who gets all wobbly-kneed when her man demands to fuck her in a parking lot in the storming rain. And I'm not going to be ashamed of that either."

Her words and the memory it brought forth jolted through his nervous system like a shot of adrenaline. His cock flexed beneath the towel.

"I'm done worrying about what other people think. And I'm done letting what Davis did define me."

He glanced down at her scars. "And the panic attacks, the flashbacks?"

She stared at him a moment, a small crease forming between her brows. "I think what scared me the most was losing control—being hurt again. But I realized the other night when I went to you without a safe word that submission is not about loss of control, it's about trust. And I trust you." She took a deep breath, but her gaze didn't waver from his. "I love you. Always have."

He closed his eyes for a moment, absorbing her words, letting the fear that had gripped his insides for the last few weeks melt away. She loved him back. *Thank you, God.* As long as he had that, everything else could be worked out.

He reached out and traced one of the scars that striped her sternum, the gentle caress making goose bumps rise on her pale skin. "I love you, too, sugar. More than anything."

"Thank you for being so hardheaded and not giving up on me," she said, her voice catching a bit and her green eyes going shiny. "Now, open that damn box before I get all weepy."

"Yes, ma'am." He didn't want her to cry—the moment was too sweet to mar with tears—so he pulled the ribbon on the box and lifted the lid. Inside, a sterling silver circle, its only adornment a simple O-ring hanging from it.

To the rest of the world, a pretty necklace.

To him—everything.

A wide grin spread across his face, the joy within him so strong, he was sure he could bleed sunshine.

She put her hands out to him, wrists up, just as she had that first night they'd made love. "Make me yours, Reid Jamison."

Brynn shivered as Reid's heated gaze caressed her naked form, heightening her awareness of every lonely inch between them. He lifted her wrists to his mouth and kissed each one. "I think it may take more than a collar for me to stake my claim."

Sharp tingles raced up her arms, her body craving him like it craved food and water. "Guess it's a good thing I sent Jace on his merry way after he let me in, then."

"Good thing." He grabbed her hips and lifted her to straddle his towel-clad lap, his hard length brushing the terry cloth against her sensitive skin. "Because you're mine now. And I don't share what's mine. Not with another person." He touched his lips to the pink line that striped the top of her breast. "And not with ugly memories. All we need is you and me."

She smiled through unshed tears as he hooked the collar around her neck and ran a finger over the hollow of her throat. "Yes, sir."

He cupped her face and kissed her eyelids, then her lips. "Don't cry, sugar."

She pressed her forehead against his and let her hands glide down his chest, which was still dewy from his shower. "I will if you don't stop torturing me."

"What do you mean?"

She traced a circle around his flat nipple. "How am I supposed to sit here and be submissive when you look so fucking hot?"

He laughed, a big and hearty sound that seemed to lighten the air around them. "We're going to have to work on your patience."

She rocked once against his lap, stroking herself along his erection. "Good luck with that."

The blue of his eyes darkened with lust, possessiveness. "Tell me now if you have any lines you don't want me to cross yet."

She smiled. No more fear. Only anticipation. And love. "Don't go easy on me, sir. I'm all yours."

He gave her butt a lightning-quick smack. "Get on your back, LeBreck. Hands gripping the slats of the headboard."

Biting her lip, she climbed off him and followed his instructions. He rose from the bed and then disappeared into his walk-in closet, leaving her wondering what the heck he was up to. When he emerged, he had a fistful of neckties and had dropped the towel. Knowing that she may soon be blindfolded, she took the chance to devour him with her eyes. No matter how many times she saw him naked, the sight of his hard angles and smooth muscles never failed to steal her breath and light up her insides.

Her focus traveled down the planes of his torso to the vee of his pelvis, honing in on the evidence of his arousal. She wet her lips, the memory of his taste alighting on her tongue. The desire to please him, to bring pleasure to the man she loved—her master—bloomed in her like a living thing. Never had she suspected that accepting her submissive role with him would feel so freeing, so undeniably right. It was as if her soul had been out of alignment, and Reid smoothed all the chinks.

He gave a dark chuckle. "You're looking at me like I'm your next meal."

"Maybe you are."

His fist wrapped around his cock, and he stroked his thumb across the head, catching the bit of liquid glistening there. "You love seeing how hard you make me, don't you? How crazy you can drive me?"

She nodded and pressed her thighs together, her own liquid heat surging in response.

He stepped next to the bed and ran his damp thumb across her lips. Automatically, she sucked the pad of it into her mouth, closing her eyes and savoring his undeniably masculine flavor. When he took his hand away, she lifted her lashes to find him staring at her with a heady combination of tender love and unrepentant sexual hunger. "Give me your wrists."

She complied and he knotted the end of a tie to one. Gently, he set her arm back on the bed, then ran his palm along the outside of her thigh. Her sex throbbed in response, and she shifted her legs in an attempt to provide some pressure to her aching clit. He gave her thigh a playful swat.

"Now, now, no cheating." He cupped the underside of her knee and drew her leg up. "I want you open to me. I'm going to enjoy that pretty pussy of yours."

She dropped her head back against the sheets and took deep breaths, trying to focus on anything but the unbearable ache between her legs. She'd longed all these weeks for his touch, his whispered commands, the feel of his mouth on her and his arms around her. The tryst in the parking lot had only whetted her appetite. She didn't know how much longer she could take it. Maybe Melody's theory of spontaneous combustion due to sexual frustration had some merit.

"Keep your arms where they are." He grabbed the other end of the tie attached to her wrist and looped the soft silk around her upper thigh, securing the two together. With one tug, the binding drew her thigh up toward her arm. He quickly trussed the other half of her body in the same manner, leaving her thighs spread wide for his perusal. Deliciously cool air licked at her damp skin as he climbed onto the bed and kneeled in front of her. A hot finger traced along the sensitive juncture between her leg and pelvis, and she shuddered from the subtle contact.

"Look how swollen and wet you are for me, sugar. I bet you would come from the littlest bit of pressure on your clit, huh?"

"Yes, sir," she said, her words coming out in a breathy rush. "Please, touch me."

He dipped his head between her thighs and she tilted her hips, begging for his mouth. For agonizing seconds, he held his lips millimeters from her skin, breathing her in, his hot exhales dancing over the needy nerves. "You have permission to come, love. I plan to draw plenty more out of you before the end of the night."

He ran the flat of his tongue over her sex in one long, languid lick, and she nearly jumped out of her skin—the sudden sensation overloading her desperate nerve endings. "Oh, God."

He didn't wait for her to inhale another breath. Bracing his hands on the backs of her thighs to keep her still, he brought his lips and tongue over her slick tissues and made love to her with his mouth. Licking, nibbling, and suckling in a sensual dance that had her screaming his name in orgasm long before he deemed it time to grant her mercy.

When he finally raised his head, her throat felt raw and her body trembled, but still she needed. Wanted. She tried to reach out for him, but the ties prevented it, and a frustrated whimper escaped. He brushed the dampened hair from her forehead, his gaze intense. "Ready for me, sugar?"

She let out a relieved sigh. "So ready."

He pulled at the knots in the bindings, releasing her legs, then reached over to the bedside table to grab one of the condoms he had laid on top of it, but she shook her head.

"What's wrong? Do you need a minute?"

She cleared her throat, trying to fight past the scratchiness. "No condom. I'm on the pill. I don't want anything between us."

His worried expression softened into one of heavy-lidded wanting, and he leaned down to kiss her, his lips still shiny with her own juices. She sucked his bottom lip into her mouth, eliciting a hoarse groan from him, and his body melted over hers. He smelled of soap and sex and *Reid*—a heady opiate that made her drunk with desire. She wrapped her legs around his hips and twined her fingers in his hair, the simple pleasure of exploring his mouth and feeling his bare skin against hers a luxury.

Reid's large palms spanned her hips, gripping hard and positioning her, his controlled demeanor fraying in the heat of their kiss. She arched against him and the smooth head of his shaft nudged her opening. She spread her thighs wider, her body begging for him.

He didn't need a written invitation. With a strangled groan, he thrust forward, his cock sliding to the hilt and filling her to delicious capacity. She sighed beneath him.

His forehead pressed against hers, his breathing labored as he held himself still inside her. "How do you expect me to maintain dominance when you completely unravel me, sugar?"

She looked up through her lashes at him. "Fuck me into submission, sir?"

His lips curled into a rapacious grin. "That's going to take a lifetime."

"Count on it."

He tangled his fingers in her hair and began to move, his eyes not leaving hers. He wasn't gentle or slow—a fact for which she was eternally grateful. Instead, he drove into her with barely restrained violence. Fucking her. Marking her. Claiming her as his.

And driving her out of her ever-loving mind.

Her thighs tightened around his waist, and sweat glazed both their bodies. She wouldn't hold out long. The rising swell of sensation hovered at the edge of her perception, ready to engulf her. She dug her nails into his biceps and clung to the last vestiges of her control, trying to wait for his permission to let go. But just as she thought she would fall apart, he slid out of her, leaving her aching and half insane.

She opened her mouth to protest, but he halted her.

"On your hands and knees, Brynn. Now."

The steel in his tone went straight to her core, her arousal climbing higher than she thought possible. "Yes, sir."

On shaking limbs, she rolled onto her belly and got into position. He gave her a low hum of approval and ran a hand over her bottom, sending her thighs trembling in response. "Spread your knees and tilt up for me. I want all of you."

She swallowed hard, knowing what he was going to do. A few weeks ago, the thought would have sent her into a spiral of terror. She'd never given herself to anyone in that way. It had only been taken. Stolen.

But now she wanted nothing more than for Reid to have her there, to chase away every last hint of darkness within her and replace it with the shining light of their love. She had reclaimed her life and now she would reclaim her body. This gift was hers to give.

She widened her knees and opened herself to him. His palms slid along her waist, and he planted a kiss at the base of her spine. Then, his hand dipped in front of her, finding her swollen clit. She jerked, the simple touch sending sparks through her, and she pressed her forehead into the sheets. His voice soothed as his hand worked her. "What do you want, sugar?"

Her body rocked against his hand, needing more of him, all of him. Everywhere. Her words came out in short pants. "Take me, Reid. All of me."

The warmth of his chest draped over her back as he brushed her ear with his lips. "I'm going to go easy, but you need to tell me if anything is too much."

He shifted away from her for a moment and dug in the bedside drawer. His hot palms caressed her ass, easing any remaining nerves before he smoothed cool gel over the sensitive opening. She shivered, the chill of the lubricant and the sharp snap of pleasure from his touch a luscious combination.

"You look so fucking sexy all spread and waiting for me," he said as he eased a well-lubricated finger past the tight ring of muscle and his other hand continued to work her clit.

"Holy shit." Her hands gripped the sheets, the intense sensation instantly pushing her closer to orgasm. "That's . . . oh, wow."

"Don't come yet, love," he said, gently pushing a second finger in, readying her. "Not until I get a chance to bury myself inside this sweet little ass."

She squirmed beneath his pleasurable assault, using all of her strength not to give in to the seductive call of release. "Please, Reid. Now."

He groaned and shifted behind her. "I don't want to hurt you, sugar."

Sweat dripped down her neck. "I'll tell you if you do, just please, I need more. I need you."

Swiftly, he removed his fingers, and added more lubrication to her and then to himself. As his other hand stroked her pussy, he placed the tip of his cock against her snug opening. "Okay, beautiful. Push out while I ease in. It will help."

She followed his directive, and the blunt head strained against the tight muscles. Oh, God. She wanted him inside her so badly, but her body seemed to be fighting against it.

"Relax, sugar. Focus on letting me in."

Taking a deep breath, she tried to relax the resistant muscles and pushed back against him. With a deep groan from him and a sharp cry from her, he slipped past the resistance and sent her into a dizzying space of sensual awareness. Every molecule of her existence seemed to light up with edgy pleasure.

His leg muscles tensed and quivered against the backs of her thighs as he held himself still inside her. "Christ, you feel good."

"Move," she begged, rocking backward. "I can't . . . I need . . ."

He began to slowly slide back and forth against the sensitive tissues, filling her in a way she'd never imagined, chasing every hint of dark memory from her system.

He pressed his forehead against her shoulder blade, words of adoration tumbling from his lips as he made love to her. But language had stopped making sense. All that was left was overwhelming awareness and rocketing pleasure. Salty tears and sweat touched her lips, and her nails grappled for a grip on the mattress as she raced toward oblivion. A desperate plea scraped across her vocal cords. "Reid!"

With a growl for her to come, Reid's pace turned urgent, and he sunk his teeth into the fleshy curve of her shoulder, putting his own brand over the one that monster had left. Her sensory system went into overload, and a scream that didn't even sound human rattled her throat. Her orgasm exploded behind her eyelids in a thousand bits of pulsing light.

Reid's voice joined the primal chorus as his own climax overtook him, releasing his liquid heat deep within her. Marking her as his.

Utterly and completely his.

After the room turned quiet and their heartbeats slowed, Reid eased off the bed and lifted her boneless body into his arms. She knew she should probably say something. *Thank you. I love you. You fucking rock.* Something. But she was too drained to even part her lips. Instead, she just let her head rest against his good shoulder as he carried her in to the bathroom and set her on the bench in the shower.

He turned on the water and climbed in with her, letting the warm water soothe their abused senses. With quiet tenderness he soaped her, washed her hair, and wiped off her tear-streaked makeup. "You okay, sugar?"

She mustered a lazy smile. "Perfect."

"Yeah, you are." He tugged on one of her wet locks.

She laced her fingers with his and kissed his soapy knuckles. "No, this is."

EPILOGUE

Brynn found a parking spot across the street from the Jamison mansion and shut off the engine, her Honda as out of place in the neighborhood as she was. "Well, we're here."

Reid smirked at her from the passenger seat. "Yeah, I noticed. What now?"

"I have no idea." She took one last lingering look at the papers on her dashboard, still not believing the words, then climbed out of the car.

She removed her sunglasses and set them on top of her head, turning her attention to the estate. Not much had changed since she'd visited ten years ago. It was still as breathtaking as she remembered.

And now it was hers—well, half hers.

Patrick Jamison had never been a father to her and never would be. But what he did know how to do was throw money at situations to alleviate his guilt. When he'd found out about what Roslyn and Davis had done, he'd signed over the house to Brynn and Reid as an I'm sorry and had taken off to his beach condo to escape the glare of the media. So now, here she was, part owner of a house that probably cost more than she'd ever make in a lifetime of social work.

The plantation-style home didn't have the proverbial white-picket fence, but in all other respects, it was the kind of house Brynn had dreamed of growing up in. All her life, she'd imagined that behind those manicured gardens laid equally manicured families. Families who ate dinner together, parents who loved each other and worked at normal jobs, kids who didn't have to wonder if their mother would make it home at night.

She'd sworn to herself that one day, she'd create one of those perfect families, create normalcy. Ensure happiness through putting all the right puzzle pieces in place. Now she had the house to do it in. But after the events of the last few weeks, she'd realized it was all an illusion. There were no perfect families. No Leave-It-To-Beaver households. Behind the pretty columns and rose-bushes of the Jamison house had lived a cheating husband and a cold-blooded killer. Deadly secrets covered with the shiny wrapping paper of wealth.

She uncurled her fist and stared at the house key in her palm.

The dream she'd sought all her life had been a false one. She could walk into that beautiful home, fill it with pretty things and find a polite husband who played by the rules. Meet lovely neighbors, attend their lovely parties, play with their lovely children. Be on the other side of envy for a change.

And be completely, out-of-her-mind miserable.

She tossed the key to Reid as he came around from the passenger side. "What the hell are we going to do with this thing?"

Reid chuckled. "Not your style, huh?"

She leaned against the hood of the car, eyeballing the ridiculous garden statues. "Hardly. What about you? I know you're used to living the high life, Prince Jamison."

He snorted. "Believe me, I've seen enough of this house to last me a few lifetimes. And I don't want all this. I'm a simple man with simple tastes."

She rolled her eyes. Reid was a lot of things, but simple would never make the list. "Liar."

"No, I'm serious." He stopped in front of her and placed his hands on the car, caging her in. "All I need in a home is a big-screen TV, comfortable furniture, and a beautiful woman—preferably you, preferably naked—to keep me company."

She laughed. "Is that right? So if I suggested we sell this gaudy thing and buy a house a third its size in a neighborhood without a gate, you'd be cool with that?"

He gave her lips a playful nip. "Have we established if you're naked in said smaller house?"

"Perhaps."

"As long as you're there, I'm sold either way." He pushed off from the car and stepped back with a smile. "Plus, think of all the money we'll have left over. We're going to be able to throw a killer party."

She raised an eyebrow. "We should probably build the house before planning a housewarming party, don't you think?"

He shook his head. "We wouldn't be celebrating a house."

"What would the party be for then?"

"I know I'm not the most traditional guy ever, but I'm not moving in with you until you make an honest man out of me."

She cocked her head to the side. "What are you talking about?"

"The collar isn't enough for me, sugar." He dug in his jacket pocket and sank to one knee, sucking all the wind from her chest. "I want it all with you. Marriage. Kids. Forever."

She blinked hard, trying to assure herself that the man before her was real.

He held out a small black box and flipped it open, revealing a simple but stunning diamond ring. "Will you have me, Brynn LeBreck?"

She gripped the car behind her, her legs threatening to collapse beneath her, and tears filled her eyes. She nodded.

"Is that a yes?"

She nodded again, trying to find her voice. "Yes."

He bowed his head and kissed her hands. "Thank God, I'd hate to have to cuff you and drag you down the aisle."

She laughed, the tears catching in her throat, and ran her fingers along the back of his neck. "You know, this is the first time I've had you on your knees for me."

He looked up at her, his blue eyes glittering in the afternoon sun, and gave her a soft smile. "Haven't you figured it out yet? I've always been on my knees for you, love."

Keep reading for an excerpt
from the next steamy novel
by Roni Loren,

melt into you

Available now from Heat Books

Evan Kennedy swigged the last of the tequila from the mini bottle as her fiancé's moans of pleasure drifted through the wall behind her. She set the bottle down and sank back onto the bed, curling her pillow around her ears. This was torture—absolute Geneva Convention–worthy stuff. Next time they stayed in a hotel, she would make sure the suite had two bedrooms that didn't share a wall.

How was she supposed to sleep with that kind of erotic soundtrack in the background? Especially when the only company she had in her room was the hotel's mini bar and a subpar selection of cable stations.

The heavy thudding of a headboard banging against the wall started up, rattling the three empty bottles on her bedside table. Oh, the guys were on their game tonight, obviously celebrating the good news they'd all gotten earlier in the evening. No telling how long their show would go on. With a heavy sigh, she threw the comforter off her legs and climbed out of the bed, happy to find she only wavered slightly.

She needed air. Or at least someplace where two happy lovers weren't sharing passionate, wall-rattling sex while she lay in bed alone.

She yanked on a pair of jeans and a T-shirt, then tucked the last mini bottle of tequila into her pocket. The bar downstairs would be closed by now, and although she rarely drank, tonight she had the urge to get comfortably numb. She just had to make sure not to run into any of the people here for her and Daniel's couples' seminar. That certainly wouldn't reflect well on the company. And the last thing she felt like doing was getting into a row with Daniel about "professional image."

After running a brush through her hair, she stepped out of her bedroom and threw one last glance at Daniel's closed door. The moans had turned to dueling male grunts. Clearly both parties were having a good time. An unexpected pang of sadness hit her in the gut, and her eyes burned as if tears were going to flow.

What in the world? Her hand went to her cheek, but of course no actual tears were there. She never cried. But that burning was the first sign she'd had in years that she was still physically capable of tears.

She shook her head. Maybe it was the tequila.

And the close quarters.

A walk would help.

She shut the door with a soft snick and made her way down to the lobby. As expected, things were quiet. The overnight desk clerk glanced up at her with disinterested eyes. She gave him a quick smile and turned in the opposite direction to head toward the pool and the beach beyond.

She slipped through the exit door, and the warm Gulf breeze wrapped around her, lifting her mood a bit. She closed her eyes and inhaled the salty air, letting it fill her lungs and hoping it would clear her head. But as soon as she opened her eyes again, the glowing swimming pool seemed to tilt in front of her. Whoa.

Maybe she had overestimated her liquor tolerance. Three shots of tequila might have been two too many. She grabbed on to the back of a nearby lounge chair to steady herself.

Evan focused on the dark expanse of the Gulf of Mexico in the distance, waiting for the spinning in her head to stop. She just needed to make it to the beach, sit down in the sand, and get her normally iron-clad defenses back in place so she could return upstairs with a smile on her face. She didn't need the guys seeing her this way. They'd want to sit down and talk about feelings and shit. And really, she didn't want to go there. The last thing she needed right now was for Daniel to put on his therapist hat with her.

After a few more fortifying breaths, she straightened her spine and made her way slowly around the edge of the pool and to the wooden stairs that led down to the beach. *Almost there.* But when she reached for the gate, the latch didn't give. "What the—"

She looked down and sighed at the sign attached to the weather-beaten wood. PRIVATE BEACH—CLOSED: MIDNIGHT TO SIX A.M. NO LIFEGUARD ON DUTY.

"Dammit."

She stared longingly at the crashing waves, the peaceful solitude of the beach calling to her like a siren song. She peeked over her shoulder at the hotel's main building. There were no security cameras out here. Who would know? And Daniel had brought a hell of a lot of business to the hotel this weekend with the conference, so even if someone caught her, she doubted they would do more than politely direct her back to her room.

Without giving it more thought, she planted a foot on the lowest railing and draped her other leg over the top, making sure to keep two hands securely on the fence so her head wouldn't start whirling again. She hoped no one was watching because she was sure she was executing the maneuver with the grace of a walrus. But at least she didn't topple down the stairs. Score.

After a careful walk down the steps, she kicked off her flip-flops and curled her toes into the cool sand. Ahh, yes, *so* worth the rule breaking.

Thunder rumbled in the distance, and the clouds far off on the horizon blinked with lightning. Damn, she should've brought her camera. The new lens she'd bought would've been perfect to catch the display. She moved closer to the water, stepping past the rows of hotel lounge chairs and closed umbrellas and not stopping until the spray from the crashing waves hit her face and the taste of salt alighted on her tongue.

The tide pooled around her feet, soaking the bottom of her jeans and sending a little chill through her. She rubbed her arms and glanced down the beach, taking in the deserted shoreline that stretched along the length of South Padre Island. The moonlight had turned the normally colorful view into silver sand and black water. But even in the darkness, she could tell she was alone on her three a.m. adventure.

No surprise there. People didn't come on vacation to wander around alone half drunk in the middle of the night. No, the people in those beautifully appointed hotels lining the beach were cuddled up to their loved ones right now, sleeping off a fun day. Or, like Daniel, having crazy monkey sex with their lovers. Lucky bastards.

Normally, that knowledge wouldn't bother her. She'd made her decisions, had created a good life for herself. For the first time, she was with someone who loved her—even if that love was only platonic. But for some reason, a hollow ache had rooted solidly in her chest tonight. And paired with the heated need that had settled between her thighs after listening to an hour of lovemaking, she was dangerously close to feeling sorry for herself.

Her fists balled. No way. Screw that. The alcohol had to be what was making her feel this way. She needed to sober up.

She looked down at the water swirling around her ankles. A dunk in the surf would probably snap her into sobriety pretty quickly. But walking back through the hotel in dripping-wet clothes wasn't exactly wise, especially when she wasn't supposed to be on the beach in the first place.

She gave the shore another quick scan, then shrugged. *Oh, what the hell.*

Evan stepped back from the water long enough to shimmy out of her jeans and T-shirt and tossed the clothes where the water's edge wouldn't reach. Despite the warm night breeze, her nipples beaded beneath her bra and goose bumps rose on her skin. A little zip of adrenaline went through her. Man, how long had it been since she'd done something like this, stepped outside the lines a little? She'd almost forgotten what it felt like.

To hell with the pity party. She was on a gorgeous beach and had the whole damn thing to herself. No more whining. She made her way back toward the waves and took her time submerging herself, determined to enjoy the luxury of owning this little piece of ocean for the night.

The water lapped at her as she moved farther into the surf— bathing her legs, sliding up her thighs, soaking her panties. *Mmm.* The gulf was deliciously warm against her skin, caressing the dormant parts of her to full sensual awareness. Her hands cupped the water and drew it up and over her breasts, soaking her bra and the tightening buds underneath. A shudder went through her.

She wanted to sink into the salty depths and allow the sensations to take over, to wash away the dark emotions that had claimed her tonight. But even in her buzzed state, she knew tequila and swimming weren't good bedfellows. So, she stopped when the waves crested at her chest and settled in to watch the light show on the horizon.

The distant storm had moved a bit closer, and though it still wasn't near enough to be a threat, the view of the flashing sky was breathtaking. She wanted to kick herself for not bringing her camera. She'd had so little time for her photography since she'd gone on this seminar tour with Daniel that she was beginning to worry she'd forgotten how to do it. Hopefully, when they returned to Dallas after this last stop, she could dedicate some time to her neglected studio.

With a sigh, she tilted her head back, closed her eyes, and dipped her hair into the water. Maybe that's why she was in such a funk. She'd spent the last few months supporting Daniel's passion and ignoring hers. She'd signed up for it, and the venture had turned out to be lucrative for them both, but it didn't feed the part of her soul that slipping behind a camera did. That part was downright starved.

Thunder rumbled, closer this time. Reluctantly, she drifted back a few feet. It was probably time to get out. The alcohol-induced fog in her head was clearing, and based on the sudden uptick in wind, the storm would be on top of her in the next few minutes. But before she could take another step, pain—sharp and sudden—shot up her thigh.

She yelped and jolted backward, her arms flailing before she crashed into the water and went under. Salt water filled her mouth, silencing her shout, and a burning sensation wrapped around her thigh and radiated outward.

Disoriented, she scrambled for solid footing, trying to get back to the surface. She knew she couldn't have fallen into deep water, but the writhing pain and the knowledge that she was out there alone had panic edging in. She spread her arms in an attempt to tread water and finally felt sand against her toes. But just as she tried to push off, twin bands of heat wrapped around her upper arms, and her entire body was propelled upward.

When her face broke the surface of the water, she sucked in a large gulp of air, half coughing, half choking. She kicked frantically, trying to make sure she didn't get dragged back under.

"Stop fighting or you're going to drown us both." The rumbling male voice came from behind her, and the grip on her arms tightened. "We've got to get out of the undertow."

Her heart jumped into her throat, but she forced herself to stop struggling so the stranger could help. His breath was warm on her neck as he pulled them both backward, but he didn't say another word. The water seemed to be fighting their progress, and the man adjusted his hold until he had his arms hooked beneath her armpits. She wanted to tell him to let her go, that she knew how to swim, but her thigh was burning like a swarm of wasps had attacked it, and her head was spinning again.

A few hard-fought minutes later, packed sand scraped against her heels and she sucked in a deep sigh of relief. The man dragged her another few feet until they reached dry land, then set her down and kneeled next to her.

"Are you okay?" he asked, his broad chest heaving beneath his soaked T-shirt.

She lifted her gaze to find concerned eyes staring down at her, an odd sense of déjà vu washing over her. "I, uh . . ."

"I heard you scream. Are you hurt?" He touched the side of her head, evaluating her.

She wet her lips. "My leg, something stung me. I lost my balance."

He glanced down the length of her—the mostly naked length of her. *Shit*. She shot up into a sitting position and scooted backward, but his hand locked over her knee as he stared down at her upper thigh, which was still burning like she'd roasted it over an open fire.

"Damn, it got you good."

"What are you talking about?" She tried to jerk her leg from beneath his grip, but he held her firm as he examined her.

"Jellyfish." He said, frowning down at her. "Your whole thigh is striped. That must hurt like a son of a bitch."

She stared down at the red tentacle-shaped lines around her thigh. "Well, it doesn't feel awesome."

He chuckled, the rich sound seeming to vibrate from deep

within his chest, and something stirred in the back of her brain. He climbed to his feet. "Here, let me help."

"Don't you dare pee on me," she said, the words slipping out before she could rethink them.

He tilted his head back in a full laugh this time, the sound echoing down the beach.

She cringed. "I'm sorry, I—"

He raised a hand, his eyes still lit with humor. "Don't worry. The urine thing is just an urban myth. And I'm definitely not going to ruin my just-saved-a-pretty-girl-from-drowning hero status by taking a leak on you. I'm not that stupid."

She couldn't help but smile. "Oh, a hero, huh? So this is all a big pick-up routine? Find drowning girls and ride in on your white horse?"

"Absolutely." He grabbed the hem of his T-shirt and pulled it off, revealing miles of taut skin, sinewy muscle, and tribal-style ink running across his shoulder and down one arm.

The view rendered her momentarily speechless. Water dripped off his soaked hair—which looked to be blond, though it was hard to tell in the moonlight—and slipped down his now bare chest. Her gaze locked on the tiny droplets, tracking their path down to the band of his shorts until they disappeared. *Oh, blessed Lord.*

He cleared his throat, no doubt catching her in her perusal, and squatted next to her. His hand slipped under her knee. "Here, seawater actually helps the sting, let me wrap this around your leg, and then we can go to my room. We'll get you feeling better."

She cocked an eyebrow at him. "Oh, really. Might want to tap the brakes there, Rico Suave. Despite my state of undress, I don't go to strangers' hotel rooms. I'm not quite that easy."

Dimples appeared as he fought a smile. "Oh, not quite *that* easy, but easy. Duly noted."

She shot him a withering look.

"For the record, that's not why I was inviting you to my room.

Although, I promise *that* certainly would distract you from the pain. But all I mean is my roommate is Mr. Prepared. He keeps a first-aid kit for the beach and always has a bottle of vinegar in it. It will help deactivate the venom."

She frowned. Two grown men on a beach vacation together? Great, not another good-looking guy who preferred other good-looking guys. Not that she was looking for anything to happen anyway. He was a stranger. An extremely pinup-worthy stranger. But still. In her sexually deprived state, a little flirting could be almost as satisfying as an orgasm. Almost.

With gentle hands, he bent her leg and wrapped his wet T-shirt around her thigh. His focus was on the task at hand, but she didn't miss the sneaky sidelong glance toward her open thighs, where her wet panties were probably revealing every detail of what lay beneath.

She cleared her throat, and his gaze darted back to her leg, but the corner of his mouth tugged up a bit.

Well, well, maybe not so gay.

Her body heated at the thought, even though her brain knew that, straight or gay, she wasn't going to do anything with her rescuer. "So how long were you out here? I thought I was alone."

He glanced up as he draped the shirt around her leg a second time. "I was here the whole time." He crooked a thumb behind him. "Was sitting in one of the lounge chairs on the far end. I thought you saw me when you looked down the beach, but I guess not."

"You could've said something, you know."

He gave her an unrepentant grin. "If a beautiful woman wants to go for a naked swim, who am I to intervene?"

"Very gentlemanly of you."

"Hey, never said I was a gentleman. Just a hero."

"Right," she said, her tone dry.

He tucked the end of the shirt underneath the first layer, securing it. "Is that too tight?"

"No, it's actually helping the burning a little."

"Hold on." He climbed to his feet and jogged a little ways down the beach, grabbed something from one of the lounge chairs, then walked over to where she had left her clothes and picked up those as well. When he returned, he held out her T-shirt. "Go ahead and put this on. You're not going to be able to put on the jeans, but you can wrap my beach towel around your waist."

"Thanks." She took the shirt and towel from him, pulled the first over her head, then got to her feet and knotted the beach towel around her hips. She tilted her head up to smile at him. "So, Mr. Humble Hero, you have a name?"

He stuck out his hand. "It's Jace."

Her body froze, the sand beneath her feet seeming to shift beneath her. Had she heard right? She stared at him for a moment, taking in every nuance of his face, the earlier whispers of déjà vu now becoming shouts.

Was it really him? His hair was longer, his body harder and more mature, the green in his eyes more wary, but the resemblance was there. It'd been years—twelve actually. The nineteen-year-old boy she'd known had become a man. "Jace *Austin*?"

———

Oh, shit. The recognition that flashed in the woman's blue eyes had Jace dropping his hand. This woman knew him? He frantically flipped through his mental Rolodex, starting with the girls-I've-slept-with file.

When they'd locked gazes earlier, he'd felt a nudge of familiarity but had dismissed it. Surely he'd remember this dark-haired beauty, especially if he had gotten the privilege of touching that sweet little body. But something about her was poking at the recesses of his mind.

He rubbed the back of his neck and offered an apologetic smile. "Uh, yeah. Jace Austin. I'm sorry, have we met?"

She flinched a bit—the move subtle, but not lost on him. Damn, well now he felt like a jackass. *Had* they slept together?

She recovered quickly, the corner of her mouth tilting up. "Don't worry. I'm sure I look a little different than I did at sixteen. Especially without that god-awful bottle-red hair and eyebrow piercing."

Sixteen? Red hair? The flashing list of names in his head suddenly flipped back over a decade and landed on one he hadn't thought about in years. One he'd purposely tried to block out. No, couldn't be. *"Evangeline?"*

She shrugged and looked out at the water, the wind whipping her hair around and disguising her expression. "It's Evan now. I stopped using my full name a long time ago."

"Wow, I don't even know what to say," he said, shaking his head. "You look great. I'm so glad to see that you're . . ." *Okay. Alive.* "Here."

She turned back toward him and smiled, though it didn't light her face the way the earlier smiles had. "It's good to see you, too. But, if you don't mind, before we go down memory lane, how about that vinegar?"

"Oh, right," he said, his mind still whirling. "Follow me."

And she needn't worry. The last thing he was going to do was initiate any reminiscing. No, some things were better left buried. And how he'd destroyed the girl he'd sworn to look out for was A-number-one on that list.

Also by Sandy Ba[...]

One Summer in Sant[...]
That Night in Pari[...]
A Sunset in Sydne[...]
The Christmas Swa[...]

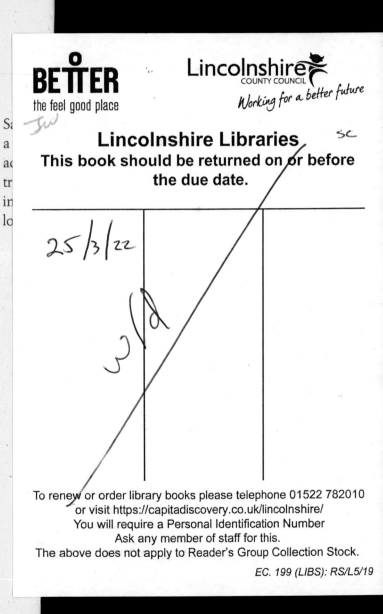

arker is a writer, traveller and hopeful romar
y bucket list. She loves exploring new places,
res, and eating and drinking like a local v
nd many of her travel adventures have four
novels. She's also an avid reader, a film bu
d a coffee snob.

🐦 @sandybarker
📷 @sandybarkerauthor
f @sandybarkerauthor
BB @sandybarkerauthor
Sandybarker.com

D0488426